BIGFOOT
DREAMS

BIGFOOT

DREAMS
Francine Prose

PANTHEON BOOKS, NEW YORK

Library of Congress Cataloging-in-Publication Data

Prose, Francine, 1947–
Bigfoot dreams.
I. Title.
PS3566.R68B5   1986   813'.54   85-43454
ISBN 0-394-54976-7

Manufactured in the United States of America.

Design by Guenet Abraham

First Edition

For Howie and Bruno and Leon

If you are afraid of wolves do not go into the forest, the Russian proverb says. We all live in the forest, and there is nothing to do but get used to the wolves.

Randall Jarrell

BIGFOOT

DREAMS

I N THE subway going to work, Vera decides to write about Bigfoot. Her story will be datelined from some backwater southern town that has been growing an acre of tobacco as a kind of vegetable sacrifice ever since Bigfoot loped into town one night and smashed up a Texaco station and made off with fifty cartons of cigarettes. Eyewitnesses describe a hairy creature, fifteen feet tall and stinking like a giant ashtray. Every fall, bathtub-sized footprints can be tracked from the woods through the clay fields to the tobacco patch where Bigfoot comes to claim his crop.

Across the aisle, a good-looking kid in white painter's jeans with a tool box tucked under his work boots sits reading *Motorcycle World* and looking worried. From time to time he takes a cigarette from behind his ear and rubs it lovingly between his fingers. He has beautiful hands, and watching them, Vera thinks of the headline: BIGFOOT LIGHTS UP. Chances are he will never see Vera's story, and yet she is writing it for him. For despite everything Vera knows, some part of her still believes that you can make someone who wants a smoke feel better by telling him how Bigfoot wants it worse.

There's a game Vera plays called Where-Did-This-Story-Come-From? Aside from the obvious—the kid, the Li'l Abner boots, the cigarette—two answers seem clear. First: Six months without a cigarette hasn't made Vera quit wanting one. Second: She's worked at *This Week* too long. UFO sightings, sex-change aliens, cancer cures in the humblest garden vegetables, new evidence of life after death. Yetis, Loch Ness monsters, live dinosaurs in hidden African valleys. Five years of writing these stories have taken their toll: Vera can't see a handsome face or boots or an unlit cigarette without thinking about Bigfoot.

It's rush hour, but the front car's nearly empty. Years ago Vera and her friend Louise used to ride the first car the way other girls rode horses. Knees braced, leaning into the turns, faces pressed against the front window so the tunnel came rushing straight at them, they'd pretended it was dangerous, and now it is. Often now Vera warns her daughter, Rosalie, to stick with the crowds and the transit cops in the middle. But Vera still rides the front out of loyalty to who she once was and because now more than ever it draws certain types: People who need room, who don't care if it's dangerous or simply don't know. In this last group are every imaginable variety of halfway house resident, shopping-bag lady, and screamer.

Vera can't remember so many people talking to themselves. Maybe she and Louise were just making too much of their own noise to hear. She can't remember when she started hearing them nor when she stopped fearing they'd start screaming at her. Vera's only half joking when she tells herself that screamers are her way of keeping in touch with her audience. They're like *This Week*: the same subjects keep cropping up—atom bombs, the environment, the whole world buried under junk cars and poisoned and finally blown up. But their great theme, the theme that underlines and transforms every word, is the suffering of the innocent, deception and betrayal by everyone from Henry Kissinger to circuit court judges, doctors, husbands, wives, parents, best friends. Vera's first byline—DEMENTO DENTIST PLANTS CB RADIOS IN MALPRACTICE MOLARS—came from something she heard on the train. On good days she likes to think of herself as a kind of screamer spokeswoman, bearing their messages to the world.

Today there's just her and the good-looking kid. If someone were screaming, she'd be listening instead of writing Bigfoot stories in her head. As the train nears 34th Street, she stands and walks past the kid, noticing only now that his mouth is beautiful, too. The regret Vera feels is so piercing and disproportionate, she knows it must be about something else. But before she can figure out what, the train lets her out and she merges with the crowd, not walking so much as letting it float her along. Perhaps none of them are moving or being moved but gliding on some sourceless energy like pointers on a Ouija board. She imagines this scene from above, a tricky aerial shot of the tops of all those heads. The image is so vivid she wonders if this qualifies as astral projection, and if so, why leaving your body always sounds so complicated, like something you have to be gifted or occult-minded to do.

It's rained overnight and the streets look fresh and washed clean, unlike the people, whose faces already have the puffed, oily shine of glazed doughnuts. Waiting for the WALK sign, Vera breathes in the sweet haze of sweat, a smell that comforts her, reminding her of summer evenings when her father would come home from work and hug her and she could believe that his smell of sweat and tobacco was all she would ever need, of nights when she and Lowell slept with baby Rosalie wedged between them and in the morning she could smell Lowell's armpit on Rosie's downy head. Sometimes she likes to think that her working for *This Week* is partly connected with her genuine love for that smell.

The lobby smells, less comfortingly, of pine disinfectant and worse. Rumor has it that bums have been sneaking in here to throw up, and it's understandable that a drunk might mistake the lobby—done in high WPA tile and marble—for something else. Vera wonders if *This Week* readers have noticed the recent run of vomit stories, including her own contribution, BRIDGEPORT BANDIT BLOWS LUNCH, about a cat burglar leaving his nasty signature in the toilets of the homes he robs.

Vera's heart skips when she spots Hazel, half hidden in her shadowy corner of the elevator. She'll never get used to the fact that this giant office building still has a semi-automatic loft-type elevator with Hazel at the helm. Though, really, it matches the rest. The whole place is a relic, its washrooms museums of antique porcelain and chain flush tanks. Half-metal, half-wood, the elevator suggests those lifts in British seaside hotels, those French wire cages, only less Art Nouveau and elegant—more in fact like one of those hot boxes in Japanese prison camp films. Maybe that's why Hazel has the zoned-out manner of a prisoner who's cracked under torture. Without acknowledging Vera, Hazel shuts the door and turns the wheel.

Hazel used to treat Vera like everyone else. She remembers Hazel saying, "Cold enough for you?" and "Couldn't get much hotter!" so she's pretty sure they went round the seasons in this period of innocent grace. Then something awful happened. Vera wrote a story about an elevator that, through some freak wiring accident, shot up through the roof and landed on a junior high next door, obliterating a science class that had coincidentally been studying asteroids. Aside from its obvious sexual content, the plot must have come from those daily trips with Hazel in that swaying, antiquated machine. At the time, though, it had seemed primally inspired. For one of *This Week*'s unspoken rules is that its stories should address the most common hopes and fears. And what are people scared of if not elevators and sex?

On the day that issue came out, Hazel stopped talking to Vera; it couldn't have been coincidence. What haunts Vera even now is that Hazel's life seems cramped and drab enough without her having to worry about faulty wiring hurtling her through space like a shooting star. Probably Hazel no longer remembers why she stopped liking Vera, but Vera rides up and down with that story every day of her working life. She's seen Hazel with other passengers, lining up with the floor so smoothly you could roll a marble across without it bouncing. But now she lets Vera watch her floor go by, then stops short a good eighteen inches later. Halfway between a step and a jump, impossible to manage with any grace, the compromise turns out to be a kind of downward stumble.

All muted browns and yellowing checked linoleum, its lighting so golden and spooky and insufficient it might as well be gas, the corridor is pure turn-of-the-century Prague. Vera used to cheer herself up by thinking about Kafka on his way to the Workmen's Accident Insurance Company until her friend Louise told her a story about a guy in her office who asked her to go to Tanglewood for the weekend and then showed up at five A.M. saying he was sorry, but two days in a motel room with Louise would drive him out of his mind. Vera asked Louise if she'd been angry or hurt and Louise said no, not exactly, mostly it had made her feel sorry for Kafka's girlfriends. Now Vera can't think about Kafka without thinking of that. Kafka with his skinny head, his bat's ears tuned to the strains of Josephine the singing mouse—how could any girl not love him! How fortunate Kafka never worked at *This Week*, where MAN BECOMES GIANT COCKROACH would be good for maybe nine hundred words.

Vera passes the office of Ehmer Verlag, Est. 1918. Having never seen anyone go in or out, she's convinced that this so-called publisher of German scientific texts is actually a front for a spy ring so sloppy about details they'd ask you to believe the Germans were establishing esoteric publishing firms in the last days of World War I. Next door to Ehmer Verlag is the American Basenji Society, where sometimes on hot afternoons the door is left open, revealing two elderly ladies typing amid a Dickensian mess of papers, folders, filing cabinets stuffed with pedigrees maintaining the purity of this rare breed of African barkless hound. Once Vera rode up in the elevator with a Basenji and its owner. The dog kept flapping its mouth in a yawning, undoglike fashion; Vera kept expecting it to talk.

The lettering on Vera's door says Magazine Marketing Management, a title that has less to do with pretension than with making it harder for the wrong people to find. Once the wrong people were creditors; now they're mainly poor souls who think *This Week* is printing their life stories or beaming directly to their brains. Every month at least one of these stumbles in; they're much more persistent and resourceful than people who want to order subscriptions or place ads. So Vera's less surprised than she might be when she walks in and finds Carmen, the receptionist, dealing with Charlie Manson's double.

Shivering visibly though he's wearing a heavy pea coat and it's

August, he grips the edge of Carmen's desk with both hands and whispers, "Please. I need to see someone."

The pop of Carmen's gum fills the silence in a companionable way. Plump and pretty even in the baggy shirtwaist dress that supposedly has some connection to her being a Seventh-Day Adventist, Carmen's known for her ability to type like a demon while soothing the troubled in spirit like Mother Teresa, and for her wonderful, crazy laugh. Now she blinks impassively at him from behind the owlish glasses that make her eyes look liquid and enormous, then puts on her earphones and rests one hand on the switchboard. "Who?" she says.

The Mansonite reaches into his pocket and pulls out a ragged copy of *This Week*. "Is this yours?" he demands, like someone trying to housebreak a pet by confronting it with its mistake.

"Not me," says Carmen. "I'm just the receptionist."

"Is this *This Week* or isn't it?"

"Yes, sir," says Carmen.

"I'm sorry I can't tell you where I found this." He glances over both shoulders, then at Carmen, then Vera, somehow managing to check them both out without seeing them at all. "Okay, I'll tell you. In the *garbage*! Guess whose."

"Whose?" says Carmen.

He looks around once more; then, so softly they have to strain to hear him, says, "Henry Kissinger's."

Of course, Vera thinks. The screamer's friend.

"No kidding," says Carmen. "Where's he live?"

The Mansonite eyes her suspiciously. It's fascinating and more than a little scary to watch the rearrangements his face goes through. "All right," he says. "Who cares whose garbage, right? Look at this." He spreads the paper out on Carmen's desk and begins leafing through it. Most of the pages are puckered and glued together and the rest keep sticking to his fingers, but somehow he finds the right one. Vera moves closer.

"Here!" He karate-chops the paper with the side of his hand. The headline says: WASHINGTON WILD CHILD: RAISED BY CATS! Vera knows the story. She wrote it. Still she reads it slowly to herself, keeping pace with Carmen, who's reading it aloud:

When D.C. police arrested a man for rummaging through the garbage in Washington's chic Northwest, little did they know that their suspect was in fact an uncivilized creature who had never known human society and had lived his whole life in the refuse-strewn alleys of our nation's Capitol.

"That's me," he says with a proud grin that might have been winning if it hadn't revealed a set of neatly matched brown stubs.

"Wow," says Carmen.

Vera knows it's not him. One thing she's sure of is that she wrote the story soon after seeing *The Wild Child* for the second time. She can't recall where she saw the film or with whom, but she clearly remembers coming home and going into Rosalie's room and hugging her sleeping body because the movie had made her feel she'd betrayed her by teaching her how to live in the world. A few days later she decided to write about a feral child in some American city and, needing a place with alleys and lots of good garbage, chose Washington.

Carmen reads on:

When first questioned, the D.C. garbage-prowler could only reply with a series of purrs and growls.

"This guy can't talk," says Carmen. "You talk."

"Go on," he says.

But after six months of intensive therapy at St. Elizabeth's Hospital, Felix Sylvester—christened by nurses after the two well-known cartoon cats—called a special press conference to tell his astonishing story.

Abandoned by his parents in infancy, Sylvester was soon adopted by a pack of alley-wise cats who taught him where to find the best garbage and the coziest sleeping places and to operate so smoothly that he was never once spotted by a fellow human. Sylvester declined to name the brand of cat food he was stealing when police caught up with him.

Carmen wrinkles her face. "Cat food! Even I could get skinny on that. Hey, maybe you could get into one of those cat chow commercials. Like Morris, you know Morris?" Suddenly she turns serious. "Listen, honey, I'm telling you. They don't pay nothing here. Public domain, you know what that means? Means they don't pay for your story unless you write it yourself."

"I don't want money," he says. "I want to meet the lady who wrote this." He chops the paper again.

"What lady? Nobody's name's on this."

"I know that," he says. "Just like I know a lady wrote this. I feel it here." He punches himself in the heart. "And whoever she is, she's beautiful, man. Maybe not on the outside, but down deep in her soul. She knows me. She understands my whole life and everything I've been through without my telling her. I don't want to hurt her. I don't want to bother her none. I just want to make contact. To say, 'Thank you, beautiful lady.' "

The line about not wanting to hurt her has driven Vera's shoulders up to her ears. She can feel the blood leaving her face. Luckily he doesn't notice; luckily Carmen does. Carmen's laugh is high-pitched and ear-splitting and lasts so long it dopplers back on itself.

"What's so funny?" the wild boy asks, his tone midway between a howl of pain and a death threat.

"I just remembered who *did* write that story," Carmen says, gulping air. "Gomez. Eduardo Gomez. Fifty, with a belly out to here and a little *maricón* boyfriend and three daughters in expensive parochial school, Our Lady of Victory, costs twelve hundred fifty a year. You want to meet *Gomez*?"

Vera thinks: She should be *writing* for us.

"You don't want to meet Gomez," Carmen's saying. "I'll tell you what you need. You need to find yourself a wild girl to keep you company. Some nice girl to run the alleys and share your Purina with you."

"There isn't any wild girl," he says. "There's just me."

"Sure there is," says Carmen. "If there's you there's another one like you. Like the Bible says, God commanded Noah to bring in the beasts of the earth, two by two. Why would it say two if there *wasn't* two . . . ?" A few more minutes of this has Vera convinced. And why not? It's what everyone wants to hear.

"Go back to Washington," says Carmen. "She's out there. Look for her in those alleys. You'll find her."

There's one last, long moment while the wild boy's face dances through all the possibilities from stabbing Carmen through the heart to asking her to marry him. Then he smiles and comes as near to radiance as those raccoon eyes and teeth will probably ever come. "Thanks," he says, and leaves without ever suspecting how close he's been to the beautiful lady of his dreams.

Vera's nearly limp with relief and at the same time charged with the strangest desire to run after him yelling, "Wait! There is no wild girl out there! Don't bother looking!" For of all her doubts about *This Week*, this—this message of false hope—is what bothers her most. Your dead loved ones aren't really dead. Cucumber slices will cure your arthritis. Elvis is alive and well on Mars. Your alien lover is at this very moment winging toward you via UFO. It's not true, Vera thinks. None of it. Searching for your long-lost feral bride will only bring further loneliness and disappointment.

It takes all she has to convince herself: This is no time to start telling the truth. She turns to Carmen and puts out her palm and Carmen slaps her five. "Who's Gomez?" she asks.

"My brother-in-law," says Carmen.

Carmen and Vera came to *This Week* around the same time but didn't become friends till a year or so later when Vera called in sick to take Rosie to the circus, and there on line for cotton candy was Carmen, clinging to some guy with slicked-back hair and a satin baseball jacket. Figuring she'd called in sick, too, Vera pretended not to see her. But they met head on in the menagerie. Carmen kissed Vera's cheek with sticky lips and said, "This is Frankie, my fiancé." Up close, Frankie was handsome in a slightly reptilian way, with eyes to match his jacket—such an unnatural, Emerald-City-of-Oz green that Vera couldn't help asking if they were real. "Hey, where's she from?" he asked Carmen. "Outer space?" The next day Carmen told Vera that Frankie played sax in a salsa band and his friends called him the Lizard.

Now, four years later, Carmen and Frankie are still engaged, though recently Frankie's had a fight with a conga drummer and, out of spite, enlisted in the army. Carmen hopes it's for the best; he's promised her and his parents he'll train as a physical therapist. Vera still wants to warn her: "Carmen, don't marry a man called the Lizard!" Still thinks of the headline, I MARRIED AN IGUANA, and a lead paragraph about a bride who discovers—too late!—her new husband's body covered with scales. But she's learned her lesson from Hazel: Some stories are better unwritten. Besides, what good would it do? Carmen believes in her soul that she and Frankie have been paired by God to walk hand in hand up the gangplank to Noah's ark.

Now she says, "Carmen, *qué pasa?* What's new with Frankie?"

"Oh God." Carmen sighs. "He called last night from Fort Benning. He's already quit physical therapy and switched to band. He's so lazy," she says, with so much love and pride that Vera has to look away, up over Carmen's head at the THANK YOU FOR NOT SMOKING sign on the wall. Those words used to make her feel murderous. But in Carmen's case, she senses something well meant and gracious and even beatific about them, something to do with purity and the body as a temple of the Holy Ghost.

"We're no good on the phone," says Carmen. "Long distance. I get things wrong and then we hang up and . . . I don't know. *Qué pasa* with you?"

"*Nada,*" says Vera.

"That's what you think," she says.

At first Vera thinks she's showing her the same kindness she's shown the wild boy, telling her what she needs to hear, that her life can't go on like this—just *This Week* and Rosalie and *nada* else except odd longings toward boys with beautiful hands on the subway. But gradually, as Carmen goes on, she understands that the news she has for Vera is anything but reassuring, is in fact so disturbing that the only way Vera can calm herself is to shut her eyes and picture that Texaco station with those fifty cartons of cigarettes just waiting to be dragged off to some safe, cool burrow in the piny woods and smoked five or six at a time.

ERA HAS a special feeling for Bigfoot. At *This Week*, everyone wants to make the front page, and Vera's first front-page story was I MARRIED BIGFOOT. It told of an Oregon housewife, missing and long presumed dead, who reappeared claiming to have been kidnapped from her kitchen by Bigfoot, whose patient vegetarian ways—so different from her carnivore human hubby's—won her heart. Bigfoot taught her the secrets of the forest; she taught him the harmony line to "Precious Lord, Take My Hand." Then gradually Bigfoot's passion cooled. He began spending more time away in the wilderness, until one night he went out for a pack of cigarettes and never came back.

Vera has no idea where this story came from, except that when Shaefer and Esposito hired her, they gave her a stack of old *This Week*s, and she noticed how Bigfoot stories appeared at least once a month. Mostly these were reports of sightings and such, so that I MARRIED BIGFOOT was a kind of landmark in Bigfoot literature, changing the focus, bringing Bigfoot home. What pleases Vera is that she was able to write it without coming close to her own Bigfoot fantasy, which is this:

Vera and the people she loves most—Rosie, Lowell, her friend Louise, her parents—are (and this is the hardest part to imagine) camping in the forest. One morning Bigfoot appears. And though they're surprised, not even Rosie is scared. His approach is so hesitant and mild, he could be a fifteen-foot two-legged dog come for love. He brings them trout and honey and watercress salad; he cooks breakfast. Then, purposely shortening his stride, carrying Rosie so she won't trail behind and fall into his footprints, he leads them to his lair. It's one of those phantasmagorical rag-and-branch kingdoms hermit folk-carvers build, only Big-foot's is better hidden. He treats them like guests from a foreign country whose language he doesn't speak. He teaches them what he can. After a week they leave, more closely bound by their memory of those seven days than by love itself.

Of course, she'll never write OUR WEEK WITH BIGFOOT. It's too private and lacks all the juicy details that *This Week* readers have come to expect. Still, Vera likes to calm herself by imagining it on nights when she can't sleep and at difficult moments like this one, when Carmen's just given her the bad news. Today she adds smoking cigarettes with no harmful physical consequences to the list of things she and her loved ones and Bigfoot will do.

The bad news is that Frank Shaefer and Dan Esposito were on the phone with some lawyer at eight this morning. Then they called their own lawyer; then they went out. What Carmen and Vera don't have to say is that Shaefer and Esposito *never* leave. They send out for lunch. They're the first to arrive, the last to go home, and when they do, you can almost see something sticking and stretching and breaking like bubble gum on a shoe.

Now Frank's left instructions for Vera and Mel Solomon, the staff photographer, to be in his office first thing after lunch. "What's it about?" says Vera, knowing Carmen's overheard more than she's letting on. "It's probably nothing," says Carmen.

It takes Vera less than a minute to walk to her office and even less than that to jump to the conclusion that she's written something libelous. She's feared—been taught to fear—this since her first day at *This Week*, when Frank Shaefer told her the cautionary tale of how her unlucky predecessor was fired for writing about a silent movie queen returning from the dead, only to learn that the actress was still alive and well enough to sue. "The bottom line," Frank had said, "is to know who's alive and who's dead." Vera assured them she was a journalist; she had principles, ethics, checked facts. Facts? Shaefer and Esposito exchanged knowing looks, and then with a rueful little smile Dan said, "Look, it's better all around if you make it up." "What Dan's saying," explained Frank, "is that we're mostly concerned with that gray area—it *could* be true, it just *isn't* true."

Since then reminders have appeared on Vera's desk, xeroxed clippings from other papers. Vera's favorite dates from when E. Howard Hunt was working for the CIA, writing spy thrillers on the side, and having to submit his final drafts for security clearance because his most fantastic scenarios so often turned out to be classified information. Scrawled over the clipping is Frank Shaefer's note: "Too close for comfort!" When Carol Burnett sued the *Enquirer*, Shaefer and Esposito called a meeting to remind the staff their search for truth need take them no further than the Teletype. Let the wire services take the heat. They hadn't started a paper like *This Week* to have reporters yelling, "Stop the presses!" Whole nations might be changing hands in the jungles of Asia and Latin America, but the only jungles that matter here are those remote pygmy hideouts where the brontosauruses still graze. And so while the competition delves ever deeper into celebrity scandal, *This Week* never mentions a famous name unless the context is innocuous or inspirational (DEBBY BOONE: I GAVE UP JAVA FOR JESUS) or, on rare occasions, disguised as letters to the editor ("Dear Sirs: If you ask me, somebody should lock up those Charlie's Angels and throw away the key till they put on underwear like decent Christian women").

Of course, for every Washington Wild Child who shows up at the office, three more write letters containing the line, "I have contacted my lawyer." Presumably their lawyers are charging stiff fees for what Carmen does for minimum wage: convincing the insulted and outraged they don't have a case. The same person rarely writes twice. So if Shaefer and Esposito are seeing their lawyer, someone has something solid.

Suddenly Vera's seized by the urge to go home and get into bed and start the day over again. She thinks of how, in primitive cultures, magicians often advise bewitched clients to undo spells by doing everything backward. She considers backing down into Herald Square, onto the subway, and up to her apartment. Perhaps she could take it even further, back before she came here to work and wound up where she is now—dreading the prospect of facing Shaefer and Esposito, of losing a job she doesn't want and doesn't want to lose.

Vera sits down at her desk and types out the Bigfoot story in roughly the same six hundred words she'd thought of on the train. After five years she can pretty much think in final-draft *This Week*-ese, and the typing is in itself a kind of pleasure that calms and distracts her. She retypes it till it's perfect, then moves on to the next best thing, which is telling herself that losing her job at *This Week* may be a blessing. She never planned on staying so long, but despite how she worries about its effect on her, she's made no move to quit. What she needs to remember and often forgets is that there's a world out there, a world in which every dog isn't eating newborn babies or posing for cute photos talking on the phone.

Pushing the Bigfoot piece to one side, Vera clears a place and climbs up on her desk. Her office dates from a time when office work wasn't supposed to feel like typing in the gondola of a balloon swaying high over Manhattan. Vera's sooty little window isn't there for scenic views—just, grudgingly, for light. She can't see out of it without getting up on her desk—an effort she saves mainly for days like today, when she so needs the sight of other lives that what's visible from fifteen stories up is better than nothing at all.

Now, looking down, Vera wonders how many of those tiny specks ever dreamed they'd be doing what they're doing. No wonder they go for *This Week*'s basic message: Fate can just pick you up and put you down someplace else. You can be eating breakfast and a tornado will move you and your family three counties over without breaking the shell on Dad's egg.

So it is with Vera. Fabricating tabloid news was hardly her childhood ambition—not that her childhood ambition was any less absurd. Vera's first love was Peter Pan, her first wish to be reborn in an Edwardian nursery with a sheepdog, frilly nightshirts, and Mr. and Mrs. Darling for parents instead of Dave and Norma Perl. Only now does Vera see how even this marked her as their daughter, DNA-encoded for desiring the impossible.

By the time Vera set her sights on something closer, her friends were setting theirs on infinity. By graduation, a girl in Vera's college class had discovered a new galaxy. Vera's friend Louise took lots of acid and wanted to write poetry and see God. By comparison, Vera's wanting to be a journalist seemed modest, yet even in this her aims were so lofty she'd settle for nothing less than telling the true stories that revealed the profound and fantastic nature of ordinary lives.

Her first published article profiled recent Russian emigrés: dour, craggy-faced Brighton Beach Solzhenitsyns. The second dealt with a family of storefront fortunetellers. After Rosie was born, the need for steadier employment drove Vera to the *Downtowner*, a weekly give-away paper consisting mostly of restaurant listings and ads for neighborhood chiropractors. Her last attempt at serious journalism reported Louise's experiences in the Ananda Devi ashram—yet one more story that would have been better untold. Recalling it makes her cringe, with guilt and with its power to suggest that her coming to *This Week* was not quite the lark, the lucky accident she likes to pretend. She was sick of the truth. Writing for *This Week* seemed much simpler—dispensing with facts while exercising her natural bent for daydreaming at the edge of probability, converting the most ordinary incidents into the most bizarre.

It all seems so distant. Ten years ago she was a fool for truth, her heart set on nothing less than all history and human connection revealed in a pattern neat and colorful as an argyle sock. Now she's just another company slob. What saddens her is not just the innocence lost, the time wasted, but that the passing years have turned her brain into a complicated trash compactor, shredding her inner life into Grade B drive-in Grand Guignol.

The spiritual implications of this have Vera fired up to quit on the spot when suddenly Carmen appears in the doorway and sails four letters Frisbee-style onto her desk. Pleased with herself, Carmen rocks on her heels like one of those huts on chicken legs in Russian fairy tales, then makes the okay sign, thumb and forefinger joined. Where else, Vera thinks, where else in the world will her mail be delivered like this? The sharp, freefall drop of loss she feels is her first hint that her five-year romance with *This Week* might really be ending. That special clarity of vision, that nostalgia before the fact, the pain itself is specific to leaving: jobs, apartments, cities, Lowell.

"Carmen," says Vera, "tell me. Are we being sued over something I wrote?"

"I don't think so," mumbles Carmen unconvincingly, and backs straight out the door.

By now Vera's reduced to folding her hands on her desk and plotting out her morning, overcarefully, like a drunk planning a trip to the bathroom. First she'll read her mail, saving the most interesting letters for last. Then she'll hit the coffee room. On the way back she'll stop and see Mel Solomon or Mavis Biretta or whoever else is around. Then she'll head for the morgue and look through back issues until she figures out which story Frank Shaefer and Dan Esposito are at this very moment dissecting line by line with their lawyer.

BEGINNING WITH the most boring, Vera starts with a letter from some politician whose name she doesn't recognize. Still, she opens it to kill time and on the chance that its bulk-rate-mailing look is deceptive, that inside is a personal note from Eighteenth District Representative Terry Blankett inviting her to write his speeches. Inside is Blankett's voting record on power-company tax credits. Though the brochure's printed in purple, Vera can tell that in real life Terry Blankett's skin is pink. Light-haired, stout in the face, he grins up at her from behind the gapped teeth and clipped moustache of a German burgher. Automatically, her mind goes to work on a story about a Hamburg city councilman busted for wearing fat ladies' lingerie. Then she remembers Howard Hunt's talent for outguessing history and the possibility that at this minute, history is dressing Herr Councilor somebody-or-other in a lace bra and pink rayon tap pants.

As Vera opens the second letter, an overstuffed business envelope from West Myra, Illinois, grease spots hint at what's inside—a sheaf of folded xeroxes and on top this note in ball-point on looseleaf paper:

Dear Vera Perl,

I write this in the hope that there will be a miracle. I hope to be rescued. I hope this will reach the courtroom. I am the victim of a Nazi KGB game to do away with my life. They have a well-hidden operation going on. They use sight and sound from a distance. There is also ultrasound, I've heard, but it is more like heavy air pressure. They can also control certain body functions via astral projection. All this is mind control. Radio and TV waves.

The xeroxed pages include a programming guide to mind-control broadcasts, the names of fifty secret operatives, all in West Myra, Illinois, and letters from the FBI, the FCC, the attorney general, and various network news chiefs. Vera's struck by the grace of their language:

> In response to your letter of August 21, the Federal Communications Commission does not have jurisdiction over communication by sound waves. Your information concerning unlicensed radio operation has been noted and appropriate action will be taken.
>
> Yours truly,
> Richard C. Craney
> Director, Public Relations

and by the knowledge that Richard C. Craney is a better person than she is. At least he bothered dictating a reply, instead of stuffing the whole thing in the wastepaper basket like Vera.

The third letter is an invitation to the annual convention of the American Cryptobiological Society, to be held this year at the beautiful Ghost Circle Lodge on the south rim of the Grand Canyon. Clipped to the top is a note:

> Dear Miss Perl,
>
> My colleagues and I wish to take this opportunity to invite you to our annual meeting. Perhaps you might check with your employer about the possibility of a tax-deductible "jaunt." If there's any information or assistance we can provide, please don't hesitate to let us know.
>
> Best wishes,
> Ray Bramlett, President
> American Cryptobiological Society

All that courtly concern for Vera's finances and travel plans—who would guess that Vera and Ray Bramlett have never actually met? Still, they're pen pals of sorts. He first wrote to Vera after her byline appeared on a story called SASQUATCH COMES HOME, about a Vancouver Indian cultural center that was having trouble keeping its employees because Sasquatch kept pressing its big hairy face against the window. Ray's letter congratulated Vera on her rare sensitivity to Sasquatch's Indian heritage, granted her honorary membership in the American Crypto-biological Society—which, it informed her, was dedicated to the scientific investigation of unexpected life forms—and, while acknowledging *This Week*'s unflagging interest in matters of cryptobiological concern, expressed the wish that such questions be taken more seriously. Had the Vancouver incident been listed as an official sighting by the Bigfoot Study Group? Vera was intrigued enough to write back.

From what she's been able to gather, Ray Bramlett's group consists mainly of academics from small colleges, forestry and agricultural schools, retired engineers and their wives. Like any scientific organization, they hold meetings, present papers, publish newsletters and journals, award an occasional grant. Now, looking over the conference schedule, she feels the presence of all those fervent cryptobiologists, each with a championed yeti or giant squid, and the effort to satisfy them all:

Thursday, August 24

8:30 P.M. KEYNOTE ADDRESS. Ray Bramlett, President, American Cryptobiological Society.

> *Sasquatch: Tradition, Authenticity, and Invention.* Professor Gerald Davis, South Oregon Community College.

Friday, August 25

9 A.M. TWO VIEWS OF NESSIE

> *Nessie: The Eco-biological Perspective.* Professor Duncan Glengarrie, University of Glasgow.
> *New Light on the Loch Ness Monster.* Professor Mona Miller, University of New Hampshire.

11 A.M. SEA SERPENT MYTHS IN THE FOLKLORE OF THE
CANARY ISLANDS. Professor Dorothy Chasteen, South
Florida State College.

8 P.M. AUDIO-VISUAL PRESENTATION: OUR SEARCH FOR THE
MOKELE-MBEMBE. Mr. and Mrs. Carl Poteet.

Once Vera might have flown out there at her own expense in
the hope that Mr. and Mrs. Carl Poteet and their search for
whatever the Mokele-Mbembe is might reveal something profound and fantastic about marriage and adventure, curiosity,
longing, and determination. But five years at *This Week* have
so jaded her, she stuffs it into a desk drawer and goes on to the
last letter, which despite its return address—Stormy Karma, Los
Angeles, Cal.—she's known all along is from Lowell. She holds
it for a moment, puts it to the light, postponing the moment of
opening it:

Howdy Sweetheart!

This letter is being written on a gangster's typewriter. He's
just gotten out of the joint and is crashing on the floor of
C.D.'s studio. Seems somebody told him how much money
The Godfather and *Honor Thy Father* made. He decided
since he used to work in the rackets in New York, he'd get
in on a good thing. But though he has this electric typewriter, he wants to tell his life story to someone who'll write
it for him. And guess who the writer's going to be? I don't
want any part of his plan but he won't take no for an answer. Rubbed out ten FBI agents . . . 2,000 kilos of pure
heroin . . . me and Lucky . . . couple more guys got snuffed.
Then he says to me, Know what, Lowell? If the big boys
knew I was telling you this, our lives wouldn't be worth a
plugged nickel.
     Last week I got so lonely I actually took a bus just to be
riding somewhere with people. I started talking to this total
stranger about how I can't go on attaching extraordinary

significance to the most trivial things when the bus collided with a truck and all us passengers looked at each other like we'd been caught in the same superstitious thinking when the guy I'd been talking to (a good audience when not interrupting with his own story) interrupted me with his own story about psychic birth pangs culminating in a robin fetus he was busily sealing into a glass display mausoleum constructed from twin percolator tops. Shows me this fetus floating in formaldehyde and just as I am trying to tell him, Hey, I know someone who'll write this up for national publication in *This Week,* he looks at me and warns me that we shouldn't push the birth.

So I don't know what's possible. I've been trying to improve my economic situation, pounding out screenplays at the cost of one million brain cells per second when the only way to get anywhere in this town is to blow Arthur Godfrey's cousin. But you know how it is, sweetheart—the winds of fortune don't seem to be blowing in this poor hillbilly boy's direction. I'd sure like to get to NY to see you and Rosalie. Maybe I can work out a deal with TWA—they'll let me ride the baggage compartment if I clean out their reusable airsickness bags. I'm hoping to figure out some way to be there by Christmas. Meanwhile say Hi! to Rosie and give her a giant hug and kiss from her Daddy.

So my dear, the lights are going off one by one in the chandeliers of Hollywood as the dawn comes. I must go now, for if the sun hits me I will shatter like fractured glass.

Love and kisses,
Big Youth

Big Youth indeed. It occurs to Vera that Lowell's letter is almost as crazy as the KGB receptor's, as single-minded as the cryptobiologists', as self-serving and loaded with meaningless rhetoric as Eighteenth District Representative Terry Blankett's. By now, though, she's come to accept it for what it is—Lowell's idea of a love letter—and it's the only one she reads twice. Then she refolds it and goes for the coffee that by this time she really needs.

In the coffee room she finds Mavis Biretta watching the coffeepot fill drip by drip. "Morning," says Vera.

"Fine," says Mavis. "I'll be just fine when I get a cup of this." They stand there staring at the coffeepot like strangers on an elevator watching the numbers light up. Finally Mavis pours two cups and brightens visibly as the coffee works on her like some subtler, less aggressive version of Popeye's spinach.

Nearing sixty, Mavis looks like one of those European character actresses who play aging ballerinas: taut, as if not just hair but also skin and sinew were pulled back in that perfect graying doughnut at the base of her skull. Once Mavis *was* an actress. At the height of her career, she was Judy Holliday's understudy in *Bells Are Ringing*. Mavis is nothing like Judy Holliday. Still, Vera can't look at her without thinking that Judy Holliday would be old now, too, and of how Judy Holliday and Gracie Allen are Lowell's all-time favorite actresses.

Had anyone but Carmen told Vera that Mavis went from the Broadway stage to a job as a diener in the Medical Examiner's Office, Vera wouldn't have believed it. Though Vera can't help watching for signs of those years spent chainsawing ribcages, sewing cadavers, doing the junky physical work of the autopsy room, the only clue is Mavis's intimate knowledge of every murder committed in New York during that time, of choice grisly stories —CRAZED KENNEL OWNER FEEDS STRAYING SPOUSE TO PINSCHER PUPS—which she recycles endlessly for fresh *This Week* copy. Yet Mavis is anything but a ghoul. When Vera started at *This Week*, she managed the sitter's sick days by bringing Rosie in to work and parking her with Mavis. And Mavis, who has no children and whose husband had recently died, seemed to enjoy moving everything sharp or halfway important out of a five-year-old's reach.

Now Mavis says, "How's Rosie?"

"Fine," Vera says. "No, that's not true. Terrible." But that's wrong, too. The truth, if she could tell it, would make her life with Rosie sound like a chilly two-career marriage. Most nights when Vera comes home, Rosie's in her room with the door shut, the radio going, busy with homework, the latest Judy Blume, and Byzantine game plans for Dungeons and Dragons. At dinner, Rosie will either stay silent or chatter on about the summer program. On cranky mornings, they'll fight about the bathroom floor, crumbs on the table, milk left out to spoil. Then they'll go downstairs and off in different directions. Put this way, it doesn't sound so bad, especially if Vera skips over the fact that she can't recall when Rosie last kissed her hello or goodnight.

"She's growing up," says Mavis. "It's difficult."

"Difficult isn't the word," says Vera. Last week she sat across the subway aisle from a young Puerto Rican father and his baby. The baby was plump and adorable, giggling wildly as its father kissed it up and down the almost invisible bumps of its spine. They were like new lovers; they didn't care who saw. Vera had to look away and remind herself of how, when her grandmother was alive, Vera complained about Rosie growing up too fast and her grandmother said, "You'd be happier if she stayed the same?" Vera thinks about Peter Pan's mother. Did *she* like how things turned out?

"I don't know," she tells Mavis. "She's got a big ballet recital Sunday night. I think she's nervous about it."

"Sunday?" repeats Mavis, with the peculiar, slowed-down pacing of someone giving you time to include them. So it's decided: Mavis and Vera will meet at the recital, then Mavis will come back to Vera's for a late supper.

Making plans helps Vera fight the urge to run back and get Lowell's letter. What little she knows about Mavis's long and devoted married life makes her want to show it to her and ask, What about this? Instead she asks if Mavis has heard anything about Shaefer and Esposito going to see their lawyer.

"I haven't the slightest," says Mavis. "Let me know."

"I'll do that," says Vera, tossing her cup into the trash and thinking how she likes this about coffee-room conversations. It's not like having company, or visiting: no getting up, no goodbyes. At any point, you can just leave.

Opening Solomon's door, Vera walks in on a crouching nun,

her mouth wide in a soundless scream. On the wall behind her is the shadow of a man with a knife. If you look closely, you can see that the shadow has a half-dozen cameras around its neck. It's the kind of detail that makes Solomon's photos transcend themselves. For even if you don't notice the cameras, you still unconsciously sense it: After this maniac kills the nun, he's planning to take pictures.

Solomon has the shutter on automatic so he can get the shot and play Jack the Ripper at the same time. When Vera walks in he puts down the knife and says, "Fuck it, it's too complicated."

"I'll stop back later," says Vera.

"No no no no no!" Solomon grabs Vera's hand and drags her into the room. "I need a break. Take ten," he tells the girl in the nun outfit. She's a dimply eighteen-year-old, and as she passes, trailing clouds of patchouli, her eyes meet Vera's and Vera can almost see her figuring out the whole story of how Vera and Solomon were and maybe still are in love. She and Vera could be two female monkeys declaring their intentions—it's strange, Vera thinks, having that sort of interchange with a nun.

As Solomon rushes around, switching off lights, Vera can see why even an eighteen-year-old might want him. In his close-cropped hair, Hawaiian shirt, and clear-framed glasses, he looks sweet and confident and sexy, an eighties-style fifties hipster, except that he's probably looked this way for twenty years.

"I told Shaefer yesterday," he whispers, "these lights get so hot, the wiring can't take it. We're gonna burn like fucking crisps." He knocks on a wooden desk, then moves closer to Vera. Solomon stares into everyone's eyes; Vera can't count the waitresses and salesgirls and supermarket checkers she's seen thrown off by Solomon's gaze.

"Where have you *been?*" he says. His Hawaiian shirt smells of cigars, and as he squeezes her against the smooth cotton, Vera presses her forehead into those tropical beaches and red sunsets and wishes she could stay there forever.

On the wall behind him is a framed print that looks like a

photo of exploding dust, which Solomon claims is the only known shot of his kneecap disappearing at Khe Sanh. Whether or not he has it on film, there's no denying the lemon-sized depression where his right knee should be; the rest of him seems slightly drawn, as if flesh and sinew and something less tangible has gone into healing it. Now as he runs for the phone, cameras bang together around his neck; his bad leg follows, bouncy and dogged as a younger kid keeping up.

"Who's this?" he yells into the phone. "Pete? Solomon. Listen, can you do me a favor and stop by in a couple minutes and kill a nun? Great." He laughs and hangs up.

"SINGING NUN HITS SOUR NOTE?" says Vera.

"Close," says Solomon. "SADO SLASHER STRIKES SEMINARY SISTER. One of Mavis's masterpieces."

"SICKO SHUTTERBUG SHOOTS SELF STABBING SISTER," Vera says.

"You got it," he says. "What's up?"

"Not me," Vera says. "We're in for it now. Didn't Carmen tell you?"

"*We?*"

"Someone's suing the paper." It sounds so right, Vera nearly forgets it's just a guess. "Over one of our stories."

Solomon grabs Vera's shoulders and backs her against the wall. "You know what we do to guys who bring bad news?" he says. Then he lets her go and grins. "Are you serious? Every crank with a dime to call a lawyer has sued us fifty times."

"This one's had Dan and Frank at their lawyer's all morning."

Solomon scratches the back of his neck. "Then it's a rich crank with fifty cents for a fancy lawyer."

"We're supposed to see them after lunch," Vera says. "I'm going to the morgue to read back and see what I can figure out."

"Needle-in-a-haystack time," says Solomon. Then he takes Vera's hands between his and says, "All right, I'll make you a deal. If it turns out to be nothing, I'll buy you dinner Saturday."

"And if it turns out to be something?"

"I'll buy you dinner Saturday to cheer us up."

Vera thinks she has reasons for not wanting to go, but before she can think of one, she sees the little nun, lounging in the doorway, sullen and wary as a high-school girl waiting for the teacher to pass so she can light up. Vera wishes she could, too; the time it would take to light a smoke is exactly the interval she needs to exit with anything approaching grace.

Leaving Solomon's, the first office Vera passes is Tom Dreier's. Tom Dreier—of the shiny suits, the three-strand-over-the-bald-spot pervert hair, the ubiquitous briefcase that Vera imagines containing handcuffs and rubber restraints for lunchtime assignations—writes the regular columns that appear near the back of the paper: "Ask Your Doctor," "You and Your Teenager," and the most popular, "Take That!" ("You know what I think about the ERA? I think those bra-burners would still be beating their laundry against the rocks if some MAN hadn't invented the washing machine for them! Take that!") According to the latest *This Week* readers' poll, more people than Vera wants to believe buy the paper just for "Take That!" 's responsible, hard-hitting journalism.

Next door to Tom is Mort Baird, a pleasant little recluse whose office has a certain entertainment value because of the illustrations he draws for every article he writes. The art is primitive, childlike, unprintable. But without it, Mort claims, he can't work. Vera's favorite is his drawing for GOD GAVE ME FIVE BLIND BABIES—a stick figure Mom with five tiny bundles, each wearing infant-size sunglasses. Visiting Mort reminds Vera of first dates with shy guys who took you to museums. You looked at the pictures while they stood there watching you look; then you both stood there.

Continuing down the hall, Vera almost stops in on Peter Smalley, their resident specialist in the ghost-occult. Lately he's been turning in articles under the byline Kuldip Kulkarni, bits about modern-day Kali cults and thousands of untouchables tossed down village wells. As usual his door's closed, bare except for a card with a typed-out quote: "Here we will talk of nothing but God."—Sri Ramakrishna. Inside, Vera knows, it's equally spartan, just Peter's Harvard diploma and a photo of

Meher Baba's "Smile Don't Worry Be Happy" goofy and comforting grin. But if it's comfort she's after, she'd do better smoking a joint with the brothers in the mail room, whose stoned
jivy conversation works better than the view of Herald Square
to remind her that there are other ways to live besides writing
for *This Week*. Any day, Vera can walk into the business office
and one of the secretaries will be wearing new shoes or a funny
hair clip and they can talk, like normal people, about that. Today, though, Vera just doesn't feel like discussing funny hair
clips.

Three offices combined into one room lined with old papers,
the morgue is the closest *This Week* comes to the Dickensian
splendor of the Basenji Society. Ever since Mary Alice, the
librarian, attended a workshop on newsprint preservation, a
whole ecosystem of fans, conditioners, and humidifiers have kept
it a perfect temperature, deoxygenated as the cabin of an airplane.

Today Mary Alice is nowhere around. Vera's on her own. She
takes six months of back issues off the shelves and then just sits
there, trying to remember one single event from six months ago.
She might as well be thinking back to the womb. Somewhat
desperately she reassures herself: her problem's not premature
senility but the amnesia of everyday life; she blames it on being
so far from Lowell and Louise. Without old friends to verify the
past, to remind you of what you've forgotten, your whole life
could blow away like the breeze from Mary Alice's fan.

In Vera's search for some marker in time, *This Week* is no
help at all. Its ageless plots could have come from the ancient
Greeks. Its NEW AIR FORCE UFO PICS might be reprints from
a decade ago. It's no surprise that the only mention of past, present, and future occurs in the syndicated column, "Karen Karl's
'I Predict!' "

One night Vera saw Karen Karl on TV, wearing a tenty black
cocktail dress with pointy witch's sleeves. David Susskind ridiculed every word she said, but that wasn't what made Vera
doubt her; she couldn't believe that a real witch would feel
compelled to flirt with Susskind. Now, reading Karen Karl's
March predictions, Vera sees that she's been batting zero in the

intervening months. Castro hasn't been assassinated, nor has Jackie O. remarried. If the Reagans have become grandparents, why would they keep it from the nation? And she seems to remember Liza Minelli—twins predicted here—having a rather well-publicized miscarriage. Vera gets no pleasure from Karen Karl's misses; instead she feels badly for readers who care about such things and who six months ago believed—as Liza Minelli must have—that there was something to look forward to.

With a batting average like that, it's a wonder she stays on the team, though probably modern witchcraft has less to do with ESP than with letting Susskind make fun of you. Not that the rest of the *This Week* staff would win any prizes for accuracy. If one of Karen Karl's predictions came true, she'd write a column about it; if theirs did, it would go round marked "Too close for comfort."

Vera leaves Karen Karl to her mistakes and starts looking for her own. All and none of the pieces look familiar; it's a tribute to the staff's ability to write uniform *This Week*-ese. The first to ring any sort of bell is DWI ON GOD:

> In an unprecedented court case, the Reverend Dewey Smoot of Sump City, Georgia, has pleaded innocent to charges of vehicular homicide on the grounds that he was driving under the influence of visions sent by his guardian angel.

Solomon's right about needles in haystacks; any one of these stories could be it. Maybe there is a Dewey Smoot testing this very case before a Sump City grand jury, and maybe his guardian angel has sent him the money to hire a smart Yankee lawyer. Would it help to play Where-Did-This-Story-Come-From? All that DWI ON GOD brings to mind is a meld of two TV shows— one on Mothers Against Drunk Driving, the other on child evangelists.

In the May 14 issue, MILLIONAIRE LEOPARD-LOVER LEAVES T-BONE TRUST TO ZOO sounds familiar. Could this really have happened? Vera remembers a trip to the zoo—steering Rosie past a catatonic gorilla and thinking she'd shielded her from that particular horror until Rosie began waking up with gorilla bad dreams for three weeks in a row. She remembers Louise writing a poem about it, Lowell telling her, there's no shielding *anyone* from the gorilla. But that was years ago. Rosie couldn't have been more than four.

What's happened to all her bylines? She can't find a one. Frustration is making Vera feel catatonic herself. Nothing seems possible. She's thirty-seven years old and, except for Rosalie, has no one but two parents still fighting the Spanish Civil War, an ex-husband writing letters on a gangster's typewriter, a sometime lover who is at this moment photographing himself sticking knives into a teenage nun. Entirely unmemorable six-month chunks are crumbling away from a life already half gone.

Pushing the stack of *This Week*s away, Vera thinks: A morgue is a morgue. Mavis should come in about now to suture up the mess. Closing her eyes, Vera listens to the air conditioner. Then suddenly the room goes silent. And when she looks up again, everything seems brighter. For in the interim she's realized: If she's fired today, she'll never forget—Friday, August something, the day she lost her job. At least she'll remember that! All at once the details of this room seem so permanent, so clear—she feels as if she's taken a photo.

In that moment Vera's triumphant; she feels like Proust. Thinking madeleines, butter, sugar, thinking lunch, she's halfway out the door before she realizes: The silence she'd heard is just the click of Mary Alice's air conditioner automatically shutting off in its search for the ideal climate for eternal newsprint life.

THOUGH VERA would never admit it, she's scared of the office at lunch. It's safe enough with Shaefer and Esposito and half the staff always there. By rights, she should be more uneasy on those occasional Saturdays when she comes in and the place is deserted. But she isn't. The office at lunch feels like one of those spots in fairy tales—the graveyard at midnight, the bayou beneath the full moon—those confluences of place and time where you just shouldn't be. So by the first rustle of brown paper bag, the first food smell, the first "Can I get you anything from downstairs?" Vera's gone, outracing any malevolent spirits to the elevator.

The elevator's so crowded Vera considers waving it on, except for the look she'd get from Hazel. Being jammed in like that feels both repellent and erotic. It makes her want to find some Himalayan cave and never see anyone again; it makes her want to strip naked and rub against all that sweet, sticky human flesh.

The lobby seems chokingly hot, then like a cool memory compared to Sixth Avenue. It's the kind of heat that feels like wearing a cast-iron pot on your head: inside, brain cells explode like popcorn. Vera has no idea where she's going. The crowd engulfs her, then casts her up like driftwood, slamming her into a bin of tube socks and shower sandals and discount-store washcloths. Stunned, Vera stares at the rainbow-colored Afro wigs bunched over the doorway like exotic, fuzzy coconuts. She tries to imagine wearing one into Frank Shaefer's office for the post-lunch showdown. Once Louise went to a Halloween party dressed as garbage, with a milk carton pinned to her T-shirt, orange peels and shredded plastic wrap in her hair; at the party she opened a toy garbage can and dumped paper on the rug. The silence, the guests' blank faces—it's how Vera pictures Frank and Dan's reaction to her in a rainbow Afro wig.

She's thinking of the winter Lowell scratched his cornea and so complained about people staring at his eyepatch that Vera bought him a grinning, pop-eyed Froggy the Gremlin mask. She was shocked when he seemed hurt by this new evidence of her hard-heartedness. If her heart were so hard, it wouldn't have been broken by this sign of how far they'd come from the days when he'd have hung that frog mask by the door and never gone out without it. Even now the memory's painful enough to make her just stop, causing a slight pedestrian pileup that leaves her directly in front of the New Napoli Restaurant.

Outside, a speaker's playing a Muzak mariachi version of "South of the Border." "Mission bells told me I shouldn't stay. . . ." Why not? Vera wonders, wishing she knew the rest of the song. Is it violence, or just faded love? Perhaps she's confusing it with "El Paso" or *Touch of Evil* or countless lurid border stories that only a trashy *This Week* sensibility would care about in the first place. Still, she can't help swaying slightly to those xylophone dips and glides.

In the window, Vinnie's spinning pizza dough on his fists. He catches Vera's eye, smiles, then looks away. Vinnie's shy and handsome and such a flirt that sometimes Vera's chest gets tight and it feels like the start of real love. Now she wonders if it's possible to build a marriage on that: shy smiles and great pizza. Last year Vinnie's pizza was written up in *New York* magazine, and for a while the place was crowded with upscale types. But the crowds moved on even before the blown-up magazine clipping came back from the printer. Mounted in plastic, gathering dust in the window, the clipping reminds Vera of a whole class of *This Week* stories, all variations on the theme of "too late": Delayed letters arriving from GIs dead fifteen years, grieving mothers receiving hospital gift portraits of newborns who never made it home from neonatal intensive care.

Vera orders eggplant parmesan and a dark Heineken and brings them to her table. The eggplant is rich and generous with melted cheese; that and the ice-cold beer should make her feel better. But just to make sure they don't, she takes Lowell's letter from her purse. Rereading it till she knows it by heart, she's trying—as she's always done with Lowell—to read in something that just isn't there.

The soundtrack has segued from "South of the Border" to "Tijuana Taxi." Shutting it out, Vera thinks back to the time she went to San Francisco to visit Louise. Substituting Vivaldi's *Four Seasons* for Herb Alpert is all it takes to bring back those New Age wood-and-hanging-plant greasy spoons where she lunched with Louise's tofu-brained friends, who would sooner have choked on their beansprouts than ask an uptight East Coast question like What do you do for a living? Unasked, Vera volunteered the fact she wrote other people's stories. Other people's stories? Really, they said. You've got to meet Lowell.

And where was Lowell? Off in some Bombay opium den, some Karachi hashish parlor, guiding some rich French junkie on a narcotics tour of Asia. While back at home, friends with barely enough energy to gum their guacamole jumped at the chance to tell his life story: how he was born to Arkansas Holy Rollers; how his father became a government engineer and was posted four hundred miles north of Fairbanks, Alaska, to work on the DEW line; how he lived ten years in a log cabin with Mom and Dad and six kids and huskies and dogsleds, until his father was transferred down to Portland, where Lowell discovered his true calling, selling pot; how this vocation financed numerous trips to Asia, three spectacular hashish deals, and as many expensive failures. How those scrubbed vegetarian faces lit up when they listed the addictions Lowell had kicked, the substances he'd abused!

So even before she met him, Vera saw how Lowell's friends loved him, how his story gave them not just the hope of new possibilities, last-minute changes, exceptions to the rule, but also the pure joy of telling it. The next part was predictable: She almost *had* to be disappointed by that big, long-faced hillbilly skulking around the edges of his own coming-home party.

Vera still likes remembering the interval when she convinced herself that her interest in Lowell was just friendly, that all she wanted was to spend time with him, to walk down the street or drive in a car and see what would happen and what he would do; followed by the period when every day she didn't spend with him seemed wasted. The morning he showed up to see her at eight A.M., and they knew what was going to happen, but the protocol of her staying on Louise's living-room couch made them wait like courting teens all day. The strangeness of hearing that hillbilly accent in the darkness, telling her stories that permanently changed her idea of what stories she wanted to hear in the dark. The night he told her about a place in Afghanistan so backward they had no musical instruments but cupped their hands in their armpits and quacked out the rhythms and solos of the Nuristani Underarm Band. Even Vera knew how crazy it was to be falling in love with someone for telling glorified Afghan Polish jokes; and she knew that was what she was doing.

Meanwhile, the same people who'd told her Lowell's life story now felt duty-bound to warn her: Lowell could go to Nuristan but not to the corner store. Send him out for a quart of milk and he'd come back with a plastic Aqua Man to wind up and swim in the tub. Yet it made perfect sense that the bazaars of Mazār-i-Sharif would spoil you for the Safeway, and Vera thanked God for sending her someone who could find the magic in the Seven-Eleven.

By then they'd rented a room in some art student's Hayes Street flat and were living on love with a food-stamp backup. Then winter came, bringing week after week of rain. One wet morning Lowell rolled up his last antique Bokhara rug and came back hours later with no rug and two plane tickets to Mérida, where, he said, they'd eat enough psilocybin mushrooms to put them in touch with ancient Mayans who'd lead them to their lost buried treasure. Soon after, Vera found herself in a cow pasture in Palenque, watching some Québecois hippies cook psychedelic-mushroom omelets, and soon after that on her knees in a tunnel under the pyramids, burrowing through the darkness lit only by bunches of sputtering wax *cerillos*. Her sharpest memory is of sitting by a *cenote* with Lowell complaining nonstop about the team of crack divers from *National Geographic* who'd got there first and dredged up a fortune in gold. How soothing it was to picture *National Geographic*'s sunny yellow borders instead of that dismal black pool, those thousands of gilded Mayan virgins sinking like stones!

So what? said Lowell. What good did all that treasure do the Mayans? They'd go to the coast and skindive for the Giant Squid and bring him back to exhibit in New York. But all Vera got skindiving was rapture of the deep before she'd even left the surface and a blistering sunburn on her back.

By this time their money was almost gone. They had twenty pesos total when Vera asked Lowell to buy some cocoa butter or vaseline, some homeopathic Mayan sunburn remedy—anything to ease the rawness aggravated by the rough rope hammock they were sleeping on in their poverty-level hippie shack on the beach. Hours later Lowell returned with a small bag of cashew nuts, its fifteen-peso price tag still attached. He was bewildered when she hid her face in her hands and cried. He'd bought the cashews as a present to take her mind off her sunburn. By then Vera was starting to suspect that all those addictions Lowell had kicked had taken their cerebral toll. The miles those cashews had traveled from Ceylon to Mexico seemed suddenly like an infinitesimal fraction of the distance between her and Lowell.

By the time Louise sent money, Vera and Lowell weren't speaking any more than it took to arrange some vague plan to fly back to New York and try to work things out. Vera's secret plan, which made her feel like one of those Mafia widows who marry their husband's killer and wait twenty years for their middle-of-the-night revenge, was to try working things out without Lowell. But when their plane ran into a storm—two very long hours of freefall plunges and dead silence except for the clicking of rosaries—Lowell put his hand over Vera's and told her stories of Royal Burmese Airways: how when the planes turn around for takeoff, the passengers pile out onto the runway and push; how a lady beside him found a chilled, semiconscious scorpion in her plastic-wrapped dinner tray. He'd just begun telling her how the Burmese pilots turn the signal lights out at night to save fuel when their plane limped into Kennedy and they looked at each other and knew that their love and bravery had brought them in for a landing.

Peter Pan and Wendy, they flew hand in hand through baggage claim, customs, straight to the marriage-license bureau. By the weekend, they'd already found an apartment and conceived Rosalie. Lowell got a Christmas-rush job on the Gimbels loading dock. Vera went to work for the *Downtowner*, cutting self-help articles to fit snugly around the ads. Rosie was born. They fell in love with her and briefly again with each other. Then Vera went back to work while Lowell took care of the baby and started a screenplay that, she realizes now, was his domestic version of digging for Mayan treasure; the script, she vaguely remembers, was a kind of Preston Sturges comedy involving the Annual Tannana Ice Derby, when all Alaska bets on the minute and second the ice in the Tannana River will crack.

She can almost graph those weeks: up on Wednesdays when Lowell bought his New York State Lottery ticket, down on Tuesdays when the winning numbers came out. She can almost smell the spoiled-milk odor of the Ninth Street Market Stop with its astronomical prices, its aisles narrow as arteries, clogged with old ladies stalled by the cranberry juice, its power to make you imagine it after closing, rats scrabbling over the cheddar cheese in the pale half-light of the dairy bin. She sees a procession of brown paper bags marching toward her like the Sorcerer's Apprentice's brooms, most filled with awful things that Lowell had bought and she wouldn't touch with a stick: sauerkraut in salami-shaped packages, rainbow-hued breakfast cereals, meat in brine with fat globules waving like sea anemones, and cornflakes, always cornflakes, the dropped-from-the-sky-by-helicopter manna of Lowell's Alaskan childhood. And still she kept sending him out, kept testing him. Because no matter how often it happened, it never seemed possible that he would really spend the money for Rosie's diapers on some new brand of rolled anchovy.

Yet now, as Vera goes for another bite of eggplant and finds she's already finished, it seems just as unlikely that you could stop loving someone for being unable to go to the grocery. Vera can hardly believe it, but she knows *This Week* readers could: SHOOTS SPOUSE FOR SHOPPING SLIPUP. Shopping slipup. Vera tries saying it aloud a few times, then notices that the people around her have looked up from their sausage heroes and are staring at her strangely. How fitting that she should be taken for a screamer! How many screamers clutch grease-stained, crumpled letters just like hers! Vera stands and slides her tray into the stack with such excessive precision that anyone watching would think she *was* certifiable, or at the very least blind drunk.

Leaving, she pretends not to see Vinnie; if she smiled, it would come out one of those rictus screamer grins. Engrossed in her *Afternoon Serial* magazine, Hazel ignores Vera, who's wondering why a woman who works all week bothers to read summaries of the soap-opera plots. Perhaps all her friends watch, and poor Hazel has to keep up. Vera's heart warms to Hazel, then cools again when the elevator stops with her floor at knee level.

When Vera walks in, Carmen holds up a tear sheet still smelling of printer's ink: REMARKABLE RADISH DIET FIGHTS FAT. DES MOINES DOC PROMISES RADISHING NEW FIGURE IN 30 DAYS.

"What do you think?" says Carmen.

"Thirty days of radishes? Carmen, please." Among Vera's reasons for distrusting the Lizard is that he's always telling Carmen how much he likes skinny girls. Consequently, Carmen has been on every fad diet known to man and permitted by the Seventh-Day Adventists. She loves talking about her diets, conversations that are theoretically about willpower and actually about food: I was doing fine till Cousin Lupe brought over her three-layer devil's-food cake. Nothing but grapefruit for two weeks till Uncle Manuel had his barbeque—chicken, ribs, rice with squid, buttered pigeon peas, coco flan.

Now she says, "No, I mean *this*." She points to two postage-stamp-sized pictures at the top of the story. Like all before-andafters, they look like no one you'd ever run across in real life. But these are both Carmen: Carmen bulging prettily out of a modest one-piece bathing suit beside Carmen with so much weight airbrushed off she looks positively anorexic.

"Did Solomon take these?" Vera asks.

"I volunteered," says Carmen, saluting. "Now listen, here's my diet. I send the 'after' shot to Frankie in Fort Benning. I say, 'Look how skinny I've got!' Then I'll *have* to lose it before he comes home Thanksgiving."

"Don't do it," says Vera.

"Relax," says Carmen. "If it doesn't work, I'll just tell him I gained it back again."

"Forget it," Vera says. "Just forget it. Are Shaefer and Esposito back yet?"

"Jury's still out," Carmen says. "Go to your office, put your feet up, take it easy. I'll buzz you when they come in."

Obediently, Vera trots off and actually puts her feet on her desk. She thinks of one of Solomon's pre–*This Week* photos— the furrowed soles of an old Mexican who'd just completed a barefoot fifty-mile walk to some shrine. Leaning back, she studies her bookcase, filled mostly with books she'd gotten in the office mail and hadn't thought worth taking home, including—she sees now—a load of material from Ray Bramlett and the cryptobiologists. She picks out *Bigfoot: Fact or Fantasy?* and, opening at random, reads:

It is nearly impossible for most city dwellers to imagine a terrain wild and vast enough for a creature of Bigfoot's size to live there undetected. In many ways, Bigfoot is a creature of the last frontier.

When she catches herself reaching for Lowell's letter again, she decides that working will make the time pass faster.

Another game she plays, a little like Where-Did-This-Story-Come-From? only more productive, is to shut her eyes and put her finger on the nearest printed matter and make a story out of whatever word she's touched. In this case it's the salutation on

Lowell's letter: Howdy! She switches on the typewriter and without thinking slugs in the head: HOWDY DOODY VICTIM OF BIZARRE KIDDIE CULT. SHOCKED MOM SUES.

When six-year-old Teddy Fedders's friends asked him to bring his Howdy Doody doll out to play, little did the Michigan tot suspect that his beloved puppet would become the latest victim in a wave of violence aimed against America's best-loved dummy.

In a schoolyard not far from his posh Bloomfield Hills home, little Teddy watched in anguish as the marionette— a legacy from his Dad, killed in a car crash three years before—was tied to a stake and doused with gasoline and burned.

When Teddy's Mom, Ariella Fedders, 29, pressed charges, she learned that this apparently isolated incident was actually the latest in a Howdy Doody crime wave culminating in last spring's raid on a Cleveland DJ's collection of Howdy memorabilia. Nationwide, collectors are fearing for the safety of their Howdy Doody holdings. There is some concern that news of this bizarre violence may be spreading via the same kiddie rumor underground responsible for last year's whisper campaign alleging the presence of rat hairs in Burger King products.

Where did *this* story come from? Vera watched Howdy Doody as a kid, but was never much of a fan. Nor does she associate him, as some do, with all the sweetness of childhood, with those last precious moments of afternoon TV before Mom called you for dinner.

Rather than pursue this, Vera drifts off till she catches herself staring into the trash basket at the letter from the ultrasound victim in West Myra, Illinois. Then she rolls in more paper and types: HOUSEWIFE CHARGES ASTRAL RAPE.

In a ground-breaking criminal suit, an Illinois housewife has charged a neighborhood man with assaulting her via astral projection.

Anything would be better than knowing where this story came from. Vera's considering another trip to the coffee room when the red light on her telephone blinks on.

"Okay," says Carmen. "They're here."

THE TABLEAU in Shaefer's office reminds Vera of moments at parties when conversation dies and you look around and see nothing but other groups who've just run out of things to say. All four men—Dan Esposito at Frank Shaefer's desk, Shaefer standing in the far corner, the two lawyers seated at opposite ends of the chapped Naugahyde couch—look slightly stunned, motionless except for the younger lawyer, whose knees pump as he dandles his briefcase in his lap.

Vera aims her thin little "Hi" at Dan Esposito, whose tan, handsome, slightly hangdog face is the easiest to look at. Tilted back in his chair, he seems at once weary and wholly at ease; if he were driving a truck, one elbow would be out the window.

"Vera," he says. "Come in."

Once at an office Christmas party, Vera drank too much punch and found herself standing very close to Dan Esposito, who had himself drunk enough to want to tell her about the camping trips he takes with his wife every fall, out into what he called the heartland to see if *This Week* was keeping in touch. As he spoke, Vera pictured a misty campground beside some Idaho lake. Gazing into the water, Mrs. Esposito is shredding a cigarette filter and wishing they'd gone to Europe like the Shaefers, while Dan sits in a lawn chair with his sleeves rolled up, his fine hands over his eyes, straining to hear what the folks in the camper next door are saying about UFO sightings and life after death.

"Vera, you know Mr. Goldblum," says Dan, and though Vera has no memory of the bald, gnomish man who rises to greet her, she nods and attempts a smile.

"And this is Mr. Goldblum's partner. Leonard Villanova, Vera

Perl." The younger lawyer unfolds himself from the couch and walks towards Vera with steps that seem rather too small for his age and height. His hand is soft and damp, and Vera can hardly mumble hello for trying not to laugh at the thought that this is the kind of guy who makes you think the Victorians were right about excessive masturbation showing up in your face. "Pleased to meet you," says Leonard, a good ten seconds after it's appropriate, then backs up and sits down.

Vera would like to sit, too, but short of wedging herself between the lawyers, there's no way. Furnished in dentist's-waiting-room chic, Shaefer's office makes no concession to comfort or beauty, not unless you count the prodigious collection of monkeys covering their eyes, ears, mouths, and nearly every inch of shelf space. At their first interview, when Vera complimented him on it—and really, you had to say something—he'd spoken with great reverence of how Gandhi received thousands of similar statues from admirers all over the world. Surely there's some hidden meaning beyond the obvious irony in the editor of *This Week* amassing these symbols of perfect discretion and tact, but for the life of her, Vera can't think what it is.

Now Frank spins toward her with a folding chair, which he snaps out like a matador flicking a cape. Above the rumpled shirt, the straining buttons, Frank Shaefer's face is round as the moon and his blue eyes peer out of it with a baby's astonishment. In a forties movie or a better world, Frank would live forever in some newsroom, Mr. City Desk chomping stogies and clacking out datelines on an old-fashioned Royal. Instead he's the eighties version, forced by an early coronary to give up cigars. Vera's always thought the heart attack had less to do with nicotine than with Frank's conversational style—firing off questions, then answering them for you. Now she wishes he'd ask her where Solomon is so maybe she could find out.

She and Solomon should have come in together. Waiting for him again recalls a bad party kept going by the hope that some new arrival may yet change everything. Finally they hear his cameras clanking out in the hall and turn toward the sound. Solomon lurches in and bounces around shaking hands. Then

Shaefer shakes open a copy of *This Week* with much the same motion he'd used on the folding chair and says, "Okay, what's the story on *this*?"

FOUNTAIN OF YOUTH FLOWS IN BROOKLYN BACK YARD. Vera remembers the headline from three or four weeks back. But when Solomon passes it on to her, she rereads every word, partly for the details and partly because she knows no one will bother her till she's finished:

Soon after a Brooklyn brother and sis started their sidewalk lemonade biz, neighbors began claiming that the youngsters' brand was having some surprising side effects.

Business boomed for 8-year-old Joshua Green and his sister Megan, 6, when word spread that their 5-cents-a-glass wonder drink was curing satisfied customers of chronic ills and restoring youth and vitality throughout their Flatbush neighborhood. In an exclusive *This Week* interview, the children's mom, Stephanie Green, 37, admitted that the beverage was concocted from generic lemonade mix and water.

Dr. Martin Green, a well-known Manhattan cardiologist, lost no time in putting his kids "out of business." But though the Greens refuse to sell samples, requests remain numerous. Daily crowds have all but ruined the front lawn and forced the unfortunate family to invest over $5,000 in additional fencing.

As the shell-shocked Mrs. Green told *This Week*, "I don't know how this happened to us. I feel like it's all my fault."

Vera knows where this story came from. Sometimes Solomon gives her photos and she makes up stories to go with them. It's a game they play, a reverse of their usual working method. The sad truth is that their collaboration has become a parody of their own dreams. For during that time they'd imagined themselves in love, they'd spoken often of working together on the perfect marriage of picture and text and all-expense-paid vacations: articles for *Geo* magazine on deserted Balinese beaches, lush coffee-table books on Indians of the Amazon and carnival in Venice.

Studying the grainy reprint, Vera's looking for what's left of that gorgeous eight-by-ten glossy that Solomon dropped on her desk. She can still see the plastic pitcher, the miniature table and chairs, the two children in front of their Flatbush Gothic monstrosity home, and above it, the dark sky and clouds that look borrowed from Kansas. But what's missing in reproduction are the hopeful, wide-open-for-business looks on the children's faces; without them, Vera finds she can't recapture the peculiar feeling that the little girl in the photo was herself as a child.

She'd set out to write about people who *weren't* like her, people who name their kids Megan and Joshua and restore the kind of house she grew up in but which in the meantime have declined into what are euphemistically called "multi-family dwellings." And she'd wound up writing about the fountain of youth, the only thing that could change her back into that child who'd imagined great fortunes begun selling lemonade.

When she looks up, everyone's watching her and Frank Shaefer's saying, "Dr. and Mrs. Green are suing."

"What Dr. and Mrs. Green?" says Vera.

"Why don't you tell us about it?" says Dan, the good cop on the interrogation team.

Vera looks at Solomon. For some reason she'd had the impression he'd just been driving by and had got out and snapped the picture. But maybe not, maybe he knew these people, had told her about them, lodged their names in her brain without her remembering. Solomon's shrugging, palms upturned; he's bugging his eyes at her. So her impression was right. For once she's glad Shaefer's answering for her:

"The Dr. and Mrs. Green who live in this house." He pokes at the paper. "Megan and Joshua's Mom and Dad. The well-known Manhattan cardiologist and his shell-shocked wife."

"That's not possible," says Vera. "I made them up."

The silence that greets this makes Vera want to climb Shaefer's bookcase and lean out the window toward the soothing traffic noise of Herald Square. Old Mr. Goldblum keeps bobbing his head and smiling. Perhaps he's surprised or embarrassed; perhaps he thinks Vera's joking. Solomon shifts his weight from one foot to the other, a process so awkward and noisy that Goldblum beckons to him and pats the couch beside him. Crossing the room, Solomon just misses Shaefer. They dodge each other like dancers in some awful modern ballet. Meanwhile Leonard Villanova has scooted forward and opened his mouth. When Shaefer stands behind him and starts talking, the moment loses its balletic aspect and takes on the aura of an equally rotten ventriloquist act.

"Vera," he says. "I just can't believe the Greens' lawyer is being retained to represent your fantasies."

"Then what?" Vera's horrified by the high whine of her voice. She's saving confusion and wonder for later. Right now all she feels is panic.

"Listen! She had nothing to do with this!" cries Solomon, like some movie Resistance hero pleading his girlfriend's case before the secret police.

"It's her byline," says Shaefer. "What the hell are you talking about?"

"It was a Sunday afternoon," says Solomon. "I was driving out to my sister-in-law's. I saw the two kids and that crazy Addams-Family house and that sky. I took the shot and—"

"Releases?" says Dan.

"What releases?" says Solomon. "We're talking tiny tots here. Then I printed it up and gave it to Vera and told her to write a story."

"Right," says Shaefer. "Then Vera made up the names and the kids' names and ages and even the good doc's specialty."

"Right," says Vera. That's what she did, and the whole thing *is* impossible. What seems even more absurd is that they're accusing her of something so unlikely. Hurt and angry, Vera feels—quite literally—the sting of injustice; it's making her eyes smart. Feeling tears come on, she concentrates on drying them with the sheer heat of her will.

Finally Leonard Villanova holds up one hand and, in a soft voice, says, "I find that hard to believe."

"No shit, Sherlock," says Solomon. Beside him, Mr. Goldblum winces.

"Meanwhile," says Shaefer, "the only thing you got wrong was the order it happened in. First the kids had their little lemonade stand. Then the issue with your story in it hit the racks. Some neighbors read it, rumors got started. The kids got swamped. Now the wife's a basket case. The lawn's a wreck, the phone rings twenty-four hours a day."

"It's damaged Dr. Green's practice," says Leonard Villanova, having saved the best for last. And then they all fall silent, awestruck by a vague, nascent sense of what damage to a cardiologist's practice might prove to be worth in court.

"Think hard now," says Dan Esposito. "You *really* didn't know? You just saw the photo, that's all?"

"Yes," says Vera. "I mean no. I didn't know."

"Jesus Christ," says Dan. "This is Kafkaesque."

The great writer's name seems to have worked some magic on Mr. Goldblum, who's suddenly gone very solemn. "I don't get it," he says.

"Well, legally it's immaterial, one way or the other," says Leonard Villanova, speaking professionally now to Mr. Goldblum.

"Sure it is," says Solomon. "It's a question of intent."

"Gee," says Mr. Goldblum. "I don't know what the precedent is; I wouldn't want to say."

"What precedent?" cries Vera. "How often do you think this happens?" As Goldblum's mild, myopic eyes crinkle in a sort of retreat, Vera regrets having said it so loud. "I'm sorry," she says. "It's all been a stupid mistake. But maybe it doesn't *have* to go to court. Maybe we could settle. *I'll* talk to the lawyer . . ."

"Vera," says Shaefer. "Shut up." Then, to Esposito: "You know what that would be like? Remember that scene in *The Godfather* where the Don and Sonny go to talk to the Tataglias and Sonny says something out of turn and the whole empire goes down the dumper?"

"Yeah," says Esposito. "Time to go to the mattresses, boys."

"Anybody got a grapefruit skin?" asks Solomon. "I'll do my Don Corleone in the tomato patch."

"This whole paper's about to do a Don Corleone in the tomato patch," says Frank. "You know what a cardiologist makes an hour?"

"Maybe if I went to Brooklyn and spoke to the Greens?" Vera offers desperately.

"I don't think that would be advisable," says Leonard Villanova at the same instant Frank Shaefer says, "I'd like to see you convince them you just dreamed them up. I'd like to see them buy *that*."

By now it's occurred to Vera that talking to a lawyer who's suing you might be like talking to a lover about to leave: some conversations cannot be brought to mutually satisfying conclusions. There's no possibility of forgiveness, no chance that the whole thing will turn out to be some simple misunderstanding. Realizing this makes Vera so helpless and angry she's up and out the door even as Leonard is standing with his briefcase at genital level and mumbling something about being in touch.

Solomon catches up with her in the hall and drags her into her office. "Jesus," he says. "What was *that* about?"

For the second time that day, Vera leans against Solomon's chest. The curve of his collarbone, the softness of his cotton shirt, are so sustaining and familiar she feels like they've been married thirty years. "I don't know," she says. "And that's the truth."

"I believe you," he says. "Just tell me this. You didn't go out there and look for the house, maybe talk to those people . . ."

"Why would I *do* that?" says Vera. "I don't go out on stories. It's not exactly *Eyewitness News* around here."

"All right," says Solomon. "You made the names up out of nowhere."

"Not exactly nowhere. Half the white kids in Brooklyn are named Megan and Joshua."

"And their mommies and daddies are all named Martin and Stephanie? You should have put the family dog in there."

"*You* figure it out," Vera says. "The dog's named Sam. He's a golden retriever. They had him long before Megan and Josh. Ten years ago, they used to tie a red bandanna around his neck."

Solomon moves her out where he can see her. "Take it easy," he says. "You're getting all worked up. Look, it's just one of those nutty coincidences that happen all the time. *All* the time. Like in 'Nam, you'd be walking through the jungle, you'd think 'snake' or 'body' and within a couple minutes you'd see a snake or a corpse. You couldn't have *seen* it; you were too far away. You just knew. And it's not ESP. ESP's bullshit. ESP's some scientist paying you three-ten an hour to sit in a padded cell and stare at picture postcards."

"Then what is it?" says Vera.

"Search me," says Solomon. "Feelers, maybe. Little antennae twitching all the time. Just like the bats have sonar. They don't *know* it's sonar; it took humans to come along and tell them what they're putting out. So maybe we need some higher form of life to tell us what we're bouncing off cobras and dead Viet Cong."

"And Brooklyn families?"

"Why not? Who says feelers don't work in Brooklyn?"

"I wish mine worked better," says Vera. "I wish they'd warned me that story would cost us our jobs." Vera stops short, struck by a vision of herself and Solomon as the tabloid Adam and Eve who've just done the one thing their grumpy but loving father forbade. "I'll bet Frank and Dan have already offered to fire us if those people drop charges. Didn't that cross your mind?"

"Not once," says Solomon. "Who's going to go for that? What if somebody gave you a choice between a half million and some reporter's scalp? Nobody's going to pass up all that dough just to see us hang. My guess is they'll settle out of court for every penny the paper's got. *Then* we'll get canned."

"Great," Vera says.

"Consider it a favor," says Solomon. "I don't want to be stabbing nuns when I'm Mavis's age."

"I was thinking the same thing this morning," says Vera, but right now she's thinking of another morning, at Solomon's place, of making coffee in that coffin-sized kitchen where everything—the walls, the artificial light, the coffee—looked watery and gray. She remembers Solomon kissing her, then stopping in midkiss to complain about having to go in to work and airbrush hair onto a child's face for WEREWOLF BOY BITES BULLET. And that was when she knew: if it had been love, that buzzing fluorescent bulb would have shone like the sun. Perhaps it was always a question of what Solomon calls feelers; they picked up each other's discontents.

"Remember our bet?" says Solomon.

"Which one?" she says.

"If this turned out to be something, I'd buy you dinner Saturday."

"It's turning out to be something," says Vera, and just then Mavis walks in. Mavis is smoking and Solomon, reminded, lights one of his cigars. Vera's always maintained that Solomon's not a real smoker; a real one would have lit up the second he'd left Shaefer's office.

"Tell me everything," says Mavis.

Solomon sits down on the desk top and lets Vera tell the whole story. Mavis blanches a little at the part about the damaged cardiology practice but quickly recovers enough to say, "Darling, these things happen. Some days I'd go into the morgue and think, 'They're going to bring in a floater.' And sure enough, they'd bring in a guy with so much cement around his neck, it took a come-along to pull him off the bottom of the Hudson."

"Lucca Brazzi." Solomon's doing his Don Corleone. "Tonight Lucca Brazzi sleeps wit' da fishes."

All three of them fall silent. Vera's recalling the day Mavis finally succeeded in getting her together with the favorite nephew she'd been talking up for years. The nephew arrived for lunch with a young man he introduced as his roommate and who was clearly his lover and fellow William Buckley clone. Everyone but Mavis immediately understood everything. How proud Henry James would have been of the way they sipped tea with thin slices of Mavis's lemon poundcake and made suitable conversation. When it ended they were all so relieved the two men offered to drive Vera home. On the way they took turns telling her how one winter morning Auntie Mavis called up and asked for a ride out to her husband's grave. Overnight, snow had fallen, burying the headstones. But Mavis led them through the graveyard straight to her husband's stone, where she knelt and dusted the snow off with her glove. "Mavis is quite a girl," the nephew had said. Feelers, Vera thinks now.

"Actually, I always liked those little premonitions," Mavis is saying. "Made me feel I was on the right track. So maybe congratulations are due. We'll talk about it Sunday. Which reminds me: is there anything I can bring Rosalie, something special for her recital . . ."

"A paper bag to put over her head," says Vera. "I think that's what she really wants."

"Bring me one, too," says Solomon.

When Mavis leaves, Vera can't think of anything to say and neither can Solomon. "I'll call you Saturday morning," is all he manages. Then he comes over to give her what he no doubt intends as an encouraging hug. Unfortunately they bump heads. Vera's reminded of a cuckoo clock of Rosie's that broke in such a way that the two apple-cheeked Bavarian dancers were stopped forever, head to head, a posture that has always struck Vera as a perfect design for cuckoo clocks in hell.

VERA'S TEMPTED to ask Carmen what the Adventists would make of all this. But the last time they talked Adventism, Carmen went on about unclean foods, the apocalypse, whether Christ's human nature was sinful, and whether his atonement on the cross was partial or complete. Her description of how each soul would be subjected to a lifelong spiritual investigation had made God and Jesus sound like some vindictive congressional committee. Vera was wondering why all this gloomy stuff appealed to Carmen when she'd started in on the Adventists' faith in self-improvement and Vera understood that for Carmen religion was in many ways a more glorious form of miracle diet. Still, Vera wonders if Carmen expects the milennium to come before Frankie gets home for Thanksgiving, and if so, how can she spend her last months on earth eating nothing but radishes?

Now when Carmen says, "You honest-to-God didn't know?" Vera can't help hearing intimation of the Big Interrogation.

"Honest to God," Vera says, and Carmen seems relieved.

"Then I don't know," she says. "My cousin Mercedes, she's Pentecostal, she'd say it was prophecy. Sometimes God speaks through you, makes you say things, write things, even . . . Maybe God wrote that story through you, and you can bet He knows the names of those people out in Brooklyn, specially if they're Jewish. They Jewish?" Carmen has often emphasized the Adventists' special affinity for the Jewish people.

"I guess so," says Vera, balking slightly at this notion of God writing *This Week* stories about revivifying lemonade. Though perhaps such a God might judge her more mercifully than

Shaefer has, might not automatically prize her soul so much lower than a cardiologist's. Like Carmen, He'd know she meant no harm.

Vera's harder on herself, particularly when the elevator comes and, at the sight of her, Hazel's face sets like milk forming skin. Vera stiffens, too. She should have considered Hazel before she wrote that piece about the elevator. She should have found that house in Brooklyn and made sure the people who lived there *weren't* named Green. But how could she have known it was possible to invent a family, move them into a house, and have it be the right family, the right house? Nothing remotely similar has ever happened to her. If it *is* ESP—some drab and small and essentially useless clairvoyance—you'd think it would have surfaced before.

Passing the discount store, Vera counts one less rainbow wig. Who could have bought it? Some other woman who wore it to her boss's office to learn she'd written a story that unbeknownst to her was true? Vera's getting woozy, afraid she's beginning to look at the world like some medieval monk: As it is on earth, so it is in heaven. Everything is a sign of something else, something usually pretty awful. It's a trap set for her at tricky turns in the road, like when Lowell first left and she saw every raindrop as a sign that the babysitter was letting Rosalie drown.

Vera remembers a story about Kafka. He and Gustav Janouch are out walking. Suddenly Kafka stops and says, "Look. There, there. Can you see it?"

"A pretty little dog," says Janouch.

"A dog?" asks Kafka.

"A small young dog. Didn't you see it?"

"I saw it. But was it a dog?"

"It was a little poodle."

"A poodle?" says Kafka. "It could be a dog, but it could also be a sign. We Jews often make tragic mistakes."

Vera almost wishes the story ended there, and yet she likes knowing Janouch's reply, likes hearing that cocky young poet with Kafka for a friend and his whole life ahead of him answer, "No, it was only a dog." It seems important to remember this now and bear in mind that the two guys nearly rolling their rack of dresses into her aren't a sign of destiny seeking new ways to mow her down. The fire-sale store, its window full of lace tablecloths, fake Chinese rugs, and tusks carved into leaning-tower-of-Pisa pagodas isn't a symbol of spiritual bankruptcy. Nor does the old man selling hot dogs to harried commuters mean that humans are just so much meat on the bone.

Vera's almost convinced herself when she walks down the subway steps and notices the wall behind the ticket booth covered with signs. Why hadn't she noticed them before? Bright-colored enameled placards with pictographs aimed at illiterates and foreign tourists. The smoking cigarette behind the diagonal slash, the crossed-out radio. The schnauzer bisected by another diagonal line, and beside it the blind man with his Seeing Eye dog and no line. A dog, thinks Vera. A sign.

And finally, a joke. By tomorrow, some kid will have drawn a penis on the Seeing Eye dog, two balls on the cigarette; in six months, the Transit Authority will take down the signs. When she was in high school, the most common subway graffiti was LAMF. Who now knows it meant Latin American Mother-fucker? People talk about archeologists excavating New York and wondering at the uses of things, but it won't take that long for most things to lose their meanings.

We Jews often make tragic mistakes. Vera knows hers is not realizing: when you're looking for signs, you see them. But how to stop? Just trying reminds her of a story she heard about some alchemists who believed that the secret of making gold was going through the process without once thinking of the word *hippopotamus.*

The train pulls in, and Vera sits down across from a fat kid with a giant hippopotamus grinning at her from his T-shirt. She thinks HUNGRY HIPPO CHEWS CHICAGO CHILD, then stops herself; such thinking is her version of waving a cross at Dracula.

Lowell was a great believer in synchronicity, a tireless collector of meaningful coincidence; he'd mention some cousin he hadn't seen in years and the cousin would call up. His attitude toward it was not unlike Mavis's: those little runs outside the laws of probability seemed to cheer him. Easy for him, Vera thought. His terrors went only as far back as the Baptists, while hers had had three thousand years in the desert to cook. It wasn't that she feared synchronicity, but that she'd rather not be the beneficiary of all that unwanted attention from the beyond. Who knew but that those little casual clusters might at any moment turn out to be black holes? This too must be part of her DNA code. Why else should she feel this way? Until today she's never seen anyone harmed by peculiar coincidence except perhaps Louise. And ultimately it's hard to say *what* hurt Louise.

A few weeks before Rosie was born, Louise came to New York and asked Vera to meet her at the Museum of Natural History cafeteria, where, over lukewarm chili dogs and parched French fries, surrounded by school trips and artsy hooky-playing teens, Louise spun out her tale of woe. Coincidence, coincidence, and all of it frightful. First a boyfriend beat her up and then she met a guy who turned out to have known her old boyfriend in grade school, and he beat her up, too. A guy who'd hassled her all along Dwight Way showed up the next night beside her at an elegant dinner. She was typing a letter to her favorite uncle in Florida and her mother called to say the uncle was dead. Just as Vera was starting to fear that Louise's story might be endless, Louise looked at her watch and said, "It's time for the planetarium."

Halfway through the planetarium show, Rosie awoke in Vera's belly, and Vera guided Louise's hand to the bumpy elbows and knees. The swimming baby, the high, starry vault, and even the swelling "Theme from 2001" brought tears to Vera's eyes, but finally it was Louise who cried. At the end, when the projector—like some alien creature itself—whirled the sky overhead, Louise turned to Vera and, with the spinning stars reflected on her face, said, "I feel like this *all the time*."

It was just after this that Louise joined the Ananda Devi ashram. Vera's thinking of how the turbans the Ananda Devis wore seemed to alter the shape of their faces when she notices something strange about the kid in the hippo T-shirt. It's not how fat he is, but the pull of his flesh—almost horizontal. He's retarded, and like certain retarded people, appears to obey a slightly different gravity.

The kid—he's thirteen or fourteen—opens his mouth as if to speak, then rounds it. Magnified by thick glasses, his eyes bulge and quiver. He looks like an undersea creature, a sea cow. He blows a fair-sized spit bubble and doesn't blink when it breaks.

Vera wants to ask him: Who buys your clothes? But she can't imagine an answer that doesn't make the hippo kid in his hippo T-shirt seem like somebody's mean joke. And then she understands why she's always seen those runs of coincidence as malevolent: because they are. Think hippopotamus and you'll come as close as you can get to one on the subway. Ask for a sign and you'll get the word made flesh of every mistake God ever made.

ON VERA'S corner is a vacant lot. Before the skyscraper condos go up, it's enjoying a brief life as some landlord's tax-credit community garden. Its nametags, its tight adjacent plots, remind Vera of a vegetable apartment house. In the spring, everyone grows a few stunted tulips; in summer, Ping-Pong-ball-sized tomatoes. In every season, the earth looks starved and hard. But it's better than a weedy lot, it's something to look at. Last May, when someone scaled the chain link fence and lopped off the tulips' heads, the whole neighborhood was demoralized.

Around that time, Vera stopped into Firbank Florists, her downstairs neighbor, just as a customer was teasing the owners, Kenny and Dick, about having beheaded the tulips to eliminate the competition. Dick turned to Vera and said, "Sweetie, *you're* the one who writes about sickos cutting little things' heads off." Vera assured them she'd nipped a tulip-slasher story in the bud. Having seen the results, she didn't want to give anyone the idea.

Kenny and Dick live below Vera and Rosie. They have terrible fights that escalate from housework to Kenny's infidelities and last all night. Vera hears every word. Sometimes this makes her feel better about being single and sometimes it makes her feel worse. When she sees the wholesaler's truck pull up on Montague Street and Kenny and Dick leaning close together over the first purple irises of the year, she feels better, then worse. At any rate, they're good neighbors, conscientious about locking the outside door and not buzzing strangers in without checking. Today Vera's especially grateful: she's had enough unpleasant surprises without finding a human one on the stairs.

Kenny even brings her mail up and slips it under the door.

Now, on the hall floor, directly under a giant, framed photo of Mount St. Helens erupting, Vera finds a phone bill and a letter from Louise. She remembers ordering the Mount St. Helens photo through the cryptobiologists during one of those times when Lowell was leaving and she was doing her best to prove she would still lead an interesting life without him. Now it seems mainly a sign of how quickly you can get to the point of walking past an exploding volcano and hardly noticing.

Louise's letter is postmarked from the small town in Washington where she lives on a farm and supports herself by teaching at a community college. Vera wonders if Louise still writes poetry. She certainly has the same typewriter, its keys so mired in ink the b's and o's print solid. She also wonders why Lowell writes to her at the office, Louise at home. Among other reasons, it's probably that Lowell wants to reach her first thing in the morning, while it's more in Louise's nature to know Vera needs a letter to keep her company while she's mixing and drinking her cocktail-hour vodka tonic.

Dearest Vera,

This morning I was out picking raspberries. Everything was wet and the low warm sun hit the berries so the red in them glowed. I thought of Monet and Gerard Manley Hopkins and that this was the light they saw. Then I thought how much better it was to be seeing it than trying to teach it to Olympic Community College students who didn't give two shits. And *then* I thought: if I'm seeing that kind of light, why do I still feel the need to justify what I'm doing? It all made me think how long it's been since I wrote you. You would be the first to tell me: Light doesn't necessarily translate. That lovely Victorian parsonage meadow and the gardens at Giverny are a long way from forty miles northeast of Seattle.

I can't remember when I last wrote you. Was it before or after my brief, stormy interlude in therapy? A few months ago my parents wrote offering to pay for therapy, and I thought: Well, why not? It's like somebody offering you free dance lessons. I thought maybe it'd get me off the anti-psychotic drugs which anyhow make me pee every fifteen seconds.

So I started going to this guy somebody recommended in Seattle. Fortyish and kind of cute. I said I was afraid that if I told him everything and he found out who I really was he'd reject me and he said, why did I think that? So I told him everything and he found out who I was and he fell in love with me and *then* he rejected me! He said nothing like this had ever happened in his whole professional career and what it most likely meant was that his own analysis wasn't complete etc. etc. etc. . . . So once again my heart's broken.

Rereading this, I think: No wonder! Here's a woman who can experience rapture among the raspberries and then come home and use the words "think" and "thought" sixty times in two paragraphs! No matter what—acid, the Maha Deviants, lithium and Stelazine and God knows what—the right brain cells never seem to be destroyed. I mean right cells, not right brain. And nothing's happening here, nothing to distract me, nothing in the mailbox . . . in other words, write immediately!

All my love and kisses to you and Rosalie,

Louise

Vera picks up the phone and dials Louise's number. "Listen," she'll say. "Wait till you hear *this*." She lets it ring long enough for Louise to come in from milking the cows or feeding the hogs or whatever she does on that farm, then hangs up.

Sipping her drink, Vera shuts her eyes and sees the kitchen drawer stuffed with old letters, phone numbers, bills, and, if the cockroaches haven't smoked it, her emergency Camel, kept there the way a spy risking capture keeps the cyanide pellet. If only she could just inhale, exhale, smell the smoke, and not have to think about fountain-of-youth lemonade, let the nicotine hold her and rock her like Lowell used to rock Rosie, doing a slow, dippy dance to the *Soul Train* show on TV.

She used to think Camel smokers had a harder time quitting because of the beauty of the package. She'd quit a dozen times but never for more than a week that ended with her telling herself a week of not smoking was better than a week of smoking and she could always quit again. Then last spring she had a sore throat for a month. Smoking hurt too much, and when she got better she thought, Why not take it all the way? This time, breaking the habit was so easy, it made her think life really is a merry-go-round, and not-smoking is one of the rings you can grab when the right moment comes. She prefers thinking about merry-go-rounds to thinking about death, about fear—that long sore throat meant no more chances, too many warnings ignored—about the certainty of mortality that came like some mean joke-gift on her thirty-seventh birthday.

Now she can practically hear the vodka persuading her it's the very nature of merry-go-rounds: miss the ring once, it will come round again. Meanwhile there's that Camel, wedged in one corner of the crumpled, beautiful pack . . .

What saves her is the sound of the front-door key: Rosie's home. Vera calls out but gets no reply; Rosie's got her Walkman turned up. How often has Vera yelled at her, "You think the Dungeon Master sneaks through the Wizard's cave with earplugs on?" As often as Vera's pictured Rosie's trip home as some kind of nightmare cartoon, her daughter ricocheting from danger to danger like a frail, childish Mr. Magoo. Vera's read about some German who calculated the logarithmic probability that one's premonitions of one's own death will come true; her premonitions about Rosie are so numerous, she's afraid the chances of accuracy must be way above the norm. Sometimes when Rosie's about to go on a car trip with a friend's parents or swimming with her summer program, Vera wakes in the night with visions of wrecks and drownings so vivid she's sure they've already happened. She would do anything to protect Rosie and suspects that her fantasies are disguised attempts at protection:

if she imagines something, it won't happen. What undoes these efforts is her irrational fear—and it's odd how her superstitiousness manifests itself almost exclusively around Rosie—that imagining something *makes* it happen, a theory that this business with the Greens would certainly seem to support.

Now as Rosie sails in and sees Vera, she stops short, so startled you'd think Vera was the lurking maniac of her own worst dreams. Vera wants to squeeze her, but they don't even touch.

"How come you're back early?" says Rosie.

"Long weekend," says Vera. "Could be really long. Capital The, capital Long, capital Weekend."

"Earth to spaceship Mom," says Rosie into her fist. "Testing. Testing." She likes to tease Vera about being spaced. Vera's tempted to bring out rent receipts and paid utility bills as proof that she isn't except she's afraid of alarming her, of letting her see the thin thread on which it all hangs.

"Bad news," she says. "I think I'm about to get fired."

"For what?" Rosie asks, and when Vera tells her, she says, "Are you *serious*?" It's not a question but a dismissal. The lawsuit part doesn't interest her at all, and she considers the synchronicity element just long enough to dismiss that, too. "I'll bet Solomon told you their names and you forgot. You forget things all the time. Otherwise it's just impossible."

Vera wants to ask how someone who spends half her life playing Dungeons and Dragons can take such a hard line about possibility. Often Vera's eavesdropped on Rosie and her friend Kirsty time-traveling over monster-filled moats into caves with magic doors concealing saviors and villains governed by the forces of Lawful Good and Chaotic Evil.

If they'd had Dungeons and Dragons when Vera was young, she'd have played it to excess while Dave and Norma lectured her about the condition of the serfs and scolded her for dwelling on mythical codes while so many real-life injustices were crying out to be righted. It's not the best thing to be thinking of when Rosalie says, "I hate to tell you this, but we're going to Dave and Norma's for dinner." Though Rosie loves her grandparents and calls them Gram and Gramp to their faces, she affects their first names and this put-upon attitude for Vera's benefit.

"I know," says Vera, though in fact she'd forgotten.

They've got some time before they have to leave—Vera should take a shower and change or do something marginally useful like open the phone bill. Instead she finishes a second vodka tonic and lets time pull the afternoon out from under her like a nurse making a bed without disturbing the patient. When Rosie comes in and says, "Ready?" she feels such a rush of pure chemical outrage that she thinks she must have fallen asleep.

Rosie's long reddish hair is pulled back in a glittery crocheted net she picked up at a rummage sale. Her T-shirt has high, puffy sleeves and she's taken to standing slightly swaybacked, so that with her long legs and delicate face, she could pass for a young lady of the Florentine court.

"Oh," says Vera, amazed as she often is by the sheer fact of Rosie's existence. "You look beautiful."

Rosie comes close and studies her mother hard for a while and then says, "Don't you want to wash up? We'll get there and the first thing Norma will say is how you're not sleeping."

Vera washes her face without turning on the light. Careful not to look in the mirror or at the photo of Mount St. Helens or into Dick and Kenny's shop on the way downstairs, she makes it out onto the street and is passing the community garden when Rosie says, "Would you eat one of those tomatoes?"

"I guess if I was hungry enough," says Vera.

"Not me," says Rosie. "Not if I were starving. They're just reprocessed car exhaust. They eat carbon monoxide all day and at night dogs sneak in and piss on them." Such talk depresses Vera, makes her think Rosie's passion for Dungeons and Dragons has less to do with what she wishes for than with what she's escaping. Once, during the Love Canal incident, Rosie yelled at Vera for picking an apple off the stand and polishing it on her jeans. Suppose the pesticide rubbed into the denim and got *her* through the wash? Around that same time, Rosie declared herself a vegetarian; she hasn't touched meat since. And though she talks about not wanting baby lambs and chickies to die for her sake, Vera suspects she's scared of being poisoned. Vera hates thinking that Rosie's fears for herself are worse than her fears for Rosie, and closer to reality. Even if Rosie survives the molesters, the childkillers waiting to pounce on little girls wearing Walkmen, what then? Other parents console themselves with memories of crouching under desks for A-bomb drills, but that doesn't comfort Vera. The fear of something falling from the sky has to be better than thinking it's hiding in your tomato.

When the train pulls in, Vera takes the middle car to set an example, though from the way Rosie's eyes snake left to right, right to left, it's clear she doesn't have to. Rosie's not looking for trouble except to avoid it. But as the train rumbles on, rocking them into something approaching tranquillity, Rosie's eyes lose their wariness and take on a blank, unfocused stare that reminds Vera of Lowell and of how much he loved the subway. One of his favorite movies was a short film about a crazy guy in a truck stop talking a trucker into taking him on a run because the bouncing of the truck would make his brain feel better. Lowell used to say that the subway made *his* brain feel better; and Rosie and Vera are both enough like him that, after a few stops, theirs feel better, too. Surely, riding with your bare arm against your daughter's smooth shoulder beats making eyes at good-looking kids while Bigfoot movies run through your head.

After a while Rosie leans over and tears a length of thick white thread from her hem. Vera's kneejerk reaction is guilt: her daughter's skirt is unraveling. What kind of mother is she? Rosie winds the string around her hands, an elegant cat's cradle. The way her fingers slide in and out of the loops seems somehow as medieval as her hairstyle and the tilt of her long, graceful neck. She's the princess in the tower, weaving her own drawbridge. Turning toward Vera in a kind of slow motion, Rosie holds out her hands. Vera's two vodka tonics must still be having some effect, for she's moving more deftly than she ever could sober as she lifts the cat's cradle from Rosie's hands onto hers.

Some motions, some sequences of gestures: the hand remembers no matter what. Vera remembers learning to spin cat's cradles on her grandmother's back porch while keeping a nervous watch on the Rose of Sharon tree so thick with bees the whole bush buzzed. She remembers her grandmother telling her how King David, on the run from King Saul's army, hid in a cave where a friendly spider quickly wove its web over the entrance to make the king's soldiers think no one could have come through.

Vera slides the web onto Rosie's fingers, then looks up and remembers what she hates about the center cars: the social life. Across the aisle, an elderly woman's smiling. And though Vera knows it's a pretty picture, a scene to make you think a Botticelli has come to life and is riding the D train, she wants to tell the old woman: "It's not like that! This is the closest we've been in months! If the subway weren't throwing us together we'd be at opposite ends of the apartment! In five years she'll be grown, gone, we won't even be riding the same train!"

But maybe the old woman knows this, at least the part about Rosie growing up. Perhaps she has grown children of her own, children *she* never sees. She's pleasant-looking, white hair, green eyes, a pretty, unlined face, and suddenly Vera wants to cross the aisle and ask her to play cat's cradle.

Rosie's emerging from her trance; they'll be getting off soon. Meanwhile they're hurtling past the ancient, half-ruined local stops—Beverley and Cortelyou—where you can look up above the track and see the great gingerbread palazzos of Albemarle and Westminster Roads. Just then Vera realizes: the Greens can't live far from her parents. And it's this realization that, through some twisted logic even she can't follow, convinces her to try and contact them. Once the idea's occurred to her, it's all she can think of—a possibility she turns over and over as she and Rosalie walk from the subway through the golden summer-evening light, the flower and fresh-cut-grass and diesel smell of the quiet Brooklyn streets.

NORMA ANSWERS the door, kisses Rosie, holds her cheek out to Vera. Though she's never used makeup, her skin has a powdery feel. In the living room, Dave's tilted so far back in his lounger that the soles of his scuffs parallel Dan Rather's face. He grunts when Vera kisses the top of his head. Vera moves on to the hall, where she finds phone and book set in their arched plaster niche like statues of saints in a shrine. She riffles through the G's, not expecting anything; a cardiologist listing his home number seems unlikely. So when she reads Green, Martin, M.D., res., she feels a slight electrical thrill, a sensation so physical, so nearly sexual, she goes upstairs, takes the hall phone into her old bedroom, and shuts the door.

It *is* somehow sexual, not unlike traveling to some distant city and calling up an old boyfriend who lives there, even though it would have been nearly as cheap and certainly more comfortable to have called from home. Proximity is the excuse—not much of one, Vera knows—so she dials before she has time to imagine herself saying, Hi, I'm the one who wrote that story, just happened to be in the neighborhood. She holds the phone to her ear and lets it keep ringing, a simple and regular background rhythm that soothes her as she looks around her room.

One disturbing thing about her parents' house is that it never changes. She's scared of nostalgia, its seductive hints at oblivion, frightened she'll fall face down on the pink chenille bedspread till her whole life since high school drops away and turns out never to have happened. At the same time she resents the slightest alteration. Downstairs there's a tapestry, a folksy bird in a geo-metrical tree that Dave and Norma brought back from last summer's course at the Institute at San Miguel; Vera's caught herself glaring at it as if it were a rival sibling, a newly adopted Mexican child.

Vera can't walk into her room without thinking of Mount Vernon, Monticello, Dickens's house, all those relics smelling of lemon polish, carpet dust, and the slightly doggy odor of earnest, rained-on tourists. What's here? A conch shell pink as a fingernail, a boxed set of Grimm and Andersen illustrated with paintings of Hummel figures lost in the landscapes of Persian miniatures. The shell, those jewellike illustrations—Vera used to stare at them till she felt she'd crossed some invisible line and climbed *into* them. Now she's lost that talent, whatever it was. Now all she sees is how much her mother's thrown out.

Her corkboard, for example. Gone are the tacked-up bits of birthday wrappings, the quotations copied out of books. Vera can't blame Norma for not wanting to live with ribbon scraps, embarrassing sentiments from Herman Hesse. At least she's saved the postcards of James Dean and Marilyn Monroe, Yeats's handsome face, the Lartigue of the guy in the inner tube, and— a present from Louise—the Brassai of two lovers in a cafe booth, the laughing woman and her Valentino-haired boyfriend holding her close. Oh, Louise. Who did they think would cup their heads in his hands like that? Washington's wooden teeth, Jefferson's dumbwaiter, the blotting paper with the faint mirror image of the first page of *Little Dorrit*—it's all the same, the same hollow feeling Vera gets from the photo of her father's Lincoln Brigade battalion hanging in her parents' room. In the faded print, the boys kneel, grinning like a high-school football team; some brandish untrustworthy-looking rifles. Dave used to lift Vera up and tell her the names: which ones lived, which ones died.

Then someone answers the phone, and Vera's so shocked she almost hangs up. A woman's strained, somewhat out-of-breath hello hints at dozens of reasons why someone might pick up on the two-hundredth ring. She'd just got home. She'd been sleeping. She hadn't wanted to answer but finally gave in. None of these bodes well for conversation.

Vera takes a deep breath and asks if this is Mrs. Green. Then she introduces herself, confesses to having written the piece for *This Week*. Her tone of voice makes that a question, too.

"Oh," says Mrs. Green.

"Is there some time I could come see you?" says Vera. "I'd like to explain . . ."

"Sure," she says. "I'd like to hear it." It's as simple and as difficult as that. Vera asks how soon she can come and Stephanie Green says she and her family are going away for the weekend. "To get away," she adds pointedly. "From our own house."

"I'm sorry," Vera says.

"Well," says Mrs. Green. "I should think so."

"Monday morning?" says Vera.

"Afternoon," says Mrs. Green. "Around two."

"See you then!" Vera says, trying her best to sound brave and hopeful and perky. Mrs. Green hangs up.

What a relief to go downstairs where it's airier, less thickly curtained, where every item of forties spirit-of-the-people decor— the embroidered piano shawl, the frayed Navajo rug, the Mexican tapestry—bespeak thick peasant fingers flying, lives spent shooing pigs and weaving bird-tree rugs in crumbling adobe hovels.

Perhaps it's that it's Friday night—Vera finds herself noticing how race and history and the DNA code have crept in around the edges of Dave and Norma's scientific materialism. How Jewish it all looks! Unfocusing her eyes, she sees the bird-tree as a menorah, the Guatemalan bark painting as a Chagall; two chunky wooden owls recall Kafka's image of the Torah scrolls: dolls without heads.

Dave sighs and so does the La-Z-Boy Norma gave him at retirement: every workingman's dream. With his thin, hunched shoulders, thick eyebrows, hooked nose, Dave looks like a condor or an eagle. His eyes are black and bright, and every so often he makes nervous, darting motions with his head. Without giving Dan Rather time to finish his goodnight, he scoots forward and switches to the twenty-four-hour-news channel.

Dave's been retired from the sporting-goods store for a year and, not counting their two weeks at San Miguel, has done nothing since but watch TV news. This worries Vera, but while Norma agrees that it's not the best thing, physically speaking, is it any worse than retirees who spend all their time playing golf and chasing young girls? Vera thinks it's lots worse than chasing young girls. But Norma—who worked thirty years as a high-school guidance counselor—insists it's a phase he'll outgrow.

Right now, a young woman is reporting a terrible story out of Arizona. A weird old loner in a trailer court tells the neighbor who's befriended him that he's found a lovely widow named Mabel and got married. Mabel's shy and never goes out, but one day she calls the neighbor and invites her for tea. So the neighbor goes next door and the old guy—dressed up in women's clothes—buries an ice pick four inches into her skull.

"The things people do," says Dave. Vera thinks, MOBILE HOME MABEL: A MANIAC'S MASQUERADE, and just at that moment Dave says, "You should write that one up for your paper."

It's by no means a casual remark. Dave's convinced Vera's wasting her talent, though he's never said what he thinks her talent is or what better use she might put it to.

"Ice picks in the skull is more Mavis's department," says Vera, trying to keep it light.

But Dave's not so easily appeased. "So, Miss Lois Lane, you're planning to write Abominable Snowman interviews the rest of your life?"

It occurs to Vera that her life at *This Week* may have ended as of that afternoon, but this is hardly the context she wants to discuss it in. When Vera was in high school, she and Dave fought constantly. Now they're like an old married couple, so rooted in compromise they no longer remember who liked the window open and who liked it closed.

She turns back to the news, where now a Russian dissident poet is arriving at Kennedy airport, rejoining his wife after five years in the Gulag. Vera leans forward and studies their kiss as if it's a clue to something she should know. But mostly what she sees are the backs of reporters' heads.

Dave points his foot at the reporters, but before he can suggest she join their number, Vera says, "Don't even think it!" And Norma—attuned, as always, to the first signs of a clinch—runs in to referee. "Vera, sweetheart," she says. "Come help me."

Just outside the kitchen, Norma—like a teenager with a younger sister she doesn't really want to bring to the party—rushes ahead, leaving Vera to stand in the doorway and watch Rosie and Norma chop salad vegetables on the butcher block by the window. "What can I do?" Vera says.

"Nothing," says Norma. "Keep us company." Company? They don't even know she's there.

The warm early-evening light recalls the paintings of Thomas Cole, the Hudson River School, the luminous pastel skies of Vera's Brooklyn childhood. Actually, it doesn't seem quite bright enough for that sharp cleaver Rosie's using. It takes all Vera's self-control not to ruin the moment by yelling, Turn the light on! Watch your fingers! Though probably Norma and Rosie know instinctively, as she does: if they turn on one less-than-absolutely-necessary light, Dave will come in and shut it off.

There's a period in Dave's life he rarely mentions: after Spain he spent two years teaching English in the Soviet Union. Stalin was in power. Vera thinks of purges, of Osip Mandelstam, of wide, bleak skies and crowd scenes from *Doctor Zhivago*. She's asked, but the only thing Dave's ever said is how the shelves in the markets were bare except for huge boxes of US-Army-issue cornflakes, and he said it every Sunday when Norma cooked big breakfasts—waffles, popovers, eggs. The first time Lowell met her parents, she'd brought it up, hoping that Lowell would tell his story about cornflakes airlifted up to the Alaskan tundra and that he and her father might come together over a shared history of breakfast cereal. But Dave just got quiet and later that evening called to ask her not to talk about his trip to the Soviet Union in front of strangers. It was then—and not at dinner, as she'd planned—that Vera told him she and Lowell were already married and she was expecting a child.

The point is: when her father turns off lights they can't see without, drives to Jersey for cheap gas, eats the hard bread heels, Vera understands that these are the habits of a man who lived two years on cornflakes. Of course she knows from living with Lowell that a cornflake diet can just as easily have the opposite effect, but the real point is: her father is generous with other things. Not for one moment can Vera remember doubting he loved her.

And besides, Rosie and Norma couldn't have found a more flattering light. With its fading, they actually seem to grow slimmer, more graceful. Their hands move surely among the strips of green pepper, the perfect circles of radish like the coins of some newly discovered country. Even as the dying light blurs the edges of things, it highlights their textures. Rosie and Norma's bare arms touch and the contrast in the surface of their skin is astonishing. What fifty years can accomplish!

Rosie and Norma lean closer, reminding Vera that a few years ago they *were* closer: as close as that. Then even Vera called them Gram and Gramp because their connection to Rosie seemed the central one, the hopeful one with its promise of continuance. Now things have fallen off. Rosie calls them Dave and Norma and complains that when she stays overnight they don't let her do *anything*, by which she means talking all night on the phone.

Nonetheless Vera knows Norma and Rosie are still closer to each other than either of them is to her. Even their comfortable silence sounds a reproach: if she were part of the scene, she'd be chattering like a finch. She can't help being jealous; it's like feeling the whole world except her is in love. So when Rosie starts talking, Vera's relieved; it's as if she's out with two lovers and is grasping at conversational straws to keep them from falling into an embarrassing embrace.

"I might quit summer program," Rosie says.

"Sweetie, why?" says Norma.

For a while it doesn't seem as if Rosalie's going to answer. Finally she says, "Carl."

"What about him?" asks Norma.

"I can't tell you," says Rosie. "It's too gross."

"Try me," says Norma.

"All right," Rosie says. "But promise you won't be completely grossed out and blame *me*?"

"I promise," says Norma.

"Okay. Remember, though. You promised. Well . . . It was water-gun day. We all got to bring our water guns in. Around lunchtime mine ran out and Carl said he'd fill it for me. He took it to the boys' room and when he brought it back it was kind of warm and . . . oh God, I can't say it . . . he'd pissed in it!"

Norma flinches. "Please, the word is *urinate*!" Then she bursts out laughing. "You know what?" she says. "Carl likes you."

Four things occur to Vera, all nearly at once. One: Rosie's never even mentioned Carl to *her*. Two: Rosie already knows Carl likes her, because Three: She's more sure of herself than Vera was at her age. Which may have something to do with Four: When Vera was Rosalie's age, Norma wouldn't have been half so forthcoming with the information that Carl liked her. Yet only now does Vera understand that Norma's reticence had nothing to do with jealousy, rivalry, meanness, but rather with the same protectiveness Vera feels for Rosie. Despite her firm belief in liberal attitudes toward children and sexual play, Norma would have hesitated—and perhaps rightly so—to encourage a daughter's affection for the kind of boy who'd pee in her water gun. With a granddaughter, it's different: perspective, more humor, and forty years to have learned that such boys may turn out to be the best.

"The dumb part is," Rosie's saying, "me and Carl have so much in common it's unbelievable. We feel the same about everything! He likes Michael Jackson, I like Michael Jackson. He hates Boy George, I hate Boy George. He loves Dungeons and Dragons, I love Dungeons and Dragons. He loves raw spinach and hates cooked spinach, I love raw spinach and hate cooked spinach . . . isn't that unbelievable?"

"Unbelievable," says Norma.

Vera imagines Rosie and Kirsty in their Dungeon Master's cave with its magic doors; now every one of them swings open, revealing Carl surprised in the act of peeing in a plastic gun. She's lost the thread of Rosie and Norma's conversation. It all grows fuzzy, until suddenly—perhaps it's the light—she sees herself as a character in *Our Town* or *Carousel*, any one of those dreadful stories about people who die and come back to watch a soft-focus, tear-blurred version of life without them.

"Can I bring the salad in?" she says. For all the response this gets, she could be one of those ghosts only Topper can see.

"Dinnertime!" Norma sings out.

Following her mother into the living room, Vera notes how Norma's embroidered blouse and dirndl skirt match the general decor, except that the clothes are fake peasant: machine work on cotton polyester. "Sit!" orders Norma, and Vera does, opposite Dave, while Rosie and Norma carry in platters and pitchers and bowls.

Though the fan's doing nothing about the August heat, Norma wouldn't feel she was feeding them without a hot meat meal. The food matches everything else: Jewish international. The lamb stew with potatoes and limas reminds Vera of *cholent*. Its muttony smell evokes Berbers dipping into a common plate. They should be cross-legged on a carpet on a tent floor, elbow-deep in grease.

Norma fills their plates and, without waiting for them to taste it, says, "How's the stew? I got it from that new book Daddy got me, *Cooking Moroccan*."

Vera used to think that such questions were Norma's demands for flattery and homage. Her reputation as a cook has never been in doubt. Every time they go out—to a restaurant, to the homes of Norma's colleagues and their old friends from the Party—Dave compares the cooking unfavorably with his wife's. The noise of all that dutiful public praise kept Vera from hearing. How long it took her to understand that Norma might need reassurance, too.

"Great," Vera says, and Rosalie says, "Really great."

"Dave?"

"It's all right," says Dave, and Vera thinks, No wonder she's got to ask every time.

"What's wrong?" asks Norma.

"The meat's a little stringy is all." Dave's teeth seem to be bothering him; it's hurting him to chew.

"Now you're getting like your granddaughter," says Norma, "She'd be happy if we never had meat."

All eyes turn toward Rosie, who's meticulously spearing limas and scraping gravy off her potatoes. "You know what they feed cows?" she says. "You know what's in this stuff?"

"Protein," says Dave, but he's smiling. Norma, too. For though like the rest of their generation they believe in the life-giving sustenance of animal flesh, they approve of Rosie's vegetarianism, in which they see a nascent understanding of the harmful excesses of capitalism.

"It really is terrific," says Vera, chewing extravagantly, heroically, as if for them all—for Dave's teeth, Rosie's fears, Norma's need for approval and love. And it is; it's delicious. The hot food makes Vera break out in a sweat and even that feels pleasant. After a while Norma clears her throat and says, "Dave, guess what Rosalie's been doing in summer program."

Eyebrows bristling, Dave focuses on Rosie. Vera wonders if her mother means Rosie to tell about Carl and the water gun, and so is relieved when Rosie says, "We went to the planetarium."

"Was there some kind of special show?" asks Norma, though probably she already knows. She's been retired from her counseling job for a year; but much remains, especially this mode of inquiry, this dogged pursuit of information her students were too timid to offer or didn't even know they had.

"It was mostly for the little kids," says Rosie. "*Sesame Street* garbage. Kermit and Big Bird up in the sky."

"For the children!" says Norma. "Isn't that wonderful!" Dave's gone back to eating. There's a silence, then Norma says, "Guess where Daddy and I went this week."

"Where?" says Rosie.

"The Whitney, they have the most fabulous show. The Ashcan School. Gropper, Marsh . . ."

Vera thinks of muddy colors, subway riders with grimy faces, shopgirls' legs splayed on spinning amusement-park rides, yet understands that Norma's affection is complex: part esthetic, part political, part nostalgic. Probably Ashcan prints were what young Lincoln Brigaders tacked up on their bedroom walls.

On the wall above Norma's head is a picture Dave painted just after McCarthy got him fired from the public-school system. It's a crowd of faces, red, brown, and black, crudely done; it looks like a UNICEF card. Vera has almost no memory of that time. Used to keeping secrets, they kept that one from her so well her only recollection is of watching daytime TV, of Norma switching channels back and forth from Joe McCarthy to her favorite cooking show, Dione Lucas, until some shadow of the senator seemed to linger on the cook; even years later, when Lowell watched Julia Child, Vera would feel queasy and have to leave the room. It's all still there, thinly camouflaged, lodged in neuron and synapse and cell. When Vera thinks Carmen's Holy Trinity sounds like a congressional committee, what else could she have in mind?

Dave's painting was only an interim distraction until he found work at the sporting goods store. Vera's never understood why, of all jobs, he picked that. He never showed any interest in games, and once at a dinner she heard him telling friends how sports were popularized by the early industrial bosses, who found that their wage slaves functioned better if allowed to toss a ball around a few minutes a day. There was just that one time at a picnic for the guidance people from Norma's school; someone brought a ball. Vera's still astonished by the agility with which Dave jumped and dunked and made the net swish with shot after perfect shot.

That's what Vera wants to ask about, but Dave won't want to answer, no more than he wants to talk about Reginald Marsh. The one story he's still interested in telling is the story of the Spanish Civil War, and they've heard it a hundred times. She remembers how Dave used to charm new people with those stories and wonders if he ever wishes she and Rosie were new people.

The last time she urged him to tell them was that first night she brought Lowell home. Her hope was that Dave and Lowell would recognize each other as fellow storytellers, and that her parents would see that Lowell was, in his own hillbilly way, as deeply in love with the spirit of the people as they were. But all that came of her hopes was one silence after another. It wasn't easy steering the dinner conversation in a middle-class Jewish household to polo, but Vera kept turning it till Lowell could tell his *buzkashi* story: hordes of mounted Afghans playing free-for-all polo with no rules and a dead goat with its head whacked off instead of a ball. Norma got up from the table, leaving them to Dave's disapproval; in his day, you traveled to save the world from Fascism, not to watch the *lumpen* play ball. Vera served up Lowell's cornflakes from heaven, but had to tell Dave's Russian cornflake story for him. Which was why he got angry and called her up; and she told him the news about Rosalie, which she hadn't been able to squeeze into all that silence.

Afterward she felt so sorry for announcing it that way, she sat down and read Karl Marx. All her friends had read Marx in college, searching their Modern Library Giant *Das Kapital* for some clue to Vietnam. But Vera was glad she waited till she was pregnant, with all her emotions so close to the surface. She remembers reading with tears streaming down her face, moved by that enormous, unshakeable faith in the coming of the Revolution, its comforts so similar to what she knew of faith in the Messiah. Some things can be done to hasten its arrival, but not much; and besides, it will come no matter what.

This is what she wants to tell her father: "Dad, don't worry! You and the boys in the Lincoln Brigade, you did what you could! History will resolve itself; the prisoners of starvation will arise without us!" But she knows it's false comfort, false cheer, the same misguided impulse that makes her want to write Bigfoot nicotine-fit stories for that kid craving cigarettes on the subway.

"Guess what happened to me today," she says, then stops, afraid they'll think she's imitating Norma and unsure of what she intends to say next.

"What, dear?" asks Norma.

"Here's another good one," says Rosie. "Now Mom's going to tell you how she's got ESP."

"Hardly," says Vera, aware that the silly smile on her face could be mistaken for modesty, as if Rosie were praising her excessively.

Norma leans forward, Dave leans back. Vera wonders why they signify interest with opposite motions and whether this is what Plato meant by finding your complementary half.

"What's the story?" says Dave.

And Vera tells them. Dave and Norma keep interrupting, making her explain. When she gets to the part about the lemonade stand, they play their own version of Where-Did-This-Story-Come-From? "You had your little lemonade stand," says Dave. "Little Miss Entrepreneur at five cents a glass." Norma's in her element, extracting information, though Vera feels less like a troubled student than a witness at a trial. So Vera testifies on, and by the end is almost satisfied—if not by the logic, at least by the conviction of her story.

Not so her parents. When she's done, they both have the foolish irritated looks of cashiers who've totaled and retotaled every item and still can't get it right.

"I'm not surprised a bit," Dave says. "I've always said your mother has ESP. When you were off traveling and I'd be sick with worry, she'd know just when you were going to call. Years ago, forty-five years ago to be exact, she'd wake up in cold sweat here in New York; and later it would turn out we'd run into some fighting."

Vera wants to say that sensing when your daughter is due to call or sweating when your husband's fighting in Spain is nothing like looking at a photo of a house and guessing the names of its occupants. But now it's Norma smiling that silly, flattered smile and neither of them are listening.

"So," Dave says at last. "What'll you do about it?"

"Nothing!" Vera wants to shout. "Sit tight and let history absolve me!" But of course she says nothing of the kind. For one thing, she can't imagine what history might do in this case except turn the Greens out of their house and fill it with fifty welfare families. For another, it's not true. She's already taken action.

"I called," she says. "I talked to Mrs. Green. I'm going there Monday."

"That's my girl!" says Dave, and Norma gives him a look Vera knows. She's about to say something technical or political and is already waiting for him to correct her. "But if they're suing you . . ." she says. "Can you mention this to the lawyers . . . ?"

"Bloodsuckers!" says Dave. "Let the lawyers mention it to her!" Vera thinks of Leonard Villanova: he *did* have a kind of ticklike quality. She's imagining a story about a lawyer for a corporate blood bank busted for taking his payment in kind—BLOOD-LUSH LAWYER APPEALS VAMPIRE VERDICT—when she hears Rosie say, "Don't mind Mom. Touchdown will be any minute."

Dave takes this as evidence that Vera can't be trusted to pilot them home, so what follows is an argument about his driving them. Vera would like a ride—the streets are deserted; not even she would dare the front of the train at this hour—but feels duty-bound to refuse. Finally Norma settles it by pushing them into the car.

Dave circles Prospect Park, over to Fourth, then down Atlantic to Court. Vera wonders why he's taking such a circuitous route, then realizes it's his old route to work, mapped for minimum rush-hour traffic. There's no need to go this way now. Near Livingston Street, he starts doing a strange thing. At every turn he brakes and says, "Do I go right here?" or "Do I go left?"

"Yeah," Vera mutters through clenched teeth. He's driven this way half his life. Turning, she looks at Rosie, who shrugs and leans forward and rests one hand on Vera's arm. Vera knows her parents' aging isn't their fault. Why does it make her so angry? And suddenly she longs to cry out, Dad, pull over! Park right there between the Board of Education and the cuchifritos stand! Cut the motor and we'll sit in the dark car and listen to your war stories all night!

But by now they're already on Montague Street, and Vera can't wait to get home. Dave pulls up to the curb, kisses Vera, then turns to kiss Rosie. "Rosie, you be a good girl," he says, and to Vera, "Call us Monday when you get done seeing those people."

"I'll see," Vera says. "If I have time." Then she's out of the car and at her door so fast that for a moment Rosie seems to recede like a small retro-rocket falling further and further behind Spaceship Mom.

E VER SINCE Vera quit smoking, she's needed to plan her arrival home, those first few minutes once pleasantly occupied by her coming-home cigarette. Sometimes magazines help stave off the homecoming panic. But tonight, in the absence of tobacco or glossy print, she decides to have another drink, not so much for the alcohol as for something to clink and hold. Then she'll ask Rosie's opinion of Dave's new driving style. She's hoping that Rosie will reassure her with the wisdom beyond her years that, Vera's learned from the media, is the curse and the blessing of the single-parent child. She remembers how, after one of Lowell's departures, Rosie had said, "If he were *my* old man, I'd just sit tight and wait for him to get lonesome." How old was Rosie then? Six? Seven? And Vera was comforted by *that?*

So perhaps it's just as well that while Vera's still playing with the lock, Rosie says, "Can I use your phone?" and takes off before Vera can reply. Vera decides against the drink and follows Rosie into the bedroom to eavesdrop. Vera's tuned in for surprises; but Rosie isn't saying much, just listening—from what Vera can gather—to some story Kirsty's telling, set in a pizza parlor. "Yuck!" says Rosie. "Anchovies?" What's wrong with anchovies? Vera wants to know. Could she and Lowell have imprinted her with that terrible anchovies vs. Pampers fight they'd thought her too young to understand? By the time Vera's persuaded herself that anchovies are an acquired taste, she's abandoned the pretense of hanging up clothes, so that when Rosie says, "Mom, could you leave for a minute, everybody hears *everything* around here!" she agrees, even though it's her room.

Lingering in the hall, Vera thinks she hears Rosie say "Carl" and puts her ear to the door. But they've gone on to Dungeons and Dragons. Kirsty's Lady Velvetina, with 158 points on the side of Lawful Good.

Vera drifts toward the living-room window, where she stands watching Kenny and Dick walk Mister T., their Lhasa Apso. They're chatting with their friend Hugh, who's walking his Rottweiler. The big dog's circling the Lhasa, the little dog's trembling, but the three men look so neighborly, so relaxed, Vera's heart constricts and takes jealous revenge in a headline: RONALD MCDONALD STRICKEN BY AIDS.

Though she knows drinking and drugs will only make her feel worse, she pours some brandy, lights a joint, and flips on the TV in time to catch a rerun of *Fantasy Island* about a con released from the slammer after thirty years with one desire—to find the bride he left at the altar when the cops nabbed him at his own wedding. Vera switches to *People's Court*: a guy who dresses up as a giant Goofy and clowns at kids' parties is being sued by some parents for failing to show. The judge speaks of broken promises, transgression, and penance. The giant Goofy's convoluted arguments remind Vera of Raskolnikov. Another dog, another sign: if *People's Court*'s sounding like Dostoyevsky, she's watched too much TV.

By now the alcohol and marijuana have so profoundly damaged her logic that what Vera's thinking is: If life is one broken promise after another, why not call the expert on broken promises, Lowell? Dialing his number, she steels herself. No one will be there, meaning Lowell's gone off with someone else and the terms of their on-again, off-again ten-year marriage will finally have to change. Or worse, a woman will answer.

"Hello," murmurs Lowell in his soft, shy telephone voice. When Vera says his name he yells, "Sweetheart! How are you? How's Rosie?"

One thing Vera's got to give him credit for: he really does care about Rosie. Once at a party Vera met a man who seemed nice until he started telling her how his wife had custody of their daughter and dressed her in designer jeans so tight she had to lie down to zip them. "She's six years old," he'd said, reaching for Vera's hand, and Vera had left him there, reaching. Lowell would never serve Rosie up so some strange woman at a party would see him as a caring kind of guy.

"Does she miss me?" Lowell's asking now. "Does she talk about her old Dad?"

"Of course," Vera says, though the truth is: yes and no. Rosie misses him so much she can hardly say his name. And Lowell, for his part, would like nothing better than to have Rosie living with him. So Vera's worst fear: Rosie is marking time, hoarding her allowance till she can run away to L.A. She's already been there three times, each time for a week or so, and come home with tales of devoted attention and sacks full of wonderful gifts—a dayglo "giggle stick" that, when tilted, emitted a slow, froggy belch; a headband with its own little battery pack and tiny, sequentially blinking lights; a green plush caterpillar that, unzipped and reversed, turned into a butterfly with glittery wings. But what surprised Vera most was that Rosie and Lowell had gone shopping for presents and wound up with something remotely like what they'd set out for. She'd tried quizzing Rosie about what they'd bought where. But Rosie clammed up. It was private. And Vera felt jealous and stung, as if Lowell and Rosie were having a love affair and decided: for Vera's own good, some things were better for her not to know.

"She's fine," says Vera. "Really."

"What's the latest?," Lowell says. "What's she into?" The latest? How long has it been since they talked? A month?

"The same," says Vera. "Ballet. Dungeons and Dragons."

"Boys?"

"Give it a break," Vera says. "She's only ten."

"Ten's getting up there," says Lowell. "Don't underestimate heredity. If she's anything like her Dad, she's probably sneaking off to play hypnotist with the little boy next door."

One of Lowell's favorite stories: when he was in third grade at the Eskimo school, he took little Nancy Senkaku behind the bleachers and said, "You are getting very sleepy" till she lay down and let him take off her pants. Vera remembers where she heard it: on Louise's couch in the dark. How proud she'd been to have a lover who'd been practising since he was eight!

Now she says, "Not in *this* neighborhood. The little boy next door is a fag." She hesitates, not quite trusting what he'll do with this information, then goes ahead anyway. "As a matter of fact, I think she does like some kid in her summer program. Not that she'd tell me. Norma wormed it out of her at dinner."

"She'll do that," says Lowell. "Talking to Norma's like taking a giant hit of sodium pentathol." Vera laughs, then thinks how few people know her well enough to make such jokes. Especially as she gets older, friends and family never meet. If she waits another ten years, then falls in love with someone new, chances are that person will never meet her parents at all.

After this cheering thought, there's a silence. "Want to hear a joke?" says Lowell. "Why did Reagan invade Grenada?"

"To impress Jodie Foster," says Vera.

"How'd you know?" he asks.

"I heard it last year," she says. "Only then it was, 'Why did Begin invade Lebanon?' "

"It's better about Reagan," Lowell says.

"I don't know," says Vera. "What's new with you?"

"S.O.S. Same old shit. I gave the script to some hotshot lady agent. She's from Canada originally, so I figured she might know what I was talking about."

Vera's read Lowell's script. Called *Polar Bear Boy*, it's about a guy from Minnesota who around 1900 took a trip to the Arctic Circle and decided there was money to be made trapping polar bears and selling them to all the new zoos starting up in the various cities of America. So he caught dozens of them and, when the market slowed down, began leading tours for rich society folk who wanted to see polar bears in their natural habitat. He married a girl he met on the tour and stayed married ten years, until it turned out she was some kind of wildlife preservationist way ahead of her time—also crazy and overbred. Finally one night she laced his after-dinner cognac with enough arsenic to kill a bear. Though it's not a bad story—utterly improbable despite the end, when a credit tells you it's all true—and has room for lots of documentary nature footage and turn-of-the-century furs, Vera knows it will never be made. Polar bear jacking is hardly the world's most commercial subject, and besides, Lowell's humor doesn't quite translate onto the page. You need to hear him reading it in your head. For starters, thinks Vera, he might consider retitling it, *Polar Bear Man*.

"Have you heard from her?" Vera says. "The agent?"

"Shit, no," says Lowell. "It blew her right out of L.A. My script was the absolute last straw. She disconnected the phone, fired her secretary, hopped the first plane back to Vancouver, and married her high-school sweetheart."

Decoded, this means the secretary gave Lowell's script back without saying anything. "She's probably better off," Vera says. "She should have stayed there in the first place."

"Probably," says Lowell. "Hang on. I need a smoke." When he comes back and Vera hears the altered intake and puff of breath, she wants a cigarette so bad she's shaking. She's thinking of mornings, coffee and cigarettes shared with Lowell in that first Hayes Street apartment—gray, uncomfortable, hung everywhere with their art-student landlady's work: a series of abstracts based on *Jonathan Livingston Seagull*. Even so, she'd rather be there than here. Than anywhere.

"Speaking of smoking," says Vera. "Yesterday I wrote this Bigfoot story—"

"Bigfoot!" crows Lowell. "My main man!" Lowell considers Bigfoot a kind of personal totem. In fact he claims to have sighted one in Oregon. One night, he and his friend C.D. were out camping. They saw Bigfoot and Bigfoot gave them the V-sign. Peace and love. How typical of Lowell's stories, that flat, understated joke. Nature at its most mysterious and elusive, every cryptobiologist's dream resolving itself in a hippie cliché.

"—about Bigfoot knocking over a gas station and stealing some cigarettes—"

"You still not smoking?" Lowell says.

"Barely," says Vera.

"Good for you!" says Lowell. There's another pause, then he says, "What else is happening with you guys?"

"Plenty," says Vera. "Listen. The staff photographer at the paper gave me a photo of an old house with some kids in front of it selling lemonade. So I made up a story and now it turns out that the names and ages I dreamed up are the kids' real names and real ages. I hit the whole family history right on the fucking head, and now they're suing me for libel and invasion of privacy."

"You're kidding," says Lowell. "Run that by me again."

Vera does, partly to make sure he's got it straight and partly because she likes the version she's telling: bizarre as ever but somehow less serious. She's left out the ruined lawn, the damaged cardiology practice, the tiny school careers nipped in the bud. Also the part about her maybe being fired.

"Jesus," says Lowell. "Synchronicity central."

"You said it," Vera says. "I'm going out there to see the kids' parents Monday, get to the bottom of this—"

"No bottom to get to," Lowell says. "Just your basic warp in the general weave. They're usually a good sign. Something special's on the way. Don't fight it."

"I don't have to fight it," says Vera. "A whole team of lawyers is fighting it for me."

"The synchronicity defense," says Lowell. "I love it. Some guy could make his career on that."

Vera tries to imagine Mr. Goldblum making his career on the synchronicity defense. She can't even imagine suggesting it.

"Their suing you is very unprogressive." Lowell sucks in the end of his sentence.

"I don't know," says Vera. "What can I do?"

"Do?" Lowell repeats, a peculiarly rounded tone. He's blowing smoke rings through the word, like the caterpillar in *Alice in Wonderland*. "Don't do a goddamned thing," he says. "Just hang on. It'll do *you*."

And so Vera's forced to confront what she's always known. Her version of what went wrong between her and Lowell is like one of Lowell's own stories: flat, understated, a joke. The truth has less to do with his unique approach to grocery shopping than with this—his hillbilly fatalism. Just hang on, it'll do you. Though it's not so different in spirit from what she wants to tell Dave,

Lowell's interpretation of events has always alarmed her. It's no accident that Lowell's favorite song is a hymn called "You Can't Hurry My God":

He's the kind you can't hurry
He'll be there, don't you worry
He may not come when you want Him
But He's right on time.

Right on time? However would one know?

What used to scare her was the possibility that Lowell would always work on the loading dock and on screenplays no one would film; she would always write for the *Downtowner*. Sometimes she thought she knew the whole future, could see their lives sped up like those time-lapse sequences in Disney films that show you all the cacti in the desert blooming at once.

Now, of course, she understands that these were the fears of youth. What's impossible, she's since learned, is for anything to stay the same. Nor has her life without Lowell been a model of forward progress. All this might seem reason enough to try once more with him, if not for the evidence: He's still waiting for some gangster to come along and lend him an old Smith Corona. Putting on your shower sandals every few months and bringing your script to an agent hardly constitutes taking active charge of your life. Lowell's not what Vera needs, not yet. Still she doesn't want to lose him and doesn't like the sound of her voice when she says, "That's a very sixties attitude. Very spiritual. You know what they call that now? Retro hippie."

"Go with the flow," Lowell says. "Don't push the river. Fuck you."

Vera would hate the conversation to end this way, but what can she say to that? Finally Lowell says, "Sweetheart? Are you there?"

"Are you stoned?" asks Vera.

"During working hours?" says Lowell. "Stoned as a Wheat Thin."

"Were you working?"

"Sure. Flat on my back in the sun." Lowell is always brown. Even in February, in New York, he'd go up to the roof and lie there in his down jacket. Perhaps he's never gotten over those twenty-four-hour Alaskan winter nights. Vera's stoned, too, but not so out of it she can't count. It's eight P.M. in California, not enough sun for anyone.

"Well . . ." She draws out the word.

"Hey," Lowell says. "Do you have a copy of that story? Fountain-of-youth lemonade?"

"I don't think so," says Vera, but when she checks in her purse, it's there. She must have taken it from Shaefer's office.

"Send it to me," Lowell says. "I'd like to see it."

"Sure," Vera says. "I'll send it right out."

"All right, then," says Lowell. "A big kiss and hug to Rosalie." It sounds as though he's ending a letter. "And to you." It *is* the way he ends his letters.

"You, too," says Vera, and hangs up the phone.

JUST BEFORE dawn Vera dreams she gets a message: GOD WANTS TO ASK YOU A QUESTION. God's holed up in a cheap motel on one of those sleazy strips you find in Western cities. Miracle Miles. Sitting on one of the double beds is a slight, middle-aged Oriental who asks her this: If you found dinosaur bones—a complete and perfectly preserved brontosaurus skeleton—what would you do? Vera doesn't even have to think. First she'd ship the main bones to the Museum of Natural History. Then she'd take half of what was left and mail it in small packages to her friends. Then she'd hide the remaining fragments all over her house—in the medicine cabinet, the silverware drawer, the spice rack—places she'd find them when she was least expecting it.

This answer seems acceptable and Vera wakes up happy despite the fact she's sprawled on the living-room couch with all the lights on, nose to nose with a sour, alcohol-smelling glass, an ashtray full of roaches, and the knowledge that the God of her dreams is the former Saigon police chief immortalized by photography in the act of blowing a suspected Viet Cong's head off; recently she saw him interviewed on *Eyewitness News* in his present incarnation as a prosperous Georgetown restaurateur. Vera's good mood lasts as long as it takes her to feel something lumpy beneath her and identify it as the crumpled copy of *This Week* she found last night for Lowell.

Already the air's hot and so sticky you'd think you could walk up the walls like Spiderman. The gray light promises to stay that gray all day. Standing up seems like too much of a commitment; without quite making it, Vera limps to the window and looks out onto the street where, even at this hour, everyone seems to have shopping carts or arms full of brown paper bags. It's Saturday; and the grocery shoppers have a demoralized, wallflower look— one drawback of living in a neighborhood in which a large percentage of your neighbors know someone with a house in Rhinebeck or Fire Island.

Years ago, when she was freelancing and all seven days were the same, she used to hate weekends, when everyone else seemed so happy; used to envy the secretaries' Saturdays and even the Monday-to-Friday toil that glorified their days off. And later, when Rosie was small and Lowell was with them, she had some sense of what such weekends could be. Trips to the zoo, the Tibetan Museum, Sleepy Hollow; though she knows it can't be accurate, her memory is of all those outings taking place on bright autumn afternoons. Then she went to work full-time and back to hating weekends, understanding then that the secretaries' Saturdays weren't idyllic at all but occupied with survival, with laundry, shopping, paying bills, with all the essential and tedious chores that the rest of the week left no time for. Often Vera felt like the subject of some cruel experiment, a cat prevented from licking itself five days out of seven.

Some things she likes about weekends: One, not going to work. Two, small, manageable activities like cleaning her apartment. What a strain it was with Rosie toddling at her heels, messing up everything she'd just straightened. Perhaps that's why God gives you small children: for the rest of your life, certain things seem effortless. Now Rosie's asleep, will stay asleep till eleven or twelve, then get up and and pick up the phone and—depending on everyone's ballet lessons and divorce settlement visitation rights—get a game of Dungeons and Dragons going. Vera wonders if she's dreaming of Haunted Thickets or of Carl.

Vera pauses outside the kitchen, contemplating the drainboard, imagining how nice it will look without that bowl of soggy corn-flakes on it. She knows Rosie will just leave another one there this morning, but somehow that doesn't bother her, no more than it bothers her to know that all her bustling around will just be tidying, not cleaning. She's not interested in dirt she can't see.

The dark brown, copper-flecked oven hides grime and probably always will. The drawer stuffed with bill stubs and phone numbers won't get emptied or sorted out. If she dies in this apartment, someone else will have to come in and excavate. *That* bothers her; she hates thinking of things she'll never do: see Africa, live in London, learn Italian, have a son.

Still she has her rituals, her little compulsions like everyone else. Everything that doesn't belong in the apartment—garbage, dirty laundry, letters and bills to be mailed—has to be out before she can start cleaning.

She puts on jeans and an enormous cotton shirt, which, though certainly too hot, will save her from having to put on a bra. Then she rushes through a preliminary cleanup, throwing out roaches and cornflakes—which remind her of Lowell and of her promise to send him that article from *This Week*. Probably she should reread it every five minutes between now and her visit to the Greens, but she already knows it by heart. So she finds a large manila envelope and stuffs the whole issue in. Of course it would be cheaper to send just the story, but that would mean finding scissors and being more steady-handed than she feels. The next problem is Lowell's address. It's on his letter, in her purse; the danger there is of sinking onto the couch and reading it all day. So she looks C.D.'s retro hippie pottery studio up in her address book and considers writing "Big Youth," but realizes that at any one time there are usually five guys staying there who might answer to that description.

Vera returns to ministering to the garbage, calling on all her willpower to keep from tossing the envelope in. Knowing better than even to look for the wire ties, she knots the tops of the trash bags and takes them downstairs.

Behind a locked door in the first-floor hall are the garbage cans; behind these another locked door leads to the basement and to yet another locked door to the alley where the garbage trucks pull up. The lids are chained to the cans so the Rastafarians can't steal them and hammer them into drums. All these locks should make Vera feel secure; in fact she can't throw anything away without expecting some giant hand to grab the back of her neck and push her face in the can. She's seen too many horror films about mad janitors. CRAZED CUSTODIAN'S BOILER-ROOM BARBEQUE: DINES ON HUMAN SHISH-KA-BOB.

Vera can't laugh, she's holding her breath. By the time she's out on the street, she's got spots in front of her eyes and is still fixated on the idea of people carving other people up into bite-sized cubes. She thinks of that surprising quote from Rumi, "The true seeker after God shall value his heart no more than shish-ka-bob." But what she has in mind is hardly what Rumi meant.

Waiting in line at the post office, Vera realizes she could have slapped on a dollar in twenty-cent stamps and saved herself a trip. The old man behind the counter thinks she's done the right thing by coming. He weighs the envelope and glues on ninety-six cents' worth of postage with a tenderness that makes her feel small for being unable to mail a letter herself without the sensation of dropping it into an abyss. The old man's touch makes it seem safer; his handling bears witness that her parcel exists.

On the way home she buys a paper, and after some more straightening up—a little light sweeping, mopping's really out of the question—stretches out on the couch with the *Times*. When Rosie was a baby, and later just before Lowell left and neither could pick up a paper without the other one getting mad at them for not doing something else, Vera dreamed of such moments. What she couldn't have dreamed was that her life would so soon reach a point at which no one cared if she ever put the paper down.

Compared to *This Week*, the *Times* reads like Stendhal. The attention to detail and plot in its coverage of Lebanon recalls Napoleon's generals' elegant minuet around the slaughter at Waterloo. Just the number of headlines on the first page is a compliment to its readers' intelligence, unlike *This Week*'s single, giant head, implying that its audience can only take in one thing at a time. And yet none of the heads are very interesting. It's as if the *Times* is dozing, waiting for some post–Labor Day invasion to shock it out of its slumber. The paper has a skimpy feel, the same not-really-trying look of the people on the street, as if the reporters also believe that everyone worth writing for is out of town for the weekend.

Vera turns to the page that carries the "Around the Nation" bits. Today there's a court case from Georgia, where a fundamentalist preacher's contesting a manslaughter charge with a unique defense: at the moment he rearended a van full of senior citizens, he was receiving a message from his personal saviour and Lord, Jesus Christ. The question is why Jesus would let a pickup he was in personal communication with kill two seniors and put four more in traction. It's an old chestnut—the problem of evil, free will, Ivan Karamazov and that little girl locked in the outhouse. Vera knows she's distracting herself so she won't have to face the fact that she wrote this story months before the accident occurred.

In this case she's not especially surprised. It's an accident that's been waiting to happen. With half the nation declaring for Jesus, half killing each other on the road, it was simply a matter of putting two halves together. It had better be that simple. Vera's beginning to feel like Ingrid Bergman in *Gaslight* or the heroine of an *Alfred Hitchcock Presents* she once saw, a woman who told her husband each night's dreams—and during the day they came true. In both instances, the husband was trying to drive his wife crazy. Lowell wouldn't have to go that far; if he wanted to drive her mad, he could just move back in, turn on the TV, and sit there.

By this time Vera's read the gardening guide, the police report, the high and low temperatures in Prague. What galls her is the weather report—all those euphemisms for more of the same. S.O.S., as Lowell would say. The same could be said for her day. She's read the whole paper, now what? When at last she remembers agreeing to have dinner with Solomon, she's so elated she actually claps her hands. How could she ever have hesitated?

Vera decides to invite him to dinner. Shopping and cooking will give her something to focus on till then, and besides, it's simpler. Lately her talks with Solomon have been pocked with so many silences, they don't need the additional ones that seem always to come with the waiter. There'll be no flurry over the bill nor that pressure she often feels in restaurants and that she imagines patients feel at their analysts': the minutes are ticking away, and you're paying. Say something. Anything. Talk.

When Solomon answers the phone, Vera thinks, There are two kinds of people. The first tries to sound chipper, to pretend you haven't woken them. The second goes overboard to make sure you know you have. So groggy he can barely speak, Solomon's of the second sort, but when he hears it's Vera, becomes one of the first.

After a while Vera says, "Would you like me to call you back later and repeat this whole conversation?"

"No, no, not at all. I'll be there at seven with the truckload of champagne and cocaine."

"Heroin," says Vera. "Heroin might hit the spot."

"You're joking, right?" Solomon sounds tired and a little confused, as if he can't quite remember who he's talking to.

"Only kidding," says Vera. "Don't bring anything. Just come."

When she hangs up, Rosie is standing behind her. "Yuck," she says. "Peg Leg Pete."

The whole time she's known Solomon, Vera's feared that Rosie would call him that to his face. She finds it easier to worry about this than about the implications of having a daughter who'd say such a thing in the first place. The truth is that Rosie likes him. He pays attention, tells elephant jokes, brings her jewelled combs and tiny embroidered purses, geisha-girl presents from Chinatown. It was Solomon who bought her *Thriller*. It's only the idea of him she objects to. For despite her sense of herself as a savvy single-parent child, Rosie's still hoping that Vera and Lowell will get back together permanently.

Rosie was five when they split up. Vera remembers reading how children often seem unaffected and then take up bedwetting or refusing to eat. Not Rosie, who cried and screamed and argued against the separation until wet sheets and anorexia might have seemed healthy alternatives. Her best friend Kirsty's parents went through a spectacular divorce; almost none of their friends have the same parents they started out with. They all drag their parents, separately, to the same movies: soap-operatic comedies that all end with some estranged Upper-West-Side or L.A. couple falling into each other's arms. Vera suspects them of sharing inventive ways of tormenting new boyfriends: mentioning Daddy every fifth word, the silent treatment, and its opposite, the chatter torture.

Now Rosie says, "When's he coming?"

"I'm calling him back later," Vera lies, wondering how much Rosie's overheard. "Maybe next weekend," she adds vaguely. If Rosie knows he's coming tonight, she's not above cancelling any plans she may have and staying home to safeguard her future. Sometimes she reminds Vera of Dave, interrogating Vera's high-school boyfriends to find out their class origins.

"I hope it's tonight," Rosie says. "I won't be here. I'm staying over at Kirsty's so we can practice for the recital tomorrow. Okay?"

Vera wishes that just once Rosie would reverse the order of her sentences and ask her before she tells her. She'd still agree to practically anything, but with the illusion of control. Maybe life will get smoother again after tomorrow's recital. When Rosie was little, she always got cranky before big events: walking, talking, feeding herself with a spoon.

Now from the kitchen comes the noise of the blender churning Rosie's breakfast mix, a concoction of yogurt, granola, and black-strap molasses that, the one time Vera tried it, tasted pretty much like the center of a Baby Ruth, only colder. Watching from the doorway, Vera says, "I can't stop thinking about that kid filling your water gun with pee." She knows it's a mistake, but it's out before she can stop it.

Rosie says, "God!" in a stretched-out, Valley-Girl twang. "*I* don't want to think about it at all."

"What I mean is, it seems like something he'd have to *plan*." Why can't Vera control herself? Because she can't resist making her daughter dig under the surfaces of things for their meaning. She remembers dragging baby Rosalie through the freezing March weather to see the first crocuses in the Brooklyn Botanical

Garden. Missing the point completely, Rosie ignored the flowers and focused instead on the pebbles, the black crumbs of dirt. Or maybe she hadn't missed the point at all. "I know it's like Norma said, he likes you. But beyond that, why—?"

"Why?" Vera's shocked by the anger in Rosie's voice. Of course the water gun episode was disgusting. But it's more than that. It's as if this has given Rosie some intimation of what men and women can and will do to each other. Vera knows it can't be helped, but still it seems wrong that Rosie should blame *her*, the person who most wants to shield her. "Because his friend Elijah dared him to. The same reason Carl does *everything*." Her tone gets chattier, confidential. "Kirsty says Carl's gay."

"Honey," says Vera. "Ten's a little young."

"Mom," says Rosie. "Don't be naïve. Dick and Kenny told me they knew it the day they were born. Dick had his first crush on the male nurse in the newborn ward." This seems to cheer Rosie up, and she says, "Guess what happened last night. Lady Velvetina rolled her way out of the Haunted Thicket and wound up smack in the Swamp of Desolation."

"The Swamp of Desolation," Vera repeats. "That sounds about right." It saddens her that Rosie will be Dungeon Master all weekend and first thing Monday morning go in and be held hostage to Carl and his friend Elijah. "When are you going to Kirsty's?"

"I'm already gone," says Rosie, licking the blender jar. "Kirsty's Mom's downstairs." Vera's nearly blocking the door but Rosie squeezes past without touching her. From the living room Rosie says, "Hey, you know what I saw on TV? They've got this new stuff called Pour-A-Pie. It's lemon meringue in a milk carton. One side's the filling, the other's meringue, pour it into a readymade pie crust, bake ten minutes, and bingo! What do you think of that?"

What is Vera supposed to think, except to wonder what they put in the meringue to keep it permanently whipped? Vera would never serve Pour-A-Pie, and Rosie knows it. So why does she act as if Vera invented it, another chemical horror visited by her generation on an unsuspecting world? Who *would* buy it? Lowell.

Lowell would buy Pour-A-Pie in two seconds flat. She considers the possibility that the attraction to products like Pour-A-Pie may be hereditary, and that's why Rosie is fighting it so hard.

"What time should I pick you up tomorrow?" Vera asks. But Rosie's right, she's already gone. The door clicks shut behind her.

The Pour-A-Pie discussion has started Vera thinking about food. Shutting her eyes, she lies back on the couch and meditates on what to serve Solomon. The day promises to get hotter, so anything requiring long cooking will suffocate them before they can eat. Seviche needs no cooking at all but should have started marinating yesterday. Recipes demanding more time than she has depress her; it's as if she's reached the end of her life and discovered the one essential thing left undone. Maybe some kind of pasta. Sesame noodles with scallions, or pasta primavera with its bright flecks of cut-up vegetables. The problem is all those upwardly mobiles eating pasta salad tonight in smart little eateries from the Heights to the Upper West Side. Food chic makes Vera want to serve strips of lunch meat wrapped around Velveeta cubes and stuck with frilly toothpicks, then chicken baked with orange marmalade and onion-soup mix, frozen Japanese vegetables on the side. And for dessert? Pour-A-Pie. But why would she do that to Solomon, who's anything but a food snob and would probably be satisfied with meatballs and spaghetti?

Finally she decides on curried chicken salad with walnuts and grapes. It's just as stylish, she knows; it's what Kirsty's Mom, Lynda, calls Soho Chicken Salad. The difference is, she's always made chicken salad this way and feels about it the way others claim to feel about vacation spots they went to as children and later saw ruined by fashion. Besides, she likes chopping celery, walnuts, green onions; halving grapes; peeling chicken breasts off the bone; seeing it all cohere with mayonnaise and then turn golden with curry. The prospect fires her with energy. She'll make chocolate mousse for dessert!

En route to the supermarket, she's almost always optimistic. It's as if she expects to find something there beyond food, to pick up the *People* at the checkout counter and read all the answers to her deepest unspoken questions. Suddenly Vera feels very close to Lowell. This must be what quickens Lowell's step on the way to the store: the pull of the serendipitous and hopeful.

Vera's good cheer deserts her in the poultry section of the SaveMart. Recently she read an article on how to recognize fresh chicken. It's supposed to be very yellow or not yellow at all, she can't remember which. And even if she could, what then? All the chicken on display looks to be having a long, hot weekend. She recalls a documentary about water-witching: one old man never went to the store without his forked stick, which dove for the extra water in overripe vegetables. Vera wishes she had a forked stick and the faith to use it. She throws the nearest chicken into her basket—by the time she's boiled and shredded it, color won't matter.

Turning down the produce aisle, Vera sees bunches of collards and immediately starts wondering what she'll say to the Greens. She notices her palms have started sweating. For comfort she thinks back to this morning's dream and wishes she had those dinosaur fragments now. She'd hide them behind the gourmet items, the jars of baby corn and bad caviar that no one ever buys. She'd look for them at times like this—times when she realizes that there's nothing new at the SaveMart, times she wishes she were Lowell and knew how to transcend familiarity, times when she knows beyond any doubt that whatever elusive thing she's looking for just isn't, never was, and never will be here.

BY SIX, when Solomon shows up, whatever small promises the day's held out have all been broken. For starters, there's no chocolate mousse, just a package of Orange Milanos that Vera's run out to buy. At least the chicken salad's done, chilling in the fridge. But the dream of harmonious chopping and mixing turned out to be something of a nightmare.

First Vera tried deboning the chicken before it had cooled and kept on till her fingers were puffy and burned. Grapes shot from under the knife and rolled beneath her feet. In keeping with everything else, the walnuts were rancid, a fact she didn't discover till she'd stirred them in; she'd picked through the entire bowl, extracting nut fragments like shrapnel. Enough curry powder will cover anything, she'd thought. But not so, not so. For courage she reminded herself that Solomon claimed to have eaten dog meat in Vietnam. But this only irked her more. Why was she suffering to cook for a man who'd eat dog meat? And when at last he rang the bell, she thought: The dog-meat eater's here.

Solomon's wearing jeans and his best Hawaiian shirt, a masterpiece that has probably cost him half a week's pay and should be in a museum. It's hand painted, and—Solomon has taught her a thing or two about Hawaiian shirts—there's no interruption in the design where the pocket's stitched on. Painted over and over with light variations is a long canoe filled with half-smiling island Mona Lisas swooning over ukulele tunes strummed by brown young men. Once more Vera wishes that Solomon's shirt were the physical world, that she could stow away on one of those boats and sail off, lulled by the rocking waves and the sweet strains of "Ukulele Lady."

Smiling rather sheepishly, Solomon holds out a bunch of long green stalks with wrinkled orange dead things at the ends. Vera almost regrets not telling him to go ahead and bring the champagne and cocaine, tries not to let her disappointment show.

"I don't know about these," he says. "I drove upstate to take some pictures today. They were growing by the roadside. Free flowers. At least they were flowers when I picked them. I can't figure out what went wrong. Unless they're like the floral version of exploding cigars or those birthday candles you can't blow out. Maybe if I stick them in some water it'll help."

"It won't," says Vera. "That's why they call them daylilies. Each one lasts a day." She sounds like a second-grade teacher. Suddenly she wants to start this whole scene over, wants Solomon to shut the door and ring the bell, and this time she'll say, "Oh, what beautiful flowers!"

"You're kidding," he says. "One day? How come I never knew this? Like dragonflies or mayflies or whatever you—"

"Solomon," Vera says. "Come in."

When Solomon hugs her, it's even clumsier than yesterday at work, belated and with some confusion on both sides about when to stop. Cameras clanking, he paces the living room. Then he says, "Do you mind?" and lights up one of his cheroots.

"Where's the very lovely Miss R.?" he says.

"At Kirsty's," says Vera. "Practicing for the big recital."

"That's a shame," says Solomon. "Look what I brought her."

It's a handpainted antique photograph of a ballerina. "Tinted with me own two hands," he says. "Do you know what Joseph Cornell would have given for this?"

"She'll love it," says Vera, crossing her fingers. The possibility of Rosalie turning up her nose at Solomon's generosity makes Vera want to put the daylilies in water and pray over them till they flower again. When she does take them, though, she throws them away. There's nothing else to do.

"O ye of little faith," says Solomon. As he waits politely to be offered something, Vera wishes she were living with Lowell or anyone with the range and domestic entitlement to get his own drink. Though she knows Solomon's not to blame, she lets him stand there till he asks, "Should I run out and get some beer?" At which point she's so ashamed she reaches back past the Budweisers for one of the dark Heinekens she'd been saving for something more special.

She pours herself a stiff vodka tonic, then settles down beside Solomon on the couch. He puts one arm around her and they sit staring straight ahead, as if watching TV. Finally he says, "So how's my little psychic?"

"That's not funny," says Vera. "Solomon, are you *sure* you didn't know those people's names? And you told me and—I don't know, maybe we were drunk or something—somehow we both forgot. It's important. I'm going out there Monday to talk to them."

Solomon whistles. "Don't let Shaefer or Esposito get wind of it," he says. "Or the lawyers. The shit'll really hit the fan. Anyhow, the truth is I never saw that house before I took the goddamn picture. I was just shooting the little prince and princess selling lemonade. If I'm lying, so help me God"— Solomon taps his good knee—"let this one fall off, too."

"Then what's going on here?" says Vera.

"The outer limits," Solomon says. "The twilight zone. Think of it as unsuspected talent. Like suddenly finding out you can play mental chess or you're one of those idiot savants who can tell you the weather in 1883. All you can do is get off on it."

"How can I get off on getting fired?"

"No one's fired you yet," says Solomon. "But listen, here's what I was thinking. If you really want to stay part of our one big *This Week* family, try talking Shaefer and Esposito into giving you Karen Karl's spot. 'Vera Perl's "I Predict!"' They'd love to stop paying the syndicate. It's the most popular column we've got. The mail-room guys run a numbers game based on how many letters Karen Karl gets a day—"

"Enough," Vera says. "I know." When Vera started at *This Week*, her first assignment was answering Karen Karl's mail.

Dan Esposito claimed it would give her a clearer sense of their readership, but Vera refused to believe it. If she'd admitted that's who her audience was, she'd have quit back then. Nearly every letter went like this:

Dear Karen Karl,

I lead a miserable life. I am very lonely and have no friends. My husband died fifteen years ago. My daughter and her three kids just moved back in but they won't talk to me either. I have chronic emphysema from smoking too much, though who could blame me? Everyone needs something. The doctors don't give me much time left though I am only fifty-seven. I know you can see the future so my question is: Can you see one ray of hope in mine or should I just end it right now? Thank you for your trouble.

Mary

The first few of these letters had put Vera into such a state of depression she'd called in sick and stayed home to reread *Miss Lonelyhearts* for its slant on the redemptive possibilities of all this. But West only made her feel worse. The letters Miss Lonelyhearts got were so imaginative, so extravagantly grotesque. What Vera wouldn't have given to have heard, as Miss Lonelyhearts did, from some reader telling her what it was like to have been born with no nose.

Vera knows it's flesh and blood out there, souls in pain and in such need of comfort they'll seek it in *This Week*. But she also knows how important it is to keep reminding herself it's not her pain. Mary's problems aren't hers. They're just stories, someone else's mail. Not that Vera doesn't long to help, to speak for the screamers on the train. But if what she's dealing in is mostly false comfort, she'd better not take it to heart. Her job, like a doctor's, demands some degree of professional detachment. Best not to imagine lonely girls mounting telescopes out their windows and searching that distant red star for the King. Best not to think about arthritic hands anointing themselves with sliced cucumber.

Right now the only hand Vera's aware of is Solomon's, cradling her shoulder. She wonders if they'll become lovers again. She's not sure if she wants to or not. One thing's certain: she's not in love with Solomon. If she were, she wouldn't feel so removed, off somewhere at liberty to consider whether she's got any diaphragm jelly left. She thinks probably she has, but what troubles her is how long she's had it.

She remembers buying it before Lowell's last visit two Christmases ago. She even remembers purchasing it at the Pay-Less on State Street. The reason she remembers is that the checkout clerk—a real teenage horror, his face the color and apparent consistency of cherry vanilla ice cream—picked up the package of diaphragm jelly and looked at her and said, "Great stuff. I use it on my cat every night. Are you part Indian?" Are you part asshole? thought Vera, but didn't say it for fear of what might happen next. Now she wonders if the stuff in her medicine chest is still good, if there's an expiration date or if the implications of diaphragm jelly expiring are too depressing for even the FDA to consider. Anyhow, the more she thinks this way, the less likely it seems she'll need it.

She wriggles out from under Solomon's arm and goes into the kitchen to check on dinner. She takes out the chicken salad, stirs it, puts it back. The wilted lilies sticking out of the garbage make her think of old men's scrotums.

Back in the living room, she sits somewhat further down the couch from Solomon; she's still dancing the same clumsy ballet she did with high-school dates she wasn't quite sure of. "How far did you drive today?" she asks.

"God knows," says Solomon. "Northern Rockland County, I guess. It all looks the same to me. Grass and trees. Green and boring. I don't know where I am unless there's four signs and a traffic cop and maybe a mugger or two to make me feel at home."

Vera wishes he wouldn't talk like this. She likes men who can live in the city and then go out and creep through the woods like the last of the Mohicans. Lowell's famous for his sense of direction: one winter, traveling with some Portland friends through Mexico, Lowell was fast asleep in the back of the van and the driver woke him up and asked which way to Guadalajara. Lowell said, "Turn right."

When Solomon says, "It's always a mistake to think you know what you're looking for," it takes her a while to realize he's talking about photography. "What I had in mind was that feeling you get—or anyway *I* do—that after the Fourth of July the summer's basically over. I figured I'd go up to Bear Mountain, shoot families having their little picnics, and maybe if I was lucky catch that moment when they let it all hang out and you know they know: This is it. Finished. Might as well be Labor Day.

"So there they were, the American nuclear family burning its Basic Brands hot dogs, drinking its Kool-Aid and beer; and if the summer was over, you could have fooled them. They were having the time of their lives. I shot off two rolls anyway, but I can tell you right now: Every shot is garbage, Polaroid ads except with uglier people. I guess that's what you get for predicting what you'll find."

Vera's nodding, but what she's thinking is how different Solomon is from Lowell, whose theory is: always predict, or try. If you need a salad bowl, spend Saturday morning thinking salad bowl, and that afternoon you'll find one for a quarter at somebody's garage sale.

"But get this," says Solomon, "just before I started back I stopped in one of those little cafés with the fly-cemetery screen door and the IT TAKES FIFTEEN MUSCLES TO FROWN AND ONLY TWO TO SMILE sign over the register and the waitress grinning like she believes it. I'm sitting at the counter finishing my coffee when this big, fat redneck in a Cat hat sits down beside me. He sees the camera, asks if I'm a photographer, then he says, 'Jeez, you shoulda been here yesterday.'

"What happened yesterday? His kid's hamster had babies. And just as I'm thinking about those last scenes on the Roy Rogers show when Pat Butram's dog's just had puppies and Roy and Dale are standing there smiling like they're the biological parents, he says, 'One of 'em had two heads.'

"I asked him where it is now and he says, 'Where the fuck do you think? I flushed it down the fucking toilet. All we need is the kid having nightmares, keeping us up all night. But Jesus, that would have made some picture.'

"I said I was sorry I missed it. It *would* have made some picture. It was all I could do not to tell him, Buddy, where I work that would make front-page news. HUNDRED-HEADED HAMSTER HAUNTS BIG-CITY SEWER."

Vera rubs her eyes. Then she says, "Are you getting hungry?"

"Not really," he says. "I don't want to spoil my high."

"Maybe we should smoke a joint," says Vera.

"That sounds more like it," he says.

By the time the joint's half gone, Vera's feeling better. Crazily, what's cheering her up is that she's wondering why Solomon didn't ask her to go to the country with him. And though she's annoyed at herself for reacting this way, the fact remains: the possibility that he didn't want her along is making her want him more. Once she saw Janis Joplin on TV talking about how romance was like driving a mule with a carrot and stick: the woman's the mule, the carrot's the promises the guy keeps breaking. Vera suspects that what moves her is the chance that the carrot may have disappeared altogether. Maybe she and Solomon will become lovers again.

"What *would* you do if they fired you?" asks Solomon.

"I don't know," Vera says. It's getting dark, too early for a summer evening except that it's been so gray all day. Neither gets up to turn on the light. The dimness and the marijuana give their talk the spacey tone of certain scenes in movies: stoned around the campfire. *Easy Rider*, thinks Vera. God help us.

When Solomon asks if she'll go back to freelancing, Vera remembers the chilly fall day she and Solomon went out to the old cemetery near the Brooklyn-Queens Expressway where her grandmother was buried and where, since the funeral, Vera had wanted to take pictures: the crumbling gravestones overgrown with vines, the worn Hebrew letters, and especially the enamelled cameos of the dark-eyed, rakish dead. Before Solomon could focus, an old man ran at them screaming in Yiddish as if Solomon's lens were the evil eye. But if the evil eye was open that day, it was fixed on Vera and Solomon. After that, something changed. They stopped imagining projects and devoted themselves to complaining about *This Week*. And it wasn't long until that morning Vera awoke to hear Solomon ranting about having to go into work and airbrush hair onto Five-year-old Werewolf Boy's face, and he and Vera looked at each other and knew that they couldn't go on.

She's thinking of the community garden on her corner, realizing what those squeezed-together little rectangular plots *really* remind her of when she hears Solomon say, "You might have to go back to writing the truth."

"The last time I wrote what I thought was the truth," Vera says, "I nearly lost my best friend. I MARRIED BIGFOOT seemed safer."

"Safer than what?" asks Solomon.

"Haven't I ever told you about my friend Louise joining that ashram?" Vera's almost sure she has, but Solomon's shaking his head no.

The real beginning of this story is that Lowell had just left. But Vera doesn't want to start there. For one thing, Lowell's name makes Solomon flinch. For another, she fears sounding like those dreadful people one overhears in restaurants, whining about their divorces. So she says, "About five years ago, I got a letter from Louise."

The thought that Solomon's never met Louise exhausts her. There's so much background he needs. Louise dressed as garbage, weeping at the planetarium, her poetry, her wanting to see God. But maybe Vera's mentioned some of this, and besides, the stories themselves are misleading, make that time in their lives seem cuter, less disturbed and confusing than it was.

"I knew that Louise was living in Berkeley, working some secretarial job and going to yoga classes. I hadn't heard from her for two months and was starting to get worried. And then she sent me this letter saying she was happier than she'd ever been in her life."

"That would have scared the hell out of me," says Solomon.

"It did," Vera says. "The other scary thing was that she'd moved in with the people she'd been studying yoga with. That and her using the word *community* about three times per paragraph. And *sharing*. I mean, this was *Louise*! A couple of things kept me calm. She'd included this quote about St. Joseph of Cupertino, the one who used to levitate and flap around the monastery and have to be talked down for meals. I thought, Well, if she's joined a cult at least it's one that's let her keep her sense of humor. Also, she wrote, she felt like a TV that's just had its fine tuning adjusted. Colors were brighter, sounds clearer, when she walked down the street people's flesh tones were the colors God meant them to be. I thought, Who wouldn't want that? Finally she said that every time she cast the *I Ching*, she got the same hexagrams, Return and Pushing Upward. The commentary on the first was, "Everything comes of itself in its own time," and on the second, "Pushing Upward does not fall back." These were always her favorite hexagrams, she said, though she'd always seen them as contradictory. Until now."

"The *I Ching*," says Solomon. "I thought that went out with hula hoops. I would have been on the first plane out there."

"Well, I was," says Vera, but this is the part she can't quite explain: why she couldn't just rescue Louise without feeling she had to *write* about it. She knows it was connected with Lowell's leaving, her fears for her own life, of growing old at the *Downtowner*. And maybe she thought she was helping Louise. That's what she's not sure of. She has to remind herself that Solomon's not asking for justification. For now he seems satisfied with simple mechanics, the details of how she parked Rosie with her parents and took time off from work . . .

"So there I was at the airport," she says. "I didn't recognize Louise. When she started to hug me, I ducked. I thought she was trying to sell me one of those twenty-dollar editions of Krishna's life story. She'd gained thirty pounds and turned white. Moby Dick in a turban. White sneakers, leggings, weird, shiny dress. In college they used to serve these all-white meals—chicken in cream sauce, biscuits, mashed turnips, angel food cake. I thought: If I'd eaten too many of those I'd look like her. Only Louise's eyes were the same; if she'd been wearing sunglasses I'd never have known her.

"Louise always had secondhand Saabs, not for the normal reasons—gas mileage, whatever—but because she said it was the only vehicle that sounded like its name. But now she led me to a rusty Ford station wagon. A bumper sticker said, End World Hunger, Think Food, and inside were maybe a dozen metal racks.

" 'For the bowls,' Louise explained. 'The salad.'

"As we headed onto the freeway, she told me her group supported itself making salad for Bay Area vegetarian restaurants. I kept thinking how much salad it must have taken to make Louise's hands look so chapped. The idea of all that lettuce and oil and vinegar made me feel so . . . *lonely*. Then Louise began telling me about those months she hadn't written or called.

"What happened was: she finally saw God. And guess what? He *was* the guy in the William Blake etching, the bearded one with the compass. Every night she dreamed of him drawing circles, and every night the circles grew smaller, excluding first the office, then her neighborhood, then everything except her and her bed where she'd lie, hearing voices—"

"Saying what?" asks Solomon.

"Telling her to go to dances. Square dances, parties, concerts, it didn't matter. As soon as the dancing started, the voices would, too. 'Look at the dancing skeletons!' they'd say. 'All that meat on the bone!' "

"Oh," says Solomon. "*Those* voices."

Vera looks at him, startled. One thing she likes—or tells herself she likes—about Solomon is that he so clearly doesn't hear the kind of voices that torment Louise, that send Lowell off to UFO landing sites in the Yucatan. Solomon's voices suggest he pick flowers for her by the roadside, buy presents for Rosie, pay attention to things that someone else might not notice: children selling lemonade, an old man's furrowed feet.

"Well," Vera says, "it got so the only time she couldn't hear them was when she was chewing. That's how she got so fat. And the only places she could go were the grocery and yoga class. Until one night in class she got twisted in some kind of cobra position and couldn't get out. She just lay there crying and then her yoga teacher came over and held her and told her to take fifty deep breaths. The whole class counted along and when they stopped she'd stopped crying, and the voices had stopped too. And that's when the Maha Devi people asked her to come live with them.

"I didn't know what to say. We'd reached the ashram—this big, gaudy Victorian in Twin Peaks somewhere—before it occurred to Louise to ask how I was." Vera stops. Here's another part she'd rather skip over. She's often suspected that the rest of the story turned on this interchange, that her subsequent actions weren't as pure as she likes to pretend but rather, spurred by anger at Louise's indifference. "I told her Lowell and I had split up, but she didn't respond. She didn't even ask how Rosie was. She patted my back and said personal relationships didn't matter, people just *thought* they did. I asked her what did matter, and she said, 'Breathing.' "

"Can't argue with that," says Solomon.

"Finally we went in. Nice wood floors, nice smell—that incense-cinnamon-apple health-food-store smell. Other than that, the ashram could have been a sensory deprivation tank. White and more white. Louise left me in the lobby a few minutes. I felt like a guest at some terrible party, checking out the bookshelves, the hostess's art. Except that there weren't any bookshelves, just a couple of pictures, scenes from the life of Guru Nanak done like illustrations from some freaked-out children's Bible. A letter soliciting donations to help send brother Nawab Singh to the Tokyo Olympics. Well, it made sense that a religion based on breath control would produce good long-distance runners, though the turban might be a handicap, what with wind resistance—"

"All right," says Solomon soothingly. "All right."

"Sorry," says Vera. "Louise reappeared and took me upstairs, down a corridor. Time travel back to the college dorm—the smell of shampoo, that sense of hushed things going on behind closed doors. At least Louise's room was just like Louise's room every-where, a real mess: papers, books, her Persian miniatures and yarn paintings and Mexican cross. I was looking at them like old friends when a fire alarm went off. 'Louise,' I said, 'let's get out of here!' 'Oh,' she said. 'Dinner.'

"Downstairs, the whole turbaned crew was already seated at long trestle tables, and when I walked in they started grinning to beat the band. Every one as white as Louise. The only spot of color was the head honcho's orange turban. He also had the biggest beard, the biggest belly—maybe that's how they picked him—the same weird, shiny, polyester dress, and suddenly it hit me: nurse's uniforms! Then the honcho said grace and they brought out the food—"

"Don't tell me," says Solomon. "Salad."

"Iceberg lettuce. With a couple of sprouts and pumpkin seeds and raisins. Dab of curried veggies on the side. All I could think of was how Louise always loved to eat. It was something we did together: cook and eat." Vera's remembering a week they spent in someone's beach shack on Long Island. Mussels, swordfish, arugula, fresh tomatoes.

"But there you'd have thought they cooked for noise instead of for nourishment or taste. Feeding time at the rabbit hutch. Everyone crunching, you couldn't hear yourself think. Not that anyone wanted to think; they didn't even want to look at the stuff. They all had their eyes closed so they could concentrate on all that greenery going down.

"After the meal they stood when the honcho did and trooped out to work off the lettuce by breathing through their noses. And maybe I should have breathed with them, maybe it would have changed my life like Louise's. But I couldn't. I didn't want their lettuce breath in my lungs.

"Well, that was pretty much the day. Somebody brought an extra futon into Louise's room. She turned off the light and in the dark said she had something to tell me: she was engaged to be married to some guy named Bhani Singh.

" 'Bunny Sing?' I said. 'Louise, are you joking?'

"She wasn't. The honcho had arranged the whole thing. They loved each other. This wasn't like all those pointless love affairs; this was based on deep spiritual love and trust and guaranteed for life. They hadn't even slept together yet, although at the betrothal rite they'd stared into each other's eyes and breathed each other's breath.

"The next day I met Bunny Sing and sure enough: pinky eyes, white eyelashes, little round twitchy nose . . ." Vera pauses. Here comes the worst part. There's almost no way she can tell it without revealing herself as a thoroughly reprehensible human being. So she pleads friendship, desperation ("I *had* to do something!") and bulls her way through the rest of it on selective editing and pure hell-bent narrative speed: How she stayed another two weeks, shredding lettuce, pretending to breathe, then one afternoon arranged to make a salad drop in Emoryville, just her and Bunny Sing, after which she talked Bunny into accompanying her into a bar. After three beers—his tolerance was, of course, pretty low—he told her he didn't really want to marry Louise, whom he called Sat Mukanda Khalsa. She was ten years older and not exactly his idea of good-looking, but the honcho threatened to send him back to his Mom and Dad in Denver if he didn't . . . Vera had heard enough. That same day she kissed Louise goodbye, flew home, and began writing "Among the Lettuce Lovers," its first sentence: "Bhani Singh doesn't want to marry Sat Mukanda Khalsa." A magazine editor Vera knew published it soon after. Vera folded the printed article into a copy of *The Songs of Milarepa*, in case there were ashram censors, and in a month or so got a call from Louise's mother telling her Louise was in Langley Porter mental hospital and thanking her for everything she'd done.

"Thanking you?" says Solomon. "Was she serious?"

"Absolutely," says Vera. "You don't know Louise's mother. Her feeling was, lots of perfectly respectable people wind up in the nuthouse for a spell, but only real nuts put on turbans and eat lettuce and breathe through their noses."

"Maybe she was right," he says. "Maybe you did her a favor."

Vera's always wondered if that's what Louise thought, if on some level she'd longed to be rescued. Why else would Louise have forgiven her so quickly? By the time she got out of the hospital, they were friends again. But what Vera says to Solomon is, "Louise was in Langley Porter a *year*. I think they gave her shock; she's never said for sure. She's still on God-knows-what antipsychotic drugs. Maybe I should have let her hop off into the sunset with Bunny Sing . . ." Vera takes a deep breath, and then is embarrassed for having exhaled through her nose. "Anyhow, that's when I came to *This Week*. I figured it was the furthest I could get from the facts. And it's true; I could have written I WAS A LETTUCE LOVE-SLAVE and sent it to Louise and it wouldn't have made any difference. No one ever recognizes themselves in *This Week*." Except the Greens, she thinks. No mistake likely there.

"Don't blame yourself," says Solomon. "It was better than pulling a pillowcase over her head and throwing her into a van. A whole lot less violent."

"And sneakier," says Vera. "The pillowcase might have been kinder." She's impatient with him for missing some point she's not sure she gets either. What's occurring to her now is that one reason she was so eager to tell this story was that she imagined some connection between what she did to Louise and whatever she's done to the Greens, some conclusion she might come to about responsibility and intention, some chance that confessing her crimes against Louise might exonerate her for sinning against the Greens. Now she sees she was wrong: the two situations couldn't be more dissimilar. One was intentional, and she got off scot free. The unintentional wrong is the one for which she'll apparently have to pay.

"Anyhow," Vera says, "who cares what I had in mind? It's what happened that's important."

"Come on," says Solomon. "Give yourself a break. For all you know, you saved your friend's life. How long can someone survive on iceberg lettuce?"

Vera thinks: Lowell would never say "your friend." Louise knew Lowell before Vera did. It makes Vera so miserable to hear Solomon call Louise that, she thinks she must be hungry. "Speaking of which," she says, "let's eat."

Turning on the kitchen light makes the whole world seem brighter. Vera's beginning to blame her bad mood on the vodka and grass and the dark. If they'd switched on some lamps an hour ago, she'd never have got so low. A fingerful of chicken salad—the perfect mating of sesame oil and curry—very nearly persuades her that everything's for the best. These Greens could turn out to be soulmates! And what if they do have the fountain of youth in their backyard, flowing underground, unsuspected till Vera's article brought it bubbling into light. What then!

Vera turns on the living-room light; and Solomon, though blinking a little, seems grateful. Vera serves out globs of chicken salad, then realizes she's not hungry. Still, she eats as she used to when Rosie was small, as if showing Solomon how. Halfway through the first mouthful they know the worst: too much celery, and what there is is old and tough. Even before their first swallow, they're sucking chicken through a net of soggy green string that they're then obliged to spit out.

Vera should have caught it earlier. The celery did seem stringy when she was cutting it, but not extraordinarily so; anyway she wasn't concentrating. And it's something you wouldn't notice taking small tastes; a whole mouthful's needed for the full effect. What makes it more embarrassing is that she's just spent an hour putting down lettuce eaters.

Solomon smiles and says, "Great stuff," the very same words the drugstore clerk used about the diaphragm jelly. She thinks: Dog-meat eater. So. It's worse than she thought, so bad they can't even joke about it. There's real discomfort here, even an edge of resentment, and suddenly—though neither could say just how—they both know they won't become lovers again. How can you make love to someone you can't even be honest with about dinner? Vera's gums are aching; it's painful to eat. At the same time they're both reluctant for the meal to end. Solomon asks for seconds.

Finally their plates are empty except for maybe two dozen wads of celery string. Solomon looks at the mess and says, "This is the first meal I've ever had where you eat and floss at the same time." Vera laughs, but it's too late. If only he could have thought of that earlier.

From then on it's simply dismal. Vera asks if Solomon wants

coffee, and even that's awkward. Like it or not, they can't forget how they used to stay up and drink coffee in bed so they could stay up some more. Solomon says he guesses not, and Vera says, "Me neither."

"Well, then, I guess I'll let you get some rest," he says. "Good luck Monday."

"Okay," says Vera, who's in a kind of panic, dreading their goodbye. Once more she might as well be in high school, out on a date with some less-than-special guy, half-rigid all evening at the prospect of fending off one timid good-night kiss. It's surely not like that with Solomon; she loves him. She doesn't know what's gone wrong. Finally they do kiss, and both seem relieved when it's over.

When Solomon leaves, the apartment feels like a vacuum, as if his exit's sucked out all the oxygen. It's hard to breathe. Vera goes to the window for what passes in this neighborhood for air; Solomon's crossing the street. She watches him as far as she can, then hides her face in her hands for the quiet and darkness and perfect privacy she already has more of than she could ever want or need.

VERA'S HITTING the jackpot for dreams. This morning she's in a forest. Pine-needle floor, striped sunlight, a whooshing like wind in the trees. Something's hiding in the pines, but Vera's not scared. She knows that it's Bigfoot and that he's got something to give her. The bonging of a Japanese temple gong announces the moment . . .

But it's just the phone ringing. Dave calls every Sunday, usually before nine. When Rosie was little, he'd used that as an excuse: people with babies can't sleep late. Now Rosie's not even here and he's still calling. Vera's come to see that calling's his version of her waking newborn baby Rosalie to make sure she was all right. Dave's making sure she's survived the dangers of Saturday night. It's annoying being woken, but how can she be angry at someone who's never outgrown a state she remembers as awful: that fearful, compulsive tiptoeing toward the crib. Who knows what he imagines? He's always so relieved when she's there.

"Vera," he says in the serious tone that augurs heartfelt and way-off-the-mark advice. "That conversation Friday night. This thing that's come up at your job. Did I ever tell you . . . ?" And he's started the story before she can ask, "Tell me what?"

"This was forty-five years ago. Me and Manny Satz and a couple other guys were coming back from Figueras with supplies. We kept hearing of battles up ahead, the Fascists weren't so far away. So we took plenty of detours, you can be sure.

"One of them took us through a little village. San Xavier de los Something. The Anarchists had got there the day before and were celebrating with a giant feast and promising the villagers they'd eat like that every day. This was early in the war. So they set out tables and chairs in the plaza and told everyone to bring all their food, empty the granaries and root cellars, kill the fattest lambs. They said, Go ahead. Eat. Drink. Don't worry. War? What war? Plenty more where this came from.

"Well, what the hell. Me and Manny didn't want to be kill-joys, we threw in our rations, too. But Jesus, after a while we couldn't help asking how they meant to provide. After all, it was fall and the start of a war that even then looked to be a long one. The Anarchists just shrugged: no problem.

"The next morning we left, and that night the Fascists came in and wiped out the whole goddamn village."

Vera *has* heard this story, more than once. It always reminds her of Breughel's *Peasant Wedding*, a painting she hates. That poor bride and groom, looking so terrified and sick. If that's life in all its greedy richness, count her out. Likewise, Dave's story: the more she thinks about it, the less she likes it. Eat, drink, and be merry, for tomorrow we die. Is that how Dave sees destiny? Can watching TV all day be his way of making merry?

Now she says, "I don't get the connection."

"Oh," says Dave. "I guess what I'm telling you is: You never know what'll happen. All you can do is give it your best shot. If you can't see round the corner, stay in your lane and drive like hell."

Vera's astonished. What she'd always thought was a cautionary tale about the Anarchists' lack of foresight turns out to be a story in praise of their spirit. "That's a pretty terrific story," she says.

"Isn't it?" says Dave.

"Thanks for telling me," she says.

"It's nothing," he says. "So what's new?"

"Not much," says Vera.

"Here neither," says Dave. "The usual. Your mother dragged me to Alexander's yesterday morning. They were having a sale on men's winter coats."

"Coats?" says Vera. "It's August."

"Mrs. Rockefeller," says Dave. "What's wrong with saving a few bucks?"

Eat, drink, and be merry. Vera thinks of Dave and Norma shopping, Norma standing on tiptoe, smoothing the cloth over Dave's broad, stooped shoulders, then stepping back for a look. If Vera can only step back, the picture's quite lovely: a handsome, elderly couple preparing for winter. What's wrong with that? What's wrong is the other picture Vera can't shake. In the photo of Dave with his Lincoln Brigade battalion, he's wearing a leather bomber jacket that Vera bets he didn't buy the summer before, didn't think of till his ship was due to sail and it was already cold.

Vera's imagining a story about some maniac concealing syringes of poison in the linings of brand-new jackets, thinking BARGAIN BASEMENT BEDLAM: KILLER COATS when Dave says "So?" and she wonders if it's a follow-up to some specific question or if he's just ending the silence.

"So nothing," she says. "Thanks for calling. I'm glad you told me that story, I feel better." How effortless, how instinctive it is to lie! She should take it for granted that Rosie is lying to her with every breath.

"Hold on, hold on, where's the fire?" says Dave. "What about this big recital tonight? Don't tell me you forgot." Suddenly the conversation threatens to turn into one of those exchanges that question—first implicitly, then overtly—her competence as a mother.

"I wish," says Vera. "If you'd lived with Rosie this week, you'd *want* to forget." At such moments it's important to remind Dave that he doesn't live day in, day out with a ten-year-old, and Vera does; it's why he has a brain left to remember with. "It's at seven," she says.

Dave says, "Talk to my social secretary. Norma!"

"Don't bother her," Vera says. "You can handle it."

"Okay," says Dave. "Want us to pick you up?"

"No thanks," she says. "I'm meeting Mavis, she's coming for dinner later. It's easier if we meet you there. Ten to seven?"

There's a deep and—unless Vera's imagining it—accusatory

silence through which she can hear Dave wondering why she's feeding Mavis and not them. It's like this whenever he hears she's having someone over—like jealousy, but more primitive, as if he's accusing her of wasting family food.

"*Quarter* to," he says. "That is, if we want to get seats."

"All right, quarter to. See you then."

"Where you running?" he says. "Don't you want to talk to your mother?"

"Sure," Vera says disconsolately; Norma likes news, and she has none. Just then she hears Kenny's knock—*Jumpin' Jack Flash it's a gas gas gas*—on the door. "Just a minute!" she calls.

"Who's there?" says Dave.

"Kenny," she says. "From downstairs."

"You're kidding," says Dave. "I didn't know the *feigelach* got up so early Sunday morning." It's the first indication he's ever given of knowing it's an uncivilized hour.

"Paper boy!" Kenny sings out. "Don't mind me! Just keep on keepin' on!"

But why should she? It's the perfect excuse to get off the phone. "Got to go," she says. "Tell her I'll see her tonight."

When she opens the door, Kenny's already gone. On the doorstep is a Sunday *Times*, a *News*, and a bag of croissants. Vera wants to run downstairs and tell Kenny how much she treasures him, then decides against it. For one thing, Kenny's so anxious for her to find love, he'll just be disappointed to learn that the reason she was slow in answering the door was not that she was in bed with a lover but on the phone with her Dad. For another, he and Dick are probably getting ready to go out, and that's when their arguments frequently start.

Vera picks up the papers, loving their weight, their smooth, unviolated quality, the sharp newsprint smell. Saving the *Times* for later, she steals a glance at the *News*'s front page. BOMBS BLAST BEIRUT. It's too reminiscent of *This Week*, worse for being true. She can never read the comics or *Parade*; today's entertainment page offers listings for Kung Fu movies in Brooklyn neighborhoods where not even Vera will go. Aware of the incongruity of munching croissants while trying to decide if a fifty-cent coupon is reason enough to buy a new brand of fish stick, she's trying to remember if Rosie even eats fish these days when out of the coupon section falls a glossy invitation to her local Belmontbooks, where this very afternoon Karen Karl will be here direct from L.A. to autograph her new bestseller, *I Predict: How Seeing the Future Can Help You Live in the Now*.

Last week this might have seemed a coincidence worth paying attention to: just yesterday she'd read six months of Karen Karl's columns and now here she is. But after all that's happened, it just seems like daily life. A week ago she wouldn't have crossed the street to see Karen Karl, and now she's planning a route that will take her past Belmontbooks on her way to pick up Rosie.

God alone knows why. Curiosity, certainly, and beyond that— though Vera would never admit it—the possibility that Karen Karl will say something useful or even applicable. Applicable to what? What scares Vera is the suspicion that she's becoming one of those poor souls who'll go anywhere for help, even to Karen Karl. More likely her dropping by the book-signing is simply one way of getting through a day on which she's got nothing much else to do but pick up Rosalie and cook dinner for Mavis Biretta. There, then, that's it. The lift she's getting is the one she remembers from Sundays when—faced with the prospect of a day alone with little Rosie—she'd see in the paper some mention of a clown or puppet show, a charity street fair, anything to take them out into the world of other lives. Oh, thank heaven. This day can be survived.

The book-signing is at the back of the store, but Vera sees it from the street, just as she's heard you can see Chartres or Mont St. Michel—except that what she sees is not a cathedral spire directing her spirit toward heaven, but rather the black tip of Karen Karl's witch's hat. The aisles are lined with men with the shifty faces of perverts, the kind who waits till you pick up a book on Mexican cooking or Billie Holiday, say, then presses against the shelves and slides his penis into the empty space.

They can't all be perverts, there are too many; and soon Vera realizes they're just husbands, checking to see if their wives are done chatting with Karen Karl. Karen Karl's crowd is nearly all female, all in fact except three huge boys whose identical, lumpish noses, bad skin, and fishnet T-shirts proclaim them to be brothers, possibly even triplets.

Karen Karl looks as she did on TV: same round face, blond Dutch-boy hair, same long, pointy sleeves and tenty black chiffon. Where in the world does she shop? You can't just pick two-hundred-pound-witchs' gowns off the rack. She's standing on a platform behind stacks of books with shiny black jackets, white lettering, and a spray of multicolored stars like the ones on her hat.

Flanking her are two young men in horn-rimmed glasses, pressed jeans, rolled shirtsleeves. One of them takes the books that people hand up and gives them to Karen Karl to sign. The other passes them back. When they're not doing that, they stand with their legs apart, arms folded, glaring into the middle distance like Secret-Service agents. In contrast, Karen Karl seems freakishly animated. The two-foot-long gold fountain pen she's brandishing like Cinderella's fairy godmother keeps almost cracking them in the face.

"When's your birthday?" she's asking a skinny old lady in tight stretch jeans and a beehive hairdo. "Not the year, now," she warns coyly. "Just the day and month."

The old lady mumbles something and Karen Karl calls out, "Sagittarius! It's your year!" She waves her magic wand for order. "Okay. Let's say you get up tomorrow and open your paper and your horoscope says, 'Sagittarius: Don't be surprised if loved ones seem short tempered. Drive carefully and watch for falling masonry.' What are you gonna do?"

"Go back to bed," says the old lady.

"Abso-goshdarn-lutely!" says Karen Karl. "Pull those blankets over your head. Now let's say you open the paper and it says, 'Sagittarius: An old problem will be settled. Romance in the air. Don't overlook new chance for fame and fortune.' What then? You're gonna feel like a world-beater, right?"

The old woman draws herself up and pats her hair and says, "Right." Then one of those boys in the fishnet shirts raises his fist and says, "Way to go, Mom!"

"Is that your son?" asks Karen Karl.

"They're all three my boys," says the woman. Everyone applauds motherhood, and even Vera feels warmed, as if the tightness of the woman's jeans is a statement of faith in the future.

"Say it again, son," orders Karen Karl.

"Way to go, Mom," he says, no longer sounding convinced.

"That's what I'm talking about in my book," says Karen Karl. "Positive Energy Potential. P-E-P. Pep!" As she punches the air for emphasis, her sleeve falls back, revealing an armful of digital watches set, Vera imagines, to tell the time on other planets or, at the very least, in L.A.

Karen Karl goes back to asking names and signing as fan after fan approaches with such awe and reverence they could be touching a god or the fingerbone of a saint. When they reach out, they actually pale a little, as if bracing themselves to hear their fortunes told on the spot. Vera's so moved by these women and their questions, she suddenly wants to ask Karen Karl something, too. Perhaps she should introduce herself, one professional to another, saying, "My paper carries your column." But she can't stop thinking of that scene in *Wise Blood* when Enoch Emory goes up to Gonga, the man in the gorilla suit who's shaking children's hands in front of a theater, and Enoch is so overcome with feeling he confesses his life story and all his deepest hopes, and Gonga says, "You go to hell."

Just for something to focus on, Vera lifts a book from the stack and gets as far as the title page when one of the owlish boys snatches it from her hands. "What's your name, Sweetie?" Karen Karl asks, and Vera's horrified to hear herself whispering. Karen Karl scribbles a few words and motions for Vera to follow her book down the line but Vera just stands there. She's searching for the tiny eyes in that wide face, and as soon as she finds them, she says, "Do you believe in coincidence?"

"Now what do you mean by that?" The wariness in Karen Karl's voice moves Vera all over again; it's the voice of a not-very-bright child going stiff when the smarter kids tell riddles. A dozen answers swim through Vera's head, but all seem way too complicated, and finally the best she can do is, "Yesterday I read your column—really read it—for the first time. Then I read every one—back through the last six months. Then today I pick up the paper. And now you're here!"

Karen Karl stiffens again, but the fervor of Vera's conversion—six months of columns at once!—seems to mollify her. She rubs her eyes with the heels of her palms. How tired she looks. Then she waves her wand and says, "Let's put it like this. It's all in the stars, and we earthlings don't know the teensiest bit about it. What we call coincidence may be two distant planets crossing the plane of our orbit. I don't care *what* you believe—the big bang or the little bang or God created it all in seven days. Whether you think the universe stops at a certain point and there's something else beyond it, or that it never stops but just goes on and on . . . Believe any of that and you can believe *anything*! Compared to that, your reading my column and my showing up here today is chickenfeed!"

For one brief moment, Vera feels that all her questions have been answered, wants to change places with the owlish boys and follow Karen Karl to L.A. and beyond. Barely audible music seems to be piping under her skull. She wants everything to stop so she can sort it all out, but the owlish boy's being paid to make sure it doesn't. She takes the book he offers her.

What registers first is that she's got the wrong book. The inscription reads, "To Virginia, Huey, Dewey, and Louie, Don't stop wishing on your lucky star! Love, Karen Karl." The old woman and her three sons are beside her. Vera knows it's theirs.

Without understanding precisely why, she feels that the naming of these boys is the very epitome of everything that most depresses her about human life, everything she most hates and secretly fears about the kind of people who read *This Week*. Of course their mother couldn't have known how they'd turn out.

Clearly she'd had something cuter, less swollen, more baby-duckling-like in mind. And if they're saying, "Way to go, Mom!", they must not hold her accountable. Still, how could she *do* it? What Vera's feeling is the opposite of that honeyish, sentimental glow that had her seeing these people inching toward Karen Karl as pilgrims. Perhaps if she tried hard enough she might recapture it, might see it as funny and tender and really rather sweet to name your kids after Donald Duck's nephews. But she can't. Instead she's losing patience, much as she used to at the end of a long day with Rosalie, when she'd turn on her, shrieking and chattering like a monkey. That's what she'd like to do to the old lady as they trade books and apologetic smiles. Vera hates her smeary mouth, her tiny, sharp teeth, her pleasure in having her own book at last. Vera's copy says, "To Vera, Don't stop wishing on your lucky star! Love, Karen Karl."

Vera reels out of the bookstore and into the street, where now *everyone* has cartoon-character names. Mr. Naturals, Olive Oyls, Daddy Warbuckses, Little Nemos, Betty Boops—Eighth Street on a Sunday afternoon is crawling with them. Seeing people as cartoons is one of Vera's personal horrors and one that, she fears, is yet another occupational hazard of working at *This Week*. Sometimes it even happens in Vera's dreams: people turn into Looney Tunes. It's why she's never enjoyed movies that switch between live action and animation, finds them nightmarish. Why? Because when it happens in her nightmares, she knows something terrible is hiding and waiting to pounce as she rounds the next corner of her dream.

IT'S A SHORT subway ride to Kirsty's, but long enough for Vera to envision a dozen horrendous scenarios of carnage and gore she'll find upon arriving. It's nothing she hasn't imagined before, only this time the maniac killers have the cartoon faces and sadistic m.o.'s of Dick Tracy's archenemies: Fly Face, Flat Top, Prune Face, 88 Keys.

But when Kirsty's mother, Lynda, answers the door, it's clear nothing terrible's happened. Not yet. At worst, Vera feels as she always does with Lynda—interested and uncomfortable.

Lynda works at a trendy Soho beauty salon called Skank. She's wearing black vinyl toreadors, leopard scuffs, neon pink plastic earrings, a sweatshirt big enough for three: yet another style begun as a way of offending the middle classes, who've taken to it so fanatically that women like Lynda have to wear it to keep their jobs. Lynda's bangs are peacock blue. The rest of her hair is a reddish fox color, cut against the grain so it stands straight up and looks so like an animal pelt that Vera wants to pet it. Why doesn't she? Lynda often makes free with *her* hair, hefting it in a pony tail, appraising it with that cool hairdresser's eye that always makes Vera expect the worst: ENDS SPLIT TO ROOTS—CANCER OF THE HAIR.

"Come on in," says Lynda, whose breathless, slightly charged-up voice evokes the ghost of Marilyn Monroe. She turns till she's shoulder to shoulder with Vera; it's as if they're arriving together. And in a way it's true; it's not exactly Lynda's apartment. Thanks to an imaginative custody arrangement, Kirsty stays here, and her parents move in with her for alternate weeks. Kirsty's Dad is named Richard, but Vera has never heard Lynda call him anything but El Creepo. The way Lynda talks, Vera imagines El Creepo as a masked bandit who leaves picked-over chicken bones in the refrigerator, full garbage bags in the pantry, whiskers in the sink. No one, probably not even the judge, expected this setup to last; but though the apartment has the dulled, dusty look of a child being used as a go-between by two warring parents, Kirsty seems to be thriving.

"Guess what happened to me Friday," says Lynda. "I ran into four flashers. Four exhibitionists in one day. They couldn't whip it out fast enough. One right up against the shop window, one down the counter from me at lunch, one on the subway each way."

"Ugh," says Vera. "Give me a screamer any day. The thing I hate about flashers is the surprise. I mean, you're not looking crotch level, so you've been staring at their silly faces for hours before you look down and notice. By then it's like they're your *friends*, like obscene phone callers always sounding at first like some guy you know. Then they've *really* got you—"

"Christ," says Lynda. "You know what the guy in the window said? The shop was pretty crowded, I figured I couldn't get into too much trouble, so I told him to get lost. And he said, 'Don't be offended, Missus. Me and Henry, we're just takin' the breeze' "

"Me and Henry?" Vera shudders. "Once my friend Louise was walking through Central Park and a guy came up to her jerking off. 'Please hep me,' he kept saying. And she looked him right in the eye and said, 'God heps them what hep themselves.' "

"Sure," says Lynda. "You always hear stories like that. But no one ever does it."

"The worst are the ones in bookstores," says Vera, recalling how when she'd first walked into Belmontbooks she'd thought everyone was a flasher. Now that she thinks about it, it's a wonder she didn't encounter one. She's noticed that thinking of flashers seems to attract them. Which isn't to say she believes that stuff about rape victims secretly wanting it. That's simply untrue, and anyway, desire—even secret desire—isn't the issue. It's something subtler, more mysterious. In which case, what does

Lynda's four-in-one-day imply about *her* mental processes? Well, plenty. Lynda and her friends inhabit a world where men named El Creepo want nothing more than to leave whiskers in the sink or leap out from behind the nearest subway pillar waving their penises in women's faces.

Which is to say: the real world. Or their corner of it. All Lynda's friends seem to be divorced from men who might as well be named El Creepo, and what they do when they get together is complain about their ex-husbands. In other words, romantics. None of them has stopped believing in true love; they all want to remarry. Often in their company Vera imagines she's among women on torturous diets: the one food they crave is the only one they can't have.

Beyond that, they make her miss Louise the way boring men at parties make her miss Lowell. Their talk makes her long for the common language she shares with Louise and just can't seem to speak with Lynda and her friends. One problem is: when they're telling their horror stories, Vera can never manage to come across with a suitable contribution. And it's not that she doesn't have stories to tell. Let them beat the one about Lowell spending their last peso on cashews! Still, she's never told it, partly out of some vestigial loyalty to Lowell, but more out of loyalty to herself. If she presents Lowell as an idiot, what does that make her for marrying him?

One night, bravely keeping up her end of the conversation, she told them about the S.C.U.M. Manifesto, in which Valerie Solanis, the one who shot Andy Warhol, claims the only way men can rehabilitate themselves is to sit around repeating, "I am a lowly, abject turd." Just saying it cracked Vera up, but no one else thought it was funny. Did they think she was making fun of them? She wasn't. Perhaps she was just taking it too far.

Now she asks Lynda, "Are you coming or going?", meaning the apartment. Traditionally, the changing of the guard takes place on Sunday nights.

"Leaving," Lynda says. "Can't you tell? When El Creepo's been here, the place is a total disaster."

If this isn't a disaster, Vera would like to see one. But who is she to pass judgment on anyone's housekeeping? Changing the subject, she asks Lynda if El Creepo's coming to the recital.

"Let's hope not," says Lynda. "I don't know if he knows about it, and I'm not going to tell him. When he does go, all he does is stare at Madame Svenskaya's ass."

"Madame?" says Vera. "She's eighty!"

"Don't kid yourself," says Lynda. "She's got terrific muscle tone. Madame's got a cuter ass than we do."

Strangely, Vera's a little hurt by this; pride alone prevents her from reaching back and patting her behind reassuringly. Lynda seems to know what she's thinking; it's the kind of thing she's instinctively sensitive to.

"You?" she says. "You're doing great. Me, I'm getting to the point where the highway patrol wants me to put a sign on my skirt, 'Caution. Wide Load.'"

Vera laughs and asks where the girls are. "Listen," says Lynda. Vera hears a scratchy version of "The Dance of the Sugarplum Fairy" coming from down the hall and follows Lynda toward it. The girls don't hear them come in. They're twirling round the cramped bedroom, each holding one hand in the air like show-off waiters balancing trays. At the recital there will be trays, and on them lit candles. Vera's never approved; the girls' long hair whips back and forth at tray level. One night she asked Rosie if they were planning to dance in asbestos tutus: another mistake. Rosie can't stand any questioning of Madame's authority and taste. "*Mom*," she said. "*It's the St. Lucia dance.*"

Vera knows for a fact that St. Lucia has something to do with Christmas in Sweden, with fresh-braided cardamom loaves glazed with sugar and raisins. But then, ten-year-olds waltzing with open flames in mid-August fits right in with Madame's vague Mittel Europa origins, her trailing Isadora Duncan scarves and Isak Dinesen makeup job. What sympathy Vera has comes from knowing that all this, accent included, is Madame's uniform, as much a part of her job as Lynda's blue hair. In five years, Rosie's had three ballet teachers, all of them called Madame.

As soon as the music ends, Vera says, "Okay, Anna Pavlova,"

and immediately regrets it. She hopes Rosie's never seen the same film clip she did. Thrashing and flopping about, the great Pavlova looked more like the victim of some scabrous poultry disease than a gracefully dying swan. Wondrously, Rosie seems pleased and graces her mother with a smile. Vera almost tells her about the photo Solomon brought her, but no; admitting she even *saw* Solomon is perilous. "Let's hit the road," she says.

Before they can leave, the girls go through an elaborate hand-slapping ritual Vera hasn't seen the likes of since 1968. Soul-sister ballerinas. Vera notices rings under Rosie's eyes. But when she asks if she's sleepy, Rosie ignores her, says nothing all the way to the subway and then, as if no time's elapsed, replies that she and Kirsty were up till one A.M. watching a horror movie. Running on Sunday schedule, the train takes so long coming that Rosie has time to tell the entire plot:

"It's about a guy who buys this windup doll for his girl-friend. He takes it home and—oh, yeah, he has this real nosy landlord—one day when he's not there, the landlord comes snooping around and suddenly the doll starts gnashing its razory little teeth"—Rosie demonstrates—"and eats up the landlord. Then a detective comes to investigate and the same thing happens to him. By now the guy knows the doll's pretty weird, and he can't decide whether he should still give it to his girlfriend, but he does. Except the doll's jealous of the girlfriend and the last thing you see is the girlfriend pinned against the wall screaming and the doll taking little nibbles from her leg. Really gross."

"Gee," Vera says. "I wonder where we could get one."

Rosie's delighted. "Who would we sic it on?" she asks.

Vera can't think of anyone she'd like to see digested by a mechanical doll. Maybe life isn't so bad. Finally she says, "What about Carl?"

"Mom," whines Rosie. "Why are you so hung up on Carl?" When the train comes, she sits across the aisle. And that's it for conversation.

They're home in no time, or anyway before Vera remembers she's forgotten to buy food for Mavis's dinner. She so hates the idea of going out again, she actually considers recycling last night's chicken salad. Perhaps it could be salvaged, every shred of offending celery hunted down and removed. What restores her to sanity is remembering that Mavis has problems with her teeth. She's even given up meat—for dental reasons. To invite someone for dinner and serve food that causes them physical pain seems like something Ghengis Khan would do. She'll make the pasta primavera she should have made last night—a resolution that gives her heart to throw out the leftover chicken salad.

Scraping the nearly full bowl into the garbage, Vera tenses. If there's any time lightning seems likely to strike, this is it. Her mother will eat anything—hard rice, stiff gravy—rather than throw it out. Long before Vera had ever heard of Marx, she believed her parents were working toward some ideal world in which all leftovers were divided in neat little packets and distributed evenly among the nation's poor. Before she knew anything about Judaism, she intuited the presence of that angel with the flaming sword guarding the garbage to make sure nothing marginally edible got thrown out. She thinks, TERROR IN THE TRASH: HOW LEFTOVERS CAN KILL, and to go with it, a story about a woman who makes the mistake of cleaning her refrigerator and taking her metal garbage can out during an electrical storm. All afternoon, shopping and cooking, she rewrites it in her head and is just putting the finishing touches on pasta and story when it's time to leave.

THE ACADEMY of Classical Dance meets in a loft on a bombed-out block of Flatbush Avenue Extension. In the year Rosie's gone there, three different furniture stores have opened and failed in the storefront below. For what Vera pays, the Academy could own the whole building; but in fact they share space with the Ken-Do Karate Dojo, the Kings County Country Dance Society, and several other physical-culture groups. One drawback of this is the smell. Even with the windows open, the loft seems to have trapped a whole weekend's worth of heat and humidity and revved-up martial-arts sweat, sharper and sourer than little-ballerina sweat or even that subway-commuter smell that Vera sort of likes.

Vera deposits Rosie backstage, then goes back out to find Mavis. In her white linen blouse, skirt, shoes, Mavis is dressed for a garden party, a croquet match—for anything but a kids' ballet recital and dinner at Vera's. Vera wants to run home and dust every surface lest the true extent of her disaffection leave its mark on Mavis's white bottom.

"Darling!" says Mavis. "Good evening! How was your weekend?"

"Weekend? What weekend?" says Vera, fighting the temptation to tell Mavis everything: last night's dinner and how, just before falling asleep, she had a vision of herself and Solomon wrapped round and round with celery string like two pale green mummies or some awful conceptual vegetable art. One problem is how to explain this without making Mavis apprehensive about some similar culinary disaster happening tonight. But that's not what's stopping Vera.

Sometimes, after a few glasses of wine, Mavis takes Vera's wrist between her thin fingers. "Passion," she'll whisper. "That's what's missing nowadays. You girls go from one man to another. In *my* day, you loved a man, and if that man died, you carried that love to your grave." Now, remembering that and the story about Mavis beating a path to her husband's headstone, Vera can't stand to tell her about Solomon. She knows Mavis won't let her pretend that what came between them was just celery.

"How was *your* weekend?" asks Vera.

"Don't ask," says Mavis. "I'm ashamed to tell you. Going home Friday night, I found a book on the subway seat and though it wasn't the sort of novel I'd normally read—"

"Called what?" asks Vera.

"*The Burning Pyre,*" says Mavis.

Vera vaguely remembers an ad for a paperback bestseller, a woman in deep Regency decolletage beside some dark, scuzzy, mustachioed type in a dishrag turban. "India?" she says.

"More or less," says Mavis. "Sabu the Elephant Boy. I started it Friday night and finished this morning. How's that for a wasted weekend?"

It's just occurred to Vera that Mavis has made up the part about finding it on the train. Mavis's lying to her is disturbing, but less so than the idea that Mavis bought *The Burning Pyre* and read it in one weekend with nothing to distract her.

"And really, what for?" ask Mavis. "At the end of the book, she hurls herself on her husband's funeral pyre. Eight hundred pages for *that?*"

"Oh, no," Vera says.

"What's the matter?" asks Mavis.

"I guess this is kind of a rotten time to tell you we're having barbeque."

"You're kidding," says Mavis.

"I am," says Vera. "Pasta."

"Marvelous," Mavis says. "Now let's go in."

The first person Vera spots is Madame, fluttering stage left, winding and unwinding the yards of chiffon scarf encircling her head and neck. Vera's afraid she'll get carried away and her eyes will pop. DUNCAN DIES AGAIN. DANCER'S GHOST RE-TURNS, REPLAYS BIZARRE DEATH SCENE. What a bad night this would be for what's left of Madame's brain cells to go. Vera's looking forward to seeing Rosie dance. She's nearly convinced that Rosie won't incinerate herself and that watching her perform may partly undo what damage Vera's sustained from her dinner with Solomon, her audience with Karen Karl.

Eventually Vera sees that Madame's watching Lynda, who's walking down the aisle in a hat that's a multicolored plastic umbrella attached to a matching beanie. Vera can't tell if Madame's panic is esthetic or superstitious. Opening an umbrella indoors is bad luck; it makes Vera nervous, too. She wishes Lynda had left her hat upside down on the floor in the hall.

Lynda catches Vera's eye and nods. The umbrella swoops wildly. Vera gives her a friendly "talk to you later" grin that feels like something a baboon would do. "Should we get seats?" asks Mavis, but Vera hangs back, looking for her parents. Finally she spots them, sitting down. They turn and wave at her—the smooth, distant waves of people in old home movies, people who don't intend their waving to *do* anything. It's the wave of the dead, Vera thinks, remembering a recent movie about a woman who dies and comes back to tell the tale of how death's like falling down a rabbit hole lined with one's loved ones and the newly deceased, all waving just like that.

Even from this distance, the tilt of Dave's head signals one of his famous—and mercifully infrequent—bad moods. Vera's always envied him the freedom of these moods, the freedom to say anything. It's enough to make Vera want to be anyplace else, yet she and Mavis have really no choice but to sit down directly behind them. Although they've met Mavis several times, Vera introduces them again. Norma smiles, as does Mavis.

Dave smiles the thin, sharky smile that has always meant trouble and says, "I can't believe anyone but a relative would come to this kind of thing."

It's an insult to Mavis and Rosie. All three women look down. Vera wants to take Mavis aside and tell her, It's just passion, love for his family gone wrong. But Mavis doesn't need Vera to tell her about passion. Smiling sweetly, she says, "I wouldn't miss it for the world."

"You're a better man than I am, Gunga Din," says Dave.

Dave turns around and Vera's left staring at his back till, losing focus, she's seeing the back of Rosie's neck when Rosie was a baby. That most fragile and lovely and vulnerable part—Vera would stare at it for hours! And now what she wants is to rest her face against Dave's neck and search for the smell of his sweat, to pretend he still smells of tobacco and that they are thirty years younger.

The house lights blink on and off. Vera sits back in her chair. In the darkness, something pokes her in the head so hard she stands halfway up. This outrage, this pain and intrusion—this is what it must be like to be stabbed. But it's only Lynda, taking off her hat as she slides in next to her.

"Jesus Christ," says Vera. "You almost took my eye out."

"Oh, dear," says Lynda, dropping the hat and pawing maternally at Vera's head. "I'm sorry."

A ragged spotlight comes up center stage, illuminating Madame. The grimy edge of chiffon she's running through her hands reminds Vera of the washcloth baby Rosalie couldn't go to sleep without. "Good evening," says Madame in a sepulchral voice. Down the aisle from Vera, a boy of eleven or twelve—some ballerina's brother—repeats "Good evening" in a deep, Boris-Karloff *basso profundo*, and his pals fall off their chairs laughing.

"Tonight vee are pleased to velcome you to zee Claseek Ballet Kedemy." Madame's accent careens like some manic, desperate tourist through half a dozen different European countries. "Vee veel start tonight veeth zee top." It takes Vera a while to realize she means tap dancing. Nor is Madame making it any easier. In any language she can barely bring herself to pronounce the hated words. It is the shame of Madame's existence that for economic reasons she must concede to the uninformed, vulgar little girls and offer modern dance and tap.

There's a bark of electronic sound, then the unmistakable swooping moan of a tape recorder breaking. "Gott in heaven!"

cries Madame, pressing her hand to her forehead. Another blast of painful white noise has the boys down the aisle hissing and booing like a movie audience reminding the projectionist to focus. "Don't those children have mothers?" whispers Mavis.

Miss Rossen, the pretty former beatnik who plays piano, crosses the stage and whispers in Madame's ear. Madame brushes her off like a bug. She must be hell to work for, thinks Vera. Not once has she breathed the name of Bonnie Kleckner, the little Sohoite who's teaching tap. Even Vera gets bylines. To choose this limping reel-to-reel over the rich, woody overtones of Miss Rossen's upright is madness on Madame's part, a reflection of her attitude toward anything but classical ballet; the scratchy tape represents both her continuing humiliation and her revenge.

Finally a blare of noise makes the children squeal with joy and the adults' blood pressure jump. Gradually sounds organize themselves, first into rhythm, then in tune: "Nothing could be finer than to be in Carolina in the mo-o-orning." A double row of girls shuffle out carrying canes, wearing black leotards, tap shoes, white dickeys, bow ties, and black bowler hats. Every one's a mite awkward, tall for her age, though it's hard to tell how old they are since they're all in blackface except two spindly girls in the center who seem to be genuinely black.

Don't these children have mothers? Vera knows they do. Intelligent, political women who go to peace encampments and evacuate their children when anyone in the neighborhood is having the exterminator in. Though there are lots of space-outs like Lynda, who wouldn't turn her umbrellaed head if Kirsty came home done up like some nymphette Aunt Jemima.

The audience takes it like a punch in the kidneys. You can practically hear the jaws drop. How could a fairly hip person like Bonnie Kleckner have visited this upon them? You'd have thought she'd sneak in something by the Talking Heads or even, being conservative, from *Fame*.

As soon as the dancing begins, it's clear that these little minstrels are all at the age when every step in public is torture; electric cattle prods could be driving them in this grim buck and wing. Still, most boys and girls this age are, despite themselves, graceful. These seem *unusually* gangly, uncoordinated, cursed with pot bellies and premature dowager's humps. They must be a freak cross section of the population, these children who ask to take tap, or whose parents suggest it the way some well-meaning, heartless Mom might suggest a more flattering hairstyle for her homely daughter. Faced with this group, now grinning white-lipped smiles and bravely rolling their eyes, Bonnie Kleckner must have lost her nerve and reverted, as people will, back to childhood, resurrecting instinctively and in perfect detail the long-lost "Carolina in the Morning" recital piece of her own childhood tap school.

At long last it's over. The dancers go down on one knee. If the applause lasts one second too long, they'll pitch over on their faces. The girls wobble to their feet and straggle off, and out comes an unbelievably tiny girl wearing glasses with Coke-bottle lenses. From a distance her candy-striped tutu resembles a swirl of toothpaste. Her cane is candy-striped, too, and long before the music starts, Vera knows it's going to be "The Good Ship Lollipop." The tiny girl rotates her cane in full circles as she skips to the right, then the left.

Vera thinks back thirty years to *Ted Mack's Amateur Hour*, to the one-legged vet tap dancer who won for weeks with his two crutches and tap versions of military favorites. His grand finale, "Off We Go Into the Wild Blue Yonder," ended with him standing on his one good leg and raising the crutches like wings. Every time he got to this point, her father burst out laughing. And Vera, young enough to take such things seriously, was shocked. Once more she wants to lay her head on her father's neck and see if he's laughing now. Chances are he's not. He might even be moved by this little girl, having come full circle back to the point at which you take these things as they're meant.

The little girl's making her last candy-cane rotations when suddenly there's a commotion; loud conversation comes from the back of the loft. The house lights flash on and everyone wheels around to see twenty guys in white karate *ghi*s stamping their feet and doing warmup maneuvers behind the last row. Madame and Miss Rossen and even little Bonnie Kleckner go back to confer with a small, rather beautiful Japanese man. Vera can't help noticing how helpless and ineffectual the women look. Some men in the audience notice, too. They stand up and hover about in case the women need them. And maybe the women will. Because the longer Vera looks, the more obvious it seems that what's just walked in is a karate school for psychotics.

It's the Baldies, the Bishops, the Young Lords, the Jets, the street gang of your wooliest fifties nightmares, the kind you don't hear about any more unless they go in for break dancing or graffiti. They're like the rotten parody of those multiethnic UNICEF cards or one of Dave's ·paintings, an all-star dirty dozen chosen for sheer ugly nastiness. All the little ballerinas' fathers put together are no match for this bunch. Vera's read the stories: parties full of people mugged by unrepentant crashers.

If the parents survive, they'll have a story to tell. ROBBERS ROUT RECITAL. BANDITS BLAST BABY BALLET. But the children, the poor children. Vera imagines them grown, laughing young women telling their lovers how their first ballet recital was held up at knifepoint. Even the older brothers in Vera's row have fallen silent. Mavis leans toward her and whispers, "Well, if it isn't the Bad News Bears!" On her other side, Lynda's saying, "Don't worry. I've got Mace in my purse."

"That's the city for you," says Norma. How sad and ironic that Norma's turned into one of those people who criticize the city when what they really mean is blacks and Puerto Ricans. But it turns out that Norma really does mean the city and its blind stabs at social improvement, for there, powwowing with Madame and the *sensei* are three bearded social-worker types, clearly some sort of counselors. So, then. It's not the ultimate Bad Boys at all, but some pathologically misguided bad-boy rehabilitation scheme. Vera marvels at the ingenuity of the grant hustler who got funding to make those juvenile killers' bare hands lethal weapons. What little she knows of karate is enough for her to be unnerved by the fact that the counselors are all white belts, their charges brown and black belts.

Perhaps it's the language barrier—Madame's accent, the

sensei's Japanese—but there's an awful lot of discussion going on, when anyone could see what the conflict is: the little girls want to dance, the guys want to kick and punch and scream from the gut. Finally some agreement's reached; everyone looks at the clock. Then the boys slink out.

Meanwhile the tiny girl has left the stage. "Continue," orders Madame in a voice like a stick being rapped on the stage.

"Thank God," says Vera.

"Amen," says Lynda. The tension of sitting through this is moving them to prayer.

As those first high Sugar-Plum-Fairy harp plucks crackle through the speakers, Vera's knuckles turn white. She's Ethel Merman in *Gypsy*, she's Brooke Shields's mother: essence of corny stage Mom. Bubbles pop in her chest when Rosie and Kirsty come on. They're up on their toes, moving smoothly and so slowly it seems less like human motion than like tense, trembling Jello. Their filmy costumes make them look airy, insubstantial, drawn with the finest pastel. Rosie's gliding and turning is the most graceful and beautiful process Vera's ever seen. Vera thinks of Barbara Stanwyck at the end of *Stella Dallas*, spying on her daughter's wedding, every imaginable and many unimaginable human emotions registering on her face. Afraid that something similar may be showing on *her* face, Vera remembers to worry.

The flames! They're carrying their trays, and this time—Vera cannot believe that Madame has really gone through with this—the candles are lit. Their long hair whips dangerously near the fire. Vera closes her eyes and waits for the screams. Then she opens them and sees: they keep missing each other, it's magical, like watching someone dance through burning hoops. The lights flicker but don't go out and instead make a pattern like sparklers waved in the dark. It seems a kind of miracle, and if it weren't *her* daughter up there risking immolation, Vera would be on her feet applauding Madame's brilliance.

Well, it's a good thing she's not: the dance isn't over. One thing she's learned from hearing Rosie rehearse is that the music always lasts ten times longer than you expect. Then suddenly—and like so many terrible things, when everyone's least prepared

—loud music blares from the back of the room, a back beat that doesn't just drown out the Sugar Plum Fairy but pulls it out of the water and stomps it: Michael Jackson singing "Beat It" on a ghetto blaster turned up to full volume.

Rosie and Kirsty stop in midtwirl. There's no way they can go on. All at once their costumes look silly—dingy and worn, like rummage-sale nightgowns. The candles take on the fore-boding air of lights that some weak-lunged birthday boy or girl can't manage to blow out. There's no telling if the ballet music's still playing; maybe it's just as well. The Tchaikovsky would sound fussy and overdone, a pale second to Michael Jackson's energy, fake anger, and real youth. It's how Vera feels at office parties when she and Mavis are wearing their next-to-best clothes, and the secretaries flash by in their satins and ankle socks and tarty plastic barettes.

First Kirsty, then Rosie burst into tears. Vera and Lynda link arms so they won't run up on stage and embrace them. Short of that, Vera would like to go back and engage the radio-playing karate kids in hand-to-hand combat. Meanwhile she watches her daughter cry. Thank God *someone* takes action. The music stops as suddenly as it started. The girls stand there, their eye makeup smeared so badly they look like junior replicas of Madame. A couple of curtseys and brave, teary smiles would bring down the house. But how could they know that? They're only ten. They back offstage, and not one soul in that audience of adults is grown up enough to clap into all that silence. They're all paralyzed, even Vera, who's afraid that if she starts the ap-plause, Rosie will somehow discern this and never forgive her.

Madame comes out and says, "Thank you," but it's not the kind of thank you meant to start the crowd cheering in agree-ment. "And now for our last number, 'Zee Flight of Zee Boomblebee.' " Vera steels herself for more white noise. But now Miss Rossen slides onto the piano bench so awkwardly and self-consciously, *she* could be ten years old and this her first recital.

It's "The Flight of the Bumblebee," all right. Miss Rossen's pounding away; the piano's got at least forty different unwanted

138

overtones buzzing at once as the little girls swarm on. They've got bobbing antennae, wings out of some stiff net, tutus that seem to have been sewn from alternating strips of brown and yellow bath mat. Hardly the stateliest costumes, and worthless at disguising the fact that all the little bumblebees are terribly overweight. Nor is theirs the smooth, tight flesh of most plump little girls. Everything over those toe shoes jiggles and shakes.

Watching their scowling, determined buzz, Vera has never felt so gloomy. Putting them all together this way seems like the most barbaric cruelty. They simply can't move as fast as the music insists, and as they strain and trip and mortify their poor flesh, she understands that this is what the whole weekend's been leading up to. No solace anywhere, not in love or food or media witches, not even in Rosie's grace. Everything's a cartoon, and Vera even knows which one this is: the hippos' dance in *Fantasia*. No use telling herself these ducklings will grow into swans. There's no guaranteeing the future, no denying the present and past. According to a recent *This Week* poll, half the American people think everything that happens on earth may be stored forever in some galaxy, and Vera hates thinking that this moment may survive for eternity.

Eventually the dance ends. The lights go on. Vera blinks grumpily, as if it's a camera flash and she's been immortalized in her present state of mind. The piano keeps buzzing forever, or at least that's how long it seems before the clapping begins. It gives Vera some satisfaction that the applause peters out before Madame gets on stage and doesn't start up again when she does. Everything's slightly hurried. The karate boys are shadowboxing the empty spaces in back; the crowd can feel those black-belt eyes drilling the backs of their heads. Everyone talks at once and, in the general nervousness, seems to say the wrong thing.

"Goodness," says Mavis. "Somebody should have covered that for *This Week*."

"The bastards," Dave keeps saying, "the bastards," though it's unclear whether the bastards in question are Madame or the radio-players or whatever forces of nature and society make some little girls fat.

By now the karate group's jumped on stage, where they're chaotically bashing each other while they wait for their teacher to join them. All over, little minstrel girls and bumblebees are finding their parents. Quite a few are in tears; the rest get their kisses and hugs and then stand around in stiff, unnatural groupings as if posing for some invisible graduation photographer. Vera doesn't see Rosalie in the crowd, but for once she's not worried. In fact, she's rather grateful; she hasn't quite decided what to say.

Ignoring the NO SMOKING signs, parents are lighting up. Vera checks out the fire exits. But Lord, how wonderful it smells!

"I'm going outside for a second," she tells Mavis and her parents. "If you see Rosie, say I'll be right back."

Outside it's hot and dark and, except for the traffic, deserted. Moving shadows augur worse than the karate group inside: teenage killers with some awful violence yet to commit before they'll even reach the rehabilitation stage. But Vera doesn't care.

She's thinking about Bigfoot, about how much worse she'd feel if she were Bigfoot now, stranded on Flatbush Extension. And suddenly she understands that the reason she thinks in Bigfoot stories is not that she writes for *This Week* but because on some level she wishes she *were* Bigfoot—huge and strong, self-sufficient, her dignity and privacy insured because no one's even sure she exists. If she were Bigfoot, she'd never have to see another flasher or screamer or ballet recital again. She'd steal cigarettes by the caseload till her lungs turned black and she died. Branches and leaves would cover her, keeping her secrets in death as in life, hiding what's left and what's already gone as flesh and bone and fur sifted quietly into dust.

I T'S BEEN a rough Monday. Rosie sulked through breakfast and wouldn't speak to Vera, who went off to work to find Hazel mysteriously gone and in her place a young guy with slicked-back hair and a tight muscle T. When Vera asked about the logo on his shirt—WANNA SEE SOMETHING REALLY SCARY?— she was treated to a frame by frame description of *Twilight Zone: The Movie*, while she prayed for Hazel's quick return and made a solemn vow: If Hazel comes back while Vera's still at *This Week*, she'll apologize for writing ELEVATOR LIFT-OFF SMASHES SEVENTH GRADE. The elevator stopped, no closer to the floor than Hazel ever got; and Vera's longing for her old friend swelled as she understood that what she'd always seen as malice might just be a question of tricky alignment. Then into the office, where Vera spent the morning hiding at her desk for fear that Shaefer and Esposito might look at her and guess the secret of where she's headed now.

A block from the Greens', Vera sees a flashing blue light and has no doubt about whose house it's turning in front of. She's equally sure that whatever the cop car's doing there doesn't bode well for her visit. So she slows down, hoping they'll leave while she cases the territory for some jangle of familiarity, some clue to suggest she's been here, met this family, forgotten.

But for all its showy gingerbread, its turrets and swirling verandahs, this neighborhood reveals nothing. Its residents don't order personalized name plaques from mail-order catalogues, wrought-iron silhouettes of Mom and Dad, the right number of kids and pets. Nor are they the kind who sink bathtub grottoes in the front yard to shelter their private visions of sanctity and grace. The lives inside these homes are as opaque as their mottled Victorian diamonds of leaded glass. The brownish, going-to-seed hydrangeas, the rhododendrons curled against the August heat could be on any lawn, anywhere.

Once she must have biked down these streets; her parents' house isn't far. She remembers a story about Jean Cocteau revisiting his childhood village, recalling nothing till he got down on his knees and, child-sized again, recovered all the lost sensations. Vera's ready to try anything but that. The sight of her approaching on her knees would probably drive the Greens over the edge.

Though the cop car's still there, Vera decides to go in anyway. She feels like a child selling Girl-Scout cookies or paying a first visit to some idolized school chum. She's looking so hard it takes her a while to register what she *doesn't* see: grass, shrubs. Her tour of the neighborhood's given her some sense of what this lawn must have been. Now it's fine dust, gravel, ruts—a sandlot kids have been trampling for generations, except even sandlots have patches of hardy, unkillable weeds.

The cops' presence turns out to have one advantage. The front door's wide open, so there's no ringing the bell and waiting around like some Jehovah's Witness. From the doorway Vera can see the policemen's broad blue backs. She knocks, then walks in, counting on the officers to witness her innocent intentions. What murderer or thief would enter a house full of police?

The cops turn. One of them is middle-aged, that dark, potato-colored, handsome style of Italian. The other one, younger and gap toothed, looks like Eighteenth District Representative Terry Blankett. They barely acknowledge Vera, assuming she's family or neighbor—until they catch the Greens' blank stare. Then the younger cop tenses and says, "Yes? . . ." as if it's his house.

Vera feels like the heroine of an espionage drama with ten seconds to locate the one sympathetic double agent at a crowded party. Luckily, it takes her less than that to fix on Stephanie Green, who's one of those New York mothers she'd recognize anywhere. Angular, bright, intense, they all look like twenties vamps, the young Anito Loos. Where do they get such lovely wrists, such straight, obedient hair?

"I called Friday evening," says Vera. When this gets no response she introduces herself, and that works fine. Now everyone knows her, everyone but the cops. Still playing secret agent, Vera stands erect, waiting for someone to denounce her to the authorities. But the Greens just exchange long looks, and after awhile Stephanie says, "We'll be right with you," as if Vera's come on some innocuous business like new upholstery or reseeding the lawn.

"What's *she* doing here?" asks eight-year-old Joshua Green, whose skin has the rubbery look Vera associates with overindulged, chubby children and polyvinyl dolls.

"Hush, darling," his mother says.

"Doc? . . ." The Italian cop makes a let's-get-back-to-business gesture with his clipboard. Vera can't see a cop write anything without feeling a tightening in her chest—a legacy from when Lowell's old Volvo was always missing some vital sticker or part.

"If this is a bad time . . ." Vera mumbles.

"It's *all* a bad time," snaps Dr. Green, a slight man with moist amber eyes that must inspire his patients' trust and might seem winning now except that they're contracted—two pinholes beaming lasers of accusation at Vera. As if it's his wife who needs calming, he reaches out and takes her delicate wrist. The tops of his hands are matted with hair; he's probably hairy everywhere beneath that neat jacket and tie. When the phone rings and Stephanie goes to answer it, his hand's left encircling air. His shiny head, his little moustache, his odd, pear-shaped face all suggest a thin, Jewish Oliver Hardy, just as his obvious exasperation recalls those moments when Hardy would straight-arm Laurel up in the air and slam him down on his feet; that's what Martin Green must wish he could do to Vera.

"It's unbelievable," he says. "We got off for two lousy days to my brother's place in Connecticut. To get away, you know?" Vera nods. "We get home this morning and what do we find? The house has been broken into!"

"Oh, Jesus," says Vera. "What did they take?"

"That's the hell of it," says the gap-toothed cop. "Nothing."

Vera almost says something conciliatory and inappropriate like, "Oh, then, that's not so bad," but manages some self-control and asks, "How do you know they broke in?"

"Crowbarred the back door off its hinges," the other cop says. "Laid it neat as a pin against the back wall. That ain't something that just happens. I mean, that ain't the wind."

"That *is* weird," says Vera, feeling a shiver along her nerves. Down the same synapse comes a premonition; she's just a step away from figuring out what this break-in's all about when Stephanie reappears with a weird tan dog. The dog's as thin and intense as Stephanie, only sniffier and with a tinier head.

"You had the dog with you?" asks the Italian cop.

"No," says Martin Green. "The dog was here. My brother has a male dog, too; it's a mess when they get together. Ibo's fine here, we leave plenty of water and food—" He goes on, describing his pet's happy life as if clearing himself before some investigative committee from the ASPCA.

"Ibo's the dog?" says gap-tooth.

"Funny," says the other cop. "Funny he didn't tip off the neighbors."

Suddenly Vera knows why and wants to cover her ears so she won't have to hear Martin say, "It's a Basenji."

"Beg your pardon," says the younger cop.

"That's what kind of dog it is," young Joshua explains. "It doesn't have a voice, it can't bark."

The two cops do double takes and look at each other: how could anyone *do* that to a dog?

"They're born that way," little Megan pipes up. "They're *all* born that way."

"Great watch dogs, huh?" says the Terry Blankett cop, chuckling at his own humor. He knows it's a tad mean under the circumstances, but seems to feel the Greens deserve it for feeding and housing an overbred, parasitical dog that can't even do a dog's job.

Vera's been shying away from the dog ever since it came in;

she, too, thinks it's a freak. At the same time she's filled with the strangest desire to move mountains in its defense. Like some canine-loving Clarence Darrow, she'll rivet the jury with tales of nights on the African veldt, packs of silent Basenjis streaking beside the Masai, trusted not to cry out in the heat of the chase and warn their prey. The Greens will ask her how she knows all this, and she'll say, "I work next door to the American Basenji Society! What a coincidence!" Another meaningful cross-connection that may, with luck, prepare the way for what's next.

But if she says that, the cops will say, "Next door where?" Then the whole story will emerge, revealing her—and not the burglars—as the true culprit. Better to pretend she's the upholsterer, or the gardener, or better yet, the caterer, her purse full of sample quail's eggs and kiwi fruit for nouvelle cuisine cocktail hours.

"Don't kid yourself," says Martin Green. "Ibo's pretty tough. Silent but deadly. I wouldn't be at all surprised if he gave those sonofabitches the shock of their lives . . ."

Some way for a doctor to talk. Any minute now someone's going to tell that story about the Doberman that dropped dead after a break-in, choked on a human finger. A few years ago you heard it everywhere; everyone claimed to know someone who knew someone who'd seen it.

"Let's take another look," says the handsome cop, and the phone rings again. "Busy busy," says gap-tooth.

Vera knows what the calls are about. Why haven't the Greens changed their number? Stephanie goes into the kitchen to answer, and the two policemen follow. Vera's so dazzled by the profusion of *things*—fish poachers, paella pans, woks, crocks, food processors with funnels and smokestacks and pistons like sets from *Metropolis*—she's slow to notice what everyone's looking at: dusty footprints leading from the missing door across the dark green linoleum to the sink and back out.

"Perfect," says the Italian cop, and it is. Perfect that the lawn should have turned to dust and that the linoleum is the perfect color to show it. Perfect that Stephanie's house is so perfectly clean. The footprints themselves are perfect—sharp as footprints in children's cartoons, as those tracks that lead the Pink Panther to the villain's lair.

"Perfect," the cop repeats. "They're like the guy leaving his name and address and home phone." But if that's so, why aren't they dusting and tracing and measuring, performing those painstaking rituals TV detectives go through? They're not even bending down. If this is the guy's number, they might as well crumple and toss it in one of those kitchen-drawer graveyards where phone numbers disappear.

Hanging up the phone, Stephanie shudders visibly, reaches out, and hugs the children close. Despite everything, Vera's moved. These aren't footprints in a cartoon—they're in this woman's kitchen. How awful to come home and find evidence of some stranger's filthy feet on your clean linoleum floor!

The prints go from door to sink, sink to door. The Greens and the cops and Vera keep looking back and forth, as if the tracks were the feet that made them, still moving.

"I don't know," says the younger cop. "Seems like an awful lot of trouble for a lousy glass of water."

And then Vera sees what she should have seen all along. Whoever broke in was some larcenous Ponce de Leon in search of the main ingredient in fountain-of-youth lemonade. The only thing she can't figure out is why the Greens haven't told the cops about her article or that the neighbors believe the key to health and happiness can be theirs for five cents a glass. You'd think such facts would be key clues in *any* investigation! Perhaps they're just sick of the story. Vera can sympathize with that. Maybe they're afraid of losing the cops' good opinion, afraid this holy-water business will make *them* look like a bunch of religious nuts. But anyone could see that's not true. Has some lawyer enjoined them to keep quiet?

Here's the likeliest explanation: There's no reason to go into it. Because finally, they're not interested in seeing the water thief brought to justice. They know who the real thief is: *This*

Week. By calling the cops, they're just registering one more grievance, strengthening their case. Upping the legal ante. A million? Why not make it two?

The older cop raises his thumb and aims his index finger at the missing door. "How's your insurance?" he asks.

"Top of the line," says Martin Green. "You think I'd be this calm if I wasn't covered?"

"Well, then," says the cop. "I know it's a lousy thing to come home to. But I wouldn't worry. Looks to me like kid stuff. Mischief. Saturday night, kids get bored, have a couple beers, dare each other to break in, drink a glass of water, get out. Anyone else would at least grab the TV. It won't happen again, I can practically guarantee it. Certainly not while you're here. But look, if it'd put your minds at ease, I'll tell you what. How often you think the guys drive by here, John?"

"Gee, Angelo," says John. "Once an hour, maybe?"

"All right, look," says Angelo. "I'll ask the guys in the patrol car if they'd mind rerouting a little, drive by here every half hour or so for the next couple weeks. How's that?"

"Thank you," says Stephanie. "We'd appreciate it."

"Sure," says John. "I know how you feel, I got kids myself. Seven of 'em."

There's a moment of silence, and then little Megan says, "Seven! Holy shit!"

"Megan!" says Stephanie, but she's laughing, the cops are laughing, even Martin's laughing; the kids are giggling hysterically as they walk the cops to the front door and wave while they get in their car. It's all so chuckly and convivial, it *is* like the coda of a Roy Rogers show, only where are the newborn puppies? Suddenly Vera doesn't want them to leave; she feels like some thriller victim whose captors have just managed to send the cops away, convinced nothing's wrong. Now the police are gone, all that camaraderie gone with them; and Vera's alone with the Greens.

Vera's so busy looking at everything but the Greens, anyone walking in would think she *was* the upholsterer, checking the art and the furniture with an eye toward a suitable match. There must be a name for this style, she thinks—polished wood, exposed brick, fine Oriental rugs, good furniture, a dot-printed velvet couch. The pile on the Persian carpet is so thick she could lose her mind in it, and all at once she remembers: the party Louise went to dressed as garbage was in a house like this. When Louise tossed her play trash on the rug, the hostess brought out a vacuum, though the room was full of masked revelers and the hostess was dressed—in a trampy pilgrim getup with a giant red cardboard A—as Hester Prynne. The painting above the Greens' couch is an original that must have set the doctor back a couple of triple bypasses, by that painter whose name Vera forgets: an American flag, half-erased. She's always valued his work, not for its artistic but for its instructive value. Once when Rosie came home in tears because her second-grade teacher scolded her for spoiling her papers with too much rubbing out, Vera marched her to the museum and stood her in front of a similar picture and told her it was worth twice what her teacher made in a year.

Once more the phone rings. "You answer it," Martin tells Vera in a tone which makes Vera go and answer it.

"Hello?" Vera says.

"Hello?" says a voice so quavering and cracked it sounds like an imitation old person, a kid disguising his voice. The voice has no sex, only age and illness as it spins out its history of degeneration, operations, masses, lesions, organs repaired and removed and given up on, death sentences and reprieves. No frightening detail of the body's mutiny is omitted, yet the telling has the weary, oddly mechanical quality of business calls requiring one to repeat the same story again and again until the right person comes on the line. "One drop," the voice says, thinning now to a not-quite-human scratch, like the dry cry of certain newborns. "Water's free . . . Anything's worth a try . . . send my boy . . ."

"I'm sorry," Vera says. "It's all a mistake, it's not true." How tempting to confess everything to this anonymous, ancient voice: Believe me, I wrote it, I *know* it's a lie. Except that this caller has even more at stake than the Greens—and less desire to believe her. How tempting just to hang up. But Vera can't, no more than she can stop thinking she's getting what she deserves. The voice knows how selfish she is, asks, "What would it cost you, what?"

By the time Vera hangs up and goes into the living room, she's so upset she's yelling at the Greens. Why *don't* they get an unlisted number? An answering service at least!

The Greens are perched on the edge of their couch, side by side and so wrought-up they could be two teens she's just interrupted necking. The children are gone—bribed to stay in their rooms, if Vera knows anything about kids. Stephanie starts to answer but Martin jumps in for her. "Stephanie's Mom's in the early stages of Alzheimer's. I assume you know what that is."

"Sure!" Vera prattles on, as if possessed. "Do *I* know Alzheimer's? I think I've *got* it. Plain old-fashioned senility, only now it's got somebody's name, Herr Doctor Professor Alzheimer immortalized, you'd think he invented it. Like everything else these days—everyone wants to take credit." She's horrified and entirely out of control. Is this how screamers perceive themselves?

The Greens just look at her. Could they possibly not have heard? Well, God isn't *that* merciful. Now Martin is rounding his vowels, pronouncing his consonants very distinctly as if Vera does indeed have Alzheimer's or worse:

"My mother-in-law's neurologist thinks it's a tricky time to make changes. Particularly the phone. Calling here's her lifeline . . ." This sounds to Vera like exactly the sort of lame, temporizing plan a doctor would come up with. Six months from now the poor woman will still be able to call, she just won't remember who she's calling. She wonders if Martin felt compelled to tell his neurologist buddy *why* they needed a new number. How embarrassing, confiding in your colleague: the whole neighborhood thinks you're raising Lazarus from the dead. If it were *her* mother, thinks Vera, she wouldn't be sitting here quoting some neurologist, she'd be pouring fountain-of-youth lemonade down her throat by the gallon, praying for it to dissolve that arterial plaque . . .

"I'm sorry," says Vera, who's sorrier than she can say. She's sorry for Stephanie's mother, sorry for being in this dark living room on a bright August afternoon. She's sorry for writing that story, and sorry that even now, despite everything, she wishes it were true.

"You goddamn well ought to be," says Martin. "Why would anyone pull a nasty stunt like that? You people must be pretty goddamn hard up for news."

"We don't report news," Vera says. "We write fiction. We make it all up so things like this don't happen."

"Of course it's made up," Martin says. "You think we've got the fountain of youth flowing in our goddamn backyard? My question is, why you would write that? And the picture, the photo of my kids. Is that made up, too?"

"The picture's real," Vera says. "But I made up the rest to go with it."

"Then what does that make us?" demands Martin. "Figments of your imagination?"

This is what it means to lock horns, Vera thinks. Heads lowered, bash, bash. Then Stephanie graces them with a smile so literally disarming, they're just as suddenly unlocked, left gazing at her with the awe due St. Francis or the Bird Man of Alcatraz or any of those peace-making animal magicians.

"Martin," she says. "Remember when the kids used to run around saying, 'We're Fig Newtons of your imagination'?"

"Sure," says Martin. "The hippie babysitter taught them that, the same one who used to make Josh change Meggie's diapers so he wouldn't be uptight about his sister's bodily functions."

"Oh, what a mess," says Stephanie, laughing. "Baby shit *everywhere!*"

Vera feels a prickle of envy: marriage, even marriage to controlling, hairy Martin Green. Such envy's nothing she can't transcend. Besides, she's just noticed: something about Stephanie —her smile perhaps, or her laugh, that bony, angular grace— reminds her of Louise. It's possible that under other circumstances, she and Stephanie might have been friends, making plans to pick up the kids after school, after dance class, drinking coffee and gossiping while Rosie tolerated and occasionally lowered herself to play with Megan and Josh. Stephanie rises abruptly and leaves the room, then comes back with a pack of low-tar cigarettes. When she lights up, Vera eyes the smoke so hungrily Stephanie asks if she wants one, and it takes every ounce of will Vera has to say, "No thanks. I quit."

"So did Stephanie," says Martin. "Up until last week. And I'll tell you something else. Steph's father died of lung cancer when he was forty-five."

Vera's "I'm sorry" is less an expression of sympathy than another apology. Is this her fault, too? Perhaps she should start counting: when she's said she's sorry a hundred times, she can leave. Perhaps by then she'll have a better idea of what she's sorry for. She's come out here to apologize to the Greens; she still wishes she'd never written that piece. But that voice on the phone has saddled her with a new set of regrets—responsibilities for hopes raised and dashed—and a vision of heartbreak to make the Greens' troubles look like everyday inconvenience. It almost makes her feel better. In six months, the Greens' life will be back to normal, lawn thriving, kids in school, patients lined up for their pacemakers and vein grafts. But where will the phone caller be in six months? *That* makes her feel worse.

"Can I hold one?" she says, sliding a cigarette out of the pack and rolling it between her fingers. "I know this story may be hard for you to believe," she begins. Imagine Clarence Darrow convincing the jury with that one. "But it's true."

Somehow she expected telling it to be easy; she's certainly had enough practice. But after a sentence or two, she stumbles. This is uncharted terrain. She's talking about *their* house, their kids, their lives—it's their story too, a dubious distinction no one else she's told it to can claim. They're all together in this: Martin and Stephanie. Megan and Joshua. Vera.

Finally she's finished. Stephanie stubs out her cigarette; Vera counts three in the ashtray. Could so much time have elapsed, or did she smoke them all at once? Vera's own unlit cigarette is broken in half. Martin's giving her the kind of attention she imagines him giving a housefly he's sneaking up on to swat. After a while he says, "You know, you're wrong. I don't find it hard to believe at all."

"You don't?" says Vera. "Oh, I'm so glad . . ."

"I find it fucking *impossible*."

Vera's cheeks flame the same red they turn when she's just spent five minutes smiling at the subway flasher, chatting up the obscene phone caller, the same shade they must have turned the first time some playmate said, Guess what? and Vera said, What? and the kid said, *That's* what. Meanwhile she's casting wildly about for oaths to take. Is there a Bible in the house? The only lasting symbol she can see is that rubbed-out Stars and Stripes. Should she lay one hand on her heart and point to that?

"Listen," she says. "You can't imagine how often this happens when you write for an outfit like *This Week*." Outfit? She's never used that word in her life, except to mean clothes. "Write a story about anything—Bigfoot, say—the next week you get a letter from the cryptobiologists telling you it's old history."

"Cryptobiologists?" Stephanie goes for the bait. For years now, Vera's been dining out on the cryptobiologists; she's never known it to fail. So she's more than a little discouraged now when Martin looks very obviously at his watch. Then, in case Vera's missed that, he turns toward Stephanie and rolls his eyes.

"Now *you* listen," he says. "Let me tell you about *my* day's work. I go into the hospital to make my rounds, the nurses are so busy snickering I can't get a dressing changed. I can't get one of my patients a bedpan—the orderlies are in on it, too. You don't know what a grapevine *is* till something like this happens. Then it's *unbelievable*. The janitor knows, the chief of cardiology knows, the president of the A.M. fucking A. probably knows. Now I'll tell you something else. There's going to be some kind kind of inquiry. All very discreet and professional, no reason to get alarmed, just a procedural matter . . . so next month I get to go before the board and explain. And what am I supposed to tell them: some two-bit sleazo Lois Lane made me up?"

That's what he calls her and this is what Vera says: "I'm

sorry." Can she leave now? She can't understand why she's come here. In light of the damage she's done health care and the doctor's career and medical science in general, she wouldn't dream of being so small as to ask them not to sue.

Stephanie takes a long drag on her cigarette. "We have a neighbor," she says. "Betty Anne."

"Please," says Martin. "Betty Anne stories. Spare me."

"A horror story for every occasion," says Stephanie. "You know the type. When we moved here, I was pregnant with Meggy; Betty Anne came over and introduced herself and got going about how her second cousin just gave birth to a kid with no arms and legs and its head growing out of its liver. Lately it's mostly stories about kids who seem okay till they're Josh's age, then wake up one morning with forty-pound tumors in their stomachs.

"A couple of weeks ago, the doorbell rings and it's Betty Anne, batting a newspaper in my face. When I saw what it was, I thought, Well, it's just the kind of junk she'd read. Sorry."

"That's all right," says Vera. "Go on."

" 'Look!' Betty Anne's saying. 'Look!' And there's a picture of the house. The kids. My heart just sank. 'Betty Anne,' I say. 'Why would someone write this?' "

" 'People will do anything for a buck,' she tells me. 'I got you an extra copy.' She's waiting to be asked in. But I say, 'Excuse me,' and practically shut the door in her face and go inside and call Martin . . . who needless to say is in surgery. So I make myself a glass of iced tea, a Swiss cheese sandwich on French bread with fresh tomatoes from the garden . . ."

Vera trusts people with that kind of memory for food. Like Carmen. It makes her forgive Stephanie her kitchen equipment and think once more how in another lifetime she might have been friends with Stephanie, who's saying:

"By now I'm talking to myself like I'd talk to the kids: 'There, there, don't worry, nothing will come of this, no one will read it . . .' Just then the doorbell rings. It's Mrs. DiPaolo from down the block, a real sweetheart, Martin takes care of her for free.

She's always bringing presents, afghans, dolls with crocheted dresses for Meggy, those hard little anise cookies—"

"I tell Steffie, 'Watch out, they're Mr. DiPaolo's gallstones,'" says Martin.

Vera forces a smile. Does that count as another apology? It's an effort not even Stephanie makes, but she does say, "Mrs. DiPaolo worships the ground Martin walks on. Now Mrs. DiPaolo's got some kind of crocheted square. A doll blanket? A potholder? It's tiny, the stitches are crooked. You'd burn your hand off.

"I thought, Oh, God, Mrs. DiPaolo's going downhill. Still I invite her in, sit down. She sits down and faints dead away at the table. Mrs. DiPaolo, wake up! After a minute or so she comes to. I ask, can I get you anything, brandy, a glass of water? Yes, she says, a glass of water. There's something peculiar about how she says it. Plus she's being very careful not to look at the newspaper on the table. Still I don't get it, not till she's gulped down three glasses, all the time looking at me *very* weirdly, and finally it hits me. The dolly blanket was an excuse. She's come for the water! And then, to make things even clearer, she takes a handkerchief out of her bra, dips it in the water, stands up straight, says thanks for the water, and splits.

"And still I'm not absolutely positive. I mean, it would've been too embarrassing to say, 'Mrs. DiPaolo, are you here for the *water*?' Immediately I wish I had, because then I could've said, 'Mrs. DiPaolo, there's nothing *in* the water.' Which is just what I tell Mrs. Grossman from across the street when *she* rings the bell a few minutes later.

"Poor Mrs. Grossman's apologizing a mile a minute, but she's talked to Mrs. DiPaolo; she doesn't even believe in these things, holy water's for the *goyim*, but maybe she could have a drop, see what all the fuss's about, maybe take some home to her husband, anything's worth a try. Mrs. Grossman's husband has cancer. 'I'm sorry, Mrs. Grossman,' I say." And now Stephanie's looking hard at Vera, who's thinking that "anything's worth a try" is what the voice on the phone said.

"But *you* try telling Mrs. Grossman she can't have a glass of water for her husband. So you give her some, as if you think it might work, too. And that's when it really begins.

"The doorbell keeps buzzing. You didn't know you knew so many people on the block. By the time Martin and the kids get home, the phone's rung forty times. Just to eat you have to take the phone off the hook and stuff it under a pillow, and you can still hear that computer voice scolding you . . ."

"Next morning, the kids leave, Martin leaves. By nine you've got thirty people on your lawn staring at your window as if the pope's going to appear at it any second. And the worst part is, when you go out and look in their faces, you can't even tell them to get lost."

"*I* could've told them to get lost," says Martin, but Stephanie ignores him:

"You feel like you need an *excuse* to make them leave. So you say, 'Sorry, I have to water the lawn.' That's the worst thing you could've said. The minute you bring out the hose they're holding out jars, bowls, five-gallon trash cans. 'Just give us some,' they say. 'Then we'll go away. Please.' And you give in. You have to. It's just water. It's free. It'll make them go away."

Vera imagines Stephanie in her T-shirt and designer jeans and long perfect fingernails, turning on the garden spigot as if it were the fountain of youth, each drop a potential miracle. In her fantasy, Stephanie moves solemnly from one to the other like a priest dispensing communion.

"What did it feel like?" Vera has to clear her throat and repeat herself, but still she can't ask what she most wants to know. Is false hope better or worse than no hope at all, and is it wrong to write those stories—New arthritis cure! Elvis alive!—to make promises no one can keep? She thinks she could ask Stephanie Green these questions she's never been able to ask anyone. After what's happened, Stephanie must be asking them, too. Perhaps *this* is the common bond Vera's sensed all along.

"Like shit," says Stephanie. "It made me feel like shit."

She lights another cigarette. "All the time I was filling those poor, cracked Tupperware bowls, I kept thinking, Stephanie, you're going to pay for this. And I didn't have to wait long. By the weekend we no longer had a lawn. Not that it mattered, I didn't want to go out. Me and the kids stayed holed up all day. Meggy and Josh stopped day camp, the kids were teasing them so bad. Then the neighbor kids started in. It took Josh days to tell me, but what was happening was, the parents were sending them to snitch water from our house. My *friends!* Sensible people! I sat my kids down and tried to explain, but that only made it worse. I guess because it was their lemonade, they figured it was their fault. So every day I watched Meggy and Josh's world get scarier and smaller until they were just laying around picking on each other and fighting . . ."

"I know what's it like," Vera says. "I've got a daughter. Rosie. She's ten." Searching her memory for some story to prove she *does* know what it's like, she considers escalating Rosie's humiliation at the ballet recital into something even worse than it was. But it's too long a story, and nothing else comes to mind. Stephanie studies her coolly. There's a flicker of interest in Stephanie's eyes that goes out almost instantly, and she says:

"Really, getting away this weekend was more for them than for us. We figured their little cousins could at least be trusted to be decent. Anyhow, we get on the thruway and hit the first rest stop; you have to stop every five minutes or they'll drive you batty. We go into the snack bar, and the woman behind the counter says, 'Haven't I seen you kids before, you sure do look familiar, these aren't those kids in that mashed-potato commercial on TV . . . ?' And the kids start shrieking and run out of the snack bar and on the way are almost hit by a car in the parking lot, and that's when I start screaming, too. Poor Martin."

"Wait a minute," says Vera. "That woman couldn't have recognized them from *This Week*, the picture's not that clear. I've been looking at the photo for the last forty-eight hours, and I couldn't have—"

"*We* know that," says Martin. "You tell it to the kids." Then all three fall silent, listening to the children fighting upstairs. This, too, makes Vera miserable. There's no way she can make it up to these people. And though it's not the worst that could happen—it's not as if she's got in a car and killed them—the fact remains: Vera, who spends half her waking life fearing her own child may come to harm, has ruined these kids' whole summer.

"I'm sorry," she says, one last time, thinking now of that Babel story, "The Sin of Jesus," and how it ends with the servant girl saying, "There's no forgiveness for you, Jesus Christ. No forgiveness and never will be." If some Odessa servant can say that to Jesus, what will these Greens say to her?

"Sorry's not good enough," says Martin.

Leaving the Greens, Vera hears something hiss. She thinks of escaped pet boa constrictors, alligators in the sewers, all manner of deceptively domesticated animals seeking their lost jungle home in these manicured back yards. BOROUGH BOA BINDS BROOKLYN BABY. This is just the sort of neighborhood where such things happen. Then she sees the witch from Hansel and Gretel standing on the porch next door, crooking her finger and hissing.

There's a second or two when Vera could still pretend not to notice; by the time she's turned slightly and looked the old woman full in the face, it's too late. She checks to make sure the Greens aren't watching, then heads up their neighbor's walk.

Up close, the woman's younger than Vera first thought. She's probably sixty or so, but dresses and carries herself to look older. It's as if she can't wait to be ancient, with all hagdom's gruesome authority. Above her black brogues, ochre jersey knit pants—gathered over her belly and inches too short at the cuff—expose dry, bluish-white ankles. She's wearing a faded, pebbled cardigan over what the discount stores call a ladies' polyester shell. Her face defines the word pinched, her mouth puckered around what might be a desire to spit out uncomfortable dentures; Vera can almost picture her lying to the dentist so her teeth will fit badly on purpose. She tries to imagine a *This Week* story about middle-aged women whitening their hair, having their teeth pulled, doctoring their birth certificates in a scam to collect early Social Security. Who would believe it? This woman would.

Vera's almost to the front porch when the old lady calls out, "Did you get any?"

Isn't that what high-school buddies ask after heavy dates? Vera's a little giddy as she sings out, "Get any what?"

"Water. Did they give you any?"

Vera shakes her head no, then for some reason changes her mind and says, "Yes." Now she wishes she *had* asked the Greens for a taste. She wonders what they'd have done, if that would have made things worse.

"I'm surprised," says the woman. "Mostly those folks wouldn't give you the steam off their shit. Pardon me. But *imagine* having something like that and hogging it for yourself. What's it for?"

"Excuse me?" says Vera.

"What'd you *want* it for? What's wrong with you?" Vera's trying on an array of possible symptoms when the old woman says, "Wait. I can usually tell." She looks Vera up and down, then clamps her lips around the diagnosis as if it's something tasty she's just eaten. "Lower-back pain."

"That's right," lies Vera. "Amazing."

"Thought so," says the woman. "You're the type. Care to come in for some coffee?"

Vera hangs back, wondering if all the pilgrims who come knocking on the Greens' door are offered the same hospitality. Probably not; probably most of them are in so much real pain that no low hiss or beckoning finger can turn them in their course. Yet all are sent away, while Vera's gone in and witnessed whatever went on with the cops . . . How could this woman not be curious?

"I'm Betty Anne," she's saying. "Betty Anne Apple." The horror-story teller. Now, as Vera looks harder at Betty Anne, she sees the face of a woman who eats horror stories, sucks them for what nourishment she requires. The face of a *This Week* reader, she thinks. My audience. My public.

"I'm Vera Perl," she says before it occurs to her not to. Now Betty Anne wheels on her, eyes glittering in a snaky way that goes along with the hissing. "My, my," she says. "You're the girl wrote that story in the paper." On this end of the block, Vera's something of a celebrity—hated by some, admired by others, instant recognition everywhere. My, my.

Betty Anne Apple's house is a monument to misplaced energy and hours spent home alone. Everywhere are afghans, appliqued pillows, needlepoint seat covers, decoupage waste baskets, corn-husk wreaths, stenciled wall plaques. Entering the living room is like leafing through forty years of back issues of women's magazines, faded by time and the repeated turnings of some dedicated homemaker with more enthusiasm than talent: forty years of directions read slightly wrong. All the afghans are in painful shades of puce and dayglo orange, the cut-out felt flowers have a slightly wilted tilt, the decoupage is yellow and buckled like newspapers left in the rain. Hobo clowns leer down from their plaques with the stoned, loopy grins of real bums and psycho killers.

Betty Anne sees Vera take it all in and interprets her attention as a compliment. "I hate to just watch TV," she says.

Unyielding is a euphemism for the couch Vera's shown to; it's aggressive in its lumpiness. She scoots back, not that it's any more comfortable, but to avoid calling attention to her discomfort by balancing on the edge, and finds herself surrounded on both sides by giant pillows appliquéd with fuzzy black monkeys. She thinks of Shaefer's knickknacks, of Gandhi, but mostly of the Rue Morgue. FLATBUSH FEARS MORE MONKEY MURDERS. There's no escaping it. Wedged between two chimpanzees, Vera feels as if she should put both hands over her mouth.

"Coffee?" says Betty Anne. "I'm off it myself. I read this article where scientists fed these baby rats nothing but instant coffee and water; every one of them critters got cancer of the bladder. But you're certainly welcome to some. It's instant, no trouble at all."

"No, thank you," says Vera.

"Smart girl," says Betty Anne. Sighing with relief, she settles into an equally unaccommodating chair, then slides forward as if she's imitating Vera in reverse. "I've always wanted to meet one of you people." You people? Her tone might refer to Jews or nymphomaniac single mothers, but no, she means writers for *This Week*. Vera knows what's coming next: How much of what you people write is true? But that's not what Betty Anne wants to know. Instead, she waves in the Greens' direction, sucks on her gums a minute, then says, "How did you get wind of *that*?"

"I didn't," says Vera, then tells her story in almost the exact same words she's just used at the Greens'. Explaining it twice in less than an hour makes it seem boring beyond measure. Vera wishes she had a tape of it she could run; for all the emotion or connection she feels, she and Betty Anne might both be sitting there listening. It reminds her of how, when she and Lowell split up, she'd tell *anyone*—the guy at the newsstand, supermarket checkout girls, strangers on the subway. All that distinguished her from a screamer was a softer voice and the pretense of finding someone specific to talk to. She'd hoped that repetition would trivialize her unhappiness, make it seem stale, banal, less painful. She'd called it boredom therapy, and it worked. The only problem was when it quit working: alone in her bed in the dark.

As Vera drones on, Betty Anne leans forward till her chin's nearly resting on her bony little knees. It's not really like listening to a tape, nor even like talking to the Greens. Something's crackling in the air, some wholly new electricity and it's not long before Vera identifies it: Betty Anne believes her. She's not looking for explanations, facts Vera might have overlooked or forgotten. Betty Anne *wants* to believe her. What a difference, telling your story to someone who thinks it's the truth! Vera hears her voice lose its robot edge; she's positively trilling. How charming she is, how expansive, barely controlling the urge to share her whole weekend with Betty Anne. She's recreating, making new, inventing and embroidering as if she's never told anyone before.

Finally Vera says, "That's it."

"Well, isn't that the darndest thing," says Betty Anne, and exhales with such reverence and resignation you'd think she was at church. "God moves in mysterious ways," she says. "We just always seem to know things we couldn't possibly know. It's like years ago, my brother's first wife. Out to here." She circles her arms in front of her, wide enough to accommodate a full-term pregnancy and a couple of basketballs; try as she might, Vera can't imagine Betty Anne's stingy body ever swelling to such roundness. "She kept saying it wasn't a baby in there. The doc kept saying it was. They all thought she'd gone a little off her nut, like women do when they're that way. But after ten months and no baby's come, they cut her open and guess what they found?"

A forty-pound tumor, thinks Vera, and that's just what Betty Anne says. "Poor woman. It's funny, what we know. One summer me and Art God bless him rented a little cabin up near Yankee Lakes. These people next door to us, the husband buys a little motorboat, and all night we can hear the wife screaming, 'Don't buy it, something terrible's going to happen.' And sure enough, they'd hardly got the thing in the water, their only daughter, the prettiest little girl you ever saw, ten years old, swims into the propellor, chops her head off clean as a whistle."

Now Vera does have her hands over her ears. Hear no evil, anyway. Not one more word. In the silence, she imagines the husband bringing the boat in, tying it up at the dock. Or did they just let it float away? She's infinitely depressed, not just by the stories but also by the fact that Betty Anne is the only one who believes *hers*. To Betty Anne, she's simply another freak; it makes sense that Betty Anne's spectrum of possibility should be so much broader than the norm. In her world, life's secrets reveal themselves as juicier and more horrendous than anyone could have predicted. If you can believe that a woman's body could host a forty-pound tumor, you can believe anything.

"Even so," says Betty Anne, "what throws me for a loop is how you knew it works."

"Knew what works?" says Vera.

"The water," says Betty Anne. "Listen. Two weeks ago, poor Mrs. DiPaolo had fluid on her chest, her knees swole up so bad you could push your finger in and leave a dent for twenty minutes, couldn't get her breath, couldn't move for seeing spots and this awful sinking feeling; it'd break your heart to see her walking down the street. Take a step, stop. Another step, stop . . ."

Vera feels like she's hearing Betty Anne read aloud from some hellish *Merck Manual* or one of Dr. Green's less optimistic charts . . . "And now she's fit as a fiddle. Looks healthier than I do. Than *you* do, don't mind my saying . . ."

"From the water?" Vera's voice sounds strangely effervescent. She wishes she'd remembered to eat lunch. Would food help? She feels as if Betty Anne's taking her nerves and crocheting them into some craftsy dayglo snarl.

"She got better that very day." Again Betty Anne makes that turtlelike snap of the lips.

That dizzy, tangled sensation seems to be getting worse, perhaps because Vera keeps digging through the original fountain-of-youth story, examining every word. "Neighbors began to *claim* . . ." "Word spread that the wonder drink was curing . . ." Innocent, Your Honor. Nowhere in the article does my client say it *works* . . .

"I don't know what else it could have been," is Betty Anne's conclusion. "She was telling everyone there'd been a miracle. So naturally Mrs. Grossman thinks to try some on her husband. Cancer of the sophagus, poor guy. Takes the poor fella all morning to get the water down drop by drop, and that night they drive to some Jewish-Hungarian place in the city and the guy eats a pound-and-a-half skirt steak."

"Have these people been to doctors?" asks Vera.

"Sure have." Betty Anne jerks her thumb toward the Greens. "Even that one there."

Now Vera's thinking back over her visit with the Greens. Why didn't they mention this? You'd think a doctor would be over-joyed by the discovery of a true panacea—until all his training reminded him it was impossible. Vera reviews Martin's behavior, trying to reinterpret it as that of a man who's just had his whole sense of reality challenged, not just the everyday acting out of Napoleon Bonaparte, M.D. Clues must have been dropping everywhere, hers to follow if only she'd known to look.

"That's not all," promises Betty Anne, and it isn't, not by a long shot. Who'd have thought that death would have nearly undone so many? And all in one neighborhood. All pulled back at the very last minute from the slippery edge of the grave! Not merely have the sick been healed. Broken hearts have been seamlessly mended, troubled waters calmed, crumbling marriages shored up. Water from the Greens has smoothed wrinkles, turned white hair black, or at least gray.

"I'd try it myself 'cept I don't need it." Betty Anne knocks on wood. "I'm saving it for when it counts. Anyhow, who knows if they'd give me any. Specially now that I've talked to you."

Betty Anne's fudging. In truth, she doesn't want her youth and beauty restored. She doesn't even want her teeth to fit. Still she goes on, listing the marvels with such obvious satisfaction, you'd think she'd worked all those miracles herself.

When really, it's Vera who should take credit. If not for her, they'd never have known the stuff was there. What in the world is she thinking? What Betty Anne's just told her is the strangest news of all, and yet she's less upset than she was Friday afternoon in Shaefer's office. It's all begun to seem completely routine. Completely acausal. Completely Kafkaesque. Unless, of course, there *is* an order and a plan. Why would God create the fountain of youth unless He wanted it divined? Is a miracle a miracle if there's no one around to behold it? There's something else here, something about faith and belief and the body's ability to heal itself: Lourdes, Saint Anne de Beaupré, immunology and the placebo effect . . . Vera puts these considerations off till later. All the quilting and kapok in Betty Anne's living room would blunt the fine points of anyone's metaphysic.

"There's a story for you," Betty Anne's saying. "HOLY WATER WORKS! Write that one for your paper."

And so the most depressing fact of all, the worst saved once again for last: Betty Anne thinks in *This Week* headlines, too. Their minds are perfectly in tune. So much so that when Betty Anne smiles triumphantly, Vera knows she's the kind of woman for whom triumph is always mixed with spite, knows they're both thinking the same thing: a story like that would *really* fix the Greens' wagon . . .

"Are you sure you want that?" she says. "If we ran a story like that, the whole neighborhood would be crawling with reporters . . ." Vera imagines photographers crouched in parked cars, beneath rhododendrons, leaping out at Meggy and fat little Josh. And suddenly it hits her: If that happened, the Greens would be news, public figures, their story right smack in the midst of the public domain. Stephanie might just as well be Jackie Kennedy! Invasion of privacy? They'd no longer have any privacy to invade, nor any chance of suing *This Week* for libel or anything else! For once, for probably the first time in its publishing career, *This Week* would have the truth on its side.

"The truth will out," Betty Anne's saying. "No way you or me's going to stop it."

"There might even be an investigation," says Vera, testing her now. "Would you be willing to swear to all this in court?"

"Sure would," says Betty Anne. "And so would Mrs. DiPaolo and Mrs. Grossman and her husband. *They'd* be the ones you'd want."

Vera imagines a procession inching forward, would-be witnesses pushing their own wheelchairs, carrying their crutches and bottles of pills to lay at the Greens' front door. Here's Betty Anne Apple guiding teams of researchers and newsmen on tour of this reliquary—Mrs. DiPaolo's oxygen tank, Mr. Grossman's bedpan—and all those ladies like Betty Anne, those tireless raconteurs of repulsion. Now, for the first time, it occurs to Vera that maybe they're not telling their stories to wallow and suffer and make their listeners suffer, too. Perhaps their secret hope is that someone will contradict them. Such things don't happen, life isn't so cruel, there's still hope. Cucumbers will cure your arthritis; water from some Brooklyn cardiologist's kitchen faucet will save you, mend your broken heart, fix everything that ails you. And even if they're just telling these stories to reassure themselves that this time pain's chosen someone else—the person on the phone at the Greens—and passed over them—well, that's not so bad, either. Because it's just crossed Vera's mind that the voices narrating these tragedies aren't merely the voices of hopelessness, death, and gloom, but also the thin, twisted, terrified, and unsilenceable voice of life itself.

"I'll see you," says Vera, so cheered by this that seeing Betty Anne again almost seems like a welcome prospect.

"You keep in touch," orders Betty Anne. "You let me know if there's anything else I can do."

As Vera rises to leave, it's all she can do not to kiss the monkey pillows on their hideous, woolly snouts. Vera feels as if she *has* been to someplace like Lourdes or Saint Anne de Beaupré, or at the very least drunk water from the Greens' tap. She feels as if she's been healed.

SHAEFER'S NEVER seemed so interested in anything Vera's had to say. It's the first time he's ever asked her a question—asked lots of questions—and not answered for her. Why didn't she come tell him yesterday afternoon, straight from Betty Anne Apple's? Well, Vera meant to. And should have, before her euphoria wore off. But when the train stopped at Borough Hall, she found herself getting out, going home, just as later she found herself not telling Rosie.

What Vera can't figure out now is why she *didn't* tell Rosie, didn't tell everyone, didn't buttonhole strangers on the street and tell them. What a story! If she skips the disturbing parts—how she woke in the middle of the night still hearing that voice on the phone at the Greens'—it's truly a pleasure to tell. She couldn't be happier when Shaefer asks if she'd mind going through it again for Dan, and without waiting for her reply, buzzes Esposito on the intercom.

Dan comes right in. No one's working. With a million-dollar death sentence hanging over their heads, why should they? This morning Vera arrived to find the office in a state of suspended animation that reminded her of her junior high during the Cuban missile crisis. Why do algebra when planetary destruction was imminent? The mailroom guys greeted Vera the way those junior-high schoolers might have eyed Castro. And now, as she tells Dan her story, his face softens as hers must have when the principal's voice came over the P.A., announcing, Crisis over, everyone back to work. "Congratulations," says Dan.

"One thing you should keep in mind," Vera says. "All this could be a figment of Betty Anne Apple's hyperactive imagination. The lady spends a lot of time alone with nothing to do but read *This Week* and dream."

"Who cares?" says Shaefer. "All we need is one neighbor willing to testify in court her bunions disappeared after a foot bath at the Greens, we've got a story. The mess they'll have then will make what they've got now look like surgical scrub. They know that. And as soon as they know *we* know it, game over. It won't get to court, won't get as far as *out* of court. They'll be paying *us* to keep quiet."

Shaefer picks up the phone, the veins in his forearms pumping; you'd think *he'd* got a shot of fountain-of-youth lemonade. "Carmen," he says. "Get me Goldblum. Wait till Goldblum hears this." Vera feels strangely jealous. It's her story. *She* wants to tell it. She excuses herself and slips out the door. She pauses briefly outside Peter Smalley's office, but his "Here we will talk of nothing but God" sign discourages her, and she keeps on till she finds Solomon.

"Listen to this," she says, pulling him back in his office. She hugs him—a simple hug without complexities or innuendo. He listens attentively as she tells him about the Greens, about her moment of enlightenment and human connectedness at Betty Anne Apple's. When she's done, he says, "Hot dog! Fuck the paper; let's get out there and get some of that water. I'll trade them the negative of the kids selling lemonade. One glass and my leg'll be like it was before Vietnam. We'll go dancing! Wouldn't it be wild? We could go into business peddling the stuff; we'd be raking it in like Oral Roberts." Solomon holds both arms high in the air, curling one hand to look withered. "Lord," he cries, "Lord, make this hand like the other one," and curls them both.

"That reminds me," he says. "I was watching this show on TV yesterday, some national born-again telethon where people can declare for Jesus over the phone. Anyhow, this mother and son from Texas call in and accept Jesus as their personal savior. And about ten minutes later, the father calls in and declares, too.

Wouldn't you love to have been a fly on the wall at that house for those ten minutes?"

"I don't know," says Vera. "I don't think that's any place I'd like to be."

"Tell you where *I'd* like to be," says Solomon. "I'd like to be at the Greens' when their lawyer calls and lays *this* on them."

Vera thinks of the dusty lawn, the footprints on the kitchen floor, Stephanie holding her children's shoulders. How quickly they've become the enemy. It seems important to remember they've done nothing wrong, that what's happened is more her fault than theirs. The suffering of the innocent—any screamer will tell you how often the guiltless get blamed. Vera wants to tell Solomon this, but can't. Perhaps she's afraid of sounding excessively generous, like those women who take pains to speak kindly of their ex-husbands' new wives.

"Hey," says Solomon. "Let's celebrate. Go out for dinner tonight. The two of us. And Rosie. I found this great Cuban Chinese place, the kind where you know they're chopping up boat people in the alley and serving them sweet and sour. Moo shu *marielito*. They've got this dragon lady behind the register you'd go crazy for. Real schizo. One night she's ready to stick bamboo stalks under your fingernails, the next night she's flirting. Know what she told me last week? *Won ton* spelled backwards is *not now*."

"I'll have to remember that," says Vera.

"How about it?" he asks.

"Not tonight," she says. "I'm beat. If I'm lucky I'll make it through *The Dukes of Hazzard* with Rosie."

"That's on Friday," says Solomon. "And Rosie wouldn't touch the Dukes with a stick."

"All right," says Vera. "Maybe later in the week."

Drifting back down the hall, Vera knocks on Shaefer's office door and walks in before it occurs to her she's got no excuse or reason besides curiosity to do so.

Right now, apparently, she doesn't need one. "Well," he says, "if it isn't our own Bernadette of Lourdes." Esposito laughs. Even Vera brightens.

"Goldblum nearly went down for the count," says Schaefer. "I thought I'd have to run over there and administer CPR. Then he decides he's going to make legal history. I had to say, Look, Marv, we're not trying to make the textbooks with this, we just want it dropped. *Not* making history is the whole point. If this Green's smart enough to do open-heart surgery—"

"Is that what he does?" asks Dan.

"If he's smart enough to *find* a goddamn heart, he knows what's in his best interests. And right now his best interests are to pretend he's never heard of *This Week*. To wait for those neighbors of his to die off from whatever they've got and then get back to business as usual."

"You think that'll happen?" It's what Vera's come in to hear.

"I'm betting on it," says Frank.

"Thank God," Vera says, and is halfway out the door when Schaefer calls her back. "Oh, Vera," he says. "Good work." It's such a cliché—crusty Perry White congratulating Lois Lane—Vera can't help smiling.

"What's so funny?" asks Schaefer.

"Oh, nothing," says Vera. "I was just thinking of a story I wrote Friday before all the trouble started. BIGFOOT LIGHTS UP."

"You know what?" says Dan, a little dreamily. "I hope they never catch him, I really do. Because the first thing they're going to do is dig a giant pit and invite all their friends to a Bigfoot roast." Vera imagines Dan in that misty campground, overhearing his RV neighbors plan just that. You bring the cole slaw, I'll bring the beans. Bigfoot and all the trimmings.

"Bring it in tomorrow," Shaefer tells Vera. "We've all done enough for one day."

Despite all her doubts and second thoughts, Vera's pleased to hear she still has a tomorrow at *This Week*. And when Vera tells Carmen, she seems to feel the same. She laughs her crazy laugh; light dances on her glasses as she takes Vera's hands in hers. "God's will be done," she says.

Rosalie's not surprised. At dinner, when Vera tells her the news, she just seems relieved that her life isn't turning into an unemployed-single-mom sitcom. Perhaps Rosalie's equanimity is part and parcel of the Dungeons and Dragons worldview. There *are* no losers, really. A lucky roll of the dice can turn everything around. The problem is: no worry, no relief. Had Rosie been concerned, joy might move her now to volunteer help with the dishes. Instead, she pats Vera's shoulder half-heartedly and goes off to her room.

Vera cleans up, then collapses just in time to catch the opening of a new detective show set somewhere with palms. California? Hawaii? The plot's Byzantine; she can't follow. She's glad *The Dukes of Hazzard* isn't on; she'd probably watch it. She goes into her bedroom and lies down; she'll get up in a minute and change. In less time than that, she's fast asleep, dreaming she's in the woods, still looking for Bigfoot.

This time she's with an expedition that, she's alarmed to discover, is composed entirely of old people who look barely capable of surviving a week in their own warm apartments. Their leader's the Vietnamese ex-cop from her dream about dinosaurs, except that he's not God here, just a senior-citizen tour guide. It's dinnertime, and the old men have caught a brace of fish. Their competence at campfire cooking is reassuring. At the edge of the firelight, one couple appears to be necking. Then the Saigon police chief takes out a glockenspiel, and the old people start to sing. "Many's the hearts that are weary tonight, wishing for the war to cease" . . . What war? The Civil War! It's "Tenting Tonight," from her fifth-grade songbook, her grade-school favorite song! Now she realizes it's terrible—saccharine, sentimental. But sung by these elderly voices, it moves her. She feels, as she rarely does, that there is no break in time, that she is the same person she was as a child . . .

The pain of being wrenched awake from this idyllic scene is compounded by the fact that the ringing is not a glockenspiel at all, but Vera's doorbell. At one o'clock in the morning, it can't be anything good. Already afraid of the mad killer-rapist she's sure she'll see, Vera forces herself to look through the peephole.

At first all she sees is teeth—a perfect set of sharp, white, grinning choppers. But after a while the teeth move back, locate themselves in a face—a face at once so alien and so alarmingly familiar she leans her forehead against the peephole's cool metal eye till she's sure she's not still dreaming.

Vera opens the door. "Lowell," she says. "What are you *doing* here?"

Lowell opens his arms. Vera presses against him. Her heart's fluttering like some romantic heroine's. When Lowell lifts her off the ground, she might as well be levitating. She thinks of St. Joseph of Cupertino flapping around the refectory, thinks of geese mating for life and of the possibility that humans do, too. Like it or not, Lowell's hers. No one else fits, nor will anyone ever hug her in a way that makes all other embraces seem like a medley of the most awkward moments of high-school make-out.

Eventually Vera and Lowell let go. It's either that or go on forever. Embarrassed by happiness, they're focusing slightly past each other's right ears. Vera has to force herself to look at his face; and when she does, it gives her the strangest feeling. The only thing she can compare it to is unexpectedly catching sight of herself in a mirror or shop window. Who *is* that person? Lowell's handsome, suntanned face is so familiar it's almost impossible to see. Has he aged? She can't tell. Perhaps he'll always look to her like he did when they first met.

"Like my haircut?" Lowell's saying. "It's called a Del Monte. Ever since they started filming all those TV series in Hawaii, everybody in L.A.'s trying to look like a pineapple. Some guys will do anything to get a job."

"It looks the same as always," Vera says, and it does: Ragged. Beautiful. A mess.

"It's a very organic pineapple," says Lowell. "I did it myself. With toenail clippers."

"How did you get here?" says Vera, echoing Rapunzel, Juliet, the bride of the seraglio, all those fairy-tale heroines whose lovers have braved impossible odds to reach them. The difference is Vera's unspoken question: *Why?* Rapunzel wouldn't wonder; new lovers don't. They know their prince would rather be in the tower with them than anywhere—there's no history of years voluntarily spent apart. The "why?" Vera wants to know is really "why *now?*"

"It's a long story," says Lowell. "Needless to say. First I tried hitting up that Mafioso I wrote you about, Frankie the Canary, telling him it was some kind of advance on our book. 'Frankie,' I say. 'You're a family man, I'm a family man. I need to see my wife and kid so bad it's killing me.' But Frankie wasn't going for it. 'Lowell,' he says, 'I got debts. Every dollar I get's going toward saving my kneecaps.' So I went to this other friend of mine. Sergio the Mystic. Honey, you should see the scam this guy's put together. First time I met him he was wearing these beaded bikini briefs and his hair done up in some kind of bird sculpture, and all around his place he's got deer heads with what looks like ladies' panties dangling from the antlers . . . But really, he's a good guy. All the weird trappings are just part of his act; in Hollywood you got to work a little harder to stand out . . . So anyhow, Sergio's loaded; he lent me enough for a plane ticket and then some. I promised I'd pay him back when I get the money for my screenplay—"

"*Polar Bear Boy?* Did you sell it?"

Lowell grins. "Let's put it this way," he says. "The distant trumpets of my literary miracle have turned into the blubbering of the sailors lost at sea on my ship that didn't come in."

Vera just stares at him. She'd forgotten anyone could get out a sentence like that. "We're standing in the hall," she says.

On the way in, Lowell stops to admire the Mount St. Helens photo. "Ka-boom," he says. "Where'd you get this?" Vera knows he's seen it before, considers pointing this out. But why? Why put him on the spot?

"Look!" Lowell's pointing to a speck at the base of the mountain. "That's me. Lowell's Mount-St.-Helen's hillbilly home." It's how he'd like to see his life: homesteading the volcano.

"You've seen that picture before," Vera says.

"Oh, have I?" says Lowell.

At the door of the living room they stop short, startled by a man's voice. "Hope I haven't picked a bad time," says Lowell, smiling slyly. When they first split up, they'd joke about the wild love lives each pretended to think the other was leading. For a long time, the Rich New York Playboy who'd sweep Vera off her feet was Lowell's number-one fantasy creation. But that was all bluff, as Lowell's smile is now. If there *were* a man in there, he'd be crushed. Actually, it's the TV, the emcee of *Rock Music Videos*; Vera must have forgotten to turn it off. She almost wishes it were a man, just for dignity's sake. How pathetic it seems, the dark apartment, the television blaring as if the single mom and her kid are scared to sleep without it. Vera shuts it off just as Cyndi Lauper starts throwing herself about, singing "Girls Just Want to Have Fun."

"Too bad," says Lowell. "My favorite."

"Mine, too," says Vera. "Are you hungry?" She's hoping he isn't. What will she feed him?

"No, thanks," he says. "I ate on the plane."

"Ugh," she says. "What?"

"Chewed-off fingernails," he says. "You know the red-eye. They hire these pilots that got canned from Royal Burmese. Got 'em working for minimum wage. Which reminds me, how's Rosie?"

Vera's weighing a dozen possible answers when—as if on cue—Rosie walks in. She's rubbing her eyes with her fists the way she used to when she was tiny. If that was all Lowell saw, he'd think no time had passed since he left. And maybe none has. *Rosie* doesn't ask why he's here. She jumps up in his arms, just as Vera did. The first few times they split up, Vera used to half-hope that Rosie wouldn't—or would pretend not to—recognize him when he returned. In fact she never blamed him, never held back; and now Vera's glad. Trouble between Rosie and Lowell would only make it all seem sadder.

"Sweet potato!" says Lowell. "I hear my Rose of San Antone's been dancin' up a storm!" He's flirting now, playing the shy country charmer; that's how he won Vera's heart. She remembers the first day she knew she was in love with him. They were taking a walk up Mount Sutro. Near the top, Lowell pulled ahead of her and climbed a steep boulder. "Watch this!" he cried and leaped across a deep, precipitous crevice to the rocks beyond. "Did you see *that*?" he asked, still panting when she caught up with him. "Crazy Arky risks certain brain damage just to impress his girl." His girl? Vera had been working so hard at pretending they were friends. It was the next morning that Lowell showed up so early at Louise's.

What's wrong with a little flirting? Rosie looks pretty and flattered, radiant. It's no worse than that let's-toss-around-the-football buddy-buddiness that eighties dads are so careful to adopt with their daughters. The only thing wrong with Lowell flirting with Rosie is that it makes Vera miserable, makes her envy her own daughter, makes her conscious of how much lies ahead of Rosie, how much behind her and Lowell.

"I'm hungry," says Rosie. "Walk me into the kitchen," and Lowell does. Vera waits, listening to them chatter away like teens on a date. She can't hear what they're saying, only the cadence. With each sentence, Rosie picks up more of her father's lilt, his traces of Arkansas accent. When Vera walks in, Rosie's saying, "Dad, when you were ten did you ever do disgusting things? I mean *really* disgusting?"

"Well, now," says Lowell. "One man's pig's feet and gravy is another man's disgusting. Let's define our terms."

"More disgusting than pig's feet," says Rosie. "What I mean is: did you ever pee in a girl's water pistol."

"Honey," says Lowell. "Your daddy was a gentleman, even then. And gentlemen don't pee in young ladies' water guns."

No arguing with that, thinks Vera, who's just realized that

what Norma said—Carl's doing that proves he likes Rosie—is only part of it. That's why Rosie needs Lowell around, why they all do—to remind them of the rest: there's more you have to ask about boys than whether they like you or not.

"Rosie," says Vera, more harshly than she means to. "It's two in the morning. Let's get back to bed. Your dad will still be here in the morning. Unless he's got other plans."

"Is that an invitation?" says Lowell. "If it is, I'm accepting."

"You *better*," says Rosie, kissing him, then leaves without looking at Vera.

As soon as Rosie's out of earshot, Lowell says, "You wouldn't happen to have a little something smokeable? It's just not humanly *possible* to get high in airplane bathrooms any more, I don't care how many joints you blow. Maybe it's the altitude or the pressure, or maybe they spray it with something. I don't know. You think it's middle age?"

Here's the most pathetic thing: As Vera watches Lowell roll joint after joint, she feels happy, *taken care of*, that warm bath of pleasure other women must slip into when their husbands unplug drains and pay bills. He hands Vera a joint, lights it, then lights one of his own. "I just *had* to come," he says, tight back in his throat so as not to lose smoke, the strangulated voice of the sixties. "I couldn't wait one more day to see you and Rosie. Besides, I had to check out this story. I got the paper you sent me and *jammed.*"

"Record time," says Vera. How could that package have got there so fast? Fountain of youth, Megan and Joshua: Lowell's read every word. "I want to be around for red-hot developments," he's saying. "I feel like this whole story's got my name on it."

"Oh, Lowell," says Vera. "I wish to God it was yours instead of mine." It seems absurd that anyone would fly cross-country for this: anyone but Lowell. Given the opportunity, he'd spend his life chasing the inexplicable like some hillbilly Charles Fort. What seems even more unlikely is that there was a time when Vera would, too, though certainly she would have played down the marvelous in favor of what she imagined as the profound

and fantastic heart of daily life. Meaning what? Just asking
produces the emotional opposite of that continuity she felt hearing the oldsters in her dream sing "Tenting Tonight."

"Red-hot developments?" she says. "I've got a sizzler for you."
The marijuana and Lowell's obvious delight in the story of her
visit to the Greens so revives her own interest, she wishes this
could go on all night. But finally she's finished, and Lowell says:

"Here's our plan. We go back there and sneak around till the
Greens step out. Then *we* break in. One more B and E, what's
the difference? We know how often the cops drive by—that gives
us half an hour. Meanwhile we're filling fifty-gallon trash cans
with water. Truck it out of there. Jesus Christ, darlin', it's free.
Then we take it on the road. Doctor Lowell's Magic H-two-O.
It's the product for the eighties. We'll keep jacking the price up
as the supply runs low; and by the time it's gone we'll be sleek
and fat and happy. Jeeves, bring Miss Vera seconds on the caviar.
I'll tell my Mafioso what to do with his typewriter; you'll tell the
paper likewise; we'll grab Rosie and move to Tahiti, someplace
warm and cheap we can live on jumbo shrimp and coconuts off
the trees. . ."

Vera sighs. It's the second time she's heard this snake-oil
scheme today: first Solomon, now Lowell. The difference, as
always, is how much further Lowell takes it. The glint in his
eyes remind her of their life in San Francisco, of lying in bed
and hearing him talk lost Mayan treasure. His physical presence
makes such memories so vivid they stir her in a way that feels
unmistakably like desire. And yet she can't stop herself from
saying, "Tahiti's not cheap."

"Fuck Tahiti," he says. "Mexico. Wait a minute. We did
Mexico. You know, what got me nervous was when the locals
started following us around with empty taco shells. Smacking
their lips. *Enchiladas de gringo asado con frijoles.* Yum."

Vera looks at him. As she recalls, the only Spanish word he
ever admitted to knowing was *bueno.*

"And the shits. God. Pancho Villa's revenge."

Is that all he remembers? Despite herself, Vera's stung. Her own memories are a little more romantic. And yet she can't invoke them for fear of where they'll lead: that fatal bag of cashews.

"Scratch Mexico," says Lowell. "Honduras. Costa Rica."

"Revolution," says Vera. "Mosquitoes."

"No problem," says Lowell. "We'll hire spies to warn us in plenty of time to get our butts out of there. And as for mosquitoes —we'll pay ten-year-old girls to fan us with palm fronds, keep the little bastards away. Good for the economy."

"Rosie's ten," says Vera.

"I know that," says Lowell.

"I'm sorry. It's been quite a day."

"I know that, too," he says, reaching behind her to knead the base of her neck. "That's why I'm here. To help you."

Is he kidding? After "The check's in the mail" and "Gee, you're looking thinner," that must be the third biggest lie in the world. Vera knows he'd never be here except for the chance to witness the unfolding of a story more bizarre than the ones that run through his head every minute. For the moment, though, his arm on her shoulder has more weight than anything she knows.

"Let's take it from the top," says Lowell. "How you wrote the goddamn article in the first place." In other words, Where did this story come from? That he's speaking his version of her own private language moves Vera so, she'll forgive him unlimited white lies.

"The photographer at the paper—" She's rushing so her voice won't betray the fact that Solomon's something more. Not *much* more, she thinks now. After she and Lowell first split up, she'd always work casual lovers into the conversation. This guy I was talking to, she'd say, daring him to catch her. But the impulse to walk that particular tightrope has faded along with her desire that Rosalie not recognize him. Now the last thing she wants is another reminder of all the secrets she'll never be able to tell him.

"He gave me the photo. I wrote the story. That's it. The picture reminded me of myself as a kid—maybe that's what got me started wishful thinking about the fountain of youth. I figured out the kids' ages from the photo, picked what I thought were typical upwardly mobile Brooklyn kids' names, made Dad a doctor—who else lives in those houses?"

Vera can't believe how logical this sounds. Perhaps it's the marijuana, but suddenly the whole thing seems to make perfect sense. Lowell thinks so, too. "Couldn't be simpler," he says. "If that's it, my professional opinion is we've got ourselves a real loser in the synchronicity sweepstakes."

"Come on, now," says Vera. "It's a little more than that. I mean, I was batting a *thousand*. And how was I supposed to know the stuff worked?"

"You got a point there," says Lowell. "To quote your friend Betty Anne, who knows *what* we know. I was just thinking that on the plane, sifting it through the holes in my brain how it's nearly impossible to know *anything* for sure."

"Is that retro hippie?" asks Vera. "Or just plain hillbilly epistemology?"

"No, listen," says Lowell. "Seriously. I was thinking about that day we climbed Mount Sutro and I did my Tarzan-with-a-lobotomy act across the yawning abyss. Remember?"

"I remember." Vera's tense, afraid he'll somehow diminish it the way he reduced their Mexican trip to a long bout with Pancho Villa's revenge. "What about it?"

"What about it is: You probably thought I was just this loony, spontaneous Arky doing something dangerous to impress you. When the truth was: I'd been sneaking up that mountain and practicing that jump ever since I met you. The first time I was so scared I nearly puked just looking down. But I kept on till I was pretty sure my brains wouldn't splatter with a jellied plop right in front of your horrified eyes. Because all that time the master plan was to steer you up there and make that jump and impress you so much you'd let me fuck you."

"Is this true?" Vera hopes it is.

"Cross my heart and hope to die," says Lowell.

"It worked," says Vera; and when she looks at Lowell he says, "I think it's working again."

In the instant before he kisses her, Vera remembers that kid she saw Friday on the train, the good-looking one with the work boots and the thumbed-over copy of *Motorcycle World,* and realizes that the reason his mouth and hands attracted her so is that they reminded her of Lowell's. After a while she backs off and mumbles something about the time difference and how she can never remember which way it works, but anyway Lowell must be ready for bed . . .

"If *you're* in it," says Lowell, "I'm always ready for bed."

They walk quietly down the hall, pausing at the door of Rosalie's room to peer into the darkness as if they could see. What other man would stop, look in, would care at a time like this or even recall that Rosie was there?

"Remember when she was a tiny," Lowell says, "waking up every two minutes. We couldn't get together except when she'd nap, and we'd sneak around like we were cheating on her, having some kind of white-hot, adulterous love affair. Remember?"

"Yes," says Vera. But does she? It's yet another reason she needs Lowell: for verification, proof that she's led her own life. Otherwise she might have dreamed it. They should have taken more pictures, she thinks. Bought a movie camera, a projector.

In the bedroom, Lowell takes her face in his hands and kisses her. They slip off their clothes, lie next to each other, and Vera's last thought before she stops thinking is that this is why men and women were created: to fit so well.

It's also her first thought on returning to something like consciousness. She's thinking now—regretfully and a little superiorly —of all the times this hasn't seemed so, when the design of male and female seemed to her as makeshift and purposeless as apples and oranges placed accidentally in the same bowl. She's wondering how to tell Lowell this without reference to other lovers. It's impossible, of course, and also apparently beside the point. Lowell's lying with his back to her at the opposite edge of the bed.

Vera can't believe this—the TV-sitcom honeymoon, cliché bride wanting cozy conversation, cliché husband wanting sleep; by the end of the pilot, they'll have compromised, wifey prattling on while hubby lies there rolling his eyes at the ceiling. But Lowell was never like that. The best talks they had were in bed.

"Lowell," she says. "Are you okay?"

"Completely nuts," he says. "My head's about to split like an overripe papaya."

"Nuts about what?" she says.

"Same old shit," he says. "The usual S.O.S."

Vera braces herself for whatever's coming next. Meanwhile this timely reminder: It wasn't all kisses, one harmonious moment after another. Soon after they got together, Lowell told her how a former girlfriend once accused him of making love as if he were in a Tijuana whorehouse with a taxi running its meter outside. God knows why he confessed this—perhaps to reassure her that sex with his old girlfriend was nothing special, perhaps for the reassurance that she so freely gave. How could anyone say such a thing! Nothing could be further from the truth! And then one night, just before Lowell left, right in the midst of some Tijuana-style lovemaking, Vera laughed out loud and understood what folly it is to expose the sharp and accurate barbs old lovers leave lodged in one's brain.

"I can't tell what you want," he says. "*You* don't know what you want. What it looks to me like you want is for me to fall madly in love with you again so you can say, 'I don't know, Lowell, I *want* to be with you but it never seems to work out.'"

That's not what Vera wants. He isn't being fair. But what of it? Fairness was never Lowell's strong point.

"Five years of that has made pudding of my brain," he's saying. "Shuffling around the country along various interstates, standing in the rain with my thumb out, trying to do what's convenient for you. And for what? You don't even think about me. Like tonight. We've been yakking about you for hours—your job, fountain of youth, this and that . . . You never *asked* about me."

"That's not true!" Vera says. "I asked if you sold your screen-play." But that's all she ever asks. If only they could start this night over—isn't that what she wanted with Solomon? Every time someone comes to her house, she winds up wishing they could put more film in the camera and try one more take. "Tell me now," she says. "How are you?"

"Broke," he says. "Flat-out broke. No money, no job, no love, no literary miracle. Living hand-to-butt as usual. The J. Paul

Getty of food stamps. In hock to a mystic who's out of his fucking tree and a crazy Mafioso who ain't going to get published on the bathroom wall. They don't call him Frankie the Canary for nothing. All he wants to do is sing sing sing. Frankie, I say, I'm not your father confessor, I'm a Holy Roller Baptist. Just hearing that crap should qualify me for the Federal Witness Protection Act—new name, new town, brand-new, plastic-surgery face. That might be my lucky break. I'll get them to change my name to Howard Hughes, grow a beard and toenails three feet long, spend my golden years shuffling down hotel corridors with empty Kleenex boxes for shoes . . ."

"Howard Hughes is dead," says Vera.

"Who else is rich? I don't care. Mick Jagger? I can't get me no—" Lowell wags his finger in the air. He's light-years away from talking about whatever's gone wrong between them; who knows if he'll ever orbit back. At least he's not still sulking on his edge of the bed. Vera always liked it that Lowell wasn't one of those therapy heads who'd analyze all night long. Now she sees that this, too, has its disadvantages.

"Maybe we *could* break into that house. If that stuff works, it'll sure beat writing Frankie the Canary Corsaro's life story."

"Forget it," says Vera.

"All right," Lowell says. "Just tell me the address and how to get there." Slowly it dawns on Vera: He *means* it. She's thinking of Mayan treasure, giant squid, realizing now what she knew at the time but was too much in love to admit—what was a game to her was to Lowell a statement of faith and of all his future hopes. She'd have to be completely nuts to link her destiny with his. Besides, there's Rosie to consider. Admitting this makes her feel miles away from Lowell. All this time she's mocked Lynda and El Creepo and their baroque and rancorous arrangements. Why did she think hers was better?

"Is that why you came?" she asks. "To go into the snake-oil biz?"

"No, sweet pea," he says. "I *told* you. I came here to help you. And to see Rosie."

"Then if you want to help me, stay away from there. All we

need is for you to get busted breaking into the Greens. They'd trace you back to me in two seconds flat."

"Never," says Lowell. "They'd never get it out of me. Name, rank, and serial number. That's it. Peter Pan Starkweather. oooo. Private Starkweather reporting for duty, Sir."

"Big Youth," says Vera.

"That's me," Lowell says, and sighs deeply. "Big Youth's had a hard day. Maybe we should rack up some z's." He rolls over once, and by the time Vera's found a comfortable way to nestle into his back, he's breathing evenly. Revising history for what she promises herself will be the last time tonight, Vera decides that *this* is what ruined things between them: his talent for dropping off any time, anywhere. This, too, she used to love. She remembers curling beside him on the floor of a Mexican train so crowded they couldn't find a seat, Lowell snoring peacefully while a chicken stepped back and forth over his face. Eventually it began to irk her, especially when he'd nod off in the midst of an argument with nothing settled. Lying beside him, listening to his regular breathing, she thinks: SLEEPLESS SPOUSE SHOOTS SLUMBERING SIDEKICK. Sidekick? Maybe that's what Vera needs. She's never felt so alone.

BY MORNING Vera feels better. Sunlight's streaming in; there's coffee to be made. Her head's found a comfortable place on Lowell's chest, and they're both faking sleep. Even this seems a luxury; when you're by yourself, there's no point pretending.

Nor is there much now. Vera knows she'll get up, and why not? What's to lose? No wintry cold floors, and it's long past that dreary predawn hour when Rosie used to patter in, demanding breakfast or a bottle. Some days Vera couldn't wait to see her, would jump out of bed. Some days she'd dig in, muttering at Lowell, knowing that one drop of spilled syrup, one petrified, stuck-on Cheerio would drive her into the street to scream her message of thankless overwork and the suffering of the innocent to the subway, the city, the world.

Would things have been different if someone had promised Vera that one day she'd lie here deciding to let Rosie sleep, skip summer program, spend the day with Lowell? Had told her that the morning after Lowell's return would be one of those mornings when *he* couldn't wait to see Rosie? She'd never have believed it, nor can she quite believe it now as she peers over the covers to see Lowell zipping his jeans.

He's almost out the bedroom door when he turns back and kisses her. Vera rolls over into the warm spot he's left. She needs all the warmth she can get as she hears them in the kitchen, hears Rosie saying more in five minutes than she has in the last two years.

Crafts counsellors, gym teachers, Carl, Elijah, names Vera doesn't recognize—Rosie's life has a cast out of Cecil B. DeMille.

Her world will always be wider than all Vera's eavesdropping can encompass. Vera's trying not to mind that Rosie's saved her summer up in interesting bits to tell Lowell. Vera used to do that, too. She knows things would change if Lowell lived with them. Then Rosie's view of him would broaden to include all the smaller human emotions: vexation, impatience. She might even stop talking to him for a while and start talking to Vera. Imagining this is almost as hard as imagining life with a baby when you're pregnant, as looking at your infant daughter and picturing her at ten.

Vera heads straight for the coffeepot and pours herself a cup. Mimes it, that is. The pot's empty. It's not that Lowell doesn't love his morning coffee, nor is it laziness, exactly. He simply forgets. "Good morning, sweetheart," he says, so casually you'd think he'd been saying it every morning for ten years. Another difference between them: Not only can Lowell imagine *anything*, he can convince himself it's true.

Vera watches the teakettle. Lowell and Rosie watch Vera. At the kettle's first tentative whistle, Lowell says, "Rosie, hon, remember. A watched pot *does* boil. It just takes twice as long."

"I like things to take a long time," says Vera. "At least when the meter's not running."

"Well, now," says Lowell.

"What are you guys talking about?" says Rosie.

Pouring water through the filter, Vera has another one of those low-altitude, out-of-the-body flights. This time she sees her own shoulders, their martyred, weighed-down curve, the slope of St. Sebastian's shoulders, of Norma's when she'd stand at the stove wolfing down coffee when Dave was between jobs and could dawdle over breakfast with Vera. McCarthy isn't enough, he used to say. I'm on your mother's blacklist, too. Woman at the stove, man and child at the table, the same configuration— where's the dialectic now? Maybe history isn't a spiral but one closed circle after another. Vera used to believe her marriage was better—looser and more imaginative, if nothing else—than Norma and Dave's. Now she's not sure. She thinks this is unnatural, a sign of something awry. In the proper order of things, each generation sees its love life as a giant improvement over that of its parents.

"I'm going to be late," says Vera.

"Late for what?" says Lowell. "The whole plant's on hold till you get there. Stockpiling the confetti and balloons for National Vera Day. Champagne and coke on the house. You went over the top, darlin'. Saved the whole platoon."

"Champagne and coke?" Rosie wrinkles her nose as if it's a mixed drink.

"Don't knock it till you've tried it," says Lowell.

What is he telling her? Maybe Rosie *should* go to summer program. Has Vera said this aloud? Because what Rosie says is, "Do I *have* to? It's not like we do anything. Volleyball tournaments, jewelry boxes out of popsicle sticks. Everyone knows they're just giving us lame stuff to keep busy so we don't smoke dope and break windows and shoplift from Tape and Record City. Plus I *never* get to see Dad . . ."

"Sure," says Lowell. "Maybe we'll take in the Museum of Natural History. Check out the giant squid." Lowell waves his arms and bulges his eyes. Vera can't argue with that.

"Yay!" says Rosie. "There's a Muppet show at the planetarium."

Wait a minute. Not only has Rosie seen it, she was calling it garbage Friday night at Dave and Norma's. Vera looks at Rosie, then looks away, afraid of glimpsing some troubling reflection of her own face faking interest so some boy would think her agreeable. Though maybe it's not that; maybe Rosie's pretending to be younger, *Sesame Street* age, so Lowell won't feel so bad about all those years of growing up he's missed.

Lowell stretches as if he's just now waking up and says, "Goddamn if this place isn't cozy. Ladies, take notice: I'm cashing it in. These thin old bones are just too brittle to be grinding night after nightmare-wracked night on C.D.'s cold cement floor." Vera wonders if he still plays the guitar and sings songs with titles like "All My Goodtime Friends Are Gone" and "Trials, Troubles, and

Tribulations." He used to make fun of this cornpone self-pity. Now it's no joke. He *is* too old to be camping out in some retro hippie leatherworker's studio.

"I'll bring you home a lottery ticket," says Vera.

"I'd appreciate that," says Lowell.

HERE'S WHAT kind of day it is: Vera can't find a seat. Blinking dazedly at her fellow passengers, she feels foolish, exposed, as if she's stumbled in on a surprise party they're giving in her honor. But no one's welcoming or even sympathetic. She's the only one standing, and they seem to think she deserves it. Once more Vera imagines a party, this one full of monstrous, bratty children who've just trounced her at musical chairs.

Who are these trespassers? Foreign tourists or out-of-town Baptists who'd assumed the front car was safe and now by their presence have made it so? No such exotica, not today. Just your garden-variety Gotham working stiffs, perhaps a shade more pleased for having gotten a seat at rush hour. Surely there's some simple explanation: a few brave souls at Brighton Beach made others along the line take heart. It's how Dave's always explained the revolution: first one person gets the nerve, then another. Come the revolution, the whole subway will be safe, each car with its equal share of passengers. But what will happen to the screamers? Will they adjust their schedules to travel only outside of normal working hours? Contemplating this, Vera feels like a poet facing exile, the loss of her homeland, her muse.

Already adrift, she takes the wrong exit onto Herald Square and surfaces in front of the New Napoli. What a surprise. If she's the pointer on some immense, invisible Ouija board, what's tapping it now is the heavy hand of her not-very-subtle unconscious. It's obvious what she's after. After a night and a morning with Lowell, she wants one of Vinnie's smiles more than the Pulitzer Prize.

At nine A.M., the New Napoli's a different place. A sparse and desultory late-breakfast crowd hunches over the counter, mopping up eggs with the gloomy preoccupation of barflies at last call. Vinnie's halfway back, shoving bacon around the grill as if he's mad at it. Away from his window, his floury circles of dough, he's practically unrecognizable. Vera's out of context, too. Vinnie's nod has a certain lingering unease, as if she's someone he's having trouble placing.

"Coffee to go and a cruller," she says.

"In early today?" says Vinnie. Is she imagining it, or is he eyeing her strangely? Perhaps he's surprised that her life extends beyond lunchtime. Though she knows she's overreacting, she can't help thinking he's staring at her as if he'd sighted Dracula flying around at high noon.

Vera's so happy to find Hazel back at her post, she nearly kisses her. How pitiful to be so hungry for some sign of continuity, you'll jump at the person who despises you most. Vera feels like a prerevolutionary Russian muzhik kneeling to kiss the hand that's snapped the whip all these years. Oh, it's the least she can do. How much more has been promised and forgotten. Was it yesterday that Vera took an oath: If Hazel returned, she'd apologize for writing about that rogue elevator's fatal flight? But how to begin? All the way up, Vera rehearses, tries opening gambits, starts to speak, thinks better of it, starts again. They're nearly to Vera's floor when Hazel looks at her and grunts. "Hunh," she says. "You look like one of them dogs."

Vera knows which dogs she means. And what can she say to that? Forgive me. I deserve it. But Vera says nothing, lets reticence and false pride cripple her resolution, leaves good intentions trailing behind her as she jumps from the elevator to her floor.

Carmen looks a little wild-eyed. For an instant Vera weighs the possibility that the Washington Wild Child's problem was catching. "Come on," Carmen says. "I got something to show you." Her manner is so stealthy, her grip on Vera's arm so insistent, that were it anyone else, Vera would think this had something to do with drugs. But Carmen doesn't even smoke cigarettes or drink coffee. The Lizard, however, does everything —something Carmen and Vera have often discussed. Carmen says he'll give it all up after marriage. Vera and Carmen's family say he won't. Once, in a fit of companionability, Vera told Carmen about the happy ending to Lowell's history of substance abuse. Later she wished she hadn't, regretted having given her friend another typical *This Week* nostrum of false hope.

In the coffee room, Carmen opens the refrigerator and takes out a grocery bag full of radishes, not the little radish-stuffed cellophane pillows one gets in supermarkets but huge bunches still attached to remnants of chopped-off greens. Carmen must have gone all the way to Hunt's Point to buy them.

"One thing they don't tell you," she says. "This diet makes you nuts. First it takes so much eating your jaw's tired all the time. With all that noisy crunching, you get where you don't want to eat around people any more. Plus it gives you crazy dreams." Last night Carmen dreamed she was standing at the pearly gates with a group of her Seventh-Day Adventist friends and St. Peter waving them through. "You children are free," he kept saying. And what was heaven but a foggy cafeteria, the angels in their golden wings hovering over steam trays, dishing out plates of Swiss steak and turkey tetrazzini and gummy institutional stuff like that? "You know what?" says Carmen. "After four days of radishes it looked *terrific*."

"That's a wonderful dream," says Vera.

"It didn't make *me* happy," says Carmen. "If heaven turns out to be high-school lunch, lots of people are going to be very disappointed. Another thing, Frankie wasn't there."

Vera thinks, DIETER OVERDOES IT, SEES GOD. "Carmen," she says. "You of all people should know better than to believe what you read in *This Week*."

"It works," Carmen says. "I lost four pounds in four days."

"That's too fast," says Vera. Is she Carmen's mother? One can't be too careful about appetite loss these days. When Vera first heard about anorexia, she didn't believe it; then she started seeing them everywhere, displaying their emaciated figures in short shorts and skimpy tees, taking more pride in their bodies than Vera will ever have—oh, the beauty of bone, of balls rotating in sockets.

"Careful," she says. "You'll turn into a radish. How long you think Frankie's going to stay engaged to a root vegetable?"

Carmen seems to have thought of a dirty reply that she stifles with a speak-no-evil hand to her mouth and a giggle. "Frankie?" she says. " 'Bout two seconds. Anyhow," she adds dreamily, "Aunt Gloria's barbeque's Labor Day. You think I'm going to eat radishes with everyone packing in ribs, you got another think coming."

"Labor Day's two weeks off," says Vera. "Eat nothing but radishes till then, you won't live to taste Aunt Gloria's salsa."

"Next week I add celery," she says. "All I can eat." Vera's tempted to tell her about Solomon and the chicken salad. But that will lead to Carmen saying for the hundredth time that she and Solomon should get married. Then Vera will have to announce that Lowell's here, which means that when he leaves again she'll have to tell her *that*.

Forgetting that she's already carrying coffee from the New Napoli, Vera pours herself another cup. Carmen laughs good-humoredly, but with a knowing Seventh-Day Adventist edge: that's what caffeine does to the brain.

Vera goes to her office, paces awhile, then roots around in her papers without any definite plan. When she comes up with the Bigfoot story, she understands that what she's been looking for is an excuse to go see Shaefer and find out what's happened with the Greens. On the way she clutches her manuscript just as she clutches her housekeys on certain bad nights when she comes home late, imagining she's being followed. The relief she feels locking her apartment door behind her is not unlike the feeling she has now when Shaefer says, "Come in."

"Got something for you," she says. Then, off-handedly, "Heard anything from the lawyers?" She's trying to make it sound like some casual office pleasantry.

"Ha!" says Shaefer. "I thought the guy was going to start blubbering when I hit him with the news. You could tell he'd already spent his fee a couple times over in his head. But as soon as this new evidence came up"—Shaefer raps his pen on the desk —"case dismissed!"

Still grinning, Shaefer reaches for the paper Vera's holding out. He looks disappointed to see it's a story. "Bigfoot lights up what?" he says. "A joint? BIGFOOT GETS HIGH, LOCALS GET GOING. I'd get going, too. How'd you like to run into Bigfoot when he'd just smoked a load of pot and he's seeing big green snakes wriggling in the trees? Not much, right?"

Shaefer likes to joke about marijuana, but Vera's pretty sure he doesn't smoke it. At the same office Christmas party at which Esposito talked about his melancholy working vacations, Shaefer told her how once, between newspaper jobs, he'd managed a jazz bar in Northampton. "I used to smoke in back with the musicians," he said. "This was before you were born. You know what they called it then? Boo!"

"Read it through quick," Vera says, not as an order but meaning he doesn't have to spend much time. There's something wrong here. Ordinarily Shaefer would have read it by now without prompting. Now he skims it, then files it apparently at random in a folder on his desk.

"Sure," he says. "I know how the guy felt. When I first quit smoking, every second I was on the edge of pulling some crazy stunt like that. That's what I can't stand about that bastard Solomon: the guy's got no heart, smoking those little cigars that smell like every ashtray you've ever emptied, and so delicious, when he offers you one, you want to take it and eat it."

Is this some roundabout way of discussing her story? That, too, seems wrong. Shaefer is nothing if not direct: I like this. That stinks. Take it back and redo it. How thrilled she was that first time he told her they might use DEMENTO DENTIST as a front-page head. Over the years, Shaefer's comments have come to mean less—though it's still flattering, still seems like something of a coup to have written something crazy enough to meet his exacting standards for front-page news.

"What's the banner head this week?" Vera asks, thinking how much of the morning she's spent trying to sound casual.

Shaefer takes a sheet of paper out of a folder—which, Vera notices, is nowhere near the one in which he's filed her story— and hands it to her. 91-YEAR-OLD MOM BEARS BOUNCING BABE.

> Doctors at Chicago's Cook County Hospital got the surprise of their lives this week when 91-year-old Sara Beckley checked into the emergency room with symptoms of acute indigestion and proceeded to give birth to a healthy 8-pound-12-ounce baby boy. "That's a new one on us," commented nurse Julia Clarkson, who attended the delivery.
>
> Albert Beckley, 86, apparently had no idea of his normally hefty wife's condition. On hearing the good news, the wheelchair-bound proud papa had attendants wheel him to the hospital gift shop, where he bought blue bubblegum cigars. Meanwhile Mom, presented with her brand-new bundle of joy, began to laugh.
>
> According to hospital spokesmen, mother and child are doing well and will return home after a routine stay of two to three days.

Vera has to turn away so Shaefer won't see the tears in her eyes. Moved by the realization that 91-YEAR-OLD MOM BEARS BOUNCING BABE is the quintessential *This Week* story, Vera's filled with more love for this shoddy, sensationalist rag than she could possibly say. There's nothing but hope in this story, hope and goodwill: hope for all the women who want children and can't have them, for women like Vera who already have a child and regret that they probably won't have more. Ninety-one! There's still time! False hope—but what's the harm? It's unlikely that any old woman reading this story will redo the spare room as a nursery or that any woman of child-bearing age will read it and postpone pregnancy for another fifty years.

In another mood, Vera might have sensed scorn and contempt, ill will toward women and their aging bodies behind this vision of drooping stomachs heaving in labor, babies suckling at withered, ancient breasts. But today she can't see it, doesn't think it's there. Three cheers for Sara Beckley, who didn't even need a cesarean but pushed him out herself! Between the lines of this story is everyone's longing for miracles, the hope that goes against all odds, beyond synchronicity and breaks in the natural order. The promise that your suffering leads to heaven and the cafeteria of your dreams, your forty years in the wilderness to glades of milk and honey . . . Only now—how slow she is!—does Vera realize that Sara Beckley laughing at her newborn son is Sarah in the Bible.

What an inspiration, going through the Bible, adapting its stories for *This Week* readers. A whole new source of plots. BROTHER KILLS BROTHER AT SADO SACRIFICE SCENE. GROOM WAITS SEVEN YEARS, MARRIES WRONG WOMAN. BOY SOLD INTO SLAVERY, TRACED VIA COLORED COAT. This last might need some work, but still! Not for nothing do they call it the greatest story ever told, though she can never remember if that's just the New Testament or the Old as well. TALKING SNAKE CONS WIFE, HUBBY HOMELESS. What kind of message of hope is that? She's all the way up to SEA DIVIDES, SWIMMERS SPRINT TO SAFETY when it occurs to her that this ninety-one-year-old laughing mom can't just be coincidental. Someone's thought of this already.

"Whose is it?" she asks.

"Mort's," says Frank.

Vera thinks of Mort, his stick-figure scribbles turning into Bible illustrations, growing more and more fantastic, charged with meaning, intensity, faith. She thinks of a painting she once saw by a woman named Sister Gertrude Morgan, Adam and Eve standing dejectedly by the tree of knowledge and underneath the caption, "I can't believe I ate the whole thing." Suddenly she has that feeling she gets sometimes about a person—she's missed something, some unsuspected depth of spirit. Suddenly she wants to talk to Mort, to say, "Where did this story come from?"

Then Shaefer clears his throat and says, "Look, this is going to be a little rough; fasten your seatbelts and hang on to the rails, we'll be back on the pavement in no time."

And that's all it takes for Vera to know: she won't be talking to Mort, or anyway not much and not for very long. She's being fired. It's a good thing she senses what's being said, since she can't hear a word. Her first response is disbelief, then anger. She's been so good, worked so hard, given her *brain* for *This Week*!

"This is rough for me, too," Shaefer's saying. "I was up all night thinking about it."

Right, Vera thinks. Tonight you'll sleep fine and *I'll* be up. "I don't get it," she says. "They're not even suing us."

"I know that," says Shaefer. "It's the whole thing. I can't figure it. And I don't like things I can't figure. What it boils down to is, either you're lying—" He holds his hand up like a traffic cop to stop her from interrupting. "*I* don't think you're lying. Or you've got some kind of ESP, and frankly it gives me the willies."

"I *don't*," says Vera. "It can't possibly happen again. And what if I did? Karen Karl's supposed to have ESP and she's *syndicated*, for Christ's sake; she can buy and sell us both."

"Maybe you should apply for her spot," Shaefer says. "That bimbo wouldn't know the future if it sat on her face."

"I don't want her job," says Vera. "Anyway, I told you. Lightning doesn't strike twice—"

"Try and understand my position," says Shaefer. "This time was too goddamned close. Next time we won't be so lucky. Every word you write will have to be checked. To make sure it *isn't* true. I'll wind up with another coronary."

Vera can't believe she's pleading for her job when what she should be doing is punching him in the snoot or, better yet, firing off some perfectly devastating remark and stalking out. "I'll stick to medical bits," she says. "Columns. You and Your Kitty Kat. Parakeet Doctor. How can you get in trouble doing doggie diagnosis? You're *supposed* to get that stuff right."

"Vera," says Shaefer. "Don't make this any lousier than it is." Vera wants to shout out loud, to call up everyone she knows and say, "How *could* they? I did nothing!" So when Dan Esposito walks in, she almost tries it on him, then realizes it's pointless.

Dan's been cued to interrupt if her talk with Shaefer seemed to be taking too long.

The thought of them planning this makes Vera's heart start to pound. She hopes it's not really possible to die of shame. She feels doubly betrayed by Dan, who was always so much gentler than Frank. This morning his features look slightly blurred. Vera wonders if they get that way in love and in those campgrounds echoing with the underwater murmurs of idle UFO gossip.

"Believe me," says Shaefer. "We'll do whatever we can. Stay on for a month or so while you job hunt. We'll send you off with two weeks' pay, everything but the gold watch . . ."

"Three weeks' pay," says Esposito. It's the first time Vera's ever heard them disagree.

"Keep the month," she says. "I don't think I'd enjoy it. Just give me the three weeks' pay." Oddly enough, what she really wants is her Bigfoot story back. What would she do with it? Who would print it? Judging from the way Shaefer filed it, they won't be using it here. They're probably afraid that running it will bring Bigfoot out of his lair and down to the nearest Texaco station. Could they be held liable? Does it matter? All that matters to Vera is making a full turn and some sort of exit without falling flat on her face.

Back in her office, she's confronted by the mountain of paper amassed over the years. It's worse than the Basenji Society. She feels the weight of it pushing her down till she's crouched in an undignified squat on the floor; the idea of sorting and moving it makes her burst into tears.

When at last she stops crying, Vera picks up the phone and, without thinking, dials her parents' number. She's thirty-seven, and look who she's calling for comfort. Comfort and absolution.

When Dave answers, Vera says, "Guess what."

"Don't tell me," he says. "You got a job."

"I lost this one," she says.

"Allah be praised," he says. "What happened?"

"Nothing," says Vera. "Part of what I told you about, Friday night." No need to tell him the second part of that story. The

Flatbush fountain of youth may have saved Mrs. DiPaolo and Mr. Grossman, but so far it's done nothing for her.

"Good news," he says. "The worst that'll happen is, you'll start making an honest living. Meanwhile, don't worry. Money's no problem. Your mother and I can certainly lend a hand till you get back on your feet."

Back on your feet—the phrase has a Depression ring. Rows of thirties tin soldiers on pedestals—knocked down, set up, knocked down again. "That's all right," says Vera. "They're giving me three weeks' pay. And I've got some saved up." That's one advantage of not balancing your checkbook; for all she knows, it's true.

"Well, isn't that something?" Vera can practically see him shaking his head. "You never know how things are going to work out. What looks like a tragedy sometimes turns out to be a blessing. That reminds me of a story." Vera considers pretending to have a call on another line, but can't bring herself to do it, and so Dave begins:

"One night up in the mountains near Teruel, the Fascists started shelling our camp. Heavy artillery." Dave makes whistling rocket noises into the phone. "Lit up the sky like daytime. We knew it was pretty goddamn close, we just didn't know *how* close till round about dawn the shelling stopped. I went outside to take a leak, walked a couple of steps away from my tent, and I'll be damned if I wasn't pissing into a thirty-foot mortar crater. *That* close. That's how close *you* came to not being here. I stood there looking down in that hole and right then I decided, my whole life after that was going to seem like a gift. A present. A little something extra. Borrowed time."

"Wow," says Vera, less amazed by the story than by the fact that she's never heard it before, never been told of this pivotal moment till now. Could he have been saving it for an occasion like this? Like what? Getting sacked at *This Week* is nothing like almost being blown to smithereens by Fascist mortar fire. What moment will Vera have to show Rosie as the point that made everything afterward seem like a gift, like grace? Is this what's bothering her? Not exactly. Is it the fact that—no matter how relevant it seems to Dave—her life *isn't* a story from the Spanish Civil War? That's not it, either. What's troubling her is this: How long would all this sympathy and exemplary tales and offers of money last if Dave knew Lowell was back?

"Talk to you later," she says. "Tell Norma not to worry."

"*You* don't worry," Dave tells her. "You're still our girl."

Dave's story helped, after all. Vera's decided to let the office go till tomorrow. Maybe a Fascist shell will hit it overnight and solve her problems for her. Besides, if she leaves right now, she won't have to tell anyone she's been fired. By tomorrow, when she comes in to pack up, everyone will know.

On her way out, she stops in the coffee room to refuel and finds Mavis and Solomon standing there. Vera pours herself a cup of coffee and, going to the refrigerator for milk, has to reach around Carmen's giant bag of radishes.

Vera could go for a radish right now. Like poor Louise: chomping it would drown out the noise in her head. She wonders how many radishes it would take to make you feel full. Every time Lowell left, she'd felt a similar urge. Once she sat down on the edge of the bed and ate a giant box of Familia, dry, with a spoon. Like sawdust and putty—*that* filled the hole. Then she'd smoked half a pack of Camels.

"First the good news," says Vera. "The suit's been dropped."

"O-*kay!*" says Solomon, grinding Vera against his cameras in an unusually—even by Solomon-Vera standards—awkward embrace.

"Now the bad news," she says. "You're going to have to go on without me, men. I've been hit bad."

Is it tasteless to be making wounded-soldier jokes in front of Solomon? No one seems to notice. They're too busy trying to figure out what she's talking about. Then finally the howl of outrage Vera's been waiting for all morning: How could they do this to her? The muttering and gnashing of teeth goes on and on, but not once does anyone suggest doing anything—resigning in protest or even complaining to Shaefer. Vera remembers picketing on behalf of a popular professor who'd been denied tenure. Well, guess what. College isn't the working world. Suddenly Vera feels so distant from Mavis and Solomon; her ship's already sailed, as they wave and grow smaller and smaller on shore.

"Wouldn't you know it?" says Solomon. "The first time anyone hits the nail on the head, they can her. What jerks. I should quit, too."

"What'll *that* do?" says Vera. Solomon's not going to bat for her, just joining the losing team.

"They'll change their minds," says Mavis. "Shaefer's a little hot right now; he's had a difficult weekend. He'll cool down. You'll see. All will be forgiven."

"Forgive what?" says Vera. "I'm leaving."

Knowing that she's coming back to pack makes it possible to leave Mavis and Solomon, to hurry past Carmen. Tomorrow they can all pretend it's not *adios*, that their friendship will survive outside the office. But Carmen won't let her by.

"Hey, what are you *on*?" she says. "The coffee diet?"

"That's right," says Vera. "I'm going on a long coffee break. *Finito*. I'm through." Then she turns and hurries out before Carmen can even think of telling her it's God's will.

V ERA HITS Montague Street at a run. She can't wait to get home—the only thing that'll make her feel better is finding Rosie and Lowell and hugging them so hard she shuts off the oxygen to her brain and can't think. All that's holding her back is the fear on people's faces as they wheel around to see if she's chasing them, then look behind her to see who's chasing her. No wonder joggers wear sneakers. Joggers and muggers, too.

Of course the apartment's empty; she could have taken her time. A vision of Rosie and Lowell communing with the giant squid brings on a rush of jealousy that makes her feel as if she's got her wish for a diminished oxygen supply. Telling herself that the city is full of people drinking at lunch, she pours a vodka tonic and sits down to wait them out.

Nothing like jealousy to make the time drag. As the long afternoon stretches on, Vera goes through stages. First hurt, then anger, then worry. She runs through her usual repertoire of threats to Rosie's life and well-being. Luckily, Lowell's presence precludes most of them. Even so, things happen. Madmen await little girls in ladies' rooms where their Daddies would never go, push them in front of oncoming trains with their helpless Daddies right there.

It's almost six when they finally ring the doorbell; Vera just feels drained. Rosie looks bright-eyed and adorable in her baseball cap, shorts, a green brontosaurus T-shirt Vera's never seen before. "I forgot my key," she says. "We stayed out till we were sure you'd be home."

Is that what they've cooked up to tell her? Before she can

say she's been home all day, Lowell's kissing her. "Sweetheart!" he says. "How was your day?"

"All right," says Vera. She's not ready to tell them the truth, and anyway they're too jacked up to listen. "And yours?"

"Outrageous!" Lowell says.

"Yeah, Mom," says Rosie. "Really great."

"I'm worried about that giant squid," says Lowell. "Looks a little the worse for wear. Well, who doesn't, right? Or maybe it's that they've got it in a different place, higher up. Not the most flattering angle. But Jesus, those dinosaurs! That big Tyrannosaurus gets *prettier* with age. What I wouldn't give to saddle up one of them mamas. Giddyap and away!"

Vera's trying not to think what it means that she's mated for life to a man whose supreme ambition is to be Fred Flintstone when Lowell says, "Honey, what's wrong? You look a little down. Hard day at the office?"

"No day at the office," she says. "I got fired."

It takes them both a while to process this. Lowell recovers first. "Way to go!" he says, sounding just like that Huey or Dewey or Louie. Rosie's gone pale.

"What'll you do?" Rosie asks.

"Win the Pulitzer Prize," says Lowell. "Your Mom's going to write the story of the century, and some sleazeball in Hollywood's going to option it, and your Dad'll write the screenplay, and then we're in fatback gravy! Bye-bye Montague, hello Malibu!"

Another variation on the lost Mayan treasure, but updated, and one that Vera so needs to believe, she almost does. She leans against Lowell and he hugs her, Rosie comes over and hugs them both, and for a moment it works. Vera can't think, can't worry, can't feel anything but them. Then Lowell says, "This calls for a celebration! Let's go to Chinatown! On me! I haven't been in years. Out where I've been, even the Chinese roll their moo shu pork in tortillas . . ."

While Lowell rattles on, Vera drifts into thinking how the secret, dirty habits of Chinese restaurants are another of *This Week*'s recurring themes. Cat, pigeon, squirrel—writing for

This Week meant constantly looking out for new, readily available, and disgusting animals to serve up in someone's sweet-and-sour pork. It'll take some getting used to, going to Chinatown and just being able to eat.

"Will the ladies be dressing for dinner?" asks the hillbilly John Gielgud.

"Certainly, Jeeves," Rosie says. Jeeves? Soon "Puttin' on the Ritz" is coming from the scratchy turntable in Rosie's room. It's Rosie's favorite. Vera's told her it's not really a New Wave song. Rosie says she knows. She claims to remember a cartoon she saw—as a child, she says—in which skeletons in top hats and tails danced to "Puttin' on the Ritz," then took off their leg bones and arm bones and skulls. Vera can believe it; it does sound like a song for skeletons to dance to. Now Vera does a kind of skeleton cakewalk to her room, where she stares into her closet with the unfocused gaze she ordinarily saves for the refrigerator.

Back in the living room, Rosie's put on a skirt and pink platform wedgies. Vera feels rather dowdy in her black pegged pants, her black satin thrift-shop baseball jacket embroidered with a map of Vietnam and the logo, "When I die I'll go to heaven because I've already spent my time in hell. Saigon 1969–70." Only now does Vera realize she'd bought it with Lowell in mind. She'd thought she'd stopped doing that—dressing to amuse him, saving her life up in stories she hopes he'll find entertaining.

Lowell's put on a white shirt and tie. "See this?" he says, flapping the tie at Vera. Up close, its little raised dots turn out to be naked girls. While Vera's looking, he kisses the top of her head. Then he puts one arm around Vera, the other around Rosie, and won't let go; they have to squeeze through the door sideways. Locking it behind them requires even more ingenious acrobatics.

"The subway's this way," says Vera.

"Let's walk," says Lowell. "What else are bridges for?"

They walk beside the traffic jam along Tillary Street while motorists glare at them in that furious way drivers watch pedestrians outdistancing them. Then they climb the stairs to the bridge, and they're up above everything. A breeze blows up here that didn't exist down below. Lights twinkle in the few windows not still flashing back the last rays of setting sun. The skyline shames every photo, every picture postcard, gives Vera an odd, hollow ache in her stomach.

For some reason she'd thought they'd be alone up here. It's true no one's going their way, but there's a steady procession heading in the opposite direction, Manhattan to Brooklyn, home from work. Young female execs with sporty little briefcases and full dress-for-success summer drag; giggly steno poolers tripping over each other's stiletto heels; Rastafarian mail-room types passing cigar-sized joints; and, every so often, ashenfaced older gentlemen clawing at their neckties as if it's the doctor who ordered them to take up walking: mandarins on the Long March. Then Lowell elbows Vera and says, "That's a lifer, darlin'. Forty years at *This Week*."

"Not me!" says Vera, feeling as she hasn't felt since high school, when she'd see workers trudging home and think, Not me! Not me! Where did she think she was headed? Never-Never Land? The planet Krypton? To have grown up in her family and not known that people have to eat and make money and feed their kids! Maybe that was why she chose to ignore it; maybe all children do. They look at their Dads at the end of the day and think, Not me! If there is a natural order, thinks Vera, quite possibly it's that.

Tonight everything's conspiring to make Vera feel like she's back in high school. The soft light, the hint of moisture—seductive and full of promise. She could be sixteen, heading into the city to look for love. Or she and Lowell could be teenage sweethearts, starting fresh but with the advantage of everything they've learned since. It's what every happy idiot wants: To be young again and know what I know now. She feels like they're in orbit, out of time, and—when at last they touch down on Canal Street—that mixture of relief and loss she imagines an astronaut feels on reentering the earth's gravitational field. Tonight she'd like to keep that sense of loss at bay. If she dwells on it, all the regrets of the last twenty years will start dancing in front of her eyes like the neon dragons already visible over Mott Street.

Vera can't figure out why Chinatown's not more crowded; perhaps there's a street fair in Little Italy, siren sausage smells waylaying hungry diners on their way downtown. By now every won-ton parlor should have a line spilling out on the street, but in fact it's mostly Chinese families shopping, children playing, groups of older boys and girls checking each other out, pairs of lovers. It feels like a privilege to be here. Passing a fish stall—jumbo shrimp, pans of mussels, flat, big-eyed fish arranged in a kind of mosaic—Vera says, "I should shop here. I forget."

"When we move to Malibu," says Lowell, "we'll be bagging this stuff off the deck."

The street's *full* of lovers, pressed together so tightly they could be running a three-legged race. Vera thinks of herself and Lowell in another Chinatown: San Francisco, where for months Chinese food was the only thing that could lure them out of bed. Perhaps such memories are why Vera so hates the sight of the newly-in-love. But not tonight. Tonight she and Lowell and Rosie are linked just as tight. They've got it all over new lovers, they're lovers who've lasted long enough to have a ten-year-old kid. And though she knows it's New York, where chances are better than average that a child old enough to walk and talk is the child of a previous marriage, people seem to know Rosie's theirs. A surprising number of lovers smile at them—or, really, at some happy future vision of themselves. And despite all her present happiness, Vera still wants to grab them as they walk by and say, Wait! Let me tell you about the ten years in between!

Turning the corner onto Bayard, Lowell pulls them into the kind of touristy gift shop you normally pass without seeing. Tonight it's full of treasures. They want, exclaim over, everything. The kid at the register isn't much older than Rosie. Watching them, he starts grinning, though it's hard to tell if he's laughing at them or if their enthusiasm is contagious. Rosie buys a mechanical toy, a green metal egg attached to a kind of plunger that, when pushed, makes the egg spin and open, re-

vealing a bright plush spinning bird. Lowell buys a kite in the
shape of a mythical beast: tiger, dragon, pelican. Vera buys a
pack of flash cards designed to help Chinese children to read,
lovely little paintings titled in Chinese and English: Chair.
Table. House. Mouth. She doesn't know why, she just wants it.
"For when I get Alzheimer's," she tells Lowell. "I'll put these
up to remind me." She leafs through the deck till she finds the
one that says Ear and holds it to her ear.

"Do it now," says Lowell. "Don't wait till you forget where
to put them."

Their favorite restaurant is downstairs, below street level.
The something something rice shop. The waiter who directs them
to their table looks at them like he's sizing up cats for the sweet-
and-sour pork. That's all right; it's atmosphere; it makes the food
taste better. The unexpectedness—that someone with such contempt for you could serve you something so delicious.

Only half the tables are filled, but they're all in the same
half of the room. Consider it a spiritual exercise, thinks Vera,
some discipline the Buddha might put you through: learning to
ignore what people next to you in Chinese restaurants say. The
ordering of the dishes, the jockeying to include everyone's
favorite. The etiquette! There's always the expert, and with him
the novice who makes timid suggestions—egg rolls, chop suey—
that the expert pretends not to hear, and who gets, instead of
chop suey, a free lecture on Chinese cuisine lasting the length
of the meal. Or what's worse: the first dates who can't eat because they're so busy confessing, can't taste because they've still
got their teeth in that messy divorce, still worrying it like a
bone. What Vera can't understand is why so many first dates
seem to take place in Chinese restaurants. You'd think sharing
food from a common plate was an intimacy you'd want to save
till you knew a person better. Once Vera heard a girl tell her
date how she'd gotten herpes from a guy who believed that the
way to get rid of it was to give it to someone else.

But tonight their luck holds even in this. At the table behind Lowell and facing Vera are two good-looking, freckle-faced
kids from someplace like Fordham or St. John's.

"If the nuns had told me to cut my leg off, I would've done it," the boy's saying. "But you know when it all ended? When I got my license and saw how bad nuns drove."

"In their little station wagons," says the girl. "Used to be a time, every Halloween party you went to, there'd be three pregnant nuns."

"Always guys," the boy says.

"This beef chow fun is great," she says. "I had this dream last night, I dreamed I was at Liza Minelli's wedding, and she was wearing a long, white dress and a crown of little stars like the Queen of Heaven."

"The ones I hate," he says, "are those dreams where friends you haven't seen in fifteen years come back. I don't know why. I just hate them."

"Fifteen years," says the girl. "Mary Walesko, my best friend. She was dumpy and wore these little funny glasses, and when her family moved away, I wanted to kill myself. I don't know what it would be like to run into her now. I guess you just hope the other person's not more successful or perfect or anything."

Vera can't believe so much wisdom and honesty can exist in an eighteen-year-old brain. The girl's date can't, either. "Want some more tea?" he says. He sounds surprised at himself, as if it's the first time he's ever offered to pour anything for anyone. Vera so wants to keep listening that she has to make herself talk.

"Know what?" she says. "*Won ton* spelled backwards is *not now*." As soon as she says it, she knows it's Solomon's joke. She just can't remember if Rosie was there when he told it.

"You order," says Lowell, and Vera looks up to see the same surly waiter slapping impatiently at his thigh.

Picking the dishes she wants feels like shopping in thrift stores on days when silk shirts and gabardine jackets beckon to her from seas of polyester; the choices couldn't be more obvious. Before the waiter stalks off, Vera asks Rosie if she can pick the pieces of meat out of her food or if they should order another vegetable dish. "No way," Rosie says. "I'm eating *everything*."

Behind them the girl with the Liza Minelli dreams is telling her date how her cousin's husband turned out to be a three-time bigamist. "Thrigamist?" says the boy. Vera could listen all night. But just then the waiter slams a metal tureen on their table: House Special Soup. Vera ladles out slabs of duck, pork, snow peas, won ton stuffed with spicy Chinese sausage. Vera and Rosie have two bowls apiece; Lowell has three. They're feeling pretty stuffed themselves when the waiter brings on dinner.

Dish follows dish; has she ordered too much? Vera flattens herself against the booth as the waiter shoves plates around to make room. Prawns with oyster mushrooms in a golden sauce; twelve-flavor chicken; mussels steamed with sesame paste and scallions; squares of fried bean curd with pork; beef with orange; a whole bass braised with carrot bits and tree ears—the colors, the textures, the sheen of cornstarch and oil drive Vera and Rosie and Lowell into a feeding frenzy. They lean close to their bowls so their chopsticks have less far to travel. What has Vera been eating? She's forgotten how food tastes. Now each mouthful maps new possibilities, a whole geography of places for her and Lowell and Rosie to eat. Hushed Japanese inns where they'll slip off their shoes and tiptoe in to eat sushi. Greek cafés where men even handsomer than Vinnie will carve slices of lamb off rotating spits. They'll eat linguine with calamari while little Sicilians play mandolins and out-of-work divas sing their hearts out, chow down pork chops and corn bread brought by beautiful black women who'll call them sugar, honey child, baby.

"Guy goes into a Chinese restaurant," says Lowell.

"Shh," says Vera. "If this is going to be some horrible flied lice joke, don't tell it."

"All right," says Lowell. "I'll tell another one."

"I've got one," says Rosie. "This guy's eating dinner in a Chinese restaurant. 'Waiter,' he says. 'What's this fly doing in my soup—'"

"The backstroke," says Lowell.

"You ruined it," says Rosie.

"Sorry," says Lowell. "I heard that one in fourth grade."

"*I'm* in the fourth grade," Rosie says.

"See," says Lowell. "I'll bet those dinosaurs were telling it in the fourth grade. All right, here's one." He opens his mouth, then shuts it again. "Problem is, all the jokes I know are too dirty for the ladies."

Even this embarrasses Rosie. She goes back to eating, staring down at her plate. Then suddenly she starts screaming, grabbing her throat and jerking around in her seat. It's the moment Vera's feared all Rosie's life. What flashes through her mind in the seconds before she can act is that her life is about to be destroyed forever by yet another obvious irony: Rosie *knew* she shouldn't eat meat. "She's choking!" she yells at Lowell, who says, "When you're choking, you don't scream." He grabs Rosie's arm and murmurs soothing nonsense to her until she calms down.

"Gross!" she sputters, picking something out of her food with chopsticks and laying it on the table. Dead and heavily sauced as it is, it's still got its carapace, its antennae. Sweet-and-sour Gregor Samsa.

"Life imitates old jokes," says Lowell. "Except I think this one's doing the crawl."

By now the waiter's come over. Rosie picks the bug up with her chopsticks again and waves it at him, a gesture of such purity only a ten-year-old could make it. Any adult would have left it on the table and pointed.

The waiter looks at the roach, then at them—a look of such utter scorn you'd think they'd brought it with them. Then he takes out the check pad and, pointing to the bottom of the column, says, "No tax. No tax."

When he leaves, all three of them burst out laughing. "What did he mean?" says Rosie. "No tax on the cockroach?"

"I think he means no tax on the whole bill," says Vera. "It's his way of making it up to us when he couldn't really bring himself to not charge us at all." Though Vera can't quite say why, she's enormously cheered by all this. It seems like an omen, a sign that destiny has decided to entertain her instead of just messing her up. The waiter brings cookies and, sure enough: all three of their fortunes promise long life, happiness, and friends bringing unexpected good news.

"I feel light-headed," says Vera.

"That's the MSG," says Lowell.

When the check comes, Lowell grabs it. "All right," says Vera. "I'll spring for the cab ride home."

Riding over the bridge in the dark, watching the twinkly lights on the Brooklyn side, Lowell asks the cabby if he's ever walked across.

"Are you kidding?" he says. "The only guys nutty enough to walk across are the ones who go halfway out and jump."

The cab picks up speed, and they're thrown against the back of the seat. Vera feels rag-doll languorous and decides that their sum-total elegance is far more than one might expect from a pair of pink platform wedgies, a tie with naked ladies on it, and a black satin Vietnam-era jacket. They should be heading out to West Egg, to a party at Jay Gatsby's. Puttin' on the Ritz.

Rosie's asleep by the time they get home. Lowell carries her upstairs. Snuggling into her bed, she wakes up enough to kiss Lowell, then Vera.

Lowell and Vera go into the living room and sit in the dark for a while, listening to cats yowling in the back alley. She almost tells him about the Washington Wild Boy, but she's saving it for a moment when she wants to say something interesting. Right now the lust they're feeling and not yet acknowledging is interesting enough. Not long ago she saw a French movie in which two about-to-be-lovers heard cats making similar sounds. "Fighting," said the man. "No," said the woman. "Making love." At least that's what the subtitles said. Vera can think of several terms for what cats do, but making love isn't one of them.

"You know what they're complaining about?" says Lowell. "That was their friend Fritz we ate in the sweet-and-sour pork."

"We didn't have sweet-and-sour pork," says Vera, embarrassed to hear herself sound like those Chinese-food experts.

"Excuse me," says Lowell. "The twelve-flavor chicken, then. One of the twelve was Purina."

Vera considers what depths of racism and primitive fear must lie beneath these stories of Chinese cooks serving various unappealing animals with your fried rice. Oh, the smoldering passion of dietary taboo. She's heard that's how riots start in India: Muslims suspecting Hindus of passing off rendered pork fat as vegetable oil; Hindus accusing Muslims of disguising beef as mutton. BENGALI BARBEQUE: CALCUTTA BUTCHERS BURNED. It's the first time she's thought of her job in hours; now the fact that she's lost it seems somehow less surprising than that she's gone so long without remembering. Maybe everything balances out: one kiss from Rosie makes her happier than writing the front-page headline every week.

Lowell's begun to sing. "Cats do it, dogs do it, even educated frogs do it, let's do it, let's fall in love." He pulls her to him and waltzes her around the living room, crooning in her ear. He's trying to achieve a mellow, sophisticated, Fred Astaire quality, but can't seem to lose that moony country twang. His version of "Let's Fall in Love" might as well be "All My Good-time Friends are Gone."

"Let's do it," he whispers, kissing her very gently. Then, in the midst of an embrace that leaves Vera's knees weak, Lowell breaks off and says, "Here's a fact: 'Let's do it' were Gary Gilmore's last words." And though Vera knows it's perverse to be pleased that a man on his way to bed with her is quoting a mad-dog killer bound for the firing squad, she can't help it.

Afterward, Lowell holds her head in the crook of his arm and points out the window. "Look," he says. "UFOs."

"In Brooklyn?" says Vera.

"Everywhere," says Lowell. "Aliens are among us." Then he tells her how, after they've made their fortune writing screen-plays, they'll take a piece of it and buy a mansion on the Hudson or a ranch up in Northern California—anywhere private. Then they'll clear some land, string up some lights: a landing strip for UFOs. First couple of times they'll just get the Martians to take them for rides, buzz Rosie's elementary school. Then they'll ask their alien hosts for a souvenir, a kind of goodwill present, a bit of the treasure the Mayans took with them when they hitched a ride on a UFO and sailed up past the Milky Way and off into outer space.

At breakfast Lowell can't look at Vera. She has to sneak up on him from behind. When she puts her arms around him, his voice gets husky as if his toast's gone down wrong and he says, "Maybe we should go back to bed."

"We can't," says Vera. "Rosie will be up any minute." She's thinking of the fat, jolly, aging hippie couple who run the corner deli with their six fat, jolly children nibbling knishes underfoot. Once the wife told Vera that all eight of them sleep in the same king-sized bed and then, intuiting Vera's question, said, "Oh, they're used to it. They say, 'Mommy and Daddy are making the springs bounce again.'" That's Never-Never Land, thinks Vera. Mommy and Daddy's bed forever. Rosie used to sleep with them. Why did they ever stop? If only they'd gotten a bigger mattress, maybe *they'd* have six kids and a deli, too.

As it turns out, they could have gone back to bed. By the time Lowell goes off to get dressed, Rosie's still asleep. Vera lingers in the kitchen. This morning his coffee cup and toast crumbs seem like less of an imposition—really, no trouble at all. In the bedroom Vera finds him stuffing clothes into his suitcase. She averts her eyes so as not to be reminded of how, when he'd come back after those first separations, she'd made him keep all his possessions in one place. "Don't get too comfortable," she'd said.

Now she says, "Wait. I'll clear out a drawer."

"I can't," Lowell says. "I've got to go."

"Go where?"

"Back to L.A.," he says.

Vera's sure she's misheard. Practically eight? Pack or be late?

Bactrian hay? There's nothing else it could be. She focuses on the tie he's folding away. He wore it for *her*, brought it three thousand miles to show *her*. Which means he loves her, or at least cares what she thinks. She can't believe he's leaving and that she's seeking evidence of love in a naked-lady tie. Would this be happening if they'd gone back to bed? She almost hopes that her putting him off was what did it. It's worse to consider the alternative: that his mind was made up and still he kept trying to seduce her, even as the taxi ran its meter and honked mariachi tunes from the street.

"Why?" she says. "You can stay."

"I can't," he says. "Frankie wants to get this book done in a hurry, and I promised. You don't go breaking promises to guys like that unless you want Teflon kneecaps."

"Fine," says Vera. "An offer you couldn't refuse."

"Sweetheart," Lowell says, putting his arms around her. "Please don't get upset. Don't think I just came out here because I thought you'd discovered the fountain of youth. And then when it turned out different . . ." Don't think it? Vera wouldn't if Lowell hadn't suggested it. It's not the first time he's planted wild suspicions in her mind. It used to be that the only way she knew what he'd done was by listening to what he denied.

"It's not like that," he's saying. "I needed to see you and Rosie, I love you . . ." Vera's not listening; she's too busy wondering if he was serious about that snake-oil scheme. A long shot, certainly, but after digging for lost Mayan treasure, hawking Flatbush wonder water is practically a sure thing. Vera shuts her eyes, counts silently to ten. When she opens them, she'll ask him to stay one more time. Once and no more.

"Call Frankie up and explain," she says. "He's Italian, he'll understand. We're *family*."

"It's not Frankie," says Lowell. "It's me. Remember how every time I used to come back, I'd still be picking the thruway gravel from between my splayed, bleeding toes and you'd already be telling me not to get comfortable."

"Did I say that?" mumbles Vera.

"Now I don't *want* to get comfortable. I'm afraid I'll relax, we'll have a couple weeks of hillbilly ecstasy, then one night it's, 'Lowell, honey, could you run down to the market for a minute?' " Lowell detonates a three-stage explosion in his mouth. "Our red-hot love affair goes down the dumper all over again, and I'm out in the cold howling lonely Arky love songs at the moon."

"*I'll* go to the grocery," says Vera. "I'll send Rosie. We're used to it."

"Then you'll find something else," Lowell says.

"Like what?" Vera says.

"Like you've never cut me one goddamn inch of slack. Remember in Mexico? You were all ready to go and leave me to die in the jungle. We had thirty pesos left, and I bought you that sack of cashews—?"

"Twenty," says Vera. "We had twenty pesos left."

"Thirty. All right, twenty. That's not the point. That *is* the point. Twenty pesos is nothing, we had nothing. Why hang on to nothing? I don't even like cashews. I just thought they'd make you feel better. And you carried on like I'd traded you to some three-hundred-pound Federale for the worm in his mescal . . ."

"If you were dying of thirst . . . ," Vera wishes she didn't sound like the start of some high-school ethics problem, ". . . and the last Coca Cola on earth cost twenty pesos, twenty pesos would be better than nothing."

"If there was just one can of soda between me and biting the big one, I'd pass on it," says Lowell. "Get it over with. Put this poor boy out of his misery."

"What are we fighting about?" says Vera. "Whether twenty pesos is better than or the same as nothing?"

Lowell laughs, but it's not the kind of laugh that changes anything. "Sweet pea," he says. "I meant what I said. I'm too old to keep going up to the Manson family farm to see if anyone needs a rider to share the driving cross-country."

"What happened to Peter Pan?" says Vera.

"Peter Pan's got crow's feet and a bald spot," he says. "And you don't even notice. You don't see me. All you see is some story you've been telling yourself about me since before we even met. It won't change if I leave. You won't hardly know I'm gone."

This last is unfair. She'll notice he's gone, yes indeed. She's less sure about the rest. But if she's not seeing Lowell, who is she seeing? What story is she telling herself? It's not the world-traveler-can't-find-the-grocery story; she's already given that up. The hillbilly-watching-the-river-flow story? If that were true, Lowell would stay with her, or at least in one place, would never have traveled this far to see her. Meanwhile she's checking his eyes for crow's feet. Wait, they'll get crow's feet together! But that's not possible, and here's one version of the story she can't deny: sometimes two people who love each other can't live together and get along.

Lowell hefts his bag, then sees the look on Vera's face and drops it. "I'll be back in no time," he says. "Aren't I always? I'm not saying it won't happen for us. But there's still a few things we need to work out. Everything'll be different when I sell that screenplay, or even Frankie's book, I won't have to turn in receipts for every soggy cashew. We'll get back together, Rosie'll be a little older, we'll spend all *day* in bed . . ."

Rosie! How can he claim to love her and speak so cavalierly about her getting older? If Vera missed a week of Rosie's growing up, she'd regret those seven days all her life. "Right," she says. "Two little gray heads on the pillow."

"Two sets of false teeth in the glass," says Lowell. Then he pulls her gently into the kitchen, where Rosie is drinking her two-thousand-calorie Baby-Ruth health drink and patting the overstuffed backpack beside her like one of those nervous passengers in bus stations and airport lounges who fear losing contact with their luggage.

Keep calm, Vera thinks. "What's going on?" she says.

"We thought Rosie could come to L.A. with me for the rest of her vacation and be back in time for school," says Lowell.

"*We?*" Vera says.

"Me and Dad," Rosie says.

"That's three weeks!" Vera screams.

"Two," says Rosie. "Two and a half."

"I suppose your Mafioso's paying for this, too."

"No," says Lowell. "Sergio the Mystic."

"She's not going," says Vera.

"Mom, why?"

"Because I said so!" says Vera.

"Mom, be reasonable," Rosie's saying. But how reasonable can you be with your hands over your ears? Vera's chained to the mast as they sing their California siren song. She knows better than to listen. She can't believe or trust them. Why should Rosie come back? It's warm out there, and Rosie hates the cold. It's a state full of vegetarians. Lowell won't make her go to school. They'll camp out on C.D.'s floor, making retro-hippie smalltalk with Mafiosi and mystics and all his Big Youth friends . . .

Vera's stomach hasn't lurched this way since her last trip down with Hazel. If only she'd apologized to Hazel, kept her vow, maybe none of this would be happening. Once again the unlikeliest explanation is the most comforting. The harsher truth is that this is what Vera's been fearing all along, because this—unlike those nightmare visions of Rosie pitched before speeding trains—is waking reality and inevitable. *This* is the natural order. She'd always known Rosie would grow up and leave her someday; she'd thought she was resigned. But not now, not so soon.

"I'm warning you," says Rosie. "I'll run away and go anyway."

"Try it," says Vera.

"Two weeks," says Lowell. "It'll give you a break."

"Thanks," says Vera.

"I won't stay forever, if that's what you're scared of," says Rosie. "I'd miss my room and my Dungeons and Dragons and ballet and Kirsty . . ."

"Terrific," says Vera. "What about me?"

"Of course you, Mom."

"Girls," says Lowell. "Girls. Please. Rosie, hon, leave us alone a second. I need to talk to your Mom." When Rosie leaves, he says, "Look, Rosie and I were talking. I know you two've been having difficulties, bashing horns or whatever the does do when the buck's not around to get pissed at. One day away, she'll start missing you like crazy. That's why she loves me so—I'm not here. You think I don't know that? Two weeks apart will set you guys up for a year."

Vera's already given in. The thought of Rosie and Lowell discussing their difficulties wounds her like the notion of Shaefer cueing Esposito to intervene if she spent too long in his office. She remembers how, when Rosie was little, women in line at the supermarket would say, Oh, if they could only stay that age. She thinks of all the ordinary moments she'd be cuddling Rosie or just watching TV with her and would be overcome with longing to stay in that moment forever. Now she understands that keeping Rosie from going with Lowell is as impossible as that.

"All right," she says. "If you swear—I mean *swear*—you'll send Rosie back before school."

"Cross my heart," says Lowell, then reaches for Vera and presses her against the place he's just crossed. Lowell and Vera stand in the doorway, rocking like dancing bears. It's easy to hug like that when your suitcase is packed: no danger of getting too comfortable. Then it's Rosie's turn, and as she rains tiny kisses on Vera's face, Vera sees that her eyes are wide open. Is she scared that Vera may yet change her mind, or is she—as Vera suspects—just scared? Perhaps she was hoping that Vera would continue to say no. For once Vera controls herself. "Call me when you get there," she says. "Collect." Then they're gone.

Vera picks up the blender jar with what's left of Rosie's breakfast glop in it. How good it would feel to throw it against the wall. But how would it console her to spend the next half hour sponging molasses and granola crumbs off the plaster? It's what would come *after* the crash: a silence so profound it might for one moment seem to stop time, might edge out the silence that's come with Rosie and Lowell's leaving. Vera's footsteps echo as if in an empty apartment. You'd think they'd taken everything, furniture and all.

First things first. Vera concentrates on not running after them. There's still time to catch them, persuade them they're picking the worst time to leave. Now that Vera doesn't have work they can play, take trips like when Rosie was small. Or better yet: she'll go with them! She's getting those three weeks of severance pay, she's got money saved up . . . She can't even convince herself. If they'd wanted her, they'd have asked. She imagines overtaking them by the community garden, pleading her case while Lowell and Rosie read the nametags on the chewed-looking Cut-and-Come-Again zinnias, the stunted Silver Queen corn. She sits down and grips the arms of her chair till she's sure she can't possibly catch them and then wishes with all her heart that she had.

Or does she? Vera no longer trusts herself to know what will help. Dinner with Solomon, Rosie's recital, even seeing Karen Karl—she'd thought those things would make her feel better; they'd only made her feel worse. If she'd run after Rosie and Lowell, she'd probably have been struck by a falling blender jar some other distraught person aimed at the wall and missed.

She knows Rosie's coming back and, eventually, Lowell. So that's not it, not really. It's what they seem to have taken with them: the comfortable myth that their return would ever be anything but temporary, that they'd ever be hers to keep. Their leaving today is just practice. Vera thinks of those women in the supermarkets, wishing their babies had stayed babies—oh, they meant more than that sweet, milky smell, more even than unconditional love. She's imagining a *This Week* story about some scientists—Russian, of course—who've found a way to stop time. That's the story *she* wants to hear! She's no different from and no better than the folks who read *This Week*. She needs those stories, too! She envies them their hopes: centenarian moms, eternal Elvis. All hers seems to be disappearing. The myth of a harmonious, unconventional, and never-boring family life with Rosie and Lowell. The myth of her true career revealing itself the minute she stopped working at *This Week*. Soon she'll have no stories left to get her through days like today.

If she goes on this way, she'll panic. First things first. She pours herself a cup of coffee and tries to remember all the things she used to wish she could do if not for Rosie and her job. Simple things, she seems to recall, places it would be nice to go mid-

week instead of on weekends when everyone else is going there, too. Today she can't think of one. She opens the paper and reads the listings. She'd have her pick of the new movies without waiting in line, but can't in her present state see spending hours in the dark watching giant faces talk about *their* problems. Uncrowded museums? The Met has a new exhibit of eighteenth-century French landscape painting—a period she hates. Who's showing at the Whitney? That guy who paints and erases.

Reading is out of the question. So is thinking, eating, getting out of her chair. Light filters in through the half-shut blinds, casting shadows on the floor; and as one skims past, Vera hallucinates a small, furry, black creature. If she doesn't get out of here soon, the place will be crawling with furry black creatures. Leave, says a voice in her head. Go anywhere. A voice? From where? Sometimes it's hard to distinguish the sound of her own survival instinct from the first harbinger of psychosis.

What to do? If she had a therapist she could ask, the therapist would answer, "What do *you* want to do?" They'd volley that back and forth for a while. She'd settle for an astrologer, for Karen Karl. No, she doesn't need a horoscope; she needs a friend. Maybe she should call Lynda and ask *her* what to do, say: "Lynda, you're right, they're *all* El Creepos." What would Lynda say? Buy a new outfit. Get your hair done. Let him go. You're better off. I told you so. That's life. Vera knows that herself. Louise! She needs to talk to Louise. She dials Louise's number, but no one answers, and that, too, seems like an omen as Vera sits there, listening to the phone ring and considering her limited options.

One: She could stay home and clean the apartment, which, after thirty-six hours of Lowell, sorely needs it. But the obvious danger is that she'll wind up grooming the furry black creatures. Two: She could go up to *This Week* and begin the Herculean task of dismantling her office. In terms of morale, it's probably the worst move she could make. On the other hand, it's the only thing that promises that illusory sense of accomplishment she so desires.

So she hangs up the phone, dresses, and on her way out almost stops at Firbank Florists to tell Dick and Kenny the news. Kenny will understand, but Dick will purse his lips and turn Lowell's leaving into one of life's wry, bittersweet little jokes. Which it's not—it's her *life*. What's really inhibiting her is the fear that halfway through her story Kenny and Dick, needing reassurance that something similar won't happen to them, will reach for one another's hands and unhinge her completely.

She doesn't stop till she gets to the newspaper stand by the station, where she gives the blind man a dollar and asks for a pack of Camels. She waits for her change, he waits for more money; nothing transpires till he says, "Dollar twenty," and she counts out four nickels. When she smoked, she was always shocked by how quickly the price went up. Now it seems like a bargain. Consider heroin. Cocaine.

She rips open the pack, leans against the railing, and lights up. The first one feels like she's filing her lungs with a rasp, the second's down to fine-grained sandpaper, the third smells like burning flesh, the fourth tastes just fine, so she lights up a fifth. By now the two winos loitering nearby are watching her with awe. "Got a smoke?" one says. "Sure," Vera says. "Take two." Then she hurries into the subway and down to the far end of the platform so she won't have an audience when she throws up. Even in this she's a model of delicacy and discretion, leaning gracefully over the tracks to spare the platform maintenance crew any nasty surprises. There's not much in her stomach— smoke, coffee, bile. Mostly what she's disgorging is the kind of self-pity that makes her wish she were Rosie's age, with Mommy and Daddy there to hold her forehead and bring her ginger ale.

By the time the train comes, she's feeling somewhat steadier. When she stumbles on, she finds she must have wandered back up the platform; she's in one of the middle cars. Maybe it's all to the good. If she ran into a screamer today, she'd probably outscream him. At this hour, even the middle's half-empty; plenty of room for Vera to study her fellow passengers. The trouble is, she can't see them, can't hear the train noise, can't feel anything but a vague nausea and pain in her lungs. Perhaps what's numbing her is a massive dose of endorphins: the brain's homegrown. If she were sitting across from Lowell's double or some retarded kid in a hippo sweatshirt, she'd be better off not knowing.

Likewise, in the elevator: she'd rather not know why Hazel's whistling "Stormy Weather" all the way up. Vera's sure it's because she's been fired, but some lurking curiosity about the bounds of her own paranoia makes her ask, "Why so cheery?" Then Hazel tells her how Monday the doctor removed a growth from her breast. "This mornin'," says Hazel, "his seckatary calls up, she says, 'Hazel, girl, you home free!'" A shiver crawls up Vera's spine. She's moved by Hazel's reprieve, which she sees as a sign sent by God to remind her that one can do worse than lose one's job and send one's daughter off for two weeks in California. Immediately she feels guilty for appropriating this major chapter in Hazel's life as an exemplary detail in her own, and then, in some misguided gesture of penance, finds herself thinking that now she can start worrying about lung cancer all over again.

"Who knew he got Labor Day off?" is how Carmen greets her. "Not me, not till last night he lets it slip he's going to Norfolk with his buddies . . ."

Vera doesn't ask why Carmen can't give Frankie some space. She knows being in love makes you want your lover to want to be with you. Even so, Vera's finding it hard to work up her usual sympathy for the continuing saga. Frankie and Carmen were lovers, Oh, Lordy, how they could love. She wants to tell Carmen that Norfolk is much closer than L.A., that Carmen will be seeing Frankie long before Vera sees Lowell. Carmen, be thankful he's going with his buddies and not your only child. Mostly what Vera wants to say is, Forget him. Hold out for someone who'd rather be with *you*. Sure, Vera thinks. Look who's talking.

Maybe what's irking her is the THANK YOU FOR NOT SMOKING sign behind Carmen. Vera reaches into her purse. The crumpled pack is still there, dusting keys and sunglasses with delicious tobacco crumbs. "He'll come around," says Vera, knowing how banal she sounds. Carmen does, too. She looks, if anything, more disconsolate than when Vera walked in.

And suddenly Vera feels as if yet another bolster's been pulled out from under her: the myth of her friendship with Carmen. They're nothing but a lonely hearts' club—if Lowell and Frankie didn't exist, they'd have nothing to talk about. Vera knows this isn't strictly true. She and Carmen talk religion, matters of the spirit. Meaning what? Soul investigations and angelic cafeterias. When Vera leaves *This Week*, they won't see each other again, not unless they happen to meet in line for cotton candy at the circus.

Vera goes into her office. Abandoning all pretense of having come in to straighten up—she doesn't even have boxes to pack things in—she calls Louise and, miraculously, Louise answers. "Awful," Vera says when Louise asks how she is. "Just awful."

"Well, hop on the first plane out here." It's what Louise always says, what Vera counts on her saying. "We'll talk. Eat. Get fat. Two happy fat ladies. That'll cheer you up."

"I wish I could," says Vera. "I wish I had the money . . ."

"God will provide," says Louise. "Especially if you give Him time to pay it off on the MasterCard."

Vera thinks of the severance pay she's supposed to be getting from Shaefer. "Well, maybe . . ." she says. "I don't know . . ."

"No maybe about it. Find some story you can research while you're out here. Then you can write the whole thing off on your taxes. It'll be like Uncle Sam's *paying* you to fly out."

It's why Vera so loves Louise: she can talk God providing in one breath and tax write-offs in the next. "Story for where?" she says. "I've been fired."

"Not for that rag," says Louise. "I mean a *real* story." And this, even more than the need for Louise's company, is what finally convinces Vera. Louise knows her from before *This Week*, remembers a time when she wrote real stories, led a real life.

"I'll call you back," Vera says. "Let me think." What she's thinking is that something about this tax write-off business has sounded a familiar note. And then she remembers: That's what Ray Bramlett suggested in his note inviting her to the crypto-biologists' convention. Vera looks for the letter and it's there, right in the desk drawer where she left it.

Is it possible? Why not? She could write about them, just as she would have when the everyday and the profound drew her so much more strongly than the simply bizarre. Everyone—everyone but the Greens, she reminds herself—loves her crypto-biologist stories, perks up when she tells of retired academics exploring the Congo for dinosaur tracks. What could be more ordinary than a couple named Mr. and Mrs. Carl Poteet or more fantastic than their search for the Mokele-Mbembe? And who could be better qualified to write about it? Five years trek-king after the yeti, trawling Loch Ness in Nessie's wake, seeking Bigfoot in every dream and nearly all her waking hours—it's time Vera put her own peculiar version of job experience to some practical use.

For a moment she falters, thinking it's more of the same: more Sasquatch, more giant squid and Mayan treasure, more false hope. More *This Week*. But really, she knows it's not. These people aren't looking for magic in the magazine racks by the supermarket checkout line. They're going out to seek it. Their myths are still vital to them, intact and so important they'll go almost anywhere to find out if they're true.

Vera looks down at the conference schedule, headed with the cryptobiologists' logo: a rather crudely drawn kangaroo that looks for all the world like a potbellied, biped Basenji. It's a dog, Vera thinks. It's a sign.

VERA LOVES making travel plans. Paradoxically, they anchor her in the present, ground her in the physical world. She thinks of those sixties gurus who used to talk about being here now. Maybe the reason they always seemed so calm was that they were always traveling. Even with a retinue, you don't get far without applying some degree of concentration to some amount of detail. Just having to look at maps and buy tickets and pack keeps you from thinking too abstractly about the future, which is precisely what Vera doesn't want to do.

Travel plans also keep her from facing her terror of travel, a fear she attempts to control by ritualizing every step. She never deals with agencies, only with the airlines and only certain airlines, always takes the earliest morning flight, will only make connections in warm, hospitable-sounding cities—Atlanta, St. Louis—never in cold, forbidding Chicago or Cincinnati. Meanwhile she's vigilant in watching for omens—how long it takes her to get through the airline's busy signals and Muzak, whether a flight's scheduled when she wants to leave. Once, bound for San Francisco, the zipper on her favorite suitcase broke and she nearly canceled her trip. She'd never have met Lowell.

Today things are going well. The airline answers on the first ring and not only has just the flight for her but volunteers the information that, for twenty dollars over the New York–Seattle round trip, she can buy a Super-See-America fare entitling her to fly anywhere in the continental U.S. At first she's annoyed, like when she orders Rosie fries at McDonald's and the cashier asks if she'll be wanting apple pie with that. If she'd wanted to eat apple pie or see America, she'd have said so. Then it occurs to her: It *is* what she wants. New York–Seattle–Phoenix–Flagstaff–Phoenix–New York.

Connections are smoother than Vera can believe, especially when she decides not to ask the size of the plane to Flagstaff. The intervals between flights are just right. The only rough moment comes when the clerk asks, smoking or non-smoking? and Vera gulps and says smoking—an interchange she makes the best of by telling herself that the back of the plane is statistically safer.

So. Vera's leaving tomorrow, spending two nights at Louise's, then on to Flagstaff Friday unless by then the plane's crashed and helicopters are already combing the Mohave for her bones. In that case she wants someone to know she's there, to identify the elbow she chipped falling off a swing, the molar she broke on an olive pit. She dials her parents' number.

"*Where?*" Norma says.

"Seattle," says Vera. "Then the Grand Canyon."

"And what'll you do with Rosie?" asks Norma. "Send her down the canyon on a donkey?"

"Rosie's with Lowell," Vera says. "In L.A." The pause that follows this is so long that Vera says, "Hey, are you okay?"

"Sweetheart," says Norma. "Don't go overboard."

Vera likes the conclusion Norma's jumped to, that Vera's sent Rosie off to her father's so she could cover the cryptobiologists. "Going overboard" implies conscious choice, as if Vera's kicked Lowell and Rosalie off the raft and is thinking of jumping in, too. "Mom," Vera says, "It's not like that."

"What *is* it like?" Norma snaps, then catches herself. "Look, maybe you could take a few minutes, come out here, tell me and your father where things stand, you never know . . ."

Vera knows what "you never know" means. It means that either of them might be dead by the time she comes back. *If* she comes back. Heart attacks, plane crashes in the Mohave—lightning may strike any minute. If she doesn't explain now, when will she? Vera used to hate this fatalism, this fear, so different from whatever spirit must have sent Dave off to Spain. It's only since she's had Rosie that she's understood how it's possible to see the world as the sum of all the disasters that can come between you and your child.

"All right," Vera says. "I'll come out."

But as soon as Vera gets there, she realizes her mistake. She should have waited till dinner. Evening softens the outlines of things. After five, Dave and Norma could be any older couple, relaxing. At two on a weekday afternoon, it's clear they haven't been anywhere, have nowhere to go.

Vera decides to ignore the fact that Dave is watching *General Hospital*. In the kitchen Norma's emptying an apothecary jar of cinammon Red Hots into the garbage. Vera remembers those Red Hots. She used to get them as rewards for doing household chores. The candy's faded, crusty, and white at the edges. Still, Vera's surprised to see them streaming into the trash. What of those Indian children? What would Karl Marx and God have to say?

"How *are* you?" Norma says. Vera wishes she wouldn't stress the "are" like that. Though mostly what Vera's irritated at is herself for having come here. She knows what she's doing: passing her worry along so they can comfort her. She thinks of that girl in the Chinese restaurant telling her date about the guy who believed he could get rid of herpes by giving it to someone else.

Meanwhile, on *General Hospital*, stills of Hong Kong harbor set the stage for Laura, bound and gagged, to squirm and whimper in some TV-studio opium den. Dave's so engrossed he doesn't know Vera's come in.

Vera's relieved when Norma comes up behind them and says, "Look who's here," then worried when Dave doesn't turn, then shocked when Norma strides over and switches off the TV. Dave's gripping the armrests, and Vera can't blame him. Still, she can see Norma's side: imagine if she and Lowell were approaching their golden years, and Lowell seemed likely to spend them watching TV. Imagine that? Imagine anything else. What did Vera think she was moving toward? Two little gray heads in front of the nineteen-inch screen—what more has Lowell ever promised her?

"Well," Dave says at last. "My unemployed daughter."

"That's me," says Vera. "Buddy, can you spare a dime?"

"Don't take it so hard," he says.

"I'm not. That's the least of it." Vera's shocked by the stridency in her voice; she must want her bad news to hurt Dave as much it hurts her. "Rosie's gone to L.A. with Lowell."

"California!" says Norma. "The state's full of nuts. Freeway killers, Zodiac killers, Mansons, Symbionese Liberation. And knowing Lowell, they're probably all his best friends."

"Don't be silly," says Vera. "Lowell's not out to get killed." Though, even as she says this, it's occurring to her that Rosie may right at this moment be with a bona fide Mafioso with God-knows-how-many ex-friends who don't want to see that autobiography written. Better she should ride the subway alone with her Walkman all night. "It's okay," Vera says, as much to herself as to them. "Anyhow, I can use the time. I want to get started on a story."

"Story?" says Dave. "What story?"

Describing the cryptobiologists, Vera's practically giving their resumés, emphasizing the fact that they're mainly retired teachers, engineers. In other words: respectable scientists, not your garden-variety crackpots. Dave and Norma aren't fooled. Their looks of disbelief turn to puzzlement, then back to disbelief and concern. You'd think she was going to look for Bigfoot instead of writing about people who have.

"Way the hell out to Arizona for *that*?" Dave says. "You can get better stories for a subway token."

Vera knows what kind of stories he means: South Bronx squatters banding together to do something about their block. Feisty old union maids organizing their nursing homes. Ex-Wobblies and Lincoln Brigaders still fighting the good fight. The problem is, they're not *her* stories. If she took the subway to find them, she'd only wind up writing about the screamers she met on the way.

She's glad she doesn't say this, doesn't get a chance to. Dave can't wait to get back to his TV. Norma is worrying a cinammon Red Hot between her fingers. Now more than ever, Vera wishes she could get a glass of water from the Greens and that it would really work. She'd bring it to her parents. Here, she'd say. The Spanish Civil War wasn't lost, and Dave came home victorious. Here, she'd say. Live forever in a workers' paradise complete with olive trees and geysers of Spanish red wine. Here, she'd say. Everything's different. I'll never leave you, and Rosie will never leave me. Here. Drink this. Be young.

The film on the New York–Seattle flight stars Clint Eastwood and a monkey. Vera doesn't buy headphones. Watching, not having to listen, lulled by the hum of the engines, the unchanging white-blue sky, she's feeling extremely pleased with herself. She likes how being on her way somewhere gives her a sense of accomplishment without her having to do anything but sit. She also likes feeling cut-off and unreachable, even if her life isn't exactly jammed with people struggling to reach her. Just having gotten this far—having passed through the metal detectors without emptying her pockets, then finding her gate and shuffling forward in an orderly fashion when her flight was called—seems like an achievement.

Only once did she falter: just after take-off, when she noticed how she and the other passengers in her section stared at the No Smoking sign and lit up the second it went off. And why? Because take-off was completed and they were still alive. She'd thought of old cigarette ads on TV, that couple by the waterfall, all joy in life made manifest in smoke. Now everything's changed. Cigarettes are the skull on St. Jerome's desk, coffin nails, twenty memento mori per pack.

She'd checked out her fellow smokers to see how they dealt with this knowledge but couldn't find an inch of common ground. They all looked so pale and prairie-American, long Nordic faces out of Sandburg and Willa Cather. She could be traveling with a planeload of the dead. She'd thought of Mark Rothko, Theodore Roethke, thought, Seattle's where you go to live without seeing the sun for six months and kill yourself. Though she reminded herself she was going there to visit Louise and not to stay, she was starting to get gloomy when the stewardess rolled in the drink cart. Remembering that airplane Bloody Marys never work, she ordered two bourbons and in no time was happily watching Clint Eastwood.

The best thing about drinking on a plane is how slowed-down everything feels as you cruise thirty thousand feet up, flying six hundred miles per hour in the face of every law of nature and of God. Normally, she'd never get through a magazine article on how to tell if your boyfriend's getting tired of you. Up here, she reads every word and even takes the test at the end. Adding the points up seems to take hours, but at the end she's relieved to discover that her and Lowell's score is nowhere near the Red Alert category or even the Danger Zone. They're well in the Smooth Sailing range, and yet they've split up ten times.

Vera would meditate on this all the way to Seattle, but dinner's arriving, and she puts down the magazine to give it her full attention. Given the care she lavishes on finishing every bite—the dense cube of beef, even the soggy bread square beneath it—the voice of the stewardess asking if she's done could be the cries of starving children or the clarion call of the angel who guards your garbage to make sure nothing's thrown out. "I'm done," Vera says. To do any better, she'd have to eat the styrofoam tray. The fact that she's polished off every crumb of the rock-hard amaretto cookies is making her think critically and with a certain drunken self-righteousness of Solomon. She'd thought that chicken-salad incident would shame her all her life, but now it no longer bothers her. People can eat anything. If he couldn't swallow a few strings of celery, the hell with him.

By now the aisle's full—a line for the bathrooms. As Vera gets up and joins in, the light of the bourbon shines even on this. She feels she's taking part in a communal activity, like the members of some African tribe going at dawn to perform their bodily functions at the edge of the sea.

Approaching Seattle, the pilot and the stewardess repeat the local time till it even gets through to Vera. It's three hours earlier than her watch says. She's trying to recall the reason you can't keep traveling from east to west forever and never get any older, but the effort's confusing her. As the plane lands, she's beginning to wish she'd gotten less drunk or that the landing were rougher. There's not even a bump to run the adrenaline that might have helped sober her up. She waits for the rush of joy in having survived, the happiness that used to come when she and Louise would crawl weak-kneed out of the cramped front car of the Cyclone. Instead, depression settles over her, thick and cottony as the gray Seattle sky, as she remembers that the only thing that equals her love of making travel plans and being on her way is the inevitable letdown of getting there.

APPROACHING THE reception area, Vera's afraid to look. She feels as if she's at a horror film, watching the screen through her fingers. All she can think of is the last time Louise met her at an airport, tricked out like some giant white cauliflower in a turban and nursey dress. She's also afraid that Louise won't have come and Vera will start signaling the mute, universal language of the stood-up to perfect strangers, who'll cease their own anxious search for familiar faces and focus on her. Then she sees Louise, so radiant Vera thinks she could find her, like the sun, with her eyes shut.

Vera's first impression is that living among the forests of Douglas fir has rubbed off on her. Tall and straight and dressed in pale browns and greens, Louise looks like a tree. Vera remembers that girl in the Chinese restaurant saying how her first best friend had better not be more successful or perfect. Vera and Louise used to feel that way, first when Louise was publishing poems and Vera was just a college student, then when Vera was publishing articles and Louise was just a towelhead. Now all that's passed. They've realized that the world is wide and generous enough for them both to be successful and perfect and that they will probably never be either.

Lowell's accusing her of not seeing him has made Vera self-conscious. Drunk and excited as she is, she's careful to hold Louise at arm's length and check for crow's feet. She won't make *that* mistake twice. Louise has them, all right, but she's one of those women whose eyes look brighter with wrinkles around them, whose dark hair looks thicker set off by few strands of gray.

"You look beautiful!" cries Louise. Vera says, "So do you," and then, "How could *I* look beautiful? I'm drunk." Louise tucks Vera's arm through hers and steers her off in what Vera hopes is the direction of the baggage claim. On the way, they pass a father holding his son by the shoulders and shaking him. The son, about Rosie's age, is crying; the father's fighting tears. Vera wonders if she should call Lowell from Louise's; she doesn't want Rosie to call home and worry. Let them worry, she thinks. Let them imagine the worst.

"Don't you hate airports?" says Louise, a question that Vera finds cheering. In her high-minded, towelhead, everything-is-everything phase, Louise might have claimed to see the God-head in the flight-insurance vending machines.

"I love hating them," says Vera. "I'm always so proud of myself for not losing my mind in them." Was this a tactless thing to say? Louise doesn't appear to notice.

"I just hate them pure and simple," she says. "I used to have this boyfriend who was obsessed with them. His idea of a date was to take the bus to San Francisco International and hallucinate spies reporting into their candy bars."

"Fun fun fun," says Vera.

"Loads," Louise says. "But the worst part was when I figured out he wasn't really obsessed with airports at all, only pretending because he knew it drove me crazy. Nothing can make you paranoid like someone trying to make you paranoid by acting more paranoid than you are."

Vera's forgotten how much of Louise's conversation consists of war stories, old-boyfriend stories like the ones first dates in Chinese restaurants tell, only weirder. She thinks of the guy who showed up at dawn and announced that a weekend with Louise would drive him insane. Maybe he meant a weekend of hearing stories like that and knowing he'd wind up as one. Another thing he might have meant: Louise's stories pull you into her world. Now Vera's panicking, wondering how many times her luggage might already have glided past without her having noticed. In fact it's Louise who spots it first, grabs it, and won't let Vera carry it to the car.

"We've really come up in the world," Louise says. "You've still got the same suitcase."

"You've still got the same car," says Vera.

"Yes and no," Louise says. "Same color, same year. This is the fourth identical one I've had. The only thing that changes is what's about to go. In this case, the water pump."

Vera can't remember Saabs being so small. Her legs must have got longer, or anyway, stiffer. Two inches less leg room, she'd be chewing on her knees. One thing that hasn't changed is Louise's driving style. She doesn't look back—or forward, for that matter—but only at Vera. Swerving, honking, shaking her fist, she talks constantly, and the only way Vera can quiet her own anxiety is to keep up her end of the conversation.

"Where's Rosie?" Louise asks.

"With Lowell," Vera answers.

A horn blows and Louise gives someone the finger, then turns and stares hard at Vera. "This isn't permanent or anything?"

"No," Vera says. "Anyway, I hope not." She takes out a cigarette and lights it.

"I thought you quit," says Louise.

"I did," says Vera.

"You'll quit again," Louise says, then reaches for a small square of two-by-four on the dashboard and hands it to Vera. "Here," she says. "Knock on this."

"I don't think it's permanent," says Vera, knocking. "Just a two-week vacation on the floor of C.D.'s studio."

"C.D.?" says Louise. "Still?" Meaning, still alive? Still Lowell's friend? It's hard to tell. Once, long ago, Louise lived with C.D. for a year, a very long time for Louise. Now Vera expects her to ask about him, but she doesn't. For all the interest Louise shows, C.D. could be the guy with the airport paranoia or the one who backed out of going away for the weekend.

"Where are we headed?" it occurs to Vera to ask.

"Shopping," Louise says. "There's nothing in the fridge." Moments later, she's cut across two lanes of freeway traffic and, without slowing down, onto the city streets. The sun's broken through, and it's a glorious, clear afternoon, October in New

York except without the edge; the dullest buildings glow. Louise pulls up to the curb and cuts the motor, giving Vera a funny look, as if daring her to point out that it's a No Parking zone. Vera wouldn't dare. She knows Louise isn't just lazy, reluctant to look further for a legal space. Louise believes parking here is a kind of augury. If her luck's running down, she'll get ticketed and towed. If it's in the ascendant, she won't.

It's a parking place, not a sign, Vera thinks. She wants to tell Louise about Kafka and the poodle, but to jump into those waters without testing them first would be to ignore history. You don't tell someone who's spent a year in the loony bin to start seeing every puppy as a possible omen. Especially when, as in this case, there *is* a sign: NO PARKING. But now, watching Louise rush ahead into the market, Vera thinks she could have told her. What seems to be in operation here is the other side of Louise: practical, commonsensical, the side that goes shopping for food.

Smelling and tasting, squeezing and sampling, Louise never looks more beautiful and vibrant than when she's buying food, nor does Vera ever love her so much. Vera wonders if Louise knows that and let her fridge get bare on purpose so they could start off here. It's no accident that Vera's memories of shopping with Louise are of tradesmen slipping free lamb chops and artichokes into Louise's parcels and trying to pick her up; it's why that lettuce diet seemed such a terrible waste.

Vera has to run to keep up with Louise as she tears through the Pike Street Market, past touristy croissant cafés, ersatz Nantucket seafood houses, stalls selling exquisite food. "Welcome to Seattle," says Louise, pulling Vera into a fish shop with a wall of ice like those wall-of-water fountains, and more kinds of salmon than Vera knew existed. Salmon steaks, filets, salmon smoked and pickled, poached and dressed with parsley and lemon, whole fish—seventy pounds of fin and scale and baleful eye.

Meanwhile Louise is stroking the smooth, pink salmon flesh. Don't, thinks Vera, that's somebody's dinner. Once, in an Madison Avenue gourmet shop, she watched Louise dip into a bowl of tortellini salad and pop the fattest pasta ring into her mouth. Vera can't help tensing, bracing herself to hear someone yell, "Hands off!" But nobody ever does. The man coming toward them is smiling. Vera wonders why guys who sell fish are always so sweet and good-looking. Perhaps it's universal: fisher-people all over the world. Now Vera imagines going on an all-fish diet and finding true love among the mussels and tuna and bass.

"Brought in this morning," he says. "This salmon's so fresh it just about walked off the boat."

Vera's staring at him, but what she's thinking about is a Florida walking-catfish story she wrote for *This Week*. FISH EATS DOGGIE'S DINNER, THEN DOG. She's remembering Shaefer saying that walking-catfish stories were growing kind of stale. How about a walking-talking-catfish story? Then he and Esposito began swapping jokes about guys ordering fish in restaurants and the fish starting to talk. They each told two or three. How did they know so many talking-fish jokes? Now, wishing she knew just one, Vera realizes she's still a little drunk and stares at the fish man's smile to anchor herself.

Louise points out four thick steaks. "Three and a half pounds," he reads off the scale. "But I'll only charge you for three." When Vera reaches for her purse, Louise grabs her wrist. "This one's on Uncle Sam," she says, paying with a booklet of food stamps. "I figure he owes us. If this were Japan, we'd be national treasures."

"For what?" says Vera, wondering why Louise has food stamps. She'd thought she was teaching.

"For surviving," says Louise, thanking the fish man with an astonishing smile and taking off at a run. Vera catches up with her at the vegetable stand. Louise roots among the ears of corn, shucking them, stuffing the ones with the smallest, whitest, most even kernels into a bag. "Too bad strawberries aren't in season," she says. "They'd be perfect."

"Strawberries?" says Vera. "I can hardly remember what month it is. Let alone what's in season."

"August." Does Louise think that Vera really doesn't know?

"Corn. And melons." Then she's burrowing in the melon bin, smelling them, tapping them, shaking them near her ear. "Melons always remind me of Lowell," she says.

Vera's so unaccustomed to hearing anyone else say his name, she thinks, Lowell who? She has to remind herself, Louise met him first.

"Remember how he'd talk about the melons in Afghanistan, the shapes, the colors; he'd go on for hours. Fifty, sixty kinds of melons. I used to think he was making it up, except that he knew all the different names in whatever language it was they spoke over there—"

"Pashto," says Vera. "And he *was* making it up, or anyway, the names. He never learned a word of Pashto, except he could say, Go fuck a crazy dog. Jig jig. Jig jig a something something."

"Jig jig," says Louise. "That's right. I remember a story he used to tell, how he was traveling with some French hippie girl to some godforsaken place. This nomad chief kept trying to buy Lowell's girlfriend, and Lowell kept refusing until the chief offered to throw in a dozen of his sweetest prize melons, and Lowell said, Well, maybe he could *rent* her for a while."

Vera remembers him talking about Afghan melons, but not about that. She's pretty sure he made that up, too. As much as Lowell likes melons, he's too much of a romantic to have traded a girlfriend for one. Hearing Louise talk about Lowell makes Vera see him from a new perspective, or maybe from an old perspective she's forgotten. Louise's memories of Lowell verify his existence, just as Lowell's memories verify the fact that Rosie was once a baby. Vera wishes she and Lowell and Louise could all live together. Then Lowell would never have to grocery shop; Louise would insist on doing it.

Now Louise says, "Let's go," but can't tear herself away. Watching her by the baskets of cherry tomatoes is like watching lovers postponing goodbye. Finally she says, "What am I doing? I *grow* this stuff!" and puts the tomatoes down.

Back in the car, Vera shuts her eyes and lets Louise drive. She knows they're leaving the thruway by the click of the turn signal and the fact that they're taking more curves without going any slower. They stop briefly, and Vera looks around. They're at some rural four corners, two gas pumps and a Seven Eleven. Louise tromps on the gas again and says, "Did I write you about Earl? I can't remember."

Vera can't either. She does remember a story about a psychiatrist who fell in love with Louise and then terminated her therapy, but somehow Earl doesn't sound like a therapist's name.

"Maybe not," says Louise. "I met him up in Wallaceville, in a bar. He's the local hippie carpenter, except that now all these rich people are moving out from Seattle and fixing up places, he's making a fortune. He did all the carpentry in my house. For free. He's not real complicated. It's easier. He's really a very nice guy."

"You lucky duck," Vera says. Suddenly Louise begins grimacing horribly, and Vera thinks it's in response to her answer, or to Earl, then realizes she's braking. You'd think a tractor trailer was speeding straight at them, but in fact all that's happening is they've turned off the black top and onto a narrow dirt road. The car bounces. Parts seem to be dropping off the chassis. Eventually Louise slows down enough for Vera to look around; they're driving through a valley. Surrounded by rolling farmland, green hills, stone fences, barns, they could be in the Blue Ridge, the Adirondacks, Vermont with harsher mountains in the distance. At last they turn past a mailbox and into an overgrown driveway that seems longer than the distance from Seattle. As Vera looks back to see if the car's in one piece, Louise says, "You really need a four-wheel-drive on this."

When the driveway dead-ends, Louise puts the Saab in a fancy 360-degree spin. Vera feels as if they should be wearing helmets and overalls and climbing out of the top of the car. Her knees shake slightly as she stands there breathing the cool, fragrant air and looking for the house. Then Louise takes her suitcase and the grocery bags up a small hill toward a rambling, dilapidated chicken coop sided with ragged asphalt and dark, tarry spaces that remind Vera of how she and Louise used to dress up as Mammy Yokum by blacking their teeth with ballpoint.

Years ago, when Louise got released from the hospital, her parents gave her five thousand dollars provided she never went near the towelheads again. Then, surprised and hurt when Louise chose to live so far from anywhere, they took to calling up Vera to share their suspicions that Louise had spent their money on a secret towelhead retreat. If they'd seen this place, thinks Vera, they'd have stopped worrying—at least about that. Not even the most fanatical cult would house its converts in a dump like this.

By now Louise has reached the porch and turned before Vera can assume a properly appreciative expression. She's afraid that Louise may have seen the disappointment on her face.

"Wait," Louise says, meaning, Don't make any judgments yet. "Come inside." And Vera follows her into a gigantic room so beautiful her first thought is: What Earl's built for Louise is nothing less than the counterculture Taj Mahal.

Every beam and board seems to have been specially chosen for richness of color and grain. The ceiling is high, and the sun shining down through the skylights bathes everything in golden light, like an illustration from some art-nouveau British children's classic. One wall is nearly all glass. Those mountains are what Louise sees every night when she washes her dishes! Vera tries not to think about Montague Street, or that girl in the Chinese restaurant. You hope that your friend won't be more successful or perfect or have a better view.

Vera's edging the walls like a blind woman feeling her way. She's pleased by how much of Louise's stuff she recognizes: the Persian miniature of two lovers in a garden, the yarn painting done by Indians on some weird combination of drugs, the Mexican cross studded with silver *milagros*—arms, legs, eyes, farm animals—the postcard of San Ramón Nonato preaching while levitating three feet off the ground. The difference is, every place Louise lived before, you had to excavate these treasures from under mountains of junk. Here everything has its niche.

"Hungry?" says Louise. Her kitchen is in the darkest and coziest corner, its showpiece a huge 1930s wood cookstove gleaming with chrome and sea green enamel. Its round wood table,

Windsor chairs, checked tablecloth, and green glass hanging lamp look like a set from one of those new-style Westerns in which the real star of the film is the art director. Yet it doesn't seem stagy or false country chic, but functional, broken-in.

On the table is a bowl of enormous dark cherries, a loaf of crusty bread, a jar of honey without even a speck of butter in it, and a hunk of crumbly white cheese the size of a shoe box. It's all so lovely, Vera can't imagine doing a vulgar, disruptive thing like eating. But Louise breaks off the heels from both ends of the bread, spraying the table with crumbs, then cuts a slab of cheese and hands it to Vera, saying, "Goat cheese. I remember, you love it."

"You must be getting a truckload of food stamps," says Vera.

"Don't laugh," says Louise. "But I make the cheese myself. I've got goats. And the honey. We keep bees."

"What is this?" says Vera. *"The Mother Earth News?"*

"I knew you'd laugh," Louise says. "Just don't get the wrong idea. Don't think I've turned into one of those New Age survivalists, hurricane lamps run on chicken shit, wiping my butt on pages from an old *Whole Earth Catalogue* hung up in the composting toilet. Or, worse, one of those screaming cancerophobes inspecting every label in the health-food store. It just tastes better this way, and you're right, I *can't* afford it on food stamps. The school pays so little I'm actually eligible for government assistance. Anyway, doing the work to eat like this keeps me in shape so I can keep eating and . . ." Louise breaks off in midsentence. "Earl's here," she says, though it's a good while before Vera hears a truck pull up.

First the door opens, admitting two enormous German Shepherds, Rin Tin Tin on steroids. They sniff Vera's crotch, nearly knocking her down, then run around wagging and barking, doing every territorial thing they can do but piss in the corners. Then Earl comes in, so tall he has to stoop under the doorway he built himself, a posture that makes Vera think of the giant in "Jack and the Beanstalk," especially when Earl announces his arrival by stomping several times on the floor. Vera wonders if maybe Earl isn't a country boy at all but a city kid gone so overboard in country ways he's still stomping snow off his boots in August.

Earl's blond beard and ponytail remind Vera of C.D. ten years ago, except that Earl's much handsomer. He's wearing faded, tight blue jeans and no shirt. Pressed under a round of glass on his belt buckle is what appears to be a dead scorpion. At least Vera thinks it's dead. She'd like to make sure, but is embarrassed to stare at the place where his belt meets his sun-tanned flesh; that part of a man's body's always moved her.

Earl comes up behind Louise, winds his arms around her and kisses the back of her neck. Louise stretches against him like a cat. It's not exactly lascivious, and yet it's clear that what's be-tween Earl and Louise is more than his lack of complication and his fine carpentry skills.

"When'd you get in?" says Earl, and Vera says, "This afternoon."

Fidgeting, Earl lifts the plate on the cookstove and looks down the well as if expecting to see live coals there. Then he sits down at the kitchen table and says to Vera, "Well, now. Welcome. Have a seat." He means nothing but friendliness, Vera knows, but it irks her that he's welcoming her to Louise's home. She's been sitting so long in the plane and the car, she'd really rather keep standing; yet she surprises herself by doing what Earl says. Maybe she just wants a closer look.

Earl's eyes are round and gray and vacant. Knock, knock; nobody home. They hardly even blink. It occurs to Vera that Louise's saying he was uncomplicated was putting it mildly. One thing's for sure: this guy isn't likely to drag Louise to air-ports to watch spies reporting into their candy bars, or to wake up at five A.M. scared to death of her. He's not scared of any-thing. It's his main virtue, thinks Vera. It's his main flaw.

"How was work?" says Louise.

"Okay," says Earl. "I figure another week on the flooring, then I'll get to those kitchen cabinets."

"You just gettin' home from workin' now?" says Vera, ap-palled to hear herself sound like some parody Loretta Lynn. What's happened to her normal voice, and where are her g's?

That's the power of the male, she thinks, the draw of the belt buckle and bare chest.

Earl seems slightly taken aback by her question. Does he think she's implying he skipped out early, or has social life reverted to what it was in California in the sixties, when it was considered such grievous bad taste to ask people what they did?

"Yeah," says Earl.

"Louise told me you built this place," says Vera, a little desperately. "It's beautiful."

"Thanks," says Earl.

"I wish I could do something like this," says Vera, afraid to look at Louise, who would no doubt know she's lying. Vera's never had the slightest interest in carpentry or any other manual skill except cooking and making cat's cradles, though now that she thinks of it, a house does seem like more to show for your time than a stack of yellowing *This Week*s and a peculiar resumé.

"What do you do?" Earl asks.

"Did," says Vera. "I got fired."

"From what?" From the way Earl perks up, you can tell he likes stories about being fired. Most of the ones he knows probably end with brawls. Vera's sorry to disappoint him. But when she mentions *This Week*, he slaps his thigh and says, "Hey, I know that paper. I read it in line at the supermarket. What a piece of junk! Listen, is that stuff true?" Without waiting for Vera to answer, he turns to Louise and says, "Weezy, how come you didn't tell me? Geez, here I am in a room with two beautiful lady writers and me, I can hardly read."

Something about the way Earl says "beautiful lady" reminds her of someone she can't quite place. Then it comes back to her: the Washington Wild Boy. Alarmed, Vera peers at Earl, then sits back, reassured. Earl's nowhere near rooting around in Henry Kissinger's garbage.

"I guess you've read Weezy's poems," he's saying. "She's even had a couple little ones published." Earl's tone is one of heartfelt admiration. Even so, Vera longs to say, A couple little ones? We're talking about the *New Yorker*! But what would Earl know about that? To Earl, New Yorkers are dudes who talk too fast and smoke cigarettes and lead stressful, unhealthy lives. While lady New Yorkers all wear purple Gloria Steinem glasses and talk through their noses and have many abortions and hysterical miscarriages, instead of children like Real Women in the West.

If Vera keeps thinking this way she'll never make it through the evening. She decides to distract herself by thinking of the poem Louise wrote about the nightmares Rosie had after they saw that catatonic gorilla in the zoo. In the poem, the child dreams a gorilla is stalking the mountain behind her home; and in the morning, the child's mother sends her off to school and goes up the mountain to look for the gorilla. How much more heroic than what Vera did, which was to let Rosie get out of bed and watch late-night TV. Now Vera wishes she'd gone back to the zoo or up to Bear Mountain or someplace and hunted gorilla. Is she crazy? There *are* no gorillas on Bear Mountain. It occurs to her now that maybe her version of Rosie's gorilla is Bigfoot. And here she is, right smack in the heart of prime Bigfoot-sighting territory! The thought gives her stepping-out-of-the shower prickles all down her spine and makes her extremely anxious. So when Earl repeats his question, she says, "Yeah, I've seen her little poems," much more sharply than she intended.

Poor Earl. What did he ever do wrong besides welcome her? Earl hears the meanness in that "little." There's a silence; then he says, "Know who I'm working for these days? This dude from New York, this ad man who came out here to shoot some commercials and fell in love with the place and bought some land. Gonna build a place where he can cool out. So he's putting in a landing strip so he can jet in and out and not waste a second. That's how this guy relaxes."

Vera knows that telling this story is as close to hostile as Earl will ever get. He's lumped her with this ad man, her fellow New Yorker. He's advising her to cool out. The disapproval and paranoia with which he says "landing strip" reminds her of how sixties hippies used to talk about CIA maneuvers, secret landings in the desert. At least they knew what to fear. What scares Earl is people moving too fast. In the grave, she wants to tell him, we'll all cool out.

"Wanna beer?" says Earl. It's a conciliatory offer, one that Vera would surely accept if she hadn't just realized two things. One: her high from the plane has finally worn off. And two: one whiff of alcohol will definitely make her sick, and she doesn't even know if Louise has indoor plumbing.

"No, thanks," she says. "I never drink on the job." Louise gives her a quick, searching look in which Vera reads misunderstanding and, Vera imagines, fear that she'll write about this, that she'll expose Louise's life with Earl the way she roasted poor Bunny Sing. Vera wants to throw her arms around Louise and apologize all over again, yet the idea seems no easier or more practicable than whatever similar overtures she'd dreamed of making to Hazel. So all Vera says is, "No, I mean the crypto-biologists. I'm flying out there day after tomorrow and I need to keep clear."

"The crypto-whozees?" says Earl. When Vera explains, he says, "Christ, they should have their convention here. Weezy, did you tell Vera about the Bigfoot scare, when was it, two years back . . . ?"

Finally! An interest in common! Vera's about to tell Earl she just wrote a Bigfoot story, but as soon as she thinks of Bigfoot smoking those cigarettes, it's as if she's on *You Bet Your Life* and a voice in her head has just said the magic word. Here comes that nicotine-craving duck. "Have you got an ashtray?" she says.

"Hey," says Earl. "Could you maybe do that outside? You know, they're finding out you don't have to actually smoke the stuff for it to fuck up your lungs. They x-rayed these waitresses working in diners where everyone smokes; their lungs look like they've been doing a pack a day."

"Is that so?" says Vera.

Louise puts a hand on Earl's arm. "Honey," she says. "You can open a window."

Smoking gives Vera the energy to tell her Bigfoot story. Earl's shaking his hands and going "hoo hoo hoo" like an owl.

He makes her repeat it twice, and by the end he's singing the theme music from *The Twilight Zone*, which Vera would never have guessed he'd be old enough to remember. "Great stuff," he says, sounding *just* like that drugstore clerk complimenting her on her choice of diaphragm jelly.

"Thanks," says Vera, her voice echoing so forlornly through a fog of déjà vu that when Louise suggests a swim in the stream, Vera assumes she understands her old friend's in urgent need of reviving. Still, Vera makes whiny, demurring noises; swimming seems like too much work.

"I'm joking," says Louise. "The stream's seasonal. There's nothing in it now but newts. We'll just take a walk."

Seasonal, Vera thinks, like strawberries, corn, melons. Struck by an image of herself climbing onto her desk to gauge the weather by the thickness of the overcoats crossing Herald Square, Vera agrees to the walk, especially when Earl says he'll stay inside and do in a couple more brews.

There's no way to get from the house to the streambed without knowing what season it is. The grass is waist-high, dry, and brown. Vera walks into something sticky and screams when a huge black-and-yellow spider abandons its broken web. Halfway down the slope is an orchard, branches so heavy with apples they're touching the ground. "Can you eat these?" she says, playing her city-mouse role to the hilt. If she heard Solomon say something like that, she'd want to kill him. She picks one; it's crisp and delicious. "It's paradise here," she says.

"Is it?" says Louise. "I hate August. For all the obvious reasons. Everything's dying or anyway, on the edge."

At last they reach the dry streambed and stand at the edge, staring in as if it were running and they were watching it flow. After a while Vera says, "Have you written any new little poems?"

Louise laughs, then says, "Please. Earl *loves* me," then pauses again. "I'll tell you something," she says. "If I were getting ready to go to a Halloween party dressed as garbage, Earl would lock the door and keep me inside till I came to my senses."

Vera's shocked. It never occurred to her that Louise might

have wanted to be protected from her own wacky sense of humor. At this late date it's finally coming home to her that something more than humor or charm was at issue, that Louise was making a statement she'd rather not have made. She feels she's betrayed Louise, let her down, that Earl's a better friend than she is.

"Anyway," says Louise, "the answer is no. Not one little poem. At least nothing I've finished. I keep trying to write this one poem and can't get it right and can't let it go or go on till I get it."

"About what?" asks Vera.

"Oh, God," says Louise. "Catching fireflies when I was a kid. What could be more sentimental than that?"

Vera thinks of Louise breaking down in the planetarium show, getting stuck on a poem about fireflies. Perhaps she should stay away from tiny points of light.

"I get distracted," says Louise, then kneels down and picks up a dullish-green rock. She spits on it, rubs it, and all at once it's shiny as marble, like malachite veined with white.

"Can I have this?" asks Vera.

"Sure," says Louise. "There's enough for everyone." They start off down the streambed, picking their way over the rocks—boulders when you get up close—a difficult walk made harder because Louise keeps bending down, finding bright-colored stones, some mined with fossils, glittery mica, black and white minerals swirled like a slice of rolled chocolate-and-whipped-cream cake. Vera's pockets are getting heavy. "I can't decide which ones to take," she says. "Maybe I should take all of them."

"Or none of them," says Louise. "Last week in the paper there was a story about a guy who went camping in some Indian ruins in New Mexico. One morning he wakes up and there's this big black crow that seems to be telling him something, so he follows it, and it leads him straight to this perfect, prehistoric stone axe, half-buried in the dirt. So he digs it up, takes it home to Phoenix or wherever, and the day he gets back he breaks out in this ungodly rash that stumps all the doctors. Within two weeks his business falls apart, his girlfriend leaves him—he's beginning to think it's the axe. So he wraps it up in a Baggie—

to defuse it or whatever—and sticks it on a shelf. The next day he's running to answer the phone, the axe falls off the shelf and cuts his Achilles tendon clean through. Finally he goes back to the ruins, puts the axe back where he found it. The story ended with a quote from the park ranger, saying every year they get dozens of packages from folks who've taken souvenirs from the ruins and are returning them because things began to go wrong."

Vera feels as if the stones in her pocket have turned radio-active—that's how fast she dumps them out. She waits to make sure this is as appropriate a moment as it seems, then says, "That doesn't sound strange to me. It's the story of my life. The last week of it, anyhow."

"What do you mean?" says Louise, and Vera tells her. When she gets to the part about going to see Stephanie Green, she says, "Louise, you would've liked her," and is surprised by the desperation in her voice. It's the first time she's ever told it *this* way, as a kind of plea for affection and understanding, the line about Stephanie cast out to catch Louise, who doesn't take the bait but continues drifting further and further away. By the time Vera's describing Betty Anne Apple, Louise is walking a few steps ahead of her, and when at last Vera says, "So what do you think?" Louise answers, "Oh, I don't know. It's probably a coincidence."

"Are you serious?" Vera says and grabs Louise and turns her around. Louise stares at Vera; she looks awful. The silence goes on till *someone* has to break it. Vera can only repeat herself. "What do you think?"

"What do I think?" says Louise. "I think I'm taking fifteen milligrams of Stelazine a day so I won't *have* to think about this shit."

"Lucky you," says Vera. Once more she's wishing she could start over. This time she'll tell Louise what's *really* bothering her: the voice on the phone at the Greens', Rosie and Lowell leaving, the growing sense that her life—that anyone's life—will never be anything but one loss after another. But how can she complain to Louise about losing what Louise has never had? And if she mentions her fear of having to give up all the stories she's told herself for comfort, it may occur to them both that the story of their friendship is one of them.

"Luck's got nothing to do with it," says Louise. "It's survival. I just don't let myself think about things that'll make me suffer."

Maybe Louise is right, thinks Vera. *She'd* certainly be better off if she weren't always imagining all the terrible things that could happen to Rosie. The problem is, she's not made that way. If she were an alchemist, her heart would be beating in rhythm: Hippopotamus! Hippopotamus!

"I'm sorry," Vera says. But for what? It's not the first time she's apologized when really she's been angry. Vera feels she's been led on. She can understand how someone with Louise's history might want to steer clear of the spooky stuff, but it was Louise who told that story about the axe. Still, Vera understands that reading a creepy story in the paper is good deal less threatening than hearing one from your oldest friend. Mostly what she's angry at is time and all that's happened since she and Louise started out. When you haven't seen one another in years, you can pretend everything's the same as when you were growing up together. But it isn't; it just isn't. What *Vera* doesn't want to think about it this: Having a friend for the first half of your life is no guarantee you'll have her for the second. Marriages break up after longer.

"Why should you be sorry?" says Louise. "It's your life. You just picked the wrong person to tell it to. I can't let myself dwell on that stuff. I tend to get sucked in. That's all. "

By now it's unthinkable to ask the one thing Vera's really curious about, namely, which part is it that Louise can't let herself dwell on? The possibility of healing by faith, or the pain that would drive someone to call up the Greens and beg for a drop of water? The synchronous and inexplicable, or the axe that leaps off the shelf and slices away at your heel? Vera thinks of Peter Smalley and his HERE WE WILL TALK OF NOTHING BUT GOD sign. If he honestly felt that way, he wouldn't be able to function at *This Week*. He'd be out here in the wilderness, spitting on rocks with Louise. Here we will *never* talk about God.

Louise begins walking again, and Vera does, too, not because she wants to but because stopping would make Louise turn round, and she's not ready to look at her yet. Eventually the streambed turns into the woods. It's cooler here; the light changes, grows dappled. They're going faster now. Light flashes through the spaces between the firs, striping everything with bands of darkness and sun. The effect is rather strobelike, dizzying. Vera's starting to feel light-headed.

Suddenly Vera stops. She's seen something out of the corner of her eye, something denser than shadow shifting between the trees. A deer. No, bigger. A bear? What lives in these woods?

Bigfoot, she thinks.

So this is what it's all been leading up to: the ultimate coincidence. Oh, it's perfect. Not only is this Bigfoot's home ground, he's been sighted in this very county! If he's anywhere, he's here. If he shows himself to anyone, who better than someone who's dreamed of him for years and clearly intends him no harm? Wouldn't that be news to take to the cryptobiologists? "Bigfoot!" Vera longs to cry, "come back! I've got cigarettes! You don't have to cook breakfast or take me to your lair. Just show yourself!" But that would only alarm Louise and waste all that good medication she's taking.

Vera's starting to feel desolate. In her fantasies of meeting Bigfoot, she's always with the people she loves most. And now they're all scattered, unreachable, and she's alone with poor Louise, who so wants those antipsychotic drugs to work, she probably wouldn't see Bigfoot if he tripped and fell on the path and she had to climb over him.

A breeze has come up, and the treetops are singing that high-pitched whoosh she used to hear on acid and think was the music of the spheres and later found out was just chemical. Or was it? Once more Vera feels something. A presence. Her knees go weak. Suppose it is Bigfoot out there, and he isn't the friendly, cigarette-smoking primate of her dreams but a monster with the razor teeth and claws and disposition of a killer grizzly. Feet the size of bathtubs, paws the size of rakes . . . Vera covers her eyes.

Where the hell is Louise? Vera can't see her anywhere. Riding the Cyclone, the front car of the subway, they were in it together. Now she's skipped out, leaving Vera to perish alone in the wilderness. Once nothing scared Vera, but out here she's frightened of everything, including the possibility that she may be lost. How she longs for Lowell and his trusty sense of direction! "Louise," Vera cries, but softly: the meow of a cat in a box. Not loud enough to reach anyone, not even Bigfoot with his heightened senses. Because the truth, after all, is: Vera doesn't *want* to see Bigfoot. She's frightened half to death, embarrassed, too. There's not even a headline for this. FEAR OF BIGFOOT?

Vera's never so terrified she can't rationalize. Even in this, consolation: If Bigfoot mauls her—fatally—she'll at least be spared the pain of living with the knowledge that this, too, was nothing like what she'd imagined. Standing here shaking and sweating is no more her Bigfoot fantasy than writing for *This Week* was her fantasy career. Besides, she was just playing with that dream of meeting Bigfoot and learning a better way to live. Couldn't God tell she was kidding? Vera's always hated people who say, You'd better watch what you wish for; you might get it. Now it's clear that her hatred was just the resentment she often feels when people tell her the truth.

Then a branch snaps behind her, and Vera's heart's pounding so fast she can't think. She's running now, stumbling, pushing ahead on wave after wave of pure instinct, adrenaline, and dread. She's crying a little, breathing hard. Now she *knows* something's after her. "Louise!" she screams. "Louise!"

And finally breaks through. The woods thin; she can see where they end. Vera finds herself in a broad, open meadow where her first thought is: this isn't Bigfoot's kind of place at all. No cover, no protection. She's still scared to look behind her, but forces herself: no one's watching from the woods. The only living thing in sight is Louise, who's stopped ahead, waiting.

Vera can't tell her what happened to her in the forest. Nothing happened to her in the forest. What she *wants* to say is, "Let's go home." A piercing rush of homesickness and discomfort has Vera counting the hours till she can leave, remembering the first time she ever slept at a friend's house and stayed awake hearing a grandfather clock chime the hours, pining for Dave and Norma and her own bed. That was Louise's house, too.

"I'm tired," she tells Louise now, meaning she can't possibly trek back through the woods. They'll just have to call in the Red Cross helicopter and airlift her out of here.

"We're almost home," Louise says, and Vera sees they've come full circle. This meadow is the view from Louise's window.

"I hope Earl's started the fire," Louise murmurs absent-mindedly. "There's grilled salmon and barbecued corn and salad from the garden."

AFTER A DAY and a half at Louise's, Vera feels like one of Shaefer's monkey statues: see no, hear no, speak no anything at all. She's pretended not to hear Louise and Earl waiting till they thought she was asleep at the other end of the cabin, then making love, not to hear Earl come in at three the next morning, or their rasping, angry whispers till dawn. In between Vera followed Louise as she cooked, milked the goats, and weeded the garden. Here we will talk about nothing but food. Their best time was picking blackberries side by side with the afternoon sun shining on the clusters of reddish-black fruit. Their fingers and lips got purple; the thorns didn't scratch hard enough to hurt.

What does hurt is the relief they both feel when they're back in the car and on their way to the airport. They're silent for most of the ride. When Louise asks if Vera wants her to wait for the plane, Vera says, "No, airport parking's always so difficult." Vera knows she'll always love Louise, but how often can you jet clear across country to talk about goat cheese? Something's gone wrong. But what? And how to fix it? Will bringing it up be misconstrued as an attack on Louise's life? And what if one of them says it: It's not their friendship at risk so much as the *story* of their friendship. That's all they've had for years, anyhow. But Vera can't afford to lose any more stories. She's bordering on panic again. The only thing keeping her from banging her head on the dashboard and howling is all that practice she's had in pretending not to know what's happening. By the time they've kissed and sworn to write, Vera's so desensitized she can't hear the interior voice that ordinarily starts telling midair-collision stories the minute she thinks about taking a plane.

It's a kind of anesthesia that seems to last all day. Changing planes in Phoenix, she can pretend that the ten-seat tin can flying her to Flagstaff is a perfectly sane form of transportation, though the lack of a cockpit or even a curtain dividing pilot from passengers makes it harder to ignore the fact that the pilot's drinking beer. Surely this must be against FAA regulations, even in Arizona. Vera focuses on the pilot's cowboy hat; beneath it, the nape of his neck looks wobbly and vulnerable, like a baby's.

At the Flagstaff airport, Vera's directed to the "stagecoach" stop for the Ghost Circle Lodge, a shed built of that imitation knotty pine one finds in restaurants with names life Beefburger Barn. Inside is a bench made of upended wooden kegs. Vera's expecting a haywagon or stake-sided pickup, but the van that pulls up is sleek and black, with windows tinted so dark you can hardly see in or out. The interior is carpeted, furnished with swivel easy chairs like a fifties nightclub on wheels. She's the only passenger. It does feel luxurious, having the whole thing to herself; on the other hand, there's no one to reassure her that the lettering on the side is for real, that the Indian kid in the Van Halen T-shirt who's driving will take her anywhere *near* the Ghost Circle Lodge. The opaque windows don't help, either. She has to press her face to the glass to see out, and then all she sees is blacktop, pine forests on both sides.

At last the stagecoach stops, and Vera gets out. In front of her is a sprawling fortress of rough cut stone and timber, and beyond that the Grand Canyon. Vera can't possibly deal with both sights at once. She tells the driver, Thank you, yes, he can take her suitcase inside, then walks around the hotel and up to the edge of the canyon.

It's beautiful, no doubt about it. And yet it's not what she'd hoped. The first disappointment is that she can't perceive it as a canyon, but only as some kind of sunken mountain range. She'd thought canyon meant something simpler: down on one side, up on the other. But this goes down and up and up and down again forever. The second is, it looks like every *Arizona Highways* cover she's ever seen. She knows how banal it is, this inability to perceive extraordinary natural beauty as anything more than a picture postcard. But would it be any less trite to have the wind knocked out of her by this testament to the majesty of nature and the grandeur of God? The depressing thought occurs to her that extraordinary natural beauty is in itself banal.

She'd rather be anywhere than here. Anywhere, that is, but here or inside the lodge. It takes her a moment to understand her reluctance: The canyon's a place of pilgrimage, like Lourdes or the Greens' house in Brooklyn. Everyone's come for one reason. And Vera feels as if she's been and come back, still with her wheelchair and crutches. Perhaps all the Ghost Circle Lodge's guests think and talk only of natural wonders, their hearts and spirits enlarged—if only temporarily—to Grand Canyon scale. Vera's heart's turned to stone.

What finally drives her inside is curiosity to see if her luggage still exists and the possibility that somewhere in that cavernous John Ford set is someone whose idea of a natural wonder is the abominable snowman. For this kindred soul—this convention of kindred souls—the whole canyon might be a movie set: background, that's all.

But the lobby of the Ghost Circle Lodge won't let you mistake it for a movie set, nor for one of those Johnny-come-lately Jackson Hole tourist traps tarted up like Miss Kitty's saloon in *Gunsmoke*. What's on display here is a century of western elegance, tradition, hospitality, respectful coexistence with the Indians and especially with their rugs, polished woodwork, copper hurricane lamps, oil paintings of Our Founder, and everywhere the most magnificent taxidermy: trophies of such venerable antiquity that only Our Founder himself could have shot them. And not just moose and deer but bison, antelope, elk, a giant javelina. Vera wishes these stuffed heads well; she hopes they last forever. Should these species become extinct, here's hard evidence for future crypto-biologists that the buffalo and wild boar weren't just creatures of fantasy but really did exist.

The discreet letterboard by the registration desk, WELCOME CRYPTOBIOLOGISTS, would certainly make it easy to register as one. Vera wouldn't have to say anything, just point. If she's going to write about this, though, it's better to snoop around anonymously. Being recognized as a reporter—even a former reporter—from *This Week* will throw everything out of whack. Besides, the desk clerk is one of those stern, disapproving women with tiny mouths who always intimidate Vera. Declaring as a cryptobiologist—or even their invited guest—would be like telling her you'd come to a Hare Krishna convocation or a meeting of Cocaine Abusers Anonymous.

The elderly couple ahead of Vera are wearing so much turquoise it's a miracle they can move. Perhaps the weight of his rings is what's making the old man fill out the forms so slowly. The desk clerk watches them clank off, then says, "It's like a sickness. An addiction. They can't get through a day without another turquoise fix." Though Vera mostly shares this opinion of turquoise jewelry, she can't tell if what's being criticized is the object of passion or passion itself. What would this woman say if Vera told her that her current passion is people who hope passionately that dinosaurs are alive and well in the Congo?

Vera registers in no time, the desk clerk smacks her hand on the bell, and everyone's hustling, the bellboy leading Vera at a brisk trot through the lobby and down miles of corridor to her room. The bellboy has a sweet face, a high, domed forehead, a turquoise stud in one ear. He goes to her window, waits till she's watching, then pulls the curtain, revealing her own private view of the canyon. It's a bravura performance, but Vera's a lousy audience. From here the canyon no longer looks quite so post-cardlike and insipid; as a matter of fact, it scares her. She's frightened by that ragged hole in the earth, by that limitless space, by her sense that the bellboy's let all that emptiness into the room with her; and her heart starts to pound as it did in the woods when she thought she saw Bigfoot. "That's okay," she says, "you can leave those shut."

The bellboy can't believe she means it. The accusing, suspicious look he gives her is what she's been expecting since she walked into the hotel. She feels like a double agent who's just given herself away, thinks with great sympathy that this is how that poor letter writer receiving KGB broadcasts in West Myra, Illinois must feel every day of her life. The dollar she gives the bellboy feels less like a tip than like hush money. Bribing the bellboy to keep quiet about her not liking the Grand Canyon—if that isn't Kafkaesque, what is?

All during dinner, Vera's been trying to pick out the crypto-biologists. It's almost erotic, as if she's come here to meet a blind date or secret lover, secret even to her. The only one she's sure of is a man she dubs Big Bwana: pith helmet, khakis, beard. Her next bets are some associate-professor-of-engineering types, each with a wife and three kids, short sleeves, and terribly naked-looking, pale, freckled arms, all surprised by middle age in the long youth of fifties suburban husbands.

But as Vera and her fellow conventioneers assemble in the Saguaro Room for Ray Bramlett's keynote address, she sees she was wrong. Big Bwana isn't here, and though the associate professors are, they're indistinguishable without their families; Vera can't tell if these are the same ones she saw. Indeed, the most striking thing about the cryptobiologists is their ordinariness. Old ladies in beauty-shop curls and lime polyester pantsuits. Slightly artier ones in graying pony tails, folksy skirts, and sneakers. Pasty young men of the kind no one noticed until Son of Sam put them briefly on the map. Middle-aged husbands and wives who could pass for fraternal twins; outdoorsy young couples with the sunburned, shiny faces of cultists. Turquoise, squash blossoms, bola ties, but in more restrained quantities than on those seniors in the lobby. On the way to the Saguaro Room, Vera mistakenly entered a meeting of some self-improvement group called Dare to Be Terrific. What strikes her now is that the two constituencies look almost identical.

After all those sweeping vistas, it's a relief that the Saguaro Room has no windows. Walls of gold-veined mirror remind Vera of her grandmother's house. Light comes from under the mirrors and from thousands of pinholes in the ceiling that, if you squint, suggest a planetarium, only dingier. It's a good thing Louise isn't here.

Filtering out the general buzz, Vera tunes in on the women

behind her, listening for *their* Bigfoot stories. But, like conventioneers everywhere, they're complaining about the food: how their noodles Florentine tasted funny, and how the maître d' said that many eastern visitors remark on this, but it's just the different water, different minerals; nothing they can do. Minerals, water—that shut the old ladies up; it must have seemed like sacrilege to sit perched like eagles above nature's greatest glory and dump on the minerals and water. Now they're blaming themselves for ordering butter and cheese when all a body needs for lunch is a bit of rye toast and tomato. All this talk of simple food lulls Vera into thinking of Carmen and her radishes, so it's not till the ladies stop in midsentence that Vera notices the man who's stepped up to the podium and is waiting politely for silence.

"Good evening," he says. "And welcome. I'm Ray Bramlett."

Sixtyish, with a neat, graying moustache and what looks like all his hair, Ray Bramlett evokes David Niven playing gentleman cowboy. He's wearing a string necktie, a western shirt, and over it, a boxy Navajo vest, handwoven in the palest golds and grays. Vera thinks of the Indian kid in the Van Halen T-shirt. It's as if the white man and the Indian have swapped clothes, and the clothes the Indians got are worth about as much as the land they wound up with in their dealings with the Great White Father.

"Before we begin," says Ray, "a few announcements." There's a slow, down-home gentleness in the way Ray Bramlett rolls each syllable around in his mouth. It's impossible to imagine him yelling or getting angry. At the same time it's very easy to picture him driving a wife or a child or a classroom full of students completely out of their minds with the thoughtfulness and deliberation behind every word.

"Then I'll say a bit about who we are and why we're here. I promise not to take too long, since the one thing I *know* you haven't come for is to hear me ramble on." Ray pauses for the obligatory murmur of laughter. Vera always wonders who the people are who can be counted on to chuckle at such moments, to make those sounds that have so little to do with real laughter. If Vera tried to laugh now, she'd probably bray like a mule.

"First, I'm sorry to say that Professor Dorothy Chasteen won't be with us to talk on the sea-serpent myths." Ray waits for the clucks of disappointment that finally come, as authentic as the laughter. "But I'm sure you'll be happy to hear that Dr. Chasteen's just completed a major project—the birth of her first child." Bramlett's really working the crowd now—more laughter and even a smattering of applause. "And I'd like to remind you that tomorrow, in the Mimosa Room at eight, we'll have the special event we've been waiting for when Mr. and Mrs. Carl Poteet present the first public showing of their history-making slides and tapes."

Vera can tell how history-making these slides and tapes must be: this time the applause comes spontaneously, without Ray having to work for it.

"And now on behalf of myself and my colleagues on the board, I'd like to welcome you to the Ninth Annual Convocation of the American Cryptobiological Society. I realize that most of you are familiar with our origins, but let me beg your indulgence while I say a few sentences for the benefit of our new members, who, I'm pleased to say, are more numerous than ever before."

Vera's pleased, too. There's no way of telling what numerous means, but it does seem to promise she won't be singled out as the only new face. Meanwhile Ray steps on the gas and goes into high academic gear:

"Two hundred years ago, three hundred residents of the French town of Julliac saw a shower of stones fall from the sky. Naturally, no one believed them. There were accusations of mass hysteria, cartoons in every paper from Paris to Marseilles adding Julliac to that roster of mythical towns breeding only imbeciles and gullible fools. Luckily for Julliac and for science, just ten years later three thousand stones fell on the town of L'Aigle, nearer Paris and including among its residents a member of the Institute, who brought one of the rocks in for analysis. At which point it was found to be structurally different from any known geological specimen. And science had its first meteorite.

"The tragic thing is that science has yet to learn the lessons of Julliac. Let's suppose that, one summer morning, the Lake

Champlain monster—Champy, to us—emerges from the water and tours the backyards of Burlington, Vermont. Whole families spot it from their breakfast-nook windows. And who believes them? No one except the lunatic-fringe press. Besides, the witnesses will soon convince themselves it was a trick played by light or by their imaginations or hangovers, whichever the case may be."

Though the audience chortles knowingly, Vera senses it's hardly a hangover crowd. She's smarting from that reference to the lunatic-fringe press. Even so, she wants to get up and testify: this narrative of anomaly and disbelief is the story of her recent life! Perhaps she should move to Julliac, her true spiritual home.

"And so," Ray Bramlett continues, "the American Cryptobiological Society was formed to make sure that an incident like the meteor shower at Julliac will never again be dismissed without a full scientific investigation.

"As most of you know, the gorilla wasn't formally identified until 1847. The pygmy hippopotamus was not officially collected until 1913. Until those dates, sightings of these creatures were ridiculed as crackpotism, much like contemporary reports of Sasquatch and the yeti. But we must keep open the possibility that these unexpected creatures may one day join the list now headed by the pygmy hippo and the gorilla.

"This word, *unexpected*, is critical. For the life forms we cryptobiologists study are neither 'extinct' nor 'legendary' nor 'unknown.' The extinct is for the biohistorian, the legendary for the ethnographer, the unknown for the science-fiction writer. *We* devote ourselves to the study of creatures that one would not *expect* at the times or in the places where they have nevertheless been reported to exist."

Vera's charmed by the notion of all these people gathered in pursuit of the unexpected. And yet it seems slightly disingenuous to call these creatures unexpected. The scientist combing Nepal for the yeti is on some level expecting—certainly hoping—to see one. And for all the shock of that moment when she imagined meeting Bigfoot at Louise's, Vera knows that some part of her was expecting to see him every moment she was there.

"And now," Ray Bramlett's saying, "it's a great pleasure to introduce a man we *have* come to expect, to *rely* on for the latest Sasquatch research. Professor Gerald Davis."

While the crowd applauds Professor Davis, Vera registers the obvious irony that here to address a society devoted to the unexpected is a walking cliché, exactly how you'd picture a northwoods anthropologist and Bigfoot researcher: a windburned Paul Bunyan in full beard, jeans, lumber jacket, hiking boots. Not for him the lectern, the timid, rustling paper of the prepared speech. With one broad sweep, he yanks down the screen behind him and yells, "Lights!"

The lights dim; a projector starts to whir. Numbers count down and up comes the flickering, badly lit face of an old geezer. With his whiskers, rheumy eyes, and lumpy alcoholic nose, he's the genuine article that early TV cleaned up and packaged as Gabby Hayes. From offscreen, Professor Davis asks with exaggerated politeness, Would the geezer care to tell us his name? It takes the old man so long to retrieve this information from his memory cells, the audience grows restive. "Billy Fred Dowdy," he says. "I'm a prospector. Retired. Worked seventy years in them hills round Mount St. Helens. One what finally blew."

"And what is your connection with the Bigfoot story?" asks the offscreen voice.

"Don't rightly have none," says Billy Fred. " 'Ceptin' for a joke me and my uncle played, must be sixty years back. Up in Paydirt Canyon." The frame stops halfway down Billy Fred's chest. He's wearing a plaid jacket not unlike Gerald Davis's. His shoulder's twitching as if he's scratching something off camera. "One morning me and my uncle seen these loggers come up the canyon with horses and wagons and enough axes to chop down half of Washington. Well, we'd kinda got to feel like it was our woods. So we figured we'd play a little joke on them peckerwoods. Let 'em find someplace else to cut.

"We had these blankets, see, big, hairy, black ones. And—this was my uncle's idea—we wrapped up in 'em and climbed the ridge and began whoopin' and hollerin' and thumpin' our chests. The loggers just stood there starin'. So we picked up some rocks and rolled 'em into the canyon. That got 'em movin'." The camera pulls back to show Billy Fred rubbing his knees and laughing, a death-rattle emphysema wheeze.

"And then?" says the professor.

"The next week my uncle goes into Marionville for some grub and picks up the paper, and sure enough, there 'tis 'bout these two Bigfoots tossin' boulders at these loggers. Me and my uncle like to bust a gut. We figured, Shoot, if they're goin' to flap their lips, we'll give 'em somethin' to flap about. So we carved these two feets out of pine, like this—" Billy Fred spreads his arms wide. "And we went around makin' prints in the dirt. 'Ceptin' it backfired. Next thing we knew, them woods was crawlin' with guys in monkey suits with tape measures, makin' plaster castings. Oh, we had to laugh," says Billy Fred, opening his mouth so wide that strands of saliva form a kind of cat's cradle between his five or six teeth.

"And now you've decided to come forward?" Is there something slightly accusatory in that offscreen voice? Can't the professor take a joke? "May I ask why?"

"Well," says Billy Fred, "I'm gettin' ready to meet my Maker, and I don't want to get to those pearly gates and hear St. Peter say, 'Billy Fred, what about that time you tricked those folks into thinkin' you was Bigfoot? All those lies you tell, all those little stories you make up . . . they come around.'"

Amen, thinks Vera, wondering if Billy Fred ever feared that one day he'd be panning in some stream and he'd look up and there would be two real Bigfoots hurling rocks at him. Listen, she wants to tell him. It can happen.

"Let there be light!" cries Gerald Davis. Looking around, Vera finds she's not the only one who looks melancholy—and with good reason. They've been promised the latest Sasquatch news, perhaps another sighting. Instead, one's been taken away.

Davis presses both palms against the podium and leans forward. "Science begins with hunches," he says. "And from the day I began collecting Bigfoot data, I've had a hunch that the Paydirt Canyon sighting was a hoax. Because this scenario—two

Bigfoots throwing stones—is at odds with every piece of evidence we have. Sasquatch never appear in groups. There is not one reported incident of Bigfoot attacking man.

"It is my view that Billy Fred Dowdy's confession is a tremendous gain, confirming what we've long suspected. For among the things we know best about Bigfoot are the things he does not do. Bigfoot does not talk. He does not use fire. No Bigfoot dwelling has ever been found. He is not a dangerous animal."

He does not smoke cigarettes, thinks Vera. He does not cook trout-and-watercress breakfasts. He does not pick children up so they won't fall in his footprints. As Gerald Davis drones on, she's getting steadily more depressed. There's certainly no place for her Bigfoot fantasy in the official canon. How could Bigfoot take her and her loved ones to his rag-and-branch palace if he doesn't have a dwelling? Anyway, who's she kidding? *Her* Bigfoot story is what happened at Louise's: if Bigfoot approached her, she'd run.

By the time his lecture's done, Vera's convinced: if Gerald Davis has a Bigfoot fantasy, it's of trapping Bigfoot in a net like King Kong, degrading him from the uncrowned king of the forest to a specimen to be poked and prodded and written up. Vera stays for the first questions and answers, long enough to watch Davis focus on the prettiest of the scrubbed, outdoorsy girls, addressing all his remarks to her till her boyfriend grows visibly uncomfortable. Then Vera leaves, lighting up as she does. In fact she craves fresh air, but can't make herself go out. Even facing the other way in the dark, she'd know the canyon was there.

So she paces the lobby, moving from trophy to trophy as if at a museum. How *real* they seem, even in death. This buffalo was never an old geezer in a fur blanket. Vera wants to lay her cheek beside the javelina's bristles, nuzzle her forhead against the elk's leathery nose. The prickle of their pelts on her skin would be enough for her, all the unexpectedness she'd ever need.

. . .

The next morning, it takes Vera an alarmingly long time to figure out where she is. What she finally decides is that she's in a fugue state. She used to like the sound of it: fugue state, like Bach's D Minor Toccata played in your head. Now she sees it isn't very romantic or, for that matter, comfortable, but rather like some analgesic that doesn't work, like the drug they gave her in labor that didn't diminish the pain, only her ability to transcend it.

Once she knows where she is, she need only figure out what's wrong. And gradually it comes to her: everything. In one week she's lost her job, her daughter, her husband, her friend, her buffers against pain and loss. All her consolations have turned out to be lies, all her hopes—including the crazy idea that she could write something profound about these cryptobiologists—delusions. There's no story in a geezer confessing to a sixty-year-old prank. The only publication that would print that is *This Week*.

She imagines running away, going back to her apartment. And what then? She thinks, WOMAN SITS IN SAME CHAIR THIRTY YEARS. Yet even now the voice of Vera's better judgment's coming through, reminding her of what choices she has left. One: she can lie here forever. Two: she can get up and get dressed and get coffee and go hear "Two Views of Nessie."

The Laguna Room is dark except for the glow from the screen on which Professor Glengarrie traces a graph plotting water depth against available light. Vera has to infer some reference to Loch Ness, because Glengarrie's lilting Scottish accent sounds to her unschooled ear like glunk glunk glunk, bubbles surfacing in the loch. Occasional words come through. "Plankton" she hears. "Metabolism." "Kilogram." Perhaps he's used to Americans not understanding; his charts tell the whole story. Nothing could winter over in the depths of that dark, cold lake.

Maybe it's not his accent but the bad news that makes him humble. Because when the lights come up and a man in the second row asks if Glengarrie would please address the question of a possible winter migration, his answer couldn't be clearer. "Of course it's possible," he says. "And let me repeat, my purpose here is not to deny Nessie's existence, but only to show how unlikely it is for a species to winter in Loch Ness." This brings down the house. That "possible" is the magic word, much as "terrific" must be for those self-improvers next door, and saying it has squared Glengarrie with the party line on unexpectedness. Despite Vera's touchy insistence on the noncrackpot nature of cryptobiology, she'd come expecting something a bit less . . . detached. She'd imagined believers with strong investments in the actuality of these unlikely creatures, but all that matters here is the scientific process: research and debate. If one of them captured Bigfoot, they'd be gratified: a feather in their L.L. Bean caps. If one of them disproved his existence conclusively, that would be almost as good. It's essential to their sense of themselves as scientists: objective, unbiased, clear. But what it proves to Vera is the essential triviality of their pursuits. If this were a convention of cancer researchers, someone would *care*.

During the break between lectures, Vera plays Dan Esposito on vacation. Pretending the coffee machine is some middle-American campground lake, Vera stares into it, sipping her coffee and eavesdropping. By now all she really expects to hear about is breakfast. But in fact what the two donnish fellows beside her are discussing is the sex life of Mona Miller, whose second view of Nessie is scheduled to begin any minute.

The tone of their exchange reminds Vera of the gossipy dowager elephants in *Dumbo*. Lips pursed so tight it's a wonder words can squeeze through, one's explaining how Mona Miller's been married five times, each time to an academic who was married to someone else when she met him at a scientific convention and who subsequently left her for another professor or student.

"Well!" says his friend. "Live by the sword, die by the sword. I wonder who'll get lucky this time."

"Hard cheese, old chap," says the first. "She's engaged again, I hear. Some microbiologist from UCLA she met at the AAAS meeting."

Such snickering is hardly what Vera longs to hear, but when the lecture begins, she's thankful for this insight into Mona Miller. For one thing, it makes her instantly sympathetic toward someone she might otherwise instantly hate. Vera's first impression of Mona Miller is that she's Alfred Hitchcock's type: Grace Kelly, or the person James Stewart was trying to dress Kim Novak up as in *Vertigo*. Her pale linen suit is loose-fitting and smooth, her hair blond and thick like a very expensive doll's, her thin shoulders tense and carried so high, her little hoop earrings could be epaulets. It's not that Vera has any natural affinity for this scholarly homewrecker, this scourge of five miserable academic wives. But how can she not feel something for a perfectly groomed and slightly panicky five-time loser?

In a voice modulated by a two-hundred-year prep-school tradition, Mona Miller speaks of atmospheric distortion, temperature inversions, refractions, and gradients. For Vera, her remarks have special poignancy, conjuring up images of a modern-day Lady of Shalott, seduced and abandoned by five successive Lancelots, standing on the shoreline and measuring angles of light. Slides of a New Hampshire lake—which, Mona claims, duplicates Loch Ness—show a stick protruding from the water, held presumably by some invisible swimmer underneath. In one photo, the stick looks two feet long; in another, taken later in the day, twenty. And monstrous. The contrast is impressive, but what Vera wants to know is: Who was holding the stick? Was it one of her husbands? Why did she fall in love with him, and why did he leave? Was it taken when yet another marriage was showing signs of disintegration, so that Mona was scanning that stick in the water for reassurance that things aren't always what they seem?

But finally it's Mona who's doing the reassuring. Like Glengarrie, she finishes by promising her listeners that she is in no way denying the existence of underwater creatures, merely stressing the importance of accurate optical technique in the continuing search for unexpected life forms. Her reception is a good deal warmer than Glengarrie's. Vera gets the feeling that— even knowing what they know—every man in the audience would gladly volunteer to be number six. Gerald Davis stands, applauding with his hands over his head. It does seem a little excessive, and there's a flutter of disapproval, as if Davis's colleagues had caught him propositioning the Ice Maiden of optical science.

Davis is still standing when Ray Bramlett scurries up to the mike and announces they're running late and will go on without a break to hear Frank Karsh of the Wildlife Preservation Task Force speak on "The Lesson of Steller's Sea Cow."

Vera wants a smoke, feels she's earned one. She'd like to repair to the ladies' room, which has a lobby of its own, minus the taxidermy, with mirrors and upholstered banquettes like a set for *The Women.* She wants to sink into one of those revolving, half-moon armchairs and look in the mirror, think of Mona Miller's angles of light, and smoke a cigarette. Nor is Vera the only malcontent. Lots of people drank coffee during the first break and look ready for the powder room, too.

Vera's glad she's not Frank Karsh, having to face this crowd with his pedagogical sea cows—but Frank doesn't care. He bounds up to the mike like the young Johnny Carson. Beamish boy, ex–Peace Corps or Vista volunteer, he wouldn't shrink before a roomful of NRAers with rifles or grizzled Captain Ahabs with harpoons. He'll do anything, *be* Johnny Carson if he has to; it's not show biz here, but the survival of whole species. When Frank Karsh waves for the lights to go out, it's a gesture of benediction.

A slide appears on the screen, a sepia etching of some huge, whiskered porpoise or seal. "Steller's sea cow," says Frank. Another slide follows, this time a little manatee floating in a tank, staring plaintively at the camera with the moist, shiny eyes one finds on greeting cards of various creatures—puppies, chimps, hippos—illustrating the sentiment, "Missing You."

"Two hundred years ago," Frank Karsh begins, "thousands of giant sea cows inhabited the waters near the Bering Strait. Now there is not one of them in the world, nor will there be again."

Frank goes on to tell the story of how, in 1741, Georg Wilhelm Steller, First Surgeon on the Bering expedition, discovered, christened, and essentially fell in love with this species of Sirenia, each one thirty feet long, weighing approximately four tons, and graced with a placid sweetness that was its undoing. For Bering's men were starving, and one day an especially brave or especially hungry sailor speared one, cooked it, and found its flesh to taste "like sole, only better—like sole amandine!"

The crowd titters nervously, laughter such as one might hear in a roomful of guilty ex-cannibals who've just heard human flesh described as tasting like chicken marengo.

"And then, just fifty-four years later, a certain Sergei Popoff killed the very last surviving sea cow in the waters near Bering Island." Frank goes on, making the sea cow extermination sound worse than Dresden and Guernica combined. It's what Vera's always suspected of these preservationists: if they had to pick one species to be eliminated, they'd pick man.

The "lesson" part hardly needs saying, but Frank can't stop now. As he names the species in imminent danger of meeting the sea cows' fate, Vera thinks of the Vietnam War, how the lists of dead and missing seemed to scroll down the TV screen forever. The list goes on and on, and when it ends, the crowd's so demoralized they can't move. When at last they rouse themselves to applaud, it's that chastened, dutiful clapping one hears at the end of documentaries about concentration camps and failed revolutions.

What Vera's just realizing is that the lesson of Steller's sea cow is why no one will ever see Bigfoot. If Bigfoot shows himself, just once, he'll wind up neatly packaged and labeled in some housewife's freezer, waiting to reappear as Bigfoot amandine. That *any* of these creatures might show themselves is as unlikely as Mona Miller finding a stolen husband who'll stay with her.

This is what Vera's thinking as she hurries from the Cottonwood Room, so when she rounds a corner and nearly runs into

Mona Miller, she feels as if she's summoned her. Mona's in one of those vintage stagecoaches converted here into phone booths. Riding shotgun, she's speaking intensely into the receiver, gesturing wildly with the other hand. She looks profoundly unhappy. Is she speaking to the prospective number six, or one of the previous five? Vera's seized with desire to squeeze in the booth beside Mona and tell her all about Lowell. Then together they will decide if loving and losing five husbands is better or worse than loving and losing the same one five times. If only Mavis were here. She could fit in there too and lecture them both about constancy and passion.

Vera wishes with all her heart that one day Mona Miller will be out by the lake measuring angles of refraction and suddenly the monster will lift its long neck and tiny brontosaurus head and look straight at Mona and wink. *That* will change her luck. Somehow Vera feels certain that this would make Mona stop stealing husbands who are so easily stolen; she wants to believe that seeing the Loch Ness monster would make you hold out for more. But Mona will never see it. Any creature highly evolved enough to survive on insufficient plankton is smart enough not to get caught like a Steller's sea cow.

Vera spots a small group of cryptobiologists moving slowly down the hall. Behind them is a picture window, and behind that all God's grandeur made manifest in three billion years of geology. They don't see it. And though Vera had hoped to find people like herself who just couldn't assimilate the canyon, the sight of these doesn't please her.

She's thinking about Georg Wilhelm Steller: how he must have loved those sea cows. Closing her eyes, Vera sees him, later in life, long after the sea cows are gone. He's wading in the shallows. His shoulders are hunched at an angle that takes her a moment to recognize as being just like Mona Miller's as he stands there waiting, trying, like Mona, not to search every wake and swell for what he knows is no longer there.

I N THE Mimosa Room, everyone's squinting. The only ones not blinking like moles are the crew—very L.A. for Flagstaff Cablevision; with their unbuttoned-to-the-waist shirts, their hairy chests and deep tans, they look as if they spend their lives in the glare of wattage like this. The brightness has the festive, urgent shine of searchlights outside Hollywood premieres, arcing up to pick the stars out of the sky and down to catch the ones emerging from their limos. Before Vera knows it, she's picked her head up, as if the light's aimed at her.

Not so the cryptobiologists, none of whom can deal with the cameras. They're curious and, at the same time, afraid that the slightest show of interest will make them look like those kids one sees jumping and waving behind the reporters on live-action TV news. So they find seats faster than they normally would and wait so docilely, Ray Bramlett doesn't have to move a muscle for their attention. "And now," he says. "I'm pleased to present to you, with their astonishing story—Ethel and Carl Poteet."

Arm in arm, the Poteets take hesitant baby steps toward the front. Vera's reminded of some celebrity's aged parents, dragged up on stage for a famous son or daughter's *This Is Your Life.* It's hard to imagine them in a remote African valley, traveling *anywhere*, for that matter, except perhaps as golden-age tourists, checking constantly to make sure the bus hasn't left.

By the time they've reached the front and are standing there letting the cameras roll and more dead air flow by than Vera would have thought permissable, they're looking more self-possessed. Ethel's neat and pretty in her new perm and Ladies'-Better-Dresses pale-blue polyester. Carl's seersucker suit is the same shade as Ethel's dress. Ethel turns to Carl and smiles.

"Well, now," says Carl Poteet. "The first thing folks always ask us is why we'd want to do such a Looney-Tune thing. So I'll try to answer that one, then I'll crawl back behind that slide projector and let Ethel take over." Though the lights play on Carl's steel-framed glasses in a metallic, outer-space way, he's still your Norman Rockwell grocer, the TV-commercial pharmacist you trust enough to burden with your hemorrhoid pain.

"It started when I was a kid," says Carl. "I was always fascinated with dinosaurs. Couldn't get enough of 'em. Lots of boys go through it, I know. Me, I never outgrew it. When Ethel married me, I told her she was moving back into the Mesozoic Age, and she said, Fine, long as she could take her Maytag with her."

Generous laughter here; the Poteets are warming the chilliest academic hearts. Even Gerald Davis is smiling indulgently, as if listening to a favorite dotty uncle.

"As many of you know," says Carl, "Ethel and I have been part of this organization since they first opened it to laymen." Laymen? As opposed to what? Professional cryptobiologists? Carl's humility moves Vera; he sounds like a heart patient deferring to a roomful of Houston surgeons. "So it's you folks I've got to thank for telling me about the Mokele-Mbembe and the Boxberger expedition and of course Professor Lausnitz's work. Soon as I heard about that, I got to dreaming how someday we'd retire and sell the business, so Ethel and I could go where these early sightings occurred and take a look for ourselves." Carl says this as if it's the most normal vision in the world: after supper in the heartland, Carl dozing in front of the TV while Ethel clips coupons and balances the books so that someday they can go hunt for dinosaurs.

"And last fall, that dream came true. Ethel and I closed up shop, got our passports, made about a million phone calls. And before you could say Jack Robinson, the big day came. We walked out the front door, got onto that Air Afrique jumbo jet, and were off to the People's Republic of the Congo. Ethel, take it away!"

After a brief dance in which Ethel steps forward and Carl do-si-dos back behind the projector, a blur appears on the screen that, after much anxious mumbling from Carl, sharpens into a small tidy house, a small tidy lawn. Anywhere Street, Anytown, USA. Carl and Ethel stand before it, each toting a giant suitcase and more cameras than Vera's ever seen on anyone but Solomon. Ethel's saying, "Carl makes taking off lock, stock, and barrel for Africa sound easy. But I'll tell you: it isn't."

A knowing laugh now; Ethel's listeners suspected as much. She's got them in her pocket, tucked in with her scented, scalloped hankie, intoxicated by her Yardley's English Lavender and by the old-fashioned yin-and-yang symmetry they've missed since Gram and Grandpa's day: Ethel's shaky, sincere woman's heart played off against Carl's cheery, brave glad-handing. Vera wishes she weren't so jaded. These Poteets aren't pitching anything. And yet she's holding back and analyzing their technique as if they were hawking Japanese steak knife sets on TV.

"First off, it was ages before we knew we *could* go. Everybody kept warning us, the Congolese government wasn't letting anyone in, *certainly* not Americans. But really they couldn't have been sweeter . . ." Ethel goes on, listing the Congolese's kindnesses like a small-town society page; next she'll be describing the cleverest little pygmy table decorations and what they served for lunch. "Carl's going to have my hide for saying this," she confides. "But by the time we were packed and ready, well, we were plum scared to death . . ."

It's an interesting moment, the Poteets' perky smiles unmasked as grimaces of terror. Vera thinks of the photo of Dave's Lincoln Brigaders. The audience strains forward, anxious to see what fear looks like. But Carl hurries through the next slides: Carl at the airport, Ethel in the doorway of a 747. Carl and Ethel reunited with their luggage at customs. Then nothing. The screen's gone blank. Carl clicks the switch.

Then this: Ethel in the prow of a canoe, mugging for the

camera as she ducks some little brown objects falling from the sky. In the next shot, the camera's moved closer, revealing the brown things—still falling, with some accumulation on the floor of the canoe—to be, unmistakably: frogs.

"Carl," says Ethel. "We're getting ahead of our story." The slide whips off the screen, leaving an afterimage on Vera's retina that vanishes too fast for her to be sure if what she's just seen was really a rain of frogs.

"Sorry," says Carl. "I just wanted to show the folks what we mean when we say the trip was one thing after another. Give 'em a little taste of what I'd call pretty darn unexpected."

"In time, dear," says Ethel.

Perhaps Vera's imagining this, but even the projector's click sounds obedient, subdued, and the next slide sets history back on its chronological track. Now the Poteets are posed in front of an airport tower, flanking a handsome, young black man who comes up to Ethel's armpit.

"That's Willy!" cries Ethel, with such heartfelt pleasure you'd think she was seeing him in person after a long separation. "Willy Nkbngnge," she says, or some last name that's all consonants. "Willy's one of the BaMbuti people, as they prefer to be called . . ." There's a significant pause during which you can practically hear Ethel wrestling with her weaker self and winning, deciding not to say they no longer like being called pygmies. It's the same pause one often hears in the speech of people who've learned not to say someone's Jewish or black or Italian unless it's relevant.

"Willy was our interpreter," says Ethel. "Though 'interpreter' wasn't the half of it. Willy did everything. Chief cook and bottle washer. Nature guide. Handyman. Navigator. And entertaining? The stories he could tell! The first night, over dinner at our hotel, Willy started in about the Mokele-Mbembe, the creature his people tell about that sounds so like the . . . ?"

"Sauropod," says Carl.

"Sauropod," says Ethel. "Anyway, Carl got so enthralled, he started sipping from his water glass even though our doctor at home made us swear not to touch it, not even to brush our teeth.

I kept signaling, but poor Carl didn't notice. And the next day . . ." The next slide shows Carl and Ethel in front of a run-down building painted with a Red Cross and "pharmacy" in half a dozen languages. Carl's grabbing his stomach, grinning self-consciously, but the fact is, he's holding his body peculiarly and looks about ten years older than he did leaving home.

"Ethel," says Carl, changing slides again, and now the whole audience catches its breath as a shot of the river comes on—green and wide, surrounded by jungle so lush and moist, you'd think if you touched the screen, your hand would come back wet. "Tell the folks a little about the Mokele-Mbembe, so they'll know what we're looking for."

Ethel goes bashful, like a child called on to recite a party piece that even she knows is silly. When she speaks again, it's in questions:

"All the tribes in that part of the world tell the same story about this creature—half elephant, half dragon? They say it inhabits caves in sharp bends of the river? And it's smooth and has one horn and kills hippos and anything else it can get its hands on? Hands? Feet, I guess you'd say? Or claws? What else? It's a vegetarian? And they all say it eats this little, pink, applelike fruit they call . . . help me, Carl.

"Molombo," says Carl.

If Ethel's trying to make them believe in some elephant-dragon crossbreed, she's got to do better than this. "Of course, we knew this before we even got there," says Ethel, resting her case. "Though Willy confirmed it and more. That first night at dinner, when poor Carl got so sick, Willy told us the most wonderful legend about a BaMbuti girl who got fed up with all the men in her village and went off to marry the Mokele-Mbembe."

I MARRIED THE MOKELE-MBEMBE. Now even Vera scoots forward. But that's all they're going to get of the dino-saur's bride. The next image is of the Poteets and Willy and four young blacks in their canoe. Two of the men wear T-shirts and shorts, the others, army fatigues. "That's Kampamba and Sabani, our bearers," Ethel sings out. "Auru and Mkembe, our

security guards; the government was *so* lovely . . ." The boat is
loaded with gear and seems to be riding dangerously low in the
water. Behind it is a pier, a ramshackle port, and, in the middle
distance, those boys who pop up everywhere, shoving their palms
at the camera.

"That's us at Mounguma," says Ethel. "Shipshape and ready
to sail." In fact Carl looks somewhat less than shipshape. Set
off by the glossy ebony skins around him, Carl's face is the
milky blue-white of the sky. "And for a while it *was* smooth
sailing: Big herons and parrots and crocodiles, whole armies of
monkeys. Then two days out of Mnganga, the going got thicker."

And so it must have. Now the river's so choked with weeds,
you'd think the boat had been plucked out of the water and
beached in some Kansas cornfield. Dark green, bamboolike, the
vegetation suggests young corn shoots, except that a cornfield is
planted in rows and this is chaotic and everywhere. Carl holds
the shot for longer than anyone wants to look at it. There's
grumbling when the same slide blinks off and on again. But it
isn't exactly the same—the boat's moved a few inches up toward
the right of the screen. So. There's not even the hope that Carl's
projector's stuck.

"This one was taken about twelve hours after that last," says
Carl. "We'd been pushing all day."

"Day two!" says Ethel, and the same slide with slight variations
comes on. So one image follows another, swamp and more swamp
with only the most miniscule changes to indicate progress. Carl
lingers over each one till the boredom is maddening, and Vera
feels like she's slogging through the muck herself.

"Day three," says Carl.

"The worst part was knowing we had to come back the same
way," Ethel says. "And that there's no rushing it. I kept thinking,
suppose something *happens* . . ."

"That's one way to learn patience," says Carl. "No emergencies
on that part of the Aruwimi. Life moves slow."

By day five, the plant life's got nowhere to go but up, winding
itself around vines, roots, moss; and where can the Poteets go
but deeper into the jungle? There's so little light the only sign

they haven't underexposed all their film is the barely discernible little boat and, in the foreground, the bearers, pushing, toting, and puffing their cheeks as if miming some embarrassing pre-black-consciousness rendition of "Ol' Man River." Vera thinks of Bogey pushing The African Queen, getting covered with leeches. What a punishing way to make the Katherine Hepburn character come to tend to the needs of the body!

"I thought we'd had it," says Carl.

Vera's had it, too. Suppose Carl makes them go through this again, documenting the trip back. Then in shot after slow, boring shot, the growth begins to thin; light shines through. Shown at a merciful speed, it might look like special effects: Charlton Heston dividing the Red Sea. At last! The river's wide and brown, and Willy's pointing thumbs up at the camera.

"Well, you can imagine," says Ethel. "I've never been so relieved. Was it that day, Carl?"

"Yes," says Carl.

"That day was the rain of frogs," Ethel says. "First it clouded up and started drizzling, and the drops got bigger until after a spell it wasn't water, it was *frogs*! Like something from the Old Testament. Moses and the plagues."

Vera's startled; she's just been thinking of Charlton Heston. "Except that it didn't feel like a plague," Ethel's saying. "It wasn't scary. And *I* don't like frogs. We were so glad to be clear of that swamp, and I kept thinking: even if nothing else happens, we'll have this. The truth is, it seemed like a miracle. Though really there's a simple explanation.

"Apparently there's a species of African frog—Carl knows the Latin name—that doesn't go through the tadpole stage. And every so often a storm picks up masses of frog eggs and sets them down hatched." Vera considers this newborn-frogs' version of *The Wizard of Oz*, but in the end pays it no more mind than froggy's Latin name. She thinks it's a miracle, too, as do Ethel, Willy, and the bearers, who, Ethel's saying, "just went crazy. Before that it was Bwana and Memsahib hunting the Mokele-Mbembe; who could blame them for not taking it seriously? But maybe the frogs were some omen in their culture. Because from then on they stopped joking and rolling their eyes when we asked them to do something. After that, they hopped *to.*"

Joking and eye-rolling and humoring Memsahib and Bwana? That's the first they've heard about this, and it lends a new perspective: five days in the swamp knowing everyone thinks you're a jerk. "That woke them up a bit," says Ethel. "They started looking a little harder. And so . . ." Ethel pauses so long even Carl catches it and moves on to the next slide: a bend in the river and, at the curve, a scooped-out hollow in the bank.

"Then suddenly it was like *King Solomon's Mines,* the guys all jabbering at once and pointing at a cave in the bank. 'See there,' says Willy, 'that's where the Mokele-Mbembe lives. And growing on the bank above it, the molombo . . . See?' " It's a long shot taken from so far away it's hard to see much of anything. Squinting, Vera can nearly make out blossoms, like some species of Congolese dogwood. Dinosaur food?

"That's where we decided to camp. And it wasn't till then that we realized we hadn't been off the canoe for five days."

What Vera wants to know is, how did they go to the bathroom? At first she can't picture Ethel squatting over the edge of the boat; then she can. In the slide that flashes through Vera's mind, Ethel's behind floats upriver like some enormous, white flower, not bawdy at all but vulnerable and rather touching.

"What's hardest to imagine is how enormous it is," Ethel's saying. "How vast. I think that's what upset Carl. On the scale of things out there, a giant dinosaur's no bigger than a mote in God's eye. So seeing that cave with the molombo tree above it was very encouraging, like searching for someone who's lost till you've nearly given up and then finding a footprint—"

"And speaking of footprints," says Carl.

Cut to Ethel standing on a red clay bank, sunk a foot or so below ground level in what appears at first to be a crater but is— if you look hard enough—a footprint. Once you've seen it there's no mistaking the webbing, the talons ending in sharp points. It's so large Ethel and Carl could lie down in it and take a few pygmies in with them. The audience is as silent as if they'd just discovered it themselves.

"Well, I just thanked God," Ethel says. "What a lift! What confirmation! Fine, I told Carl. Let's go home. A rain of frogs and a dinosaur footprint is enough for one lifetime! But not for Carl. 'Quit when we're just getting close?' he says." Ethel's chest swells when she says this, and Vera's reminded of the way Carmen talks about Frankie the Lizard. Has Vera ever spoken like this about Lowell? Yes, she thinks. She still does.

Carl says, "We'd come that far; I figured we might as well stay and see if whatever it was came back."

Over your stock natives-hacking-with-machetes shots, Ethel says, "It took the boys a whole day just to clear room enough to pitch tents. Then we made camp and then . . . well, then we waited." Click, click. Images go by: Ethel reading; Carl sitting on a log; the bearers playing some gambling game reminiscent of Queegqueg and his bones. "I'd brought a crossword book and a mystery; I did all the puzzles and read the Agatha Christie twice. Carl kept asking if I thought someone else would turn out to be the murderer the second time. So I teased him back, I said, 'Carl, if you'd been as patient with me as you are with this Mokele-Mbembe, our whole lives would have been different.'"

What was *that* about? wonders Vera, but it goes by so fast, no one seems to have noticed; nor is it likely that these crypto-biologists' antennae would twitch at the first hint of anyone's marital discord, except perhaps Mona Miller's. "Even the boys got bored," Ethel says, "And Willy asked if he could take off for a while. Turns out his village wasn't far from there. Lord, who would have thought, a human habitation near that!

"The days got even slower after Willy left. He wasn't gone long, but oh, how we missed him! We all felt a bit let down." For the first time Vera wonders if Ethel might have been a little in love with Willy. That let-down, wasted-day feeling is what she remembers from the beginning of love—days she didn't see Lowell. Vera's probably romanticizing. When you're stuck in the jungle with your dinosaur-crazed husband and four non-English-speaking Congolese, any absence must seem like a major loss.

"I was beginning to worry I'd *never* get Carl out of there. And maybe I wouldn't have if our supplies hadn't been limited. That evening Willy came back, right on time. We knew we'd have to leave the next day, and poor Carl was so discouraged. And Willy, bless his heart, must have sensed it. He started offering round some palm wine he'd brought back from his village. Even Carl and I—we're not drinkers at home—said, Well, sure, why not?

"Whew" Ethel whistles through her teeth. "That was some potent palm wine." There's a shot of Carl sitting by a campfire, toasting the camera from a canteen that looks as if it had been made from some sort of rhino bladder. "That evening went a lot quicker than most," reports Ethel. "I got a little loopy, Carl got even loopier, but neither of us got loopy enough to forget we were going home without having got any closer to the Mokele-Mbembe than the tracks he made leaving town.

"And then dear Willy joined us by the campfire and told the loveliest story, took our minds right off it. Not one of his people's stories, he said. One he'd heard from a sailor in Dakar:

"Well, apparently after Alexander the Great had conquered all the known world, he got it in mind that the only thing left for him to do was to find the fountain of youth—"

Vera, who's been lulled into a kind of jungle-campfire reverie herself, sits up straight. The fountain of youth? It's almost more synchronicity than she can bear. And yet nothing at this convergence seems threatening, nothing's waiting here in ambush.

"So Alexander searched all around for a cook for his expedition, but since it's well known that cooks like nothing better than tending the home fires—"

"Like Ethel," says Carl, lovingly.

"Like me," says Ethel. "But finally one came forward, a man named . . . Kezir, Carl?"

"Something like that," says Carl.

"By this time Alexander's heard that the fountain of youth can be found in the Black Land, the country of permanent darkness." Ethel shudders. "So he and his army push on through the Red Land, the Blue Land, the Yellow Land. Finally they reach the White Land where everything—the earth, the sky, the sun—is frozen and white. Alexander's whole party panics and deserts; only the emperor and Kezir, his cook, remain.

"They travel on into the Black Land, where the soil is the color of ebony, the trees are black—the leaves, the sky, the air; they can hardly see. They feel like Carl and I did that last night by the bend in the river: they can't *believe* the fountain of youth could be there. Alexander goes ahead, ordering Kezir to stay back and cook dinner. The cook takes what's left of their food—the last dried fish he's saved for Alexander's meal. He kneels by a black pond to wash it, and when he dips it into the black water, the fish comes alive in his hands and swims away."

A murmur goes through the audience, a gasp of such wonder and pleasure you'd think they'd seen the dead fish come to life. Perhaps they're not quite as cool and scientific as Vera supposes, or perhaps they're like Vera, looking for some reason to believe: Anything's possible. Miracles happen when one least expects them, most often when one has stopped looking. Perhaps all this talk of the unexpected is merely a product of the same magical thinking that keeps young girls from saying their boyfriends' names and businessmen from mentioning their big deals. Talk about it and it won't happen. Don't expect it—and there it'll be. Nor is it the same cruel joke that had the alchemists losing everything each time "hippopotamus" came to mind. For this allows for moments of grace when one's concentration is elsewhere: cooking dinner, washing fish, not worrying about the fountain of youth. Even now, Vera's still, small, jaded inner voice whispers on, insinuating baser motives, some mean-spirited private joke in Willy's parable of the clever servant beating Bwana to the punch. But who cares why he told it? The story offers such promise, such hope; if Vera could just think about it longer, everything might fall into place.

Ethel has the crowd where she wants it and isn't about to let go. The way she holds the silence as if it were a thread she could stretch or snap at will reminds Vera of a revival preacher, and it's with a sort of preachery hush that Ethel says, "That night we went down to the river. We thought we'd walk off the palm wine, rest a bit, come back; even with the full moon out, bright as day, it wasn't any place you'd want to stay long.

"So Carl and I were just turning up to the bank when we

heard a splash. Whoosh! 'Carl!' I cried. 'There it is!' We started running—and then we saw it. Diving into the water, brown, enormous, like some gigantic lizard maybe fifteen feet long—and we only saw the *tail*! And the wake it left! Good Lord, it was ten feet tall! My heart was pounding so fast I had to sit down, I . . . Carl, do you want to tell them? Carl?"

Carl takes a while answering. The screen's gone black; the whole room's dark. Carl and Ethel coo reassuringly at one another. Vera and the cryptobiologists and even Flagstaff Cablevision could be eavesdropping on the most intimate moments of their marriage, on fifty years of whispered conversations in the dark. Finally Carl says, "Isn't it awful the way you never have the goldarn camera when you really need it?" and the audience cheers.

"We were just pleased as punch," Ethel says when the crowd settles down. "But Willy and the others seemed rather concerned. After all sorts of hushhush meetings, they told us they were going to hold a little ceremony, some rite their people did in celebration and for protection . . . so the Mokele-Mbembe wouldn't eat them for breakfast is really the idea I got. More palm wine, naturally. By now the boys were three sheets to the wind, and soon they began to play the most extraordinary instrument."

Carl switches on the tape recorder and goes over beside Ethel. In a few moments the room—still pitch-black except for the light from the lectern—fills with a high, unearthly ringing, like someone playing a crosscut saw or running a finger around a wineglass; then the tone sinks to a kind of growl, like rattling gourds, shaking bones, dancing skeletons.

"We heard it before we saw it," Ethel's saying, "and of course we figured it was some kind of gourd or special wood, but guess what? It was a metal drainpipe with holes in it. We could hardly believe it, but Willy said it didn't matter, the sound itself was what was sacred."

Vera has no problem with that. The sound is so unlike anything she's ever heard, she'd believe it if Ethel told them it was the voice of the Mokele-Mbembe itself. And who's to say it isn't? Vera closes her eyes and listens, feels the sound taking her off to some dark land where everything is black and where it's possible that the dried fish you wash in the pond will come back to life.

When she opens her eyes, the crowd is on its feet, applauding. Vera joins in for a while, then leaves the Mimosa Room, leaves the Ghost Circle Lodge, and goes outside and stands on the edge of the canyon.

Tonight it doesn't frighten or disappoint her. It's so dark she can't see much, and what she can see looks manageable and tame; it could be a ditch some kid's dug in the hotel backyard, an excavation on which some neighbor lodge will soon build. In a few minutes she'll go back inside. Meanwhile she's thinking of questions she wants to ask the Poteets. The first one is: Could they have made that trip thirty years ago? Already she's answered for them: no. Thirty years ago they would have fought, like Vera and Lowell, over who spent their last peso on cashews. Thirty years ago they would have run from that dinosaur wake the way Vera ran from Bigfoot. Thirty years ago they couldn't have inched their way through that swamp; they would never have had the time.

Time: that's what she most wants to ask the Poteets about. The way lives change unpredictably with time. And suddenly the question of whether they could have made their trip thirty years ago seems less compelling than this one: When Carl and Ethel were Vera's age, did they ever imagine that in thirty years they'd be hacking a path through the jungle?

When Vera considers this, more things seem possible. Quite possibly Lowell will someday talk her into a dinosaur hunt of their own. There's no counting on it, Vera knows. No investing one's hopes in promises that may turn out to be false; no guaranteeing anyone a dinosaur-hunting old age. But if Carl and Ethel can search for the Mokele-Mbembe, why can't she and Lowell have one more go-around after the lost Mayan treasure? And what if they find it? How sweet it would be to call Dave and Norma and tell them their son-in-law had finally made good.

Vera thinks of her parents, her old room and *its* treasures: postcards, books of fairy tales, a conch shell. It occurs to her that the room she called the Greens from last week was really nothing like the room she grew up in. All the time she lived there, it was a junk heap, and she and Dave and Norma fought constantly about her cleaning it up. Why couldn't they have had enough faith in the future to have spared themselves that, to have just closed her door and hung on till she had a place and a child of her own, till she'd grown into the kind of woman who'd take pleasure in the small chores, the tidying up, her Saturday domestic life?

But, in the end, what difference would it have made? What permanent harm did any of it do? When Vera thinks of Dave and Norma now, it's with great tenderness and love, and if there are things about her parents that disturb and worry her, it's not any leftover bitterness from the fights they had over her room. She swore she'd never have such arguments with Rosie. And she didn't; she didn't have to. Rosie was always neat.

Here I am, Vera thinks, poised on the edge of eternity, of the Grand Canyon itself, and what am I thinking of? Children's rooms. Yet imagining Rosie's room is enormously reassuring. When Vera pictures Rosie's orderly bookcase, her collection of Dungeons and Dragons paraphernalia, her toe shoes and the hand-tinted ballerina print from Solomon arranged in a kind of shrine, she can almost believe that she will soon leave the edge of this yawning chasm and return to the safe, enclosed, familiar, and—from this distance—much-loved space of her home. Vera knows Rosie will come back. And leave again. She knows she can't stop time, can't hold on to Rosie—or anyone—forever. But tonight it seems possible to live with that knowledge, to listen for those moments when whispers of comfort and pleasure are louder than that voice on the phone at the Greens. What's most unexpected is grace.

A cool wind blows in off the canyon, and this too seems like a promise: this awful summer will finally end, and autumn will come. The idea of autumn brings Vera full circle, back to the Poteets: even though you know things are dying, all their color and glory almost make you feel they're renewing themselves, beginning life over again.

Vera looks up at the sky—black but for a sliver of moon and two stars. The bright star nearest the earth is Venus. The distant, reddish one must be Mars. Without thinking about what she's doing, Vera narrows one eye and winks. The red star blinks off and on. And though Vera knows that what she's just seen is most likely a trick of the moonlight, a reflection of something else, still for a moment she almost believes that it's Elvis, winking back.

FRANCINE PROSE, born in New York City, is the author of six previous novels, including *Hungry Hearts, Household Saints,* and *Judah the Pious* (winner of the Jewish Book Council Award). Her stories and articles have appeared in the *Atlantic, Antaeus, Mademoiselle,* and the *Village Voice.* She has taught at Harvard, the University of Arizona, and the Breadloaf Writer's Conference, and now teaches fiction writing at Sarah Lawrence and in the Warren Wilson MFA Program for Writers. She lives with her husband and two children in upstate New York.